PRAISE FOR
WHAT IS WRONG WITH ME

"It's rare to find a therapist and a novelist in the same person. Kris Hammoud is exactly that. She weaves her medical knowledge of countless patient journeys into a spellbinding story of self-discovery that creates an echo chamber for self-reflection and revelation. Every page is an opportunity for the reader to reflect on the influences in one's own life as a pathway to explain the present. The story of Anna is the story of us all if we are willing to be honest with ourselves and open to answers."

—**John Patton**, CEO, ProVention Health Foundation,
Author of *Brainless Health*

"Kris Hammond simultaneously destigmatizes mental health issues and weaves a compelling narrative. *What Is Wrong With Me* is a combination of women's fiction and self-help tutorial, as we follow Anna's brave journey through childhood trauma into a tumultuous adulthood, culminating in a beautiful and important message for mental health care."

—**Lori Nelson Spielman**, *New York Times* Bestselling
Author of *The Life List*

"Kris Hammoud's debut work is a riveting piece that blends a compelling narrative with insights into trauma, the footprints that do not fade despite the years, and the perils of repeated mistakes. Hammoud's prose is lean and accessible, stark where it needs to be, universally powerful and eminently readable. The story she weaves commands attention. Her insights command respect."

—**Greg Fields**, Author of *Arc of the Comet* and
Through the Waters and the Wild

"With a roller coaster of emotions, Hammoud explores the complexity of family dynamics while celebrating self-discovery. This smart, engaging book kept me guessing to the very end."

—**Elaine Holt**, MD, Author of *The Doctor Next Door*

"Following Anna's journey through formative stages of her life was deeply absorbing. Interestingly, at pivotal points in the narrative, therapeutic advice is given voice by key characters. Therefore this book goes beyond the other self-help books, entwining a riveting storyline with real, workable therapy."

—**Sarah Lepschy**

"*What Is Wrong with Me?* is the insightful story of Anna, a bright young woman with great potential who makes poor choices. Kris Hammoud carefully dissects Anna's life and her responses to events in her life, illuminating the powerful effect trauma has on children caught in its grip. Beginning in elementary school and reaching through high school, college, and beyond, Anna's story demonstrates how small, seemingly inconsequential interactions between parent and child can have a profound impact. A good read that ends with hope for healing life wounds."

—**Lyn Barrett**, Author of *Crazy: Reclaiming Life from the Shadow of Traumatic Memory*

"This is an expertly written story of a woman's journey from childhood into her adult years after enduring years of harrowing emotional abuse. The author, Kristin Hammoud, draws on her years as a professional therapist in carefully crafting this authentically based story. Hammoud engages the reader in a moving and important saga of struggle and courage to face life when carrying the scars from emotional and physical trauma. Hammoud paints a vivid portrait of a determined and spirited woman who seeks to overcome her past—a story told with keen insight and great sensitivity. Hammoud has produced a triumph in what illuminates our country's ongoing struggles with the realities of racial strife, flaring emotions, determination, and heartache."

—**Josie Olsvig**, Author of *Gullah Tears*

"Kris Hammoud walks you through the relatable dynamics of a dysfunctional family. You will find yourself rooting for the characters to initiate the needed change to promote self growth. Insightful read for anyone!-

—**Christine Williams** MS, LLP

"*What Is Wrong with Me* by Kris Hammoud is a book about how childhood trauma effects one's ability to form and maintain relationships. The protagonist Anna suffers emotional and sexual trauma as a child and without realizing, as an adult, starts using escapist behaviors to cope with her insecurities. Dysfunctional relationships leave more emotional scars for Anna. Kris Hammoud, through this story, highlights the effect of early adversities and trauma on life. She also, in her kind and compassionate way, gives hope that it is possible to come out of the shadows of the past and live a productive and meaningful life."

—**Tehmina Shakir**, Psychiatrist MD, CCP,
CCTSS, CCTP, CSOTP

"Excellent book. While reading it I realized that I was developing two types of connections with the book, one intellectual and another emotional. The intellectual connection comes as a result of reading about the interaction among behavior, emotions, and memory. The author (maybe unintentionally) made a great compilation of important principles to understand human behavior. The emotional connection came up when for moments I was not sure if the book was mimicking reality or if reality was mimicking the book. The book triggers a broad variety of real emotions. I am sure that each and every reader will find the emotion that she/he can identify in real life.

"There are no classes to become good parents, but if those classes were offered, this book would be one of the mandatory readings.

"I will recommend this book to students of human behavior. They will learn principles of applied cognitive behavior therapy, psychodynamic psychology, empathy, origins of self-esteem, and most important of all, they will learn about humans.

"I will recommend this book to mental health professionals. This book describes very well the connection between mind and body, cognitions and behavior, yesterday and today, and most mental health variables."

—**Orlando Villegas** PHD, LP, LCP

To all my clients whose stories I was privileged to hear and who allowed themselves to be vulnerable with me so they could learn how to be kind to, make better decisions for, and understand themselves in a whole new way.

To my family who have been so patient through the years of working on this novel. Thank you for always being there and supporting me.

What is Wrong with Me?

by Kristin Hammoud

ISBN 978-1-64663-475-0

This is a work of fiction. The characters are both actual and fictitious. With the exception of verified historical events and persons, all incidents, descriptions, dialogue and opinions expressed are the products of the author's imagination and are not to be construed as real.

Published by

Kristin Hammoud
PMH-CNS
KH Mental Health Wellness PLLC

what is wrong with me?

a novel

KRISTIN HAMMOUD

Between stimulus and response there is a space.
In that space is our power to choose our response.
In our response lies our growth and our freedom.

—*Victor Frankl*

Table of Contents

Introduction

Have you ever asked yourself, "What is wrong with me?" "How did I get to this place in my life?" I am fascinated by the journey each of us takes and have reviewed my own journey and how the decisions I have made evolved over time and brought me to my present situation. As a therapist, I learn about many different lives and their journeys in life and their decisions that have caused great harm or good. We all have challenges in this journey, but our decisions on how to cope can determine the consequences of our outcomes.

I wrote this novel to engage you to understand a fictional character's journey and how her experiences and internal thoughts and perceptions affect her decisions and her journey. Anna makes choices by reacting to her perceptions of the situation from past experiences and evolves into pausing and intentionally making decisions cognitively. Understanding her thoughts in the given moment, and how her perceptions have evolved based on different experiences and muscle memory, can help you make cause-and-effect connections and understand her decisions more fully.

As you follow Anna's journey, I welcome you to reflect on your own journey and what brought you to *your* present self from your earliest memories and how your memories affect how you react in current situations. Learning how to intentionally behave in one's life can help to not react to life situations.

CHAPTER 1

Anna's Early Memories

nna woke up squinting at the sun streaming from the window. Running to the window, she looked at the driveway to be sure her father's car was gone. This was her daily routine. She took a deep breath of relief and stretched her arms above her head then ran down the hallway to her parents' door, excited. It was her ninth birthday in early September, and she was in the fourth grade. She turned the knob and peeked in to see that her mother was still in bed. She then opened her brother Luke's door to find that he was playing with his cars in his bed. His curly auburn hair was longer than it should have been and was matted down on his scalp.

"Mom is sleeping," she said, "so be quiet."

Luke didn't listen. Instead, he ran to his mother's door, and before Anna could catch him, he had flung himself into the bed. "Mommy!" he cried.

Her mother's long, dark brown hair was snarled, and her bloodshot eyes, rimmed with dark circles, pierced Anna's vision. Anna said, "Luke, let's go downstairs and let Mom wake up."

"Thanks, Anna," her mother said. "You always help Mommy. I'll be down in a few minutes."

Holding six-year-old Luke's hand, Anna directed him down the stairs, knowing that if she let go, he would run back to their mother.

She put a car in front of Luke to play with and then got the cereal and milk, wondering, *Will anyone remember that it's my birthday?* After a while, Kathy finally came downstairs, her hair now in a ponytail.

"Mom, what happened to your eyes? Are you sick?"

Kathy said, "I'm okay, honey. I just had a hard time sleeping."

Luke interrupted. "Do I have school today?"

Kathy said, "No, silly—it's Saturday. And it's a special day for someone in this house." She looked over to Anna and smiled. Anna felt relief. *She remembered!*

"Mom, will Dad be here for my birthday?" Anna asked.

"Well, of course," Kathy said. "What a question that is! What would you like to do today?"

Anna wanted a birthday party with some of her friends but knew her mother felt uncomfortable with friends over. She could think of a lot of things she wanted to do, but when she looked at how tired her mother was, she said, "I'm fine playing at home, Mom."

She hoped her mother might encourage a different answer, but instead, Kathy breathed a sigh of relief and said, "Okay, whatever you want. We'll go out for ice cream after dinner."

Anna took Luke's hand and said, "Come on, let's get dressed."

As they walked up the back staircase, Luke asked, "Anna, why are you crying? Is it because I didn't say happy birthday?"

"No, I just thought this day would be better."

"You can pick out the games we play today, okay?" Luke offered. "Will that make it better?"

Anna smiled and nodded. Then she went to her room and closed the door. She opened up a journal her teacher, Ms. Papo, had given her after Anna saw it on her desk and admired it. Ms. Papo was her teacher in second grade and moved up this year to fourth. She told Anna that she kept her deepest thoughts in her journal to help her think of ways to think differently and to become happier. Anna loved that idea, and she found the same journal in her desk one day. Inside the front cover was an inscription: "To Anna, I hope writing down the events in your life and your thoughts helps you. You already seem too grown up and take on too many worries. Find your happiness. One day you will understand my words. Sincerely forever, Ms. Papo."

Anna pondered the sentences before she wrote, *Dear Diary. It's my birthday and I am nine. I am going into the fourth grade and love my teacher. She gave me this journal and I will keep it forever. I wanted to go ice-skating or roller-skating. My mom seems tired so I won't ask to go. I don't like the pills she takes. Why is she taking them? She always is sad. I am going to remember playing with Luke to remember being happy. The end.* Anna put it away as Luke was knocking on her door.

"Let's play. You pick—remember?" Anna took out her game Candy Land, thinking about how much Luke loved to play the game. She was setting up the game on her bed when she heard a car pull up. She jumped up and looked out the window.

"Luke, do you think Dad got me a present?"

"I don't know. I made you a card. Want it?"

"Sure. I'm going downstairs to check."

Anna crept downstairs, peeked around the corner, and saw her father going through the mail on the kitchen counter. He was tall and sweaty from a workout, and he had a serious look on his face and what seemed like a permanent frown line indented between his eyes.

"Hi," Anna said as she entered the kitchen.

Dan jumped. "Anna, don't sneak up on me like that. I hope you got your chores done."

"Mom gave me the day off today."

His black eyes glared over to the calendar and then at her. Suddenly, it was as if a lightbulb had gone off. He said, "Oh, she did. Could it be the one day I allow your chores to be missed?"

Anna said, "Yes, it is."

"You are growing up now. Another year means more responsibility."

"Can we do something today?" she asked. His thin face and tall, strong physique made her cower from him. She waited for his response patiently, but he seemed to forget she had even asked him a question.

He left the room and said, "Kathy, what's for lunch?"

Luke, standing nearby, said, "Anna, what about the game? You never came back."

Anna, looking to the floor, hoping her anger would subside, said, "I'm sorry, Luke. Let's finish the game."

They went back to her room, and Anna engulfed herself in the game until Kathy yelled up, "Kids, come and eat some lunch."

Luke ran down, but Anna took her time. She didn't want to see her father again. As she came into the kitchen, Dan said, "Luke, I told you to slow down. Now, sit and eat like a good boy."

Anna saw Luke slide into his seat and wait for his mother to give him his lunch. Dan was reading the paper as he ate his sandwich. Anna went over to her mother to help get some drinks ready.

Kathy said, "No, sit down. It's your birthday, so I want you to sit and relax."

Anna attempted to sit down, but it didn't feel right. "Mom, it's what I want to do. I like to help out."

Kathy put her hand on Anna's head. "Where on earth did you come from? How did I get so lucky nine years ago?"

They all sat down to eat, and Kathy seemed to hesitate. Finally she mumbled, "Dan, what do you think if we all went to the movies and out to eat for Anna's birthday?"

The silence seemed to last forever as everyone waited for his response. He seemed to enjoy how everyone waited in anticipation for his answer, and he even seemed to pause longer. He finally said, "Why don't you guys go and I'll meet you for dinner after?" Anna watched her parents and noticed that they never looked each other in the eye. Her mother's voice went down whenever she spoke to Dan, but Kathy did not do that with Anna or Luke.

Later that evening, while sitting in the movie, Anna thought, *I wish my father wasn't coming to dinner, but I should be happy.* Her thoughts distracted her from the movie. Afterward, she raced ahead of her mother and brother. "Mom, call Dad to let him know we are ready."

They arrived at Chili's, and Anna looked all around. The hostess seated them, and Anna heard her mother's phone beep. She instantly thought, *He's not coming. No, maybe he's just late. Think positive.*

Kathy read the text and said, "I'm sorry, honey, but your father is caught up with some business. He said he'd come for dessert."

Anna bit her lip to hold back her tears and wondered why she was upset. *I didn't want him to come anyway.*

"Anna, I'm here, and so is Mom," Luke said. "Who cares that he's not here?"

Kathy looked at him, disappointed. "Your father works hard so we can have a nice life and can come and eat at a nice restaurant. We have to appreciate that. Now, let's order."

Anna had lost her appetite but tried to eat her food. After the waitress took her plate away, she saw her father looking for them out of the corner of her eye.

Dan caught her eye and walked over, though his eyes were still on his phone. "How is the birthday girl? I hope you had a nice time." He handed Anna a small box that was in a bag.

"Thanks for coming, Dad. I know you're busy."

He said, "Open it."

Anna thought, *He has never given me anything before.* She carefully opened the bag and took the box out, thinking, *I don't care what it is now that he is here.* She opened the box as she looked at her father, who was distracted, texting on his phone. The present was a necklace that said "Daddy's Girl." He looked up at Kathy and said, "What is it?" Anna realized her mother had chosen the gift for him, and she felt like throwing it away.

"Did you order the cake yet?" Dan asked. As he spoke, the waitress came over with a few more employees and sang "Happy Birthday."

Anna watched Luke and her mother sing, but her father watched everyone. She made a wish: *I wish my mother to be happy.* She blew out the candles, and afterward the waitress cut up the cake and gave everyone a piece. Dan said, "Happy birthday. I'll see you later." He got up and turned around. "I'll be late tonight, Kathy."

As she bit her lip to hold back tears, Anna looked at her mother. "Listen, Anna," Kathy said. "You have to think positive in life and be happy that he came for your birthday. Remember—he is busy helping the family."

Anna looked at her sad mother and spread her lips to create a forced smile.

Kathy said, "Well, let's eat your cake and go home."

Anna rushed to eat and said, "Luke, hurry up."

They arrived home, and Anna hurried to get into her pajamas. "Mom," she said, "it's okay if I don't have a gift."

"Don't be silly," Kathy said. "Here, open them."

Anna saw two boxes, a large one with a smaller one on top. She grabbed the smaller one. "A diary with a key! Thank you."

Kathy said, "I started to keep a journal when I was your age. I wrote in it every day, and it helped me. One day you'll be able to read your journal when you're an adult and look back at who you were as a child. I know your teacher gave you a journal, and when you're finished with that one, you can write in this one. I made sure it had a lock on it."

Anna said, "I love it, Mom. I like that there's a key to keep for myself." She then ripped through the other gift and held a large stuffed bear. She hugged Kathy. "I love her so much."

Anna ran to her room with her gifts and sat on her bed with her bear. Luke came in and said, "Here, you forgot to read my card."

She opened up the homemade card with a big birthday cake on it and read, "Happy birthday. Luke." She gave him a hug. "I love it. I'm tired, so let's get some sleep." Anna put him in his bed and went to see Kathy, who was cleaning up. "Good night, Mom."

Kathy held her in her arms. "Good night, my big girl."

Anna woke later, startled in her bed, and went out to the hallway where she saw her bathroom light on. She went over and turned the knob, but it was locked. "Luke, what are you doing? Open the door." She knocked lightly on the door. "I'm going to get Mom."

Suddenly, the door opened, and it was her mother. Anna noticed she had been crying and that she was holding a towel stained with blood.

"Honey, go back to sleep. I just had a bad dream."

"Why are you in my bathroom? Why are you crying?" Anna asked.

Kathy sternly said, "Anna, I told you to go to bed." She walked down the hallway, not to her room but to the spare bedroom, and locked the door.

Anna thought, *I hope she is okay.* She went back to bed but tossed and turned all night.

In the morning, she woke, went to her door, and saw her father trying to open the door to the spare bedroom. "Open the door, Kathy. We need to talk."

Anna waited by her door and watched through the crack as Luke came out of his room. "Dad, what are you doing?"

Without talking, Dan went downstairs, grabbed his keys, and left.

Luke started to knock. "Mom, are you in there?"

Kathy unlocked the door and came out. She had deep, dark circles under her eyes, her hair was snarled, and she had a rip in her nightgown. She started to walk but seemed to be limping. "Hi, honey—can you get dressed? We have to go out."

Anna went to her room and got dressed faster than she ever had, grabbing a shirt and pants and socks. She went to Luke's room and found him sitting on his bed. "Come on, Luke, we have to go. Can't you see Mom is not well?"

Luke started to laugh. "You look so funny."

Anna grabbed some jeans and a shirt for Luke and, without looking to see what he was talking about, said, "Let's get in the car for Mom." Anna went to her mother's room. "Mom, do you need help?"

"No, I'll be right out."

Anna said, "We'll be in the car."

As they sat in the car, Anna looked down to see she had put on a bright red shirt and purple tights. She watched Kathy struggle to get to the car, but she got in and began to drive.

"Where are we going, Mom?"

"I'm hungry," Luke said.

Anna said, "Shhh."

"No, it's okay," Kathy said. "I just don't feel good and need to go to the doctor." By the time they arrived at the urgent care, she was having difficulty breathing.

Anna said, "Mom, I'll tell them you cannot breathe." She ran inside the office, and two employees came right out.

They helped her into the office, and the lady said, "It's okay, kids. There are some coloring books there. We'll take good care of your mother." She brought a machine into the office and closed the door. Anna paced around the room.

Luke said, "Sit down, Anna. Stop moving around."

The lady came out and said, "Here, would you like a lollipop?"

"Is she okay?" Anna asked. "What's wrong?"

The lady said, "She'll be just fine. She's just a little nervous, and we are going to help her. We should not be much longer."

Luke took the lollipop. "Thanks."

Anna hesitated but blurted out to the nurse, "What about all the blood?"

The nurse seemed puzzled. "It's going to be okay."

After another thirty minutes went by, Anna saw her mother come out of the room. She got up and stared at her mother, as if investigating her. Kathy was breathing better and had color back in her face, and she was walking better. Anna ran over to her and gave her a big hug. "I'm so happy you're all right."

Kathy looked down at Anna and stroked her face. "I'm much better now. Let's go get something to eat. You both must be hungry."

Anna realized they had not eaten anything. "Whatever you want to eat is fine."

That night, Anna was reading a book when she heard her father come in the back door. She looked up at the clock to see it was eight in the evening. He came into the family room.

"Anna, you have to go to bed now. You have school."

Anna nodded and said, "Good night."

She took Luke's hand, but he said, "I'm not going."

Dan stared at Luke with a stern look, and Luke hesitated but got up. Anna quickly got her pajamas on, and Kathy came up to put them in bed. She kissed Anna on the head and said, "Sweet girl. I love you."

Anna put the covers on and lay down. "Good night, Mom." She waited in her bed until she heard her mother go downstairs.

Anna got up and crept down the stairs slowly. She stopped when she could hear her parents.

"Kathy, you are accusing me of something I didn't do," Dan said.

"Dan, I'm going to sleep in the spare bedroom from now on," Kathy said.

"You are my wife, damn it. Ever since we had these kids, I come second."

"Dan, I'm telling you: from now on, I am sleeping in the other room."

Dan said, "If you want a divorce, you won't get a penny."

"No, I don't want a divorce."

"What kind of a marriage is this, then?" he asked.

"Everything will be the same except for at night," she said.

"I need to have sex with my wife."

Kathy got up and said, "I don't feel safe anymore with you in that way," and briskly walked out of the room.

Dan paced around the room and picked up a lamp and threw it, shattering the glass in a thousand pieces. Anna dashed up the stairs, jumped through the air into her bed, and felt her body shaking uncontrollably. A few minutes later, she felt a hand on her head. "Now, Anna, there's no need to be frightened," her mother said. "Your father was just letting off a little steam. Everything is going to be fine, just fine. You should not eavesdrop, my dear. It's not right to listen in on private adult conversations. Remember that next time. Now, go to sleep."

Anna blurted out, "Mom, it's okay if you get a divorce. I think it would be better."

Kathy hesitated then said, "Anna, we are a family. You don't understand everything, and you *will* love and respect your father. Now go to sleep."

Anna waited until Kathy left, and then she grabbed her journal. She turned her flashlight on under her sheets. *Dear Diary, Sorry my hand is shaking, but I'm upset. Something happened with my mom and dad and my mom went to the doctor and is now sleeping in the other room. My father is angry and says he didn't do anything. Why does my mom keep sticking up for him if she does not like what he does? If they get a divorce, it will be better. I won't have to tiptoe around all the time when he is home. Thanks for listening.* Anna turned off the flashlight and put her head on her pillow. *When he is not here, it is better,* she thought. *Things will be better if he doesn't live here anymore.* She drifted off to sleep.

CHAPTER 2

Anna's Adolescence

Anna, now sixteen years old, woke at eight on a Sunday morning in April to rain pelting her window. She went to her mirror to brush her long brown hair and put her sweats on. At her bedroom door, she listened out to the hallway, her usual routine, noting with relief that it was quiet. Luke, now fourteen, was still sleeping. But when Anna went downstairs and peeked into the garage, her heart raced. *He's home.* She quietly closed the door and went back into the kitchen to grab a cereal bar and head back to her room.

As she went up the first few steps, she gasped for air when she heard the sound of his voice coming from the kitchen. "I want to talk with you this morning, Anna. Meet me in the study when you're dressed," Dan said.

"Yes, Dad." She went to her room, even though she was already dressed. She ate the cereal bar and then knocked on Luke's door. "Luke, Dad wants to talk to us."

Luke said, "I heard him only ask for you."

"Come on, Luke—you know it's easier to deal with him when we're together."

He yawned. "You really need to get some confidence. What do you think he's going to do to you?"

Anna said, "Let's just get it over with. I don't understand why he doesn't get to you."

"I don't let him." Luke smirked as he came out of his room. "Come on, I'll protect you."

Anna followed Luke into the study. Her eyes automatically fixated on the floor. The kids sat in the chairs in front of the desk where their father was working. Her heart was pounding. She started fidgeting in her chair and twisting her hair.

"Anna, stop pulling at your hair and look at me. I saw your exams online, and I'm extremely disappointed. I expect all As, and I saw a B in American history. Luke, well, as usual, you never meet my expectations as a Ward."

Anna tried to stop the tears from coming by thinking of the summer, but she had no luck.

Dan said, "Anna, grow up. Deal with reality. You are both going to study two hours a night now to improve your grades. When you come home from school, the chores are first."

Luke started to tap his foot against hers to distract her. Anna took a deep breath to slow down her heart rate and relieve her aching muscles that were on fire. She kept her eyes on a black dot on the bookshelf behind her father so it looked like she was looking at him. Dan sternly looked at them as he stood up, hanging over the desk and staring down at them.

"You *will* respect me. You can go now."

Anna tried to move her legs, but they were not moving fast enough. Luke was a few feet in front of her, and she whispered, "Wait for me!" She followed Luke into the kitchen and watched him pour some cereal for himself. "How can you eat? I'm so nauseated."

"How many times do I tell you not to let him get to you? I don't even listen to what he says anymore. He's never here, anyway. After he leaves, I'm going over to Ted's. You need to have more friends."

As Luke was texting his friend, who lived a few houses down, he continued. "You can't be so sensitive. Stop trying to make him happy,

Anna. It won't happen. Haven't you realized yet that no matter what you do, he will never be happy or proud of you? Has he ever told you anything positive? He is an assh—"

Kathy came in then and interrupted, saying, "I will pretend I didn't hear that."

Luke said, "Sorry. I'm going over to Ted's to study."

"Or to play video games? I know what goes on over there."

"Well, we do play a few games, but they also have a friendly football game today with his dad."

"Well, have fun," Kathy said.

After he left, Anna said, "Mom, why don't you make him stay here? *I* have to be here and do the chores."

"He seems happy over there," Kathy said. "You should go to a friend's house, too, once in a while."

Anna went to her room without responding. She scrolled down on her phone and found Lucy, her classmate, one of the five numbers programmed in it. Lying down on her bed, contemplating the call, she started rocking back and forth. thinking about how Luke always did his own thing. She then pressed the button for Lucy and waited for an answer.

"Hello?"

Anna said, "Hi, Lucy."

"Who's this?" Lucy asked.

"It's Anna. I thought you would recognize my voice."

"Oh, hey. What's going on?"

Anna thought of her mother and felt guilty. "I was wondering if you wanted to come over Thursday after school?" As she waited for her answer, she hoped Thursday would work since her father was never home until late on that day.

Lucy said, "Sure. I have nothing going on that day."

Thursday came fast. Lucy came home on the bus with Anna. "Anna, don't you see Jack looking at you?" she asked.

Anna said, "What do you mean?"

"Are you that blind? All the boys think you're hot. No one knows you, though. You are way too quiet and shy."

Anna glanced over to Jack as he gave her an approving glance. "I am not hot," she protested.

"Well, with your long flowing hair, beautiful hazel eyes, and—"

Anna cut Lucy off. "That's enough."

"Do you wear makeup?" Lucy asked.

"A little blush is all," she said.

"Wow, I wish I could look like you with a little blush."

The bus was rounding the corner, and Anna saw out of the corner of her eye that her father's car was parked in the driveway.

Lucy looked at her and asked, "Are you okay? What's wrong? You're pale as a ghost."

Anna suddenly was seven again, standing in the entryway with a friend, staring at her father. "Anna, why are your shoes in the hallway?" he'd shouted at her, oblivious to her company. "How can you be so stupid? If you can't follow the rules of the house, you will always be a failure at everything." His voice made Anna's legs shake, and soon she was humiliated in front of her friend when she felt her pant legs grow wet.

Lucy grabbed Anna by the arm, and Anna returned from this momentary flash of the past. She looked at Lucy, pushed her aside, and threw up on the floor. All the kids on the bus started yelling, and Anna grabbed her bag and said to the bus driver, "Let me out, please." Lucy followed her, and she said, "Please go home. I'm too sick to have you over."

"Let me help you," Lucy said.

Anna yelled, "I'll call you!"

The bus driver pulled over close to her stop and said, "Don't worry. I hope you feel better."

Anna, shaking from her memory, wondered why her father was home. Taking a deep breath, she went in through the back door and started up the steps to her room. She heard someone crying and went to the family room to find her father crying and her mother at his side.

"Is Luke okay?"

Kathy said, "Yes, he's fine. Your father's mother has died."

"Who?"

"Your grandmother," Kathy said. "She's been sick for a while now, and she died today."

Anna stormed up to her room and slammed the door, knocking her favorite picture off the wall. She fell on her bed and cried. A grandmother she had never known, and now she was gone.

After a while, Anna felt a hand over her back. She looked up and saw Luke. "Are you okay? What's going on?"

"I assumed we never had family since no one ever talked about any family members," she said. "Why are our parents so messed up?"

Luke said, "I'm sure we wouldn't want to have known them. Why do you question everything? You'll drive yourself mad."

Anna went downstairs and sat against the wall outside the family room. She listened to her parents talk.

"Why did they have to notify me she died?" she heard her father asking. "I never wanted to hear about her again. That evil woman."

Kathy said, "She's your mother. Your brother thought you should know."

"He's no brother of mine. They can all go to hell."

Kathy got up, and Anna followed her to the kitchen. She started preparing dinner and said, "Anna, just let it go. Some things are better left alone."

"You always leave me out. I'm important, too, and she was my grandmother. Why does he hate everyone?"

"He has a different way of showing his feelings," Kathy explained. "He didn't grow up in a loving family."

"So why does he treat us the same way? It makes no sense."

"We have to love people for who they are, or else it will drive us mad." Kathy leaned over the kitchen sink, looked at Anna, and said, "It'll all be okay."

"What about the funeral? Can I go?"

"No. It's in California. I need you to let this go. Someday I will explain things to you."

She has never looked at me that way before. I guess I'll have to let it go, Anna thought. She went to her room to journal and wrote: *I now understand why my mother has lived with my father. She accepted who he was at some point in time. She gave up trying to change him or make things right or better. Maybe this is the way things really are in the world? I don't ever want to get married.*

As she was journaling, Anna's phone rang, and she answered it.

Lucy said, "Hi, Anna. I wanted to check to see if you were okay."

"You're checking on me?" Anna asked.

"Of course," Lucy said. "You left so abruptly and threw up. I was worried."

"I'm much better now. Thanks for checking."

"Can we reschedule for a different day?" Lucy asked.

"We'll see," Anna said. "I'm busy right now after school."

"I noticed you felt sick when the bus was in sight of your house," Lucy said. "You were thinking of something that made you really upset."

"No. It was something I ate."

Lucy said, "It's okay to talk about it, you know."

"Lucy, I'm fine. I'm going to lie down now. Thanks for calling."

Anna went downstairs and saw her father working. Her desire to understand overcame her fear of asking, and she knocked on the door. "Can I ask you why you hate your family so much?"

Dan, staring out the window in deep thought, said, "My family did nothing to help me."

Anna asked, "What did your mother do?"

After a long pause, he replied, "She cared more about herself than she cared for me. I have put that to rest. It's all in the past."

Anna wrote in her journal: *Why does my father have no forgiveness in him? Can someone so close to you do so much damage to you that you push that person out of your life forever? Will I want anything to do with my father when I am older? Doesn't he see he is doing the same thing to his own kids?*

A month later, Anna got off the bus and noticed a strange car in the driveway. She inspected the older blue BMW and noticed a California license plate. She saw Luke walking down the driveway and waited for him.

Luke asked, "Who's here?"

"I just got home," Anna said. "I don't know."

"Well, no one ever visits. This should be interesting."

Anna said, "I know. I wonder what's going on."

They came in the back door and saw a man around their mother's age at the kitchen table. Anna noticed a resemblance between him and her mother. He had a light beard and longer hair in a ponytail. He stared at her as he bit his lip. Anna said, "Hi, I'm Anna."

Kathy swiftly came into the room before he could say anything and said, "This is my cousin Tom. He's in town passing through." Tom smiled at Anna. Anna felt uncomfortable with his presence.

"I didn't know you had a cousin, Mom. I'm Luke." Luke offered his hand to shake.

Tom smirked. "She didn't want you to know about me. I'm a bad influence."

"Well, he'll stay for the night and move on. He is just passing through," Kathy said.

Anna felt tension between them. Her mother was pacing around in the kitchen. She said, "I'm going to do my homework and come down for dinner later."

She felt Tom's eyes following her as she left the kitchen. She opened up her journal in her room and wrote: *My mother's cousin Tom is here. I didn't know my mother had any family. Why is she so secretive? Maybe Tom can fill me in a little bit.* She started to work on her homework as Luke came into the room.

"That dude is weird. If that's what our relatives are like, I'm glad we don't know them."

"You're so cynical," Anna said. "Maybe we can find out about Mom and her family."

"When will you learn, Anna? Unrealistic expectations will ruin you. Let's go to dinner and mess with him." Luke laughed.

Anna and Luke came down for dinner together. Tom was on his phone playing a game, and the quiet tension was deafening. Luke, smiling, said, "So Tom, I see you're from California. Are you running from the law?"

Kathy gave Luke a dirty look and shook her head.

Tom replied, "Oh, so you're a comedian."

Kathy said, "He's moving to New York and passing through town. He's leaving early in the morning."

"So, where is Mr. Ward this evening?" Tom asked.

Anna and Luke both stared at Kathy, waiting for her reply. "Late meeting and dinner. I'm not sure when he'll be home."

When Kathy left the kitchen, Anna asked, "Did you grow up with my mother? What was she like?"

Tom was a tall, balding man. He had a beer gut but was otherwise thin. He tapped his fork against the table when he was not taking a bite of food. Kathy came out of the pantry and said, "Tom, can you please stop that noise?"

Tom sat back in his chair. "Well, she was quiet and shy, almost like she wanted to be invisible. I didn't know her for very long."

"Tom, I warned you once," Kathy said. "Now this is your last warning. Knock it off or you'll have to leave." Tom understood and nodded with a smirk, looking at Anna.

Tom said to Anna, "Please eat. Don't let me stop you from eating. How old are you, Anna? Are you in any sports or anything at school?"

Kathy said, "Tom, she's fine. You don't need to know about her."

"Mom, what *can* we talk about?" Anna said.

Luke was listening and eating his meal intently. He said, "Yeah, Mom, what *can* we talk about?"

Kathy said, "Just eat and go finish your homework. I'll clean up tonight."

Luke ignored his mother and said, "Well, Tom, I play chess—does that count?"

Kathy went to the bathroom. Anna followed her and asked, "Mom, what's going on? Why are you being so rude?"

"Why don't you sleep with me tonight and give him your bed?" Kathy suggested.

"Why are you avoiding my question?"

Kathy looked her in the eye and said, "Some things are better left alone."

"I'm spending the night over Todd's," Luke announced. "Tom can sleep in my bed if he wants to."

Anna sighed with relief. Luke packed a bag in his room and came down and said, "Nice to meet you." After Luke left, the three of them sat in the living room watching the news.

Anna thought, *I'll ask him questions when my mother leaves the room.* However, Kathy never left the room. Around ten, Anna gave up and said, "I'm going to bed to read. Good night."

Tom said, "Actually, I'm going to go to bed, too. I'm getting up early."

He took off his cowboy boots. Kathy got up and said, "Come, I'll show you to your room."

Tom said, "Good night, Anna. It was a pleasure to meet you." He winked at her.

Anna saw her mother say something to Tom but couldn't make out what she'd said. Tom rolled his eyes and said, "Don't worry, Kathy." He shut the door behind him in Luke's room.

Kathy said, "Good night, Anna." Anna closed her door, and Kathy paced back and forth in the hallway. She decided to stay on the couch and watch television. Around twelve, Dan came home, and she pretended to be asleep. He left her alone and left the television on. Kathy dozed off watching television.

Anna fell asleep, but she was startled awake by the weight of someone on top of her. A hand gripped tightly over her mouth, and she felt paralyzed. In an instant, she heard, "You better be quiet and not say anything, or I will kill you and your mother."

Anna froze, praying she was dreaming, but the pain was too real. She felt her underwear being ripped from her and his hands all over her.

His weight felt like a car was on top of her, and her muscles would not work. Her heart felt like it would just beat out of her chest as she laid there like an animal given up a fight. Her consciousness drifted away and transcended somewhere else. Just as his penis tried to penetrate her vagina, a surge of energy rushed into her as she felt tissue ripping. She was able to break free of his hand, and she bit his arm and wouldn't let go. He bit his lip to keep from screaming and jumped up and out of the bed. She released her bite, and he ran out of the room. Anna tried to catch her breath as she hurried into the bathroom and locked the door. She heard a noise and looked out the window to see Tom getting in his car and driving away. She saw blood on her nightgown and on the floor. She looked in the mirror and saw blood on her face. She spit in the sink and washed her face. Instinctively, she put a hot towel on her vagina. She didn't want her mother to wake up. As she sat on the floor, she started shaking uncontrollably, and a wave of nausea came over her as she quickly leaned over the toilet and threw up. Her exhaustion was starting to kick in.

Anna headed for her bed, but fear overcame her, so she took a pillow from her mother's room and put it on the floor next to her mother, who was sleeping on the living room couch. She grabbed hold of her mother's dangling hand and held onto it and closed her eyes, but she could only see Tom's face, so she lay there with her eyes open, not sure when she may have drifted off to sleep.

The next morning, Kathy woke her up and said, "Anna, why on earth are you sleeping on the floor?"

Anna woke up in a fog and quickly felt pain in between her legs and an unwanted image of Tom came with extreme tension. She thought about Tom with a gun or a knife and said with a cracked voice, "I had a bad nightmare and woke up with a headache, and I didn't want to be alone."

"Are you sure? That must have been quite a dream."

Anna said, "Frightening." She went to the kitchen and opened a bottle of ibuprofen.

"Eat something before, honey," Kathy said. "You must have a bad headache."

Anna turned the television on and lay down on the couch where her mother had slept. She smelled the pillow with her mother's scent and relaxed a moment. Kathy came into the living room and said, "I thought you were going to your room?"

Anna wiped a tear running down her cheek and said, "I'd rather stay here."

Kathy looked at her with concern but didn't seem to notice that Anna was suffering from more than just a headache. "I will make a nice breakfast for you."

Anna relaxed, hearing the comfort of her mother in the kitchen, and fell asleep on the couch.

Luke came home around ten, waking Anna up. "Good morning, Mom. Where's Tom?"

Kathy said, "He must have left early. He was only stopping through."

"Why is Anna on the couch?" Luke asked.

"She had a bad nightmare last night that is still bothering her, I think. Sit down and have some breakfast."

Anna listened to them talk and thought, *No one will ever know. He's gone and will never come back. There's no point in telling anyone since I was able to stop him, and I don't want Mom to worry about me. I will put this out of my mind like it was a nightmare and never happened.*

Anna got up for school the next day and put on sweats and a long-sleeve shirt under a sweatshirt and a jacket. She wore her hair down, and she did not put any makeup on. When she went downstairs, Luke asked, "What are you wearing? It's not that cold out."

Anna said, "I feel a chill. Maybe I'm getting sick. I have a lot to do at school, though."

She sat on the bus in the front seat alone. When she got off the bus at school, Lucy ran up to her. "Hey, how are you?" Anna tried to walk faster, but Lucy caught up to her. "Anna, why are you avoiding me?"

"What do you mean?"

"I've been calling you," Lucy said. "I want to get together this week."

Anna said, "I'm sorry. My grandmother died, and I just don't have time right now. I'll let you know when I have some time." She didn't make eye contact and kept walking.

Anna was in class when the teacher came over. "Anna, the front office would like to see you."

Anna, puzzled, left the classroom and went to the office. A woman waiting there greeted her and said, "Hi, Anna, come into my office, please. Do you want a drink?"

The counselor was a middle-aged woman and very heavy and short. "My name is Paula. You haven't come to see me all year, but I'm your counselor."

"What is this about?" Anna asked.

"Well, one of your classmates is concerned about you."

Anna said, "Why? I'm fine, really. No need to worry." She looked at the floor.

"This is a safe place to talk if you want to," Paula said. "It's nice to have a friend that cares so much." Anna kept silent. "If you want to talk, maybe I can help."

Anna, knowing that she had to say something, said, "Oh, I lost my grandmother and just have been wanting to be with my family. That's all."

"Loss is a difficult thing to go through."

"I really am okay," Anna said. "My mother and I talk a lot. Can I go back to class now?"

Paula said, "Well, I'm available when you want to talk. Call me to schedule a time." She handed Anna her card with her number.

Anna went home and to her room. Opening her journal, she wrote, *Why is everyone so concerned? Why don't people just mind their own business? I am just going to focus on my schoolwork the next two years, and then I can go to college and everything will be better, away from my father and this place.*

CHAPTER 3

Anna Goes to College

Two years later, Anna raced off the bus to the mailbox for the fifth brisk afternoon in April. Her heart was pounding in anticipation of a letter from one of three schools she had applied to.

Kathy yelled out to her from the house, "I already got the mail. No letters from any schools yet."

Anna, now seventeen, had grown to five feet, nine inches tall and wore her hair long to cover her face. She walked slowly to the house and thought, *I need to get away from here. I can't wait to move away to college. My whole life will be so much better.*

Luke, a sophomore now, came over to Anna. "Why are you so worried about getting into nursing school? You are one of the smartest in the class."

"What if I don't?" Anna asked. "What will I do then?"

The next day, Anna raced home off the bus again with Luke behind her. She quickly took the mail out of the mailbox, weeded through the pile, and saw an envelope with the seal of the University of Michigan on it. *This is it.* Anna allowed Luke to grab it out of her hands as they still stood by the mailbox. "I'll open it for you." He tore it open and said, "Looks like my sister is in."

Anna stood there, frozen, and a tear traced her cheek. Luke hugged his sister and said, "Now you can have a life for yourself, sis."

"Luke, when I leave, can you look after Mom? You can't spend all your time at Ted's anymore."

"But Ted's family is so normal," Luke said. "You have no idea how messed up our family is, Anna."

"I don't care," Anna said. "Whether you like it or not, it's the family you have. Mom will need you even more." She walked into the house with a smile on her face.

Luke followed her, saying, "Just because *you* feel responsible for Mom doesn't mean I have to. She makes her own choices, Anna, and I have to be happy with my life. I won't let the tension and stress at home control me like you have. I won't give in to the same guilt that controls you."

Anna started to make a salad for dinner while she waited to give the news to her mother. Kathy came in from the hallway.

"You don't have to do that, Anna," Kathy said.

Anna grabbed her hands and said, "Guess what! I got in to U of M, my first choice."

Kathy, holding back her emotions, paused and cleared her throat as she looked at the ground. Anna watched her mother and realized, judging by her facial expression of pursed lips, that she was sad. "I'm happy for you, Anna."

Anna let go of her mother's hands and grabbed her shoulders, looking into her eyes. "I'll only be a twenty-minute drive away, Mom."

"I know, honey," Kathy said. "I knew this day was coming. A mother is a mother. You don't quite understand about changes yet. You are growing up, and it's difficult to let go." Kathy then held onto Anna's hands and looked back at her eager daughter wanting her mother's approval and excitement. "I am so very happy, honey. You must know that."

Anna nodded and embraced her mother with a tight hug. "Thanks, Mom. I love you."

Anna walked to her father's office and put the acceptance letter on his desk on top of all his papers. She thought, *Now he will be proud of me. I worked so hard to prove to him that I could make something of myself.*

After dinner, as Anna cleaned up the kitchen, she asked, "When is Dad coming home?"

Kathy, smiling, said, "I'm not sure. He'll be proud of you, Anna, even if he doesn't react the way you want him to. I know he doesn't always show it, but he loves you."

Anna said, "Mom. Don't speak for him or stick up for him. You always do that, and you never understand what I'm feeling or thinking." She noticed tears in Kathy's eyes and changed her tone. "I'm sorry, Mom."

Kathy walked off before Anna could hug her.

Later, as Anna lay in bed yawning, she looked at the clock. It was already ten, and her father still wasn't home. She decided to go to sleep, but first she wrote in her journal. *What does my father do with all his time? Is he really at a meeting or out with clients? Is this how things are for other families? I am not going to get involved in a relationship like this if I ever decide to have a relationship. Is Luke right?* As she was writing, she heard her father pull into the driveway.

Anna heard her father in the office and went to the kitchen to get some water. She sat at the table, pretending to read the paper. He came out of the office and turned to go up the stairs. She sat at the table for a while and cried. Then she wiped her tears and went up the stairs to her bedroom.

Anna woke up the next morning at seven. Knowing her father usually left for the gym early on Saturdays, she didn't want to miss him. She came down the stairs and saw that his car wasn't in the driveway. *Wow, I already missed him,* Anna thought. She did her chores and kept herself busy in anticipation of her father coming home.

Luke watched Anna and could see her anxiety as she kept looking out the window and aimlessly pacing around. "Anna, he isn't going to give his approval. I hate watching you do this to yourself. I'm going to Ted's."

Since Kathy had gone to the grocery store, Anna grabbed a broom and started to sweep. Dan came in and grabbed the newspaper and started to read. Anna took a deep breath and asked, "So, did you see my acceptance letter?"

Dan, still sweaty from his workout and with dark scruff on his beard lines, looked up from his paper, squinting, and said, "Oh, is that what the paper was? That's good. We have to talk about the cost."

Anna bit her lip to avoid the flow of tears. *I feel so angry. Should I say anything?* Facing the window in preparation to walk away, she turned around with her eyes closed. "Why aren't you going to congratulate me? Aren't you proud of me? I worked so hard to get into that school."

"It's expected that my kids will get into a good school. I expect nothing less from you," he said.

Luke suddenly came in the back door, going to the fridge and grabbing a drink. Dan continued without acknowledging Luke. "I think it's good for you to take some responsibility for the cost," he said. "I was thinking I'd help out and pay for half. What do you think?"

Luke slammed his drink on the table and looked Dan straight in his eyes. "Anna has worked so hard for your approval, and you have the money. She is so good to you and Mom. Why would you strap her with all that debt?"

Dan rose from his chair and stood straight, as if he needed a position of authority. "I disagree, Luke. I paid my way and think it's good for you kids to be invested in your own education."

Luke backed down and sat on the bench, looking to the floor. "If that is the case, I'd like you to give Anna my half for college, so she won't owe anything."

Anna, cowering in the corner of the kitchen, appeared to wake up. "No, Luke. I won't let you do that."

Dan looked at Luke with a smirk. "If you want." Luke nodded his head to Dan and left the room.

Anna followed Luke to his room. "What are you doing?"

Luke jumped on his bed and opened a comic. "No worries, sis. I would never take a dime from that jerk. I have my own plan. You have tolerated living here and looking after Mom, while I've escaped to a normal environment. You deserve to have your college paid for. It's the least thing I can do."

Anna woke up on the day of her high school graduation and spent the morning like any other. She was eating cereal when Kathy came in and said, "So, graduate, what do you want to do after your graduation, and why aren't you dressed?"

"Oh, I decided not to go."

Kathy, still in her pajamas, sat next to Anna and held her hand on the kitchen table. "You didn't go to your prom, and now you don't want to go to your own graduation! These are important events, and you'll regret this when you're older."

"Mom, it's no big deal. High school isn't really an accomplishment to me. All those functions are so silly."

Luke had his face in the fridge, listening in. Kathy nudged Luke by bumping into him, hoping he'd offer encouragement. "Luke, what do you think?"

"It's a once-in-a-lifetime event. I'd like to see you get your diploma. Aren't you best looking or something?"

Anna blushed and slapped Luke's arm. "Yeah, right. It's too late, anyway. I don't have my cap and gown."

Luke turned serious and said, "Are you *sure* you don't want to go? I can get you a cap and gown. I have connections."

Maybe they're right. Will I regret this? I don't even have any friends. I haven't been awarded anything. "No, I'm sure. Let's go out to lunch when they're graduating."

Kathy motioned to Luke. "Why don't you two watch the ceremony for a while? I'd like to at least get a picture then we'll go for lunch."

Anna started to pace the kitchen. *How can I get out of this? I can't go and watch my own graduation!* Luke picked up on her anxiety.

"Mom, it's okay. If she doesn't want to go, we'll get a picture at home. We can make this a special day for her to remember."

Anna mouthed to Luke, "Thank you." She grabbed her purse and remembered she needed some razors. "I'm going to the store if anyone needs anything."

Kathy shook her head. "Think about where you want to go when you're out," she suggested.

As Anna drove past the site of her high school graduation, she decided to pull over and watch from her car. She saw her classmates all lining up, laughing and smiling. *Is this really my class? How could I have spent all that time with them and not have any real connections? College will be different.*

She saw Lucy with her parents, taking a picture of her and a few other girls. They looked very proud. Anna remembered how Lucy was the one girl who had tried to reach out and be her friend. *I'm happy for her. I wonder where she's going to college.* She looked over at the other side of the event and out of the corner of her eye saw him, her own father, leaning against a tree, looking around for someone. Could it be for her? Suddenly, she wished she had her cap and gown on. *Why is he here? Why is he pretending to care? Why can't I have a normal family?* She hit the steering wheel, surprising herself, then drove to a nearby parking lot and cried.

Anna calmed herself down by deep breathing and drove home without going to the store. She ran up to her room and immediately started to write in her journal. *Does he actually care? Is my mother right when she says he just does not know how to show it? It doesn't matter now because my life is going to be different. I'm going to have friends in college and not feel embarrassed by my family. I have lots of questions about my family, but I don't want to hurt my mother by asking her. She seems to get upset when I want to know about her past, so I will have to let it go, for now at least. I hope Luke will step up and take care of her. She is alone, and my father is never around. I won't have that type of relationship. I'd rather be single and do my own thing than be in an unhappy marriage. I would really like to know how she ended up this way.*

Anna got another letter from the school a few weeks later that contained information on her new roommate. Lori Bowman was from northern Indiana, only a few hours away from the university in Ann

Arbor. Anna, in Northville, was only a twenty-minute drive away. The letter gave her the phone number and address of her new roommate and listed all the rules and regulations of the dorm.

She went to her room, closed the door, and sat at her desk, feeling her heartbeat speed up as she dialed the number into her cellphone and waited. "Hi, is Lori there?"

"Speaking."

"Hi, Lori. I'm Anna, your roommate next year."

Lori said, "Oh, hi. How did you find out? I haven't gotten anything yet."

"I got a letter in the mail. I guess I'm excited for next year, and I called you right away."

Lori said, "I am, too. I could use a nice summer first, though. I'm not too eager to start all that work. Well, I'm meeting up with my boyfriend now. Can I call you later?"

Anna got up and started to pace in her room. *Should I have called so soon? Do I appear too excited?* "Of course. Take your time. I'll catch up with you later. Have a nice summer. Bye." Anna hung up before Lori could respond.

One day at the beginning of August, Anna looked out her window after waking up later than usual and saw her father drive up in a brand new black BMW M4. She saw her mother race out of the house and gasp. "Dan, what's this? You never told me you were thinking of getting a new car."

"I don't need your permission to spend my money, Kathy," Dan said.

Anna threw her hair up, grabbed a sweater and pulled it on over her pajamas, and ran out the door. She looked over and saw her father's Mercedes coming up the driveway, and a guy with long hair in a ponytail and a big belly hanging out of his shirt got out and shook Dan's hand. "Hope you like it." He got in a car that had pulled up behind him. They drove off, and Anna, puzzled, remained quiet.

Dan came over to her and handed his car keys to her. "You need a reliable car at school, so this is for you to use. But not to have—I'll expect you to return it to me in good condition when you are finished with your degree."

Anna choked on her saliva and coughed. After she caught her breath, she mumbled, "Thank you."

Kathy nodded to Dan in a pleased fashion. "Good idea."

Dan walked into the house and headed upstairs to take a shower. Anna waited until he was out of sight and turned to Kathy. "He didn't say anything to you about the car?"

"I had no idea," Kathy said. "Now you can come home anytime."

Anna thought of asking her mother why her father seemed to make so many decisions without consulting Kathy, but she did not want to spoil the mood.

She woke the next morning early and sat at her desk, writing a note. *Dear Dad, Thank you for the car. I really appreciate the thought, and it will help me get back and forth to school.*

As she wrote, Luke came in and said, "Hey. Mom told me about the car. Have you asked him about what kind of strings are attached? He always has strings."

"I don't want to think about that now," Anna said. "Help me pack the car for school."

Luke brought some boxes to help pack the car. "I'm going to miss you around here," he said.

Anna said, "You were never around here. You will be now, right?"

"Relax, Anna," Luke said. "Things don't change around here. You go and start building your life and find some happiness." He hugged her for a few minutes. Luke was now four inches taller than she was, and his long bony arms wrapped around her. Anna got in the driver's side, and as she pulled away, she looked in the rearview mirror at the house she'd grown up in. *This life as I know it is over, and I will build a better one for myself. All the bad memories are in my past.*

Kathy followed Anna in her own car to help her move in. When they reached the dorm, they both parked right outside the dorm building. Anna went to her mother's car. "Let's check out the room first." There were a few other cars on the street but not many. They carried a few bags and climbed the stairs and down the hall until they reached her room number, 214. They noticed that the door was locked, and just then, they saw the RA walking toward them.

"Hi, I'm Aiden, the RA. What's your name?"

"Anna Ward."

He looked at his clipboard and checked her off then handed her a key and a bunch of papers. "Here you are. If you get locked out, I can always let you in. I'm supposed to tell you to read that carefully because of our strict rules for the dorms. Any questions?" Kathy and Anna both shook their heads.

He said, "Great. Let me know if anything comes up. Welcome to college."

Anna opened the door and looked at an empty, stuffy room with two bare mattresses atop two small beds. There were two desks, a wastebasket, and a small sink with a mirror by the door.

"Wow, fancy." Kathy laughed. "You'll make it your own. I wish *I* had this opportunity. Honey, make a lot of friends and enjoy yourself."

After a few trips back and forth to the car to unload Anna's things, Kathy said, "I'm sorry, but I'm late for my doctor's appointment and have to run. Please have fun and work hard."

Anna grabbed her mother and held her. "Okay. I love you. Take care of yourself. Make sure Luke is around more."

"Don't worry about me," Kathy said. "Live your life and make your journey. Don't let life just happen to you, but make good, sound decisions to take responsibility for your own journey. And be honest with yourself every step of the way, even when it's difficult to look at your reality, for what it is not what you want it to be."

Anna stared at her mother and grabbed the journal she kept in her purse.

"What are you doing?" Kathy asked.

Anna jotted down her mother's words. "What did you say after 'honest'?"

Kathy tried to repeat it. "'Be honest with your decisions and look at your life the way it is.' Honey, this will save you a lot of undue suffering in the long run."

Anna grabbed her mother. "You have suffered a lot."

Kathy said, "This is about you, not me. I am going to go before I cry. Call me anytime, honey." She left, and Anna looked around and thought, *Freedom*.

Anna was putting her sheets and comforter on her bed when she heard the door open and loud voices start to fill the room. A girl with long, curly blond hair and pleasant, friendly eyes came in and said, "Hey, girl, you must be Anna. I'm Lori. This is my dad, Scott, and mom, Dawn."

They were short of breath from carrying many suitcases and bags. Her father put his on the floor then helped Dawn with the ones she was carrying. When his hands were free, he turned to Anna. "Hello, it's so nice to meet you, Anna." Then he did something that really surprised her—the six-foot-three older man gave her a hug.

Anna stood there with her arms down at her sides and thought, *This is what a father's hug feels like.*

Lori looked embarrassed, oblivious to what this meant to Anna. "*Dad*, don't hug people you just met!"

He said, "This is your new roommate who is going to look after you." And he winked at Anna.

Anna said, "Of course I will." Feeling uncomfortable, she kept busy unpacking and listened to Lori's parents talk while they helped her unpack and get organized.

Scott said, "So, Anna, where are you from?"

Anna said, "Northville."

He said, "What's your major?"

Looking to the floor, Anna said, "Nursing."

Lori interrupted, "Dad, please, don't drill her." He rolled his eyes. "Why don't you guys go so Anna and I have a chance to get to know each other?" she asked.

Scott said, "You're not going to eat with us? I thought we would take you out." He looked hurt. Anna couldn't believe how differently he talked to Lori than her dad talked to her. It actually seemed to matter to him whether he got to spend one last meal with his daughter before she began her new life at college.

Lori said, "Dad, I'm gonna eat with Anna."

Dawn interrupted. "Hon, let's allow these girls to get acquainted. We have to cut the cord sometime." She smiled at her husband, and he nodded in agreement.

Scott said, "I'm so proud of you and all that you have become. Whatever you decide to do, we love you and are so proud. Remember to call us with any problems you have, even if you think we will be disappointed. Remember to FaceTime me every other day at least. I'm going to miss you."

Anna had stopped unpacking and was now sitting on her bed, watching this family as if it was a play unfolding in front of her. Lori gave her a strange look, and Anna, realizing she was staring, said, "Oh, I'm sorry. I'm just tired and in a daze. I have to tell the RA, Aiden, something." Anna pretended to leave but shut the door and listened from the hallway.

Scott said, "I'm sorry for embarrassing you, but you are my baby and always will be. It's hard to let you go."

Lori said, "I know. I'll miss you, too. I'll call you often—I promise."

Her mother said, "Your father said it all. I love you, my Lori. Take care of yourself and eat healthy, and no drinking, please. I don't need another incident to happen."

Lori said, "Mom, we already talked about this. Please relax and don't worry. I learned my lesson. I'll be fine."

Anna dashed off down the hall. She sat in the living room on the floor and looked out the window just in time to see Lori's parents get into their car. She went back to the room, and Lori said, "Wow, I hope you don't have overbearing parents, too. They are suffocating sometimes."

"They seem so nice to me," Anna said. "It must be nice to be missed so much."

Lori said, "What are your parents like?"

"Nothing like yours," Anna said. "Would you like to go to dinner tonight?"

"Sure, we have a lot to talk about," Lori agreed. "Is six o'clock okay with you?"

Anna said, "Sure."

Lori was rushing around the room as if she was looking for something, and she found her phone. "I'll be back at six, then. I have some things to do."

"Okay." Anna grabbed her journal from under her mattress when Lori left. She wrote, *First day of my new life. Lori's father was so nice and cared so much for his daughter. How many fathers are like that? I have a feeling I have a lot to learn in my new world. I am so excited but scared to death of making friends, finally, now that I don't have my father to destroy any friendships I make.* She put down the journal and finished unpacking.

Anna opened her laptop to look up her classes. She was eager to get to dinner and needed a distraction. Finally, Lori came in at ten after six, and Anna asked, "Can we go? I'm starving."

Lori said, "Okay. I just have to pee."

Walking to the cafeteria, Anna thought, *What should I say? Is she going to like me?* Lori broke the silence and asked, "Do you have any brothers or sisters?"

"Just one brother, Luke. He's a junior in high school now. What about you?"

Lori said, "Yes, I am the oldest of three girls. I'll miss them." Entering the cafeteria, she added, "I heard they have good food, since we'll be eating here all the time."

Anna got a salad and a sandwich and used the card that her mother put money on for her meals. As they sat down to eat, Lori said, "I have to tell you something, Anna. I have a boyfriend, Carl, and he goes to school here, too, but he has an apartment off campus. My parents don't know, but I'm mostly going to be living there, and I would appreciate it if you'd cover for me."

Anna felt her mood deflate, and sadness filled her.

Lori, picking up on Anna's body language, said, "I'm sorry, Anna. This has nothing to do with you. I have been waiting for a year. But look on the bright side—you'll have your own room."

Anna thought, *I've had my own room my whole life*. But when she replied to Lori, she tried to sound indifferent. "Whatever works for you!"

They walked back to the room, and Carl came over to help Lori move some of her clothes to his apartment. Lori introduced them, and Carl said, "Nice to meet you. You'll have to come to our party. Lori will give you the info."

Anna nodded in agreement and said, "Nice to meet you. We'll see. I'm going to go out while you move stuff."

Lori said, "I'll see you for dinner tomorrow?"

Anna nodded yes. When she came back later, the room was quiet.

Anna sat on her bed, reading a list of events scheduled to help the new students meet each other. She opened her journal and wrote: *I thought my roommate and I could go to some events together. I hoped she would give me some courage to go. Why don't things work out for me? I thought I would have an automatic friend, but now I am even more alone. I need to overcome my shyness and meet other people. I will get a job to meet new people and get some added money to help myself. That will help me.* That night, alone in the room in her new bed, Anna tossed and turned, the building's unfamiliar noises keeping her awake.

Anna woke up exhausted the next morning at eight and made instant coffee from her hot water pot. She washed her face in the small sink and brushed her teeth. She read through the list of activities one more time and then threw it in the trash. She put her hair up and carried her bucket of toiletries out into the hall then checked to make sure the coast was clear before she walked down to the shower. She wanted to be sure she had the communal bathroom to herself. After her shower, she turned the water off and dried herself then briskly walked back to her room and got dressed with her towel wrapped around her head.

Anna took her class list she printed a month ago and went to the bookstore. She noticed a "help wanted" sign hanging on the glass door to the store and thought that would be a great job to meet other students and maybe get a discount on her books. She went to the counter and asked for an application. The guy behind the counter was a middle-aged man who was awkwardly tall and lanky, with dark brown, suspicious eyes that seemed to follow her. He gave her the application and said, "I'm Evan, the manager. Fill that out here and give it back to me right away."

Anna looked around and saw a long line and only one other counter open and no other employees. She filled out the application and put it on the counter behind him. Evan said, "Excuse me for a moment," to the customer he was waiting on. To Anna, he said, "Are you a student?" Before she could answer, he asked, "Are you a felon?"

Anna nodded and then shook her head, laughing a little at the idea of herself committing the kind of crime that would rise to the level of a felony. She couldn't even bring herself to leave her dorm room to attend a social event.

"I need you to go back and make sure the books are all lined up and sorted back on their shelves. I just had a guy quit, and two other workers didn't show up this morning. I'm really in a jam—this is the busiest week of the year. If you do well helping me today, the job is yours."

Anna thought, *This is a lucky break—I have no experience, but he doesn't care.* She said, "Sure. Okay."

He left her to figure out her work and started ringing up customers who were becoming agitated with the wait. Anna kept her purse with her and went over to the shelves, where she started to line up books that hurried customers had left disorganized. Some of the books, most worth hundreds of dollars, were even scattered on the floor. She picked up the books and started to line them up in the correct places. One towering stack was too big and started to slip from her arms. But before they dropped, another set of hands appeared and helped her lift them onto the shelf.

She looked up into the eyes of a man—way up because he was well over six feet tall—who had wavy brown hair and strong facial features. He said, "You should be careful not to lift too many at once to save your back. You think you can do it today, but trust me—it will catch up with you in a few weeks." Then he walked away as Anna stood there staring after him. He looked back and gave her a grand smile, shaking his head.

When he was out of her sight, Anna thought, *Was I staring at him? What is wrong with me? I should have introduced myself. He was so cute and nice. Why is my heart racing like this? I feel faint!*

Evan came over and interrupted her thoughts. "Hey," he said, "the shelves look great. Do you want the job?"

Anna said, "Yes, but the hours have to be flexible with my classes and studying."

Evan nodded. "The pay is nine dollars an hour, and I do expect a minimum of twenty hours a week. You get a discount on the books, though. That can help significantly."

Anna said, "Okay, I can work with that."

Evan seemed to mumble something and handed her a W-2 form. "Fill that out for today. You really helped me out. Thanks. Can I have your schedule for school so I can work around that?"

Anna said, "Sure, and can you ring me up for my books as well?"

Evan rang her up, and she said, "Wow."

He said, "Yeah—fifty percent discount for employees. You can also return the books at the end of the semester and get some of your money back."

Anna walked back to her dorm in a better mood than she'd been in for weeks. *Maybe things really will be okay*, she thought.

When she arrived at her dorm, she took her key out and was starting to put it in the door when it opened.

"Hi, Anna. I came over to say hi. I hope it's okay?" Lori said.

Anna said, "It's your room, too. Of course it's okay. Are you ready for classes tomorrow?"

Lori said, "Yes, I guess so. I'm feeling guilty about lying to my parents, though."

"Why don't you just stay here, then?" Anna suggested. "You can go over to Carl's anytime."

Lori said, "No, I want to live with him. I love sleeping with him and waking up with him."

"I got a job today at the bookstore. The manager was the only one working so he had me start right away," Anna said.

Lori, appearing distracted, said, "That's great. Carl is having a party this Friday night, and I want you to come."

Anna said, "That's really nice, but I think I am going to stay in and focus on my studies."

"Anna, you're in college, and I won't take no for an answer," Lori said. "I will come over here at eight and get you. Just come for a few hours at least. If you want to leave, I'll take you back. You have to come, though."

Anna thought, *Well, as long as I can come back anytime.* "Okay, I'll come for a while."

Lori looked in the mirror and started putting her long hair in a ponytail. "Great. Why don't we go to dinner tomorrow? I'll come by with Carl." Before Anna could answer, Lori left.

Anna opened her journal and wrote, *Things may be turning around. I met a handsome, nice guy at work, and I have a party to go to. I'm scared to go, but I have to push myself. I have no idea if I will see that guy again, but he knows where I work. Why didn't I say something? I should have introduced myself at least. What is wrong with me? I may never see him again.*

CHAPTER 4

Anna's First Relationship

Anna went to class the next day and entered the large auditorium for her health and assessment class for nurses. She was fifteen minutes early and saw a girl sitting in the middle, and she took a deep breath and sat next to her. She paused then said, "Excuse me. I'm Anna. Are you a nursing student?" *What a stupid question,* she thought.

The girl had long, flowing blond hair and was writing something down. She looked up and smiled at Anna with a friendly and kind look. "Yes, I am. I'm Jen. Nice to meet you."

Anna felt immediate relief and said, "I'm a little nervous, sorry. It's nice to meet you, too."

The professor came bouncing into the room, and an echo filled the auditorium. She put a pile of books and papers on the large desk in front of the whiteboard and fixed her hair. Jen looked at Anna and said, "I've wanted to be a nurse for the last few years, and I feel nervous now, too. I hope I'm making the right decision. Have you known you wanted to be a nurse for a while?"

Anna said, "I guess so. My mother's a nurse, and I never really gave any other thought to it."

The room appeared to fill up and became loud with people unloading their backpacks, preparing for class. The teacher started to talk, and Anna attempted to focus on the lesson.

A little later, she felt a vibration from her phone with a text from Evan. "Work schedule: Tuesday 2-8, Thursday 2-8, Friday 2-7, Saturday 10-5, Sunday 12-5. Does that work?"

Anna looked at all the hours and thought, *I won't have much time for myself, but maybe that will help me focus on my studies.* She texted back, "Yes, that will work for now."

She watched Jen gather up her things as class was ending, and she noticed how graceful her movements were. "Are you okay, Anna?" Jen asked. "You seem to be in a daze."

Anna blinked her eyes and said, "Oh, sorry. I didn't get a lot of sleep last night. It was actually too quiet with my roommate not actually being my roommate because she is living with her boyfriend."

Anna paused as Jen stood up and said, "So, are you free for dinner tomorrow? I'd love it if you would meet me and a few other people. I could use a friend in nursing school."

Do I sound that desperate? Anna thought. "Yes, that would be great, thanks." Then she remembered her work. "Oh, I actually can't tomorrow. I have to work."

Lori said, "Maybe next week, then. I'll see you in class, though. Gotta run."

Anna got up and looked at her class schedule. Class Monday from one to four and Tuesday from nine to eleven thirty. *I can't wait to go back to work. Maybe that guy will come in again*, she thought. She went to class and then to her dorm, got ready for dinner, and had started reading a chapter in one of her textbooks when there was a knock on the door.

Anna opened the door to find Lori there. "Hey, how are things going?" Lori greeted, coming in and jumping on her bed.

"They're okay," Anna answered. "Classes are going to be busy and challenging. What about you?"

Lori, taking a breath, said, "They're good. I love living with Carl.

I think I'm getting much closer to him. I just still feel so guilty about my parents. Have they called here?"

Anna shook her head. "No, I don't know why they would call here when they have your cell phone, anyway. I think you're worrying too much about it."

Lori said, "Maybe you're right. They are giving me some space. Besides, my dad is coming here to take me to dinner. Hey, do you want to come?"

I would love to come to see and feel what a father's love is really like, Anna thought. But she answered, "No, you go and enjoy your dinner with your dad. He misses you, too, I'm sure."

"Well, I'll see you on Friday night, then?" Lori asked. When a long pause followed, she continued. "Carl's having a party, and you need to come. Just for a little while, please. I really want you to come. There are going to be some cute guys there."

Anna smiled, seeing that Lori appeared sincere. "Okay. I'll see you Friday. I work till seven."

Lori said, "You're so funny. The party starts at ten. I'll come around at nine. Have a nice week." She twirled her hair as she was putting her lipstick on in the mirror. "Oh, and look your hottest. I am sure you can wear something sexy," she added, laughing as she closed the door behind her.

After work on Friday, Anna went back to her dorm and faced her closet. She pulled out every item of clothing she had and agonized about what to wear to Lori's party. She tried on many things and settled on her best pair of jeans and a black shirt. Next, she combed out her hair so that she could wear it down and put on some light makeup. To calm her nerves and distract herself as she waited for Lori, she opened her books and tried to study.

Lori knocked on the door a little past nine. Anna opened the door, and Lori said, "Wow, you look great. You're going to have men all over you!"

Anna's cheeks flushed. "No, I won't. You're making me feel I should change. I'll change my shirt."

"No. Relax," Lori said. "I'm messing with ya. Come on, let's go. I need a beer first thing."

"I don't drink. I never have," Anna said. "Actually, I have never even been to a party before."

"Really?" Lori said. "That is hard to believe. Well, we're going to change that. You have to go to a party at some point. You don't have to drink, but you'll have fun watching people get drunk—trust me."

As they walked the five blocks to Carl's house, Lori asked, "What's your family like? I never got a chance to meet them."

"Well, like I told you, I have a younger brother, Luke," Anna said. "My parents . . . they are not as close to me as yours are to you. Let's leave it at that."

"You should be happy they are not all over you, that they give you some space," Lori said.

"No," Anna disagreed. "Your parents are great. They love you and care so much about what happens to you. Cherish that forever." Lori bit her lip and nodded.

Anna followed Lori into the house, and Carl came over to them. "Hi, Anna. I'm so glad you could make it. There are some beers over there. Can I get you one?"

Anna nodded, surprising herself. She noticed some people she had seen in class and in the cafeteria. She looked over and saw Jen in the other room. "Hey, Lori. I'll be right back."

Carl handed her the beer, and she said, "Thanks." She made it over to Jen and greeted her with, "Hey, how are you, Jen?"

Jen stumbled and looked at her. "Where do I know you from?"

"We're in nursing school together," Anna reminded her. "I met you in class."

Jen said, "Oh, that's right. How are you doing? I'm sorry, but I'm a little under the weather, if you know what I mean? We're heading out to another party if you want to come."

Anna felt someone tapping her shoulder, and she turned around. When she turned back to look for Jen again, she was out the door.

Lori said, "Come on, Anna. I'd like you to meet some of Carl's friends."

Anna took another sip of the beer and felt her body relax and her rapid-cycling thoughts dissipate. She looked at the beer and thought, *My new friend. Wow! I should have done this before.* She looked at Lori and said, "Lori, I have to go pee first. I think this beer is hitting me fast."

Lori laughed, saying, "Okay, it's over there," and pointed the way.

Anna zigzagged through the crowded room on her way to the bathroom. When she was nearly there, she tripped over someone's foot and fell to the ground. Someone grabbed her shoulders with a strong, forceful grip and helped her to her feet again.

"You ought to be more careful when you make a mad dash in a crowded room," he said.

Anna looked up to see a pair of familiar sweet, piercing eyes looking down upon her once again. "It's you," she said.

The man looked at her, biting his bottom lip for a moment. "The bookstore," he said. "I never forget a face. It must be destiny that I happened to be next to you when you needed help again. However, in this case, I probably caused the problem by tripping you with my big feet. Were you going somewhere?"

Anna said, "To the bathroom, but it's no longer vacant."

"May I wait in line with you, then?" he offered. "I'm Jeff, by the way."

Anna thought, *Could I be dreaming?* "Sure."

Jeff seemed to be waiting for something. "And . . . what's your name?"

She laughed. "Oh, I'm Anna."

"Do you know Lori?" he asked. "I see she is staring at you."

She said, "Oh, yes. She invited me tonight. We were supposed to be roommates—well, I guess technically we are, but she mostly lives here with Carl."

Jeff said, "Small world. Carl was my roommate my first year here. I'm a senior now."

"So what are you studying?" Anna asked.

"Pre-law. Oh, look, the bathroom is all yours, Anna. I'll get us some drinks, if that's okay?"

Anna nodded. She closed the door and rushed to the toilet, barely making it. As she washed her hands, she looked in the mirror, thinking, *Wow, I look awful.* She tried to fix her hair and put some water on her face. *He cannot possibly like me. What are the chances he does? I need to go out there and talk to him.* She opened the door and saw Jeff talking with Carl. He noticed her and motioned to her to come over.

Jeff said, "I hope this is okay?" He handed her a beer.

"It's fine. Thanks," Anna replied.

Carl said, "What a small world—Jeff was catching me up. You know, Jeff has the nicest family in the world, I think. I love going over for their family dinners. Great conversations."

Jeff rolled his eyes. "That's because you're an only child."

Lori came over and said, "Okay, so when is the double date?"

Carl smiled. "I think Lori has had a little too much to drink."

"I told you that you looked beautiful," Lori whispered in Anna's ear. "He's such a nice guy, and hot, too."

Carl said, "I'm going to take her to bed. Have a nice night, you two. Anna, do you want me to walk you home?"

"I can walk her," Jeff offered, "if you're okay with that, Anna."

Anna said, "It's okay, Carl. Take care of Lori."

"I always do."

"Would you like to get some coffee?" Jeff asked.

"Coffee sounds great," Anna agreed.

He opened the front door for her and waited for her to walk out. "My car is over there, but if you're more comfortable walking, there's a café down the street."

Anna—thinking, *I've had a lot to drink, I don't feel so good on my feet*—said, "Can we drive, if that's okay?"

Jeff said, "Sure."

He ran ahead and opened the passenger door. Anna suddenly felt uncomfortable. "I can open the door for myself."

He said, "Yes, but then my mother would be thinking she didn't raise me correctly."

Anna thought, *I have only seen this in the movies.*

After five minutes of driving in silence, he said, "Are you warm enough?"

"Yes, I'm fine." But she couldn't help but wonder what he wanted from her. *Is it possible he can really be this nice? He probably just wants to have sex.*

She got out of the car before he could open the door for her, and he managed to open the door into the café. "What would you like? I'll order for us."

Anna said, "A hot chocolate would be nice." She sat down and watched Jeff as he ordered their drinks. She thought, *He is quite cute and nice.* He came over with a number. "Thank you."

"You're welcome. So, Anna, tell me something about yourself?"

"There is not much to say, really," Anna said. "I'm a nursing student. I have one younger brother, and I grew up in Michigan. Your turn." *Why is he staring at me like that?*

He said, "I'm sure there is so much more, but I can wait. I'm the youngest of five. My three older brothers are all pretty successful, and my one sister is in medical school. Once my father knew I was interested in law, he assumed I would follow in his footsteps. I wanted to go into law to help people who have not been as fortunate as I have. You know, it's so strange that we are all born and randomly selected to a family or a parent. I know how lucky I was to be born in my family, and I want to help those who have not been as fortunate. Now I am rambling on."

I guess there are thoughtful, nice people in the world, Anna thought. "Wow, I guess I've never thought of it that way. But I guess I'm one of those less fortunate." Jeff gave her a saddened look, and she elaborated with, "It's just that, well, I didn't have such a good childhood." She felt comfortable with Jeff, but still she tried to change the subject. "So, when did you know you wanted to be a lawyer?"

"I've always found the rule of law fascinating," Jeff said. "I know we have too many lawyers in this country, but I think it will lead to other doors for myself."

"I was wondering if you have a girlfriend. Someone like you must have one," Anna mused.

Jeff said, "Well, I hope not or she would be mad at me right now. Anna, one thing you should know about me is that I would not be here with you if I had a girlfriend. I'm not like that. My last relationship was last summer, and we ended it because we were in different phases in our lives. What about you?"

Anna looked down as she said, "I've actually never had a boyfriend."

"That's respectable," Jeff said. "Maybe we can change that in the near future."

Smiling, Anna said, "I'm trying to find some friendships and focus on school. I'm not sure about the other thing." She pursed her lips.

"I'd love to be friends with you," Jeff said.

"I'm getting tired," Anna admitted.

Jeff got up and said, "Let's go, then. I'll drive you back."

He opened the door for her, and Anna felt uncomfortable. She told him the way to go to get back to her dorm, and he stopped the car out front. Before she knew it, Jeff was around the car opening her door. She said, "You really don't need to do that, especially if we're friends."

Jeff shook his head as he took her hand to help her out. "Don't you understand my parents taught me well? I actually do this for all the women." He walked her up the steps to the door. "Can I have your number so we can hang out?"

Anna took out a pen, and he took his phone out. "You're my new contact, Anna. You'll be the first one on my list, since your name starts with an A. I like that." Anna blushed and rambled her number. She felt butterflies in her stomach and wanted him to kiss her, but she got her keys out and opened the door.

Before he could say anything, she said, "I had a nice night, Jeff. See you soon."

Anna washed her face and got ready for bed then opened her journal and sat in her bed to write. *Dear Diary, I had a wonderful night, and I met that guy from the store like it was fate or something. He caught me as I was tripping again, and his arms are so strong. He is such a gentleman, but should I trust that he wouldn't hurt me? He opened the door for me, and I felt so uncomfortable. It's like a fairytale, and I have always wanted someone to do that for me, but it does not feel right. Maybe it's because I don't trust him. I'll have to wait and see what happens, but he is cute. Well, I'm tired, and I have to work tomorrow. Good night for now. I hope I can get some rest.* Anna lay down and took a deep breath and fell fast asleep more quickly than she had in a long time.

Anna woke the next morning startled by a dream she could not recall, but she knew her mother had been in it. She looked at the clock to see that it was already nine, but it was Sunday, and she figured her mom would be home. She picked up the phone. "Hi, Mom?"

Kathy said, "Hi, Anna. How is my college girl?"

"Good, thanks. Mom, I was wondering why you haven't called me?"

"I thought you would call once you got settled in," Kathy said. "I wanted to give you some time and space."

Anna heard some despair in her mother's voice. "It's okay, Mom. I understand. It has just been a difficult adjustment. I miss you and Luke."

Kathy said, "Well, we certainly miss you here. It's so strange not having you at home."

"What are you up to?" Anna asked.

"Just the usual weekend laundry and cleaning up."

"Is Luke home?"

"No, he's at Ted's. Don't worry, Anna. He's been home more often. You'll be happy to know that I'm doing more things now that you moved out."

"Oh, Mom, I went to my first party last night. I'm slowly meeting more people. Classes are good, and the professors are helpful and nice."

Kathy said, "I'm so happy you're going out and having fun."

"Well, I guess I'd better go," Anna said. "I have a lot of homework, and I'm working later today. I got a job at the bookstore. I figured it would help me with some spending money and a discount on books."

"That's great," Kathy replied. "When will you be coming home? No pressure, of course."

"I'm not sure yet, but I'll let you know, since I'm working a lot on the weekends now."

Kathy said, "Okay, I'll wait to hear from you. Take care."

As Anna walked to work that day, she thought, *I feel so much better, not feeling the tension and worrying when my father is coming home. It's so strange not being on eggshells. It is a different kind of uneasy.*

When Anna got to work, she greeted Evan with, "Hey. How are you?" He looked extremely tired.

He said, "I'm okay. Can you stock those shelves in the back? We had a shipment come in, and it's a mess back there." Anna nodded and got to work.

After about an hour, she felt a hand on her shoulder. "Now, don't move. I'm checking your posture."

Anna looked over and smiled. "What're you doing here, Jeff?"

"I'm shopping, of course. However, you are a hard person to stop thinking about." He smiled back at her flirtatiously. "Wanna go to the movies when you're done?"

Anna hesitated. "As long as it's not a date."

He said, "Then it's a not-a-date date."

Smiling again, Anna said, "I have to get back to work now. Go!"

He said, "Well, okay, but only because you said yes."

"I'm done at five," she told him.

He nodded and dashed off.

Evan came over to Anna and said, "I know that guy. Are you dating him?"

"He's just a friend," she said.

"He is a great guy."

Anna said, "How do you know?"

"He built houses with my son for Habitat for Humanity," he said. "My son was doing community service, but he was helping the troubled youth turn their lives around while building houses for people in need. And my son actually *did* turn his life around because of Jeff's advice. He's a humble guy, though. When my son went to thank him, Jeff said, 'No thank-you necessary. You taught me, more.' My son has never forgotten that, and I guess I haven't, either."

When Jeff came to pick her up, he said, "I'm so glad you said yes. Wanna get a bite to eat first? You must be hungry."

Anna said, "Sure."

"Well, what do you like to eat?"

"I like most everything, so you can decide," she said.

Jeff said, "Oh, you failed. Now I have to guess and watch your body language, which is a lot of work."

Anna smiled. "Okay, you win. Let's get Italian."

"Great. We have an hour till most movies start. Here," he said, giving her his phone, "you can pick the movie while we drive to the restaurant." Anna started fidgeting in her seat, feeling uncomfortable again like she had when Jeff held the door for her.

Jeff grabbed her hand and said, "Anna, relax. Remember—it's not a date." He put her hand down but did not let go. Anna wanted to hold his hand, but part of her wanted to run away. *Why am I feeling like this?*

A month went by in which they saw each other almost daily. Anna had finally caught up with Jen in class, and they sat next to each other from time to time. She fell into a new routine that involved double dates with Lori and Carl and some parties. One night, Jeff picked her up and took her to one of Carl's parties, and she saw Jen with a gorgeous guy next to her. Anna suddenly drank a whole beer down as if it were eight ounces of water. She went to get another one because her heart was beating with excitement. She couldn't believe that she finally had friends.

Jeff grabbed her hand and pulled her to the back hallway and said, "Now, Anna. I have to kiss you. I can't wait anymore." He grabbed her and kissed her lips and down her neck, and Anna kissed him back and felt a tingling up and down the inside of her legs. "Let's go now." He took her to his car, and they drove to his apartment.

In his bedroom, Jeff slowly took off Anna's jacket and said, "Wow, you're so beautiful, Anna. I've wanted you since I first saw you at the bookstore. Are you okay with this?"

Anna nodded, but inside, she felt tense. She allowed him to kiss her lips and her neck as her tenseness grew. She tried to relax as he started to take her shirt off, and she felt him grow hard against her leg. Her heart was beating so loud that it was all she could hear, and a wave of intense fear rushed over her as a flash of light filled the room. She pushed him away, ran to the bathroom, and locked the door as an impulse. She sat on the floor and cried.

Jeff quietly knocked on the door and whispered, "Are you okay, Anna? I am so sorry for that. Please tell me what I can do?"

Anna laid on the floor and desperately tried to calm down. She suddenly felt stupid and humiliated and wanted to run out of the house and find some place she could get herself together. She listened intently and heard him say, "Take your time, Anna. I'll just be in the family room. I put some water for you on the counter. I just want you to know you can always talk to me and you have nothing to fear here."

Anna waited a few minutes before she came out of the bathroom. She put her jacket on and drank the water. "Jeff, I'm just going to go back now. Can we talk later?"

Jeff said, "Of course, but can I take you back, please?" Before he finished speaking, she was out the door, walking down the street.

As Anna walked, she felt a wave of exhaustion come over her that she'd only felt once in her life but could not remember when. She felt confused and so ashamed when she thought of Jeff. *There's something so wrong with me. He'll never want to see me again*, she thought.

Someone called her name, and she stopped and looked back. Jeff was hurrying toward her, waving. "Anna, you walk so fast," he said. "I'm just going to walk you home. I can't have you go by yourself in the dark." They walked in silence for a while, then he put his arm over her hand and stopped her. "Just so you know, you are beautiful and an amazing person, and I'd be honored to be your boyfriend, if you are okay with that?"

Anna said, "Stop. I'm none of those things. I don't understand. I am so messed up."

Jeff said, "Well, you are to me. I know things that have happened in your life have affected you, but that's not how I see you. Maybe it would help to talk about it."

Anna started walking, and Jeff fell quiet as he walked next to her. They arrived at her place, and Anna surprised herself by saying, "Want to come in?"

Jeff looked puzzled. "Are you sure?"

Anna nodded, and he followed her in.

Jeff reached over to kiss her forehead. "It's okay, Anna." He held her close, and for a moment, Anna let her shoulders down and felt safe. He walked her over to her bed, and she sat down as he said, "Get some sleep. I am not going anywhere, unless you want me to. I really care about you." He then turned and walked to the door, blowing her a kiss before he left the room. Anna laid down and passed out with exhaustion.

Anna woke up the next day still feeling tired and realized she was going home for Thanksgiving break. She had not been home since she arrived in August and was happy to see her mother. She thought of Jeff and quickly put yesterday out of her mind.

As she was driving, she felt her phone ping. She looked at her phone at a stop sign and saw, "Hope you drive safe and have a nice time with your family." She thought, *Why would he still want to be with me? There must be something wrong with him.*

She quickly sent a text, "You too."

As she drove up to her house, she scanned her driveway like she had done a million times before. She quickly dropped her shoulders with relief. *He's not here. Thank God.*

She went in the back door and found Kathy in the kitchen making a salad. Kathy threw down the tongs and threw her arms around her. "Hi, Anna. How are you? Let me look at you! You look so thin." She held Anna close, as if something was wrong.

Anna said, "Hi, Mom. I'm good. I've missed you. I'm sorry I haven't been home, but with working on the weekends, well, I don't have much time."

Kathy put her fingers over Anna's mouth. "You are busy and living your life, and I can't wait to hear all about it. Go get settled in your room."

"I'm only staying a few nights because of the inventory coming in at work. I don't have much with me." Anna started to peel the cucumbers. "So where's Luke?"

"He'll be home by five. He's excited to see you."

Anna and Kathy were side by side in the kitchen, cooking together just the way they had when she lived at home. *It feels like I never left*, Anna thought. She heard a car pull up and saw her father come up the back steps with a pie in his hand.

He came in with jeans and a shirt on, unusual for a work meeting, and went to the sink without looking at her. "Hi, Anna. How's school?"

Anna, not wanting to talk with her father, said, "Fine. My grades are good."

Dan said, "Here, Kathy, a client gave this to me today."

"Can you put it in the fridge, please?" Kathy asked. But before she finished speaking, he had already left the room for his study. The pie sat on the counter.

A little bit later, Luke came in and grabbed Anna. "Hey there. I missed you. Do you know how quiet it is now that you're gone? And it was quiet when you were here! You must have a boyfriend already?"

Anna, blushing, said, "None of your business."

Luke said, "That's a yes, so I want to meet him."

"Luke, that's up to her," Kathy said. "Wash up for dinner."

When dinner was ready, Kathy called, "Dan and Luke, come have dinner."

Dan came in and grabbed a plate. "I have to go into the office in a while. Something came up."

"Dad, it's Thanksgiving," Luke protested. "Anna is here, too."

Kathy said, "Don't talk back to your father, Luke. Since he took a higher management position, there is more responsibility."

Anna, listening, understood no one was communicating to her. She said, "What? Congratulations, Dad."

"It's no big deal, but hard work does pay off—remember that, Luke."

Anna thought, *Some things never change, I guess. It seems to have gotten worse.* The four of them sat down, and she studied her mother's face. "Mom, the meal is delicious. I forgot what home cooking tastes like."

Dan said, "Well, you don't live far. You could come see her once in a while."

"Well, with school and my job, it takes all my time."

Dan abruptly looked over to Anna, puzzled. "You're working? No one told me. I guess you don't need spending money, then."

Kathy said, "She doesn't work that much, Dan."

"She can appreciate what she has more if she earns it herself. Luke, you can learn from your sister."

He got up and said, "Happy Thanksgiving."

As he rushed off, Luke said, "Why did you open your mouth? You knew what was going to happen. Seems like nothing has changed." He got up and put on his jacket. "I'm going next door to have dessert with a normal family!"

Anna sat there, wondering, *What just happened? Why did I bother coming home? I'm so glad I'm going back to school.* Before she started to put the dishes in the sink, she noticed her mother went to the bathroom. She grabbed a beer from the fridge she saw earlier and quickly drank it down before her mother came out. She grabbed another one and put it in her purse and started to clean up. Anna made some tea and cut some pie up for her and Kathy. "Mom, are you lonely?"

"Anna, I'm happy being alone. Some people may not see it that way, but I enjoy being with my thoughts. Your generation never has time to be alone in your thoughts. You're always on your social media or internet. I feel best alone. It may be difficult for you to understand that."

Anna fidgeting in her chair, deflecting what her mother said. "Why don't you get a job? Get out of this house?"

Kathy said, "Anna, you focus on yourself and I will worry about me." She started washing up as Anna kept sitting at the table.

Anna thought, *I feel different now. I feel guilty for leaving, but I can hardly breathe when I'm in this house.* "Mom, I'm going to go read for a paper I have to write." *Wow, now I'm lying to her*, she thought. Kathy looked tense and was aggressively scrubbing the plates. Anna wanted to go back to school, as she felt uncomfortable in her own home even more now.

Anna went to her room and laid on her bed, looking around as her boring childhood memories of being lost in all her books came up as she always imagined being someone else and having someone else's life. Her phone rang, and she saw Jeff's number appear on the screen.

"Hi, Anna. How's your Thanksgiving going?"

Anna said, "It was okay." She looked at the clock—it was already eight in the evening.

"I'm so full," Jeff said. "Hold on."

Anna overheard someone say, "Hey, I'm glad you forced me to help in the kitchen today. I see now why you do it. See ya later."

Jeff said, "Sorry about that. So, what did you eat?"

Anna said, "The usual turkey dinner. I'm sort of tired, though."

Jeff said, "I just want you to know I am so sorry for yesterday. There is no rush for anything physical like that."

Anna felt angry and said, "I want to be physical with you."

After a long pause, Jeff said, "I am confused, Anna. Your reaction earlier was, well . . . it scared me."

Anna sat up in bed. "I am sorry about that. I just had a moment. I've never had sex before, and I guess I freaked out. It is something I want, though, with you. I am going to go now. Can we talk tomorrow?"

"Of course," he said. "Have a nice night."

Anna hung up and picked up her journal. *Dear Diary, I don't understand why I reacted that way with Jeff. He is gentle and so calm and nice to me. Why did I flip out on him? I constantly feel there is something wrong with me. I want to have sex with him, and I am going to relax the next time I see him and just let it happen. I am going to make this right.*

Why does my mother stay with my father? Why does she stick up for him? I have so many questions with no answers. Jeff is so unlike my family. Why would he want to be with me? Why don't I let him in, and why do I feel uneasy with him? It is hard to pinpoint, but I want to run away when he does nice things for me. I must be crazy. Right? Good night.

The next six weeks went by fast. Anna spent most of her time studying with Jeff and working. She went to the cafeteria with Lori one lunch and saw Jen there with a few friends and noticed that guy she had been with at that party.

Jen called her over. "Hey, Anna, how are you? Come sit with us."

Anna motioned to Lori to follow her, and they sat down at the end of the table. Jen said, "Anna, this is Dave, Brooke, and Pete."

Anna said, "Hi, everyone, this is Lori, my roommate."

Anna thought, *Why is my heart beating so fast? That guy is so hot. He seems to look right through me.*

Jen said, "So, how do you think classes are going?"

"It's difficult but manageable so far."

Dave got up from the table as Anna stared at his dark brown hair and bright blue eyes. He said with a smirk, "Well, maybe you need to study with Jen so she can have manageable grades and not get kicked out of school."

"You're horrible, Dave," Jen said. Then to Anna, she added, "I actually would like a study partner if you're interested?"

Anna said, "Of course. I'd like that."

Pete, who had a thin face and almost sad eyes, said, "Where are you from?"

"I'm from Northville, not far from here, actually. Lori's from Ohio."

Jen got up with her tray as her long blond hair brushed over Anna's shoulder. She said, "I'll be texting you for sure this time."

As they were walking out the door, Lori said, "Wow, did you see that guy?" Before Anna could respond, she looked at her watch and added, "Oh, I have to go to class so I can dream about that hunk."

Anna bit her lip and then laughed. "Don't forget about Carl. See ya later."

Anna's phone rang, and she answered it. It was Jeff. "Hi, hon," he greeted. "Just calling to make some plans for later. Can I take you to dinner?"

Anna suddenly felt sick with guilt. "I don't feel so well, so I'm gonna stay in tonight."

"I'll bring you some soup, then," he said. "What's wrong?"

"I don't know—just need some rest. I'll be okay. No need to come over."

"I'll call you later," Jeff said.

That evening, he knocked on her door. "Soup man."

Anna fumbled to the door in her pajamas like she was faking sick and unlocked the door. "You didn't have to do that."

"I wanted to. If I can make your day better, I am happy to help you. How are you feeling now?" he asked.

"A little better now," she said.

He lay on her bed, staring at her with puppy-dog eyes, and she thought, *Why is he looking at me like that? It makes me uncomfortable.* Later that night as they sat together studying, she thought, *I am keeping him at a distance. Something is keeping me from getting too close. He is almost too nice, and it's hard to trust him. No one can be that nice.*

Just as these thoughts were going through her mind, Jeff pulled her book from her hands and stroked her hair. "Are you feeling better? Good enough to fool around?"

"I would rather just get some rest," Anna said.

"Okay, lie down and I'll give you a massage."

Anna laid on her stomach and put her head on her pillow as he started rubbing her shoulders. "Wow, you are so tense," he remarked. "Close your eyes and relax."

As she did, a spontaneous image of Jen's friend Dave came into her mind. Anna opened her eyes and suddenly felt awful. She started to kiss Jeff's neck and ear, and before Jeff could speak, she put her finger on his lips as if to quiet him. He remained quiet and took her shirt off, kissing her body for the first time. Anna let herself go and kept telling herself, *Relax, Anna, relax. It's Jeff, and you can trust him.* She laid back as he stroked her and kissed her and looked at her.

"Is this okay, honey? I want you to be okay."

Anna just nodded her head and took a deep breath as he entered her for the first time. She felt pain but kept breathing and thinking, *I am safe, I am safe.*

He released himself halfway inside her as he had a condom on and came out and laid down on the bed. "Anna, you are amazing. Are you okay?"

Anna nodded and said, "Wow, I am so tired now." She laid her head on him and fell asleep.

Jen called her the next day. "Hey, can we set up a study day and time that is consistent each week? That helps me plan the week."

They came up with Monday from seven to nine. Anna said, "Can I ask you something about your friend Brooke?"

Jen said, "Let me guess: she made you uncomfortable. She is good at dirty looks. She is strange with new people and jealous, I guess. Dave seems to think it's strange, too. I'm sorry about that."

Anna said, "I was actually just wondering what her major is?"

Jen said, "Oh, too much information. She is pre-law. Why?"

"Just wondering. She looks familiar to me."

On Monday, Anna met Jen at the library on time. She waited inside the library for Jen and saw Dave walking with her up the front steps. Anna immediately felt her heart race.

"Hey, Anna, what's up?" he said.

Anna felt as if she was slurring her words as she said, "Nothing much."

"Well, you ladies get some studying in," he said. "Catch you later."

As he walked away, Anna was unaware she was staring until Jen hit her shoulder. "Come on, silly. Remember—you have a boyfriend."

Anna said, "Oh, was I staring?"

Jen started to laugh. "Everyone does."

Why am I looking at another guy? Anna thought. *I feel so bad for doing that. I'm going to call Jeff.* During a study break, she went outside and dialed Jeff's number. "Hi, Jeff. Can we go out for a late dinner tonight?"

Jeff sounded excited. "Of course—wherever you want to go. I'll come get you at six."

When Jeff showed up that evening to pick her up, he took her hand and gave her a big hug. "So, where are we going?"

"Can we go to Shalimar for Indian food?" Anna asked.

"Of course. I'm so glad you asked."

At dinner, Jeff seemed to hesitate, but finally he said, "Anna, I don't want to pressure you, but I would like you to meet my family over the holiday if you're comfortable with that. I'm just so excited for them to meet you."

Anna suddenly shifted in her chair and looked down, and Jeff understood. "No problem. It can wait for a better time. But you have to promise me we will see each other over the break. I can't go a whole month without seeing you. Agreed?"

Anna nodded in agreement. As they ate dinner, she thought, *He really is a nice guy. What does he see in me?*

As finals were in sight, Jen and Anna started studying together more often. One day, Anna said, "How do you know Dave and Pete?"

"Well, my father and Dave's father knew each other," Jen answered. "They were childhood friends, then business partners or something, and they used to have these big summer parties when I was a kid. I had the biggest crush on him. Well, everyone did. We actually dated a little in high school, but when my father found out, he was so angry he made me end it. I'm glad he did."

Anna, intensely listening to every word, asked, "Why?"

"Well, we're much better as friends. He's used to getting what he wants, and he likes girls. He's not the monogamous type, if you know what I mean? Even in high school. Pete, he's a good guy. He looks after Dave. I'm glad because I used to have that job."

"I don't understand," Anna said. "Why does he need someone to look after him?"

Jen took a deep breath as if annoyed and rolled her eyes. "It's difficult to explain, but he's his own worst enemy. I have been down this road with other girls. Please don't flirt with him. He is a good friend but not a boyfriend."

Anna was becoming fidgety in her seat. "I was just curious, that's all. It seemed that you two were a couple to me."

Jen said, "Well, we do spend a lot of time together, but like I said, we're just friends. I want to be single and study and have fun. I don't want a relationship now, never mind one with him ever. I guess I know him too well."

Anna thought about Jeff and how she felt she was the one making things difficult and said, "I'm in my first one, and he is always so nice that he makes it easy."

Jen said, "Don't ever give that up, then. That's so hard to find. Sorry, I have to get going. See you soon."

Anna took her finals that next week, and when they were finished, Jeff came over to help her pack her bags to leave for home. "I'm going to miss you so much, Anna," he said.

Anna was surprised that she felt relieved and not saddened. "Me too," she said. "Call me later." She kissed him, but he held onto her tightly. "It's only a little while, Jeff."

He said, "Okay, okay. I'm too sentimental—I know. Drive safe and call me when you get home."

Anna just shook her head in disbelief and watched as Jeff waved to her as she drove away, thinking, *Why do I feel so suffocated? What is wrong with me that I want to run away?*

As Anna pulled into the driveway, an overwhelming unhappiness came over her. She took a deep breath and got out of her car to see Luke running over. He gave her a hug.

"Hey, sis. I'm so glad you're back."

"How's Mom?" Anna asked.

Luke grabbed her bag from her arms. "She's fine. I'm good, too, by the way."

Anna rolled her eyes and felt grateful she had him there. "Sorry, Luke. How are you—really?"

He waited for her to go in the house and followed behind. "Okay, I guess. It was quiet when you lived here, but now it's a ghost town. I can't wait until I graduate so I can get the hell out of here."

"How are Mom and Dad?"

Luke said, "Well, Dad's never home. He comes home late and never eats here anymore. Not sure where he goes, but I'm sure it's not good."

Anna sat down and looked at the floor. "Mom must be so lonely."

Luke grabbed a Coke from the fridge. "Anna, she has choices. You act as if she is a child. She is an adult. Feeling bad for her doesn't help anyone. She isn't a victim."

Anna felt anger well up. "I'm aware of that, but I'm also aware that change is difficult for some." She hated feeling angry. "I don't want to argue with the only ally I have in this house. I'm glad to see you anyway."

Luke gave her a hug. "Me, too."

Anna went to the fridge and grabbed a beer, chugged it down, and took a breath. She went up to her room and put her suitcase down then went to her mother's room, where her mother was lying down, sleeping. Anna lay down next to her, closed her eyes, and fell asleep.

When she woke up, her mother was gone. She went downstairs to find her making a salad and some chicken legs. She put her arms around Kathy and said, "Hi, Mom. That smells so good. Is Dad coming home to eat?"

Kathy moved to get a dish. "I'm not sure," she said. "I didn't know when you were coming, so I haven't said anything to him." Anna helped her mother finish preparing dinner.

At dinner, Anna said, "Well, Luke. What's new? Any girlfriends?"

Luke turned to her and said, "Wow, Anna. *You* have a boyfriend."

Anna smiled. "Well, I met someone that I spend time with, but that's all." Just as she said this, her phone rang. She said, "Excuse me," and answered it. "Hello. I'm fine. I got home a few hours ago and lay down and passed out. It's so nice to sleep. You, too. Goodbye."

Luke said, "He was checking in that you got home safely. That's a great guy."

Anna gave Luke a snide stare.

Kathy said, "I think it's great if you have a boyfriend."

"Let's change the subject," Anna suggested. "What are you doing with all your time, Mom?"

She said, "Well, I took a cooking class online, and I have been redecorating the house and reading a lot. I keep really busy."

Dan pulled into the driveway as Kathy was talking. Anna took a deep breath and started rocking back and forth in her seat. Kathy put her arms on Anna's shoulders to stop her.

Dan came in the back door. "Hi, Anna. Can you park in a different place when you come home? You're taking up all the room."

Anna wanted to pretend she didn't hear that. "Hi, Dad. How are you?"

Dan came over to the table and looked at the food. Kathy asked, "Aren't you going to eat?"

"No. I have a conference call. Besides, I already ate." He went to his office and closed the door.

Anna thought, *He hasn't changed a bit—I think he's even worse.*

After two weeks, Anna was pacing in her room. *I cannot take this anymore. I have to get away from this house. I have to go back to school, but my poor mother. How can she live like this?* She went to the fridge and grabbed a beer then went to her mother's bathroom, where she remembered her mom kept her "nervous pills." She took one with the beer she chugged and then took a few more and put them in her pocket.

She took a deep breath and found her mother. "Mom, I'm going to go back to school today. They need me at work."

Kathy said, "That's too bad, but I understand."

Anna scoured the comment to try to determine what Kathy really felt. *She says that to my father all the time when she really isn't okay. But I don't care. She is choosing to live like this, like Luke says.* "Mom, you seem so sad here," she said. "Dad works all the time, and you're left here. Luke is so busy."

"Anna, some things are hard to understand," Kathy replied. "I'm a homebody and enjoy my time. Go and enjoy yourself."

Anna said, "Well, maybe you can come for a visit soon."

Kathy said, "I'd like that."

It is futile to push her, Anna thought.

As Anna was packing her bag, Jeff called. "Hi, Anna. Can we meet today?"

"Actually, Jeff, I'm driving back to school," she said. "I'm going to work at the store and, well, I just feel more comfortable there."

Jeff hesitated but said, "Can I meet you there and we can go for dinner and talk?"

Anna paused a moment and said, "Let's do it tomorrow night. I'm not sure when I'm leaving here yet."

Jeff said, "Okay, I'll come over early afternoon, then. Call me later and drive safe."

They hung up, and Anna thought, *Why am I lying to everyone? I just need some time alone, to myself. I just want to take a few relaxing pills and have a glass of wine and go to sleep and not worry about anything.* She grabbed some bottles of wine and snuck them in her bag.

Anna went to the kitchen, and Kathy said, "Do you need anything before you go?"

"No, thanks, I have everything I need," Anna replied. "Where's Luke?"

"Next door," Kathy answered.

Anna kissed her mother and said, "Say goodbye to him for me. I'll call you soon." She drove away, thinking, *Why did I lie to her? I feel so relieved to be leaving this place. I never thought I wouldn't want to come home.*

When she got to her dorm room, she lay on her bed in the quiet of the dorm and thought, *I will enjoy this night.* She took some wine and two pills.

Jeff called and said, "Hey, good, you got there okay. I can't wait to see you tomorrow. Have a nice night."

Anna said, "Me too. Good night." She then passed out.

The next few months passed by, and Anna spent all of her free time with Jeff. She wrote in her journal, *It is hard to believe that someone like Jeff wants to be with me. I am confused by this and not sure how I feel about things. Why is he so nice to me? Is this what relationships are supposed to be like? Why does he always want to talk and see how I am doing? Is this what my parents were like until they got married and had kids? Was my father like this? I don't know what to believe. He consumes all my time, and I have no more free time to meet other people. I don't want to mess this up, though. If he stops liking me, then it will be my fault. I don't want to lose him, but why do I feel so uncomfortable when he always tries to make me happy and help me? This is confusing.*

A few nights before spring break, Jeff said, "What do you want to do tonight?"

Anna thought, *I want to be alone, but I cannot say that to him.* So instead she said, "Whatever you want to do."

Jeff said, "Why do we always have this conversation? I *care* about what you want to do. Just tell me."

"Let's just go to the movies," Anna suggested.

At dinner, Anna was biting her nails and pulling at her hair and drinking some wine.

Jeff said, "Are you anxious, Anna?"

"No. Why?"

He looked at her in disbelief.

"Okay, I just was hoping you would not ask about spring break and meeting families."

Jeff said, "I actually wasn't. I'm leaving that up to you. When you are ready, you can just let me know. I don't ever want you to feel pressured,

Anna. We are a team. I hope you don't feel I would look at you differently after meeting your family."

Anna said, "Why are you so nice to me? I don't understand why you are so patient with me and always say the right thing."

Jeff said, "Anna, I love you." Anna became silent and speechless. "I'm sorry. You may not be ready to hear that, but it's true. I want to be the one to make you happy. I understand you need time, and we have plenty of time."

Anna started to cry, and Jeff went over to her side and held her tightly. He whispered, "I'm here for you. I'll always be here if you want me to be."

Anna was quiet on the ride back from the movies. *I want to jump out of the car*, she thought. *I need some space, some air, some time to think.* She finally said, "I think I need time alone."

Jeff pulled the car over and looked at the radio, and a tear fell down his cheek. Anna felt bad and quickly took back what she'd said. "It's okay. I don't need time alone."

Jeff said, "No, we all need time alone to think. I know I'm your first relationship, Anna. You take all the time you need." He kissed her on the forehead and drove silently to her dorm.

"This is moving so fast for me," she said.

He took her hand. "It's okay, really. I will be here when you want to talk."

Anna took a deep breath and opened the door. "I'll call you soon."

She went to her room and wrote in her journal, *I'm actually happy to be going home and taking a break from Jeff. I feel so guilty for feeling like I need a break. Is this normal? He is so nice to me, but I don't know what it is. I should be happy to be with someone like him. I will have some time over the break to think about it.*

Anna packed a bag the next day and drove home. She thought about how she wanted to look forward to going home, but that was not the case. She arrived at noon on a Saturday. She walked in the back door, and there was no one around.

She went upstairs and heard her mother crying in her bedroom. She slowly opened the cracked door, and Kathy jumped to her feet and wiped her tears. "Why are you sneaking up on me?" she asked.

"I texted you that I would be home soon," Anna said. "I'm not trying to do anything. I heard you crying."

"I just need a little release now and then. It's therapeutic for me," Kathy replied. "Are you hungry?"

"Mom, why don't you talk to me?" Anna asked. "I'm an adult now. I can be here for you. I know things are difficult."

Kathy said, "Anna, you always do that. You make assumptions that aren't true. Let's go downstairs."

Anna went to her room to put her bag away. She went across the hall and heard her mother in her bathroom. She went over to ask if she would like to go out for lunch and saw her mother in the mirror taking some pills. Anna felt bad that she had left her mother to go to college. She went into the hallway and down the stairs then called up, "Mom, want to go out for lunch?"

"Maybe some other time," Kathy said. "I have to start getting dinner ready."

Anna made some grilled cheese sandwiches for her and her mother, and when Kathy came down twenty minutes later, she looked much calmer.

"Here's a sandwich, Mom. Do you feel better?"

"Why don't you eat it? I would rather have something else," Kathy suggested.

Anna thought, *Why can't she let someone do something for her? Why is everything so difficult with her?* "Are you feeling better?" she repeated. "Do those pills help?"

"I just take supplements. I'm fine, really," Kathy said. "How are you?"

As Anna ate her sandwich, she said, "Everything is the same. School is good."

Luke entered the house through the back door. "Hey, Anna," he greeted. "Thanks for the text earlier that you were coming back." Anna took a deep breath when she saw him, relieved, as he added, "Oh, are you still dating Jeff? Can we or I meet him?"

"No, I'm actually thinking of ending it," she said. *Why did I just say that?*

"That's too bad," Luke said. "What happened?"

Anna wanted to say, *Absolutely nothing,* but instead blurted out, "We're just too different. I'm not ready for a serious relationship."

"Different is probably good, Anna," he said. "Is he nice to you?"

"He is *too* nice." She paused for a moment, wanting the conversation to end, and said, "Really, Luke, it's not your business."

Luke grabbed the sandwich Anna had made for their mother and ate it. They sat in silence until Anna said, "Sorry, Luke. How are you doing?"

"Same old, same old," he said.

"Well, I have a paper to work on, so I'll be in my room." Anna, glad to have an excuse to leave the room, returned to her bedroom and wrote in her journal: *Things are so different. My mother is so distant. I am feeling so much tenser.*

She heard her mother say, "I'm going to the store for a minute. Do you need anything?"

"No, thanks." Anna looked out the window and saw Luke walking over to his friend's house and her mother driving away. She went into her mother's bathroom and looked into the drawer with her pills. She saw bottles labeled Prozac, Xanax, and hydrocodone. Anna ran to her room and got a paper and pen. She looked them up and wondered why her mother was on pain pills. She took a few out and took one.

Anna went back into her room and looked up the drugs on her iPad. She had been taking her mother's Xanax, but hydrocodone, which was for pain, was new and also addictive. *Maybe this is how my mother copes with her own life.* She was still reading when she heard a car pull up in the driveway. She got up from her bed and felt dizzy and nauseated. She went downstairs and saw her father sitting at the kitchen table reading the newspaper. She felt much calmer and lightheaded and said, "Hi, Dad. How are you?"

Dan looked up from his paper and said, "Oh, what are you doing home?"

She said, "It's spring break and Easter tomorrow."

He mumbled but went back to reading.

Anna thought, *Wow, that pill does help. I don't feel much tension or anger. It must help my mother, but I do feel tired.* She went back to her room and stretched herself out on her bed and fell asleep.

At dinner, Dan came in the kitchen after five thirty and seemed to be getting ready to go out.

Kathy said, "I made you your favorite. I thought we could have a family dinner. You never told me you were going out."

Dan said, "Oh, a dinner meeting just came up. Save some for me; I'll eat later."

Kathy never responded. She just looked down the hallway after him as he left the house.

Anna said, "Why do you tolerate that?"

"Anna, please don't start," Luke begged.

"It affords us this life and your college," Kathy replied.

Anna regretted saying anything.

Luke asked, "Want to go to a movie tonight?"

"I would love to," Anna agreed.

Kathy said, "That's great. My kids at the movies together."

Anna said, "With you as well."

Kathy said, "No, I'd rather stay home. Thanks."

Anna looked at Luke and rolled her eyes. Luke mouthed, "Let it go, Anna."

Anna grabbed a beer and snuck it in her bag, and they drove to the movie theater in Ann Arbor. She saw Jeff out of the corner of her eye, and he saw her and smiled. As they stood in the popcorn line, Jeff came up to them. "Hi, Anna. How are you?"

Anna swallowed a few times to keep her tears at bay. "Hi, Jeff. We were going to the movies and came out here. This is my brother, Luke. Luke, this is Jeff."

Jeff said, "Hi, Luke. I've heard a lot about you. My parents went on a vacation, so I decided to stay here, and my brother came for a visit. Well, I hope you're enjoying the break, Anna. Luke, you are lucky to have such a great sister."

Luke laughed and said, "At times." Then he said, "I need to go the bathroom."

As he walked away, Jeff said, "Anna, don't be nervous. It's just me. I want you to go out and have a nice time. Take care of yourself and drive back safely." He walked away before his brother came over.

When Luke rejoined her, he said, "He seems nice. I take it you asked for some time."

Anna just shook her head. As she tried to watch the movie, she thought, *Why don't I want to be with him? What is wrong with me?*

She drove home, and Luke said, "Anna, you need to be with someone who treats you well. Guys like us do exist. We are not all like Dad. You deserve some happiness."

"You don't know the whole story," Anna said.

"No, but I do know you. You have always wanted Dad's attention and approval, and you've never gotten it. You have unrealistic expectations of him. That can affect future relationships in your life, and I want you to be happy."

Anna got out of the car after she pulled into the driveway, and she turned to Luke. "I am happy, Luke. Don't worry about me so much. I know what I'm doing." She went to her bedroom and took one of the pills out of her pocket and went to bed.

On Friday morning, Anna snuck into her mother's bathroom and took a few more of her pills. She hoped she was being careful not to take too many and hoped her mother wouldn't notice. Anna told Kathy she was going back to school because she had to work. As she was driving back, she decided to text Jeff. "Hi, Jeff. I'm coming back and was hoping we could meet."

Jeff texted, "Are you sure?"

Anna said, "Yes, can you come over around eight?"

Jeff said, "Of course. See you later."

Jeff knocked on the door, and Anna let him in. She gave him a brief hug and said, "I'm sorry about my reaction the other day."

He said, "Anna, please don't be sorry. Your brother seems like a nice guy."

"He always disappears to leave me and my mother. He's never around, just like my father," she said.

"I'm sorry, Anna. I would never do that to you."

"I believe you, Jeff. You're a great person," Anna said. "Could we just not talk about serious things? I just missed you and wanted to see you."

"Does this mean we're still together?" he asked.

Anna hesitated and looked to the floor. "Yes."

Before she could continue, Jeff embraced her, and she noticed how happy he was. He started kissing her neck and massaging her back. She took his shirt off and they made love, and a picture of Dave came into her mind as Jeff said, "I'm so happy right now. You make me so happy."

The rest of the year went by quickly as she and Jeff fell into the same routine. Anna wrote in her journal: *I don't understand why I don't feel the same as Jeff does. I feel suffocated by him. He is so nice and kind and wants to take care of me. I feel I am not doing him any good. I think I need to end it before summer.*

The week before summer started at the end of May, Jeff came over after her last final exam. He knocked on her door, and she answered. "Oh, hi. I didn't know you were coming."

Jeff said, "I wanted to surprise you. I want to take you to this cool bar and take you dancing."

She took a deep breath and said, "Jeff, we have to talk. Come in." Jeff's body immediately deflated once again. Anna, looking at the floor, said, "I'm sorry, but I think when we go home for the summer, we need to take a break." She waited for his response, but he held her hand and remained silent. "I just don't think . . ."

He interrupted her. "Anna, I understand. I was hoping this would last but knew that you don't feel the same for me as I do for you."

With tears coming down his face, Jeff opened the door. "Anna, I hope you find happiness. I will always love you and wish you well."

Anna fell on her bed. She had to take multiple breaths to calm down. She went to one of her dresser drawers and took the last of her mother's pills. She waited for the pill to kick in as she drank a few glasses of wine. She wrote in her journal: *How can he just understand when I don't? I hope I did the right thing. Maybe he does understand me after all? I felt overwhelmed with him all the time, and he was so nice to me, it didn't feel right. Maybe there is something wrong with me. I am sad but relieved. I'm sure he will move on and find someone else.* As the pill made her drowsy, she fell asleep.

CHAPTER 5

Anna's Sophomore Year

Anna was coming home from work as an aide at the hospital one afternoon when her phone rang. She answered it; it was Lori. "Hi, Lori. How are you?"

Lori said, "Great, thanks. How has your summer been?"

"I've been working as a nurse's aide and spending time with my mother, mostly," Anna answered. "How about you?"

"Great. I have been going out a lot. I was wondering if you want to be roommates again this year? I know you'd rather have an actual roommate, but . . . "

Anna interrupted her. "Yes, I would like that. I got used to my space. I'm sure you heard that Jeff and I broke up."

Lori paused. "No, I had no idea. Jeff hasn't said anything to us. What happened?"

"Have you seen him? How is he doing?"

"No, I haven't seen him, but Carl has," Lori said. "Why won't you tell me what happened?"

Anna said, "I guess I wasn't ready for something so serious, since this was my first relationship."

Lori said, "I get that. He's a great catch, though. You may never find someone like him again."

Anna, wanting to change the subject, said, "The summer is flying by, and I took some classes to be able to graduate early. So, will we be in the same dorm?"

"I'm not sure, but I'll see if we can be," Lori said. "That was a great location. I'll see what I can find out and let you know."

When Anna woke up the Sunday morning she was planning to leave for school, Kathy came into her room and asked, "Can I bring anything for you?"

Anna said, "No, thanks, Mom. I got it."

She went downstairs. Her father was at the kitchen table reading the paper. As she carried some boxes down, he asked, "Are you moving out already?"

"Yes. Back to school."

He said, "Good grades."

He packed up his workout clothes and headed out. Anna grabbed her mother and said, "Mom, please meet some friends and reach out to others. You don't have to be alone all the time."

Kathy said, "Don't worry about me."

Anna drove off and waved to Luke in the window.

She arrived at school and unpacked her belongings by herself. An urge to call Jeff came over her, but she averted the thought and looked at her schedule. Her first nursing class would start Monday morning. She was leaving the room when she saw Lori and her parents from the window. *I don't want to bump into them again*, she thought. She took a long walk out the back door, and when she got back, Lori was on the phone sitting on the bed and smiled when she saw Anna.

She gave Anna a hug when she got off the phone. "Hey, Anna. I'm glad you got my text. It's nice to be in the same room again."

Anna said, "Yes, it's fine."

"I hope we can spend more time together this year," Lori said.

Anna said, "That would be nice. Will you be around more?"

Lori said, "Probably. You will have to come to more parties, too, and not just date the first guy you meet like the last party." They laughed, but then Anna felt sad for a moment.

Lori said, "I did see Jeff after I spoke to you, and it seems like he took your breakup pretty badly. He really fell for you."

"Why are you trying to make me feel bad?" Anna asked.

Lori said, "I'm sorry. I guess I was hoping you would get back together."

"There are things you don't know," Anna replied. "He's better off without me."

Lori looked puzzled but kept quiet. "I should go now, but I'll call you later in the week. Bye."

The next day, Anna got up, got dressed, and went to her nine a.m. nursing class. She saw Jen and sat down next to her. "Hey, stranger. How was your summer?"

Jen said, "It was okay. I'm glad to be back at school. Not for the work but just to be independent. I go home, and my parents still think I'm twelve. How is Jeff?"

"We actually broke up before the summer started," Anna said.

"He was suffocating, wasn't he? He wanted to be with you all the time."

Anna felt defensive. "I think I wasn't ready for it. He's a great guy. I'm sure I won't ever meet someone like him again."

Jen said, "Maybe he wasn't the right one. It was only your first relationship, right?" Anna nodded. "I know relationships can be difficult. That's why I'm not in one." The professor came in then, and Anna opened her notebook.

After class, Jen said, "We're meeting for dinner if you want to come."

Anna said, "Sure, what time?"

"Usual time, six."

Anna's heart started pounding when she was getting ready. *Why does the thought of seeing Dave make me like this? At least I don't have a boyfriend anymore.* She got ready and walked to dinner. Anna looked at her watch and saw that it was just five forty-five. She took a deep breath. She got herself a salad and sat at a big empty table and waited for a while, looking down at her phone as if she were reading. She looked up and saw Jen come in with a group of people. She looked at her phone quickly as Jen yelled her name. "Hey, Anna. We'll be right over." They got their food and came over.

Anna was watching out of the corner of her eye and noticed Dave flirting with the girl across the counter giving him a pizza. They came over, and Anna said, "Hi, Jen, sit over here," pointing next to her.

Dave came over and sat across from Anna. "So, Anna, nice of you to join us. I haven't seen you in a long time. I thought maybe you transferred."

Anna said, "Hi, Dave. No, just busy with work and school."

"She *was* consumed with her boyfriend, but they broke up now, so we'll see more of her. Right?" Jen said.

"Sure," Anna agreed.

"What happened?" Dave asked. "Why did you split up?"

Anna thought, *Why is he staring at me and asking these personal questions? Those eyes are so piercing.* "Well, I guess I wasn't ready for a serious relationship."

Dave shifted in his chair and seemed to become more intrigued. "Oh, so you ended it."

Anna said, "Yes, he wasn't the right one or the timing was off."

"Dave, leave her alone now," Jen said. "How was your summer?"

"I worked as a nurse's aide and babysat all summer, as well as coming back and forth for summer classes," Anna said.

They all looked at each other.

"What? I really want to finish early and get working."

Jen said, "Why the rush? Enjoy college. You're going to work the rest of your life."

"I don't really party or anything," Anna said. "I just want to get my education and move out on my own."

Dave said, "Sounds like you don't want to go back home."

Anna, rattled that he could see through her so easily, asked, "How was your summer?"

Brooke interrupted with, "Well, mine was fun. I'm having fun in college because I'm only young once."

"You're always having fun, Brooke," Pete said. "Anna is mature and knows what she wants. That's great."

Anna said, "I'm not sure about that. How was your break?"

Pete said, "It was nice. I spent time partying and worked with my father. He has a store that I help with when I'm around."

"That sounds nice," Anna said. "Well, I'll catch up with you later, Jen. I have to work tonight."

"Are you at the bookstore still?" Dave asked.

"How did you know that?"

Jen looked at Dave, waiting for a response. "Well, I saw you there last semester."

Anna said, "Oh, I don't remember seeing you, but a lot of people come in there." She was thinking that she certainly would have remembered seeing him. "Well, catch you in class."

Jen said, "Before you go, Dave and Pete are having a party Saturday night. You have to come."

"I'll check my work schedule," Anna said.

Anna went into work and handed Evan her availability list for the semester. Evan said, "I'm glad you're still working here. It's nice to have consistency."

"Well, I like working here," she said. "It's helped me, too."

Evan said, "I'm glad you think like that. A lot of people don't like working here. I have a lot of turnover."

Anna looked at Evan and saw a fifty-year-old guy with graying hair and a beer belly. He seemed sad. "Why didn't you ever get married, Evan?" she said, surprising herself with the question.

Evan appeared angry at first, but after a minute, his face relaxed. "Well, it hasn't worked out that way for me. I was engaged once, but she left me a few weeks before our wedding. I guess I never got over that. Life, as with people, is not always predictable. I really loved her, but years later I found out she had met someone else. He had the type of money I never would have. She married for money, I guess. It really hurt me. I'm used to being alone now. I have my family and take care of my mother. By the way, how is Jeff?"

"We broke up at the end of last semester," she told him.

"I'm sorry to hear that," Evan said. "You two seemed like such a nice couple."

"Where should I start today?"

Evan said, "Why don't you work the register? Todd is leaving soon, and you can take over for him."

Anna was on her way back to the dorm when Jen texted her. "Remember, Dave is having a party Saturday night. Come to my place and we can go over together."

Butterflies filled her stomach. *What is wrong with me?* Anna thought. She texted back, "I'm working till eight but can come after that."

Jen replied, "Great."

Saturday came, and Anna, trying to get dressed after work, pulled all her clothes out of her drawer, unhappy with everything. She finally decided on her first outfit of jeans and a tight black shirt. She thought, *I'd better leave before I change my mind again.* She walked over to Jen's rental house and knocked on the door.

Brooke answered and quickly said, "Jen, it's for you."

"Hi, Brooke," Anna greeted. "I came to see you as well."

Jen came bounding down the hallway. "Hey there. Wow, you look amazing with your hair and your makeup and your big chest sticking out with that tight shirt."

Anna's face turned bright red.

Jen said, "I'm just kidding. Come on."

Anna followed her and saw her room had clothes and books everywhere with nothing in order.

"Excuse the mess," Jen said. "Well, I'm a slob—nothing to really excuse. It sort of always looks like this."

Brooke yelled, "Yes, it does. She's not exaggerating."

"It doesn't bother me. I wish I was more laid back," Anna said.

Jen said, "No, you don't. I can't find anything, and I'm completely unorganized." Then she called down the hall, "Are you coming, Brooke?"

Brooke called back, "I'll meet you there."

As they walked to Dave and Pete's house, Anna said, "I don't think Brooke likes me."

"She's hard to warm up to. She's a lot of fun once you get through that outer shell. It just takes a while. I think she's in the closet and hasn't figured it out yet, but that just stays between us," Jen said. Anna smiled.

They walked a few houses away and opened the door. Anna saw about ten people already there, and Jen ran over to get a beer. "Want one?"

Anna followed behind her and said, "Thanks." She drank half the beer in a few seconds.

Jen said, "I see my old roommate. I'll be right back."

Anna looked around the room, thinking, *I'd like to go home. Maybe I just don't fit in here.*

Pete suddenly appeared. He was an inch taller than Anna, who was about five eight. He had dirty blond hair on the longer, wavy side and lots of scruff on his face, with a friendly smile. He said, "So what is a nice girl like you doing in a place like this?"

Anna laughed. "Cute."

Dave came over before Pete said anything else. "You made it. I wasn't sure you would. So now maybe I can get to know you? How do you like the party?"

Anna said, "It's fine. I'm really not into partying "

"Do you like movies?" Pete asked.

Dave jumped in. "Pete, some of your friends came in and were looking for you."

He rolled his eyes at Dave like that happened often and said, "Excuse me, Anna."

"Are they really here?" Anna asked.

Dave smiled at Anna and said, "Now, why would I lie about that?" Then he added, "Anna, if you hear anything about my character, don't listen to rumors. Please make your own judgment."

"Why would someone talk about your character?" Anna asked.

Dave paused. "Well, it has been my experience that people seem to talk about me. I do have a history of liking women, but women tend to like me, too. I would like a chance to get to know you, and I would like you to get to know me without any preconceived notions."

Anna was intrigued and curious and said, "Well, I feel you've already pre-judged me, thinking I listen to gossip."

"Point taken," Dave said.

Since Dave was standing next to Anna, she could smell his cologne. She thought, *I just want to take him in as he holds me.* She looked at him out of the corner of her eye, trying not to stare, but noticed his strong physique and short dark hair with piercing blue eyes and cherry-colored lips.

"Have you heard anything about me?" Dave asked.

"Yes, but I won't tell you what I heard."

Dave nodded with a smirk. "I'm sure it was positive."

Anna thought, *He really cares what people think of him or what I think of him.* She said, "I guess I can get to know you for myself."

Dave smiled, and the air that had been so heavy suddenly lifted. "You are smart. I always knew you were." He laughed. "You can ask me anything, and I will answer you honestly."

Pete came over, handing them each a beer. Anna drank half of hers down.

Dave said, "Slow down. You want to be lucid when we talk."

Pete rolled his eyes. "Dave, why don't you leave her alone?"

"It's okay, Pete. Really. I'm fine," Anna said. Pete shook his head and walked away.

Dave said, "Don't pay attention to him. He has a crush on you."

"I'm sure you're wrong about that," she said.

Dave shifted in his shoes and bit his lip as he leaned up against the wall, hovering over her. "Well, you're beautiful and nice, so I'm sure that's a common thing in your life. How do you feel about dating now?"

Anna thought, *Is he asking me out? Why did he say that?* Wanting to say the right thing, she paused and, as he was looking at her as if examining her, said, "I'm focusing on school and work and meeting new people. Excuse me. I really need to go to the bathroom."

Anna saw an open door and almost sprinted to the bathroom. Dave laughed.

Anna felt her heart beating very fast, and she quickly finished her beer before she peed. She put some cold water on her face and took a deep breath. "Dave would never like you with all his charm and good looks," she said out loud to her reflection in the mirror. "You need to go home."

Anna flipped her golden brown hair back and opened the door to two girls stumbling into the bathroom. She noticed Dave had moved on and was talking to a few girls she didn't recognize. She slipped out the front door and texted Jen. "I'm fine, Jen. I'm going home and didn't want you to worry. I'm tired. Talk to you later."

Anna went to the library and to work the next day, thinking, *Don't think about him. Focus on your school and getting your degree.* She started sorting through the new arrivals of books in the back. Evan came over and said, "Hey, I need you out front. It's too busy to be unloading right now."

Anna said, "Sure."

When she rang up the last person in the store, she looked at the clock to see that it was already eight forty. *Wow, my time went fast today; only twenty minutes to go,* she thought.

She was coming out of the bathroom when she looked over and saw Dave looking through some books. Evan walked over to him and said, "Hey, we're closing at nine."

Anna snuck over to the cash register to start closing out and pretended not to see him. He walked over to a shelf closest to her and kept reading a book he had in his hand. He looked up and, with a stunning smile, said, "Oh, do I know you?"

Evan looked over and shook his head. Anna said, "How are you, Dave?"

"Much better now," he said.

"Can I ring you up? We're closing soon."

He said, "Well, only if you agree to a coffee after work."

"I'm not sure that would be a good idea," she said.

"Anna, it's not a date. It's two friends having a coffee. Besides, you owe me. You blew me off after you went to the bathroom."

Anna surprised herself by saying, "No, you were flirting with other women. I was tired and wanted to leave."

Dave quizzically turned his stare to his books. "I see. Now I understand. I still won't leave until you have some coffee with me."

Anna smiled. "Okay, for a little while." She rang him up, and he handed her a hundred-dollar bill. She thought, *Well, for a college student, he is not hurting for money.*

Dave went outside to wait for her to finish up. When she came out, he pointed. "Okay, my car's over here." He walked toward it, and she saw a BMW.

"Nice car," she commented.

He smiled. "It's fun, too."

He got in the car and unlocked the door, waiting for her to get in. *If this were a date, would he open the door for me? Jeff would have never done that.* He drove a few blocks to Starbucks. "I'm glad I ran into you, Anna."

She said, "Why's that?"

He smiled at her in a flirtatious way without saying anything. She looked at the menu at the counter. Dave was already ordering his drink. "And the lady will have . . ." He waited for her response.

She said, "Café latte with French vanilla."

Anna started to take out her wallet when his hand gently glided over hers and he shook his head. Anna thought, *His hand is so warm and strong, and I don't want him to take it away.* He paid the attendant and said, "Let's go sit by the fireplace."

Anna followed behind him, and he sat down with his back toward the wall. She sat down and said, "Remember this is not a date, but thank you for my drink."

He smiled as he put his hand over hers and said, "You seem so tense. Are you stressed?"

Anna fidgeted in her chair and looked to the floor. "No. Well, you sort of make me uncomfortable."

Dave said, "Good. I like a woman on her toes."

Anna smirked, thinking, *Now I'm more uncomfortable. It seems like he likes to intimidate.*

He smiled and said, "Come on. You can't take a joke?"

Anna said, "Of course, but it didn't seem like you were joking."

Dave, ignoring her, said, "So, Anna, tell me about yourself."

"Well, first tell me about you," she countered.

He said, "You want to play this this way. Let's see. I come from a wealthy family. My father is a corporate banker and wants me to join his firm when I'm finished with school. I'm already working with him now to learn the business and so the clients get to know me better. I have an older brother who's also in the business, but he's a lawyer and handles that end of things."

Anna listened to every word like her life depended on it and asked, "How about your mother?"

"That's not a good subject. She died over a year ago now." He stood from his seat. "I'll be right back."

Anna tried to see his face, but he turned so fast she was unable to read his emotions. *Why did I ask him that? Jen never told me about that. What do I say now?*

He came back after five minutes in the bathroom that felt like half an hour to Anna. He sat down, and she put her hand over his and said, "I'm so sorry."

He looked at her hand and took a breath. "You're very comforting, Anna. No one knows what to say when I share that, but you're different. You really are special."

Anna blushed and took a deep breath to build up the courage to ask, "Can I ask what happened?"

Dave looked into the empty fireplace and said, "We think she had a brain aneurysm because she fell down the stairs. It was all so sudden that my father didn't get an autopsy, but that's what the doctors think."

Anna paused and imagined if she lost a parent.

He held onto her hand and looked deep into her eyes. "You have done more than you know. Most people don't know what to say and aren't able to stay with me, but you are beautiful inside and out."

Anna blushed and shook her head as a coy gesture.

She stopped and said, "We all have some difficulties in our lives. I have parents and a younger brother. I have lived sort of isolated, in my own world, until now. Well, they don't have a good marriage, but my mother stays with him. He works all the time and is never really around, and when he is there, there's a lot of tension."

"What does your father do?" he asked.

"He's an executive at Ford and travels a lot," she said. "He doesn't talk about it with us. Anyway, my mother keeps to herself and gardens and tends to the house. She doesn't have much of a life to me."

"Does she work?"

"No, she actually was a nurse but never did work and lost her license, if she ever did get one. I guess I'm following in her footsteps, but I can't wait to work and help people." Anna noticed his hand on hers; she removed her hand, and her face turned red.

He turned his face sideways and said, "Now you're blushing. That's good."

Anna took a breath and said, "Jen told me you and her have been friends all her life."

He said, "Our fathers were friends but had a falling out. I never did understand what happened with that, but it was after my mother died. Jen and I have been friends forever, it seems. We've always been there for each other."

"What about a relationship?" Anna asked.

He smirked and said, "So, you have been talking to Jen about me! I hope my story is consistent with hers." He paused then said, "I don't have feelings for her in that way. We both thought once it would maybe work, but soon after we dated, we knew it wasn't right. I do think with you it may be different."

Anna looked down at the floor with her heart beating so loud she thought he would be able to hear it.

"Anna, I know you must know I'm interested in you, as more than a friend. I know you recently got out of a relationship, and I'm willing to give it time for you to be comfortable with the thought of dating me."

Anna laughed. "Why would you be interested in me?"

He nodded. "Okay, Miss Insecure." He looked at his phone and read a text. "Sorry, Anna. I'll have to take you back now."

"I hope everything is okay," she said.

"Yes. I have to meet up with my father."

"Now? That's strange," she commented.

Dave looked at Anna sternly. "I work all the time. Unfortunately or fortunately, I'm at my father's beck and call because these clients have needs all the time."

Anna said, "I'll just walk back, then."

"No. It's okay," he said. "I can drive you home."

They got up, and Anna rushed to get her coat on. Dave threw his cup away and turned around. "I'm glad I got some time to get to know you today. I hope we can do this again soon."

Anna walked out the door and thought, *I feel strange and want to get home.* He reached her dorm, and she opened the door. "Thanks for the ride and the drink."

He said, "You owe me now. I'll take payment in the form of coming to my party in a few weeks."

"We'll see," Anna said. He drove off before she went in the dorm, feeling butterflies in her stomach.

Anna went in her room and opened her diary. *Dear Diary, Dave has been through so much with losing his mother and is so busy with making a life for himself. He is so gorgeous. He could have anyone. What does he see in me? I feel on top of the world with him, but there is something that doesn't feel so right. It feels different than with Jeff. I need to focus on school.*

Anna woke up the next day, got a protein bar, and made some coffee before she headed to class. *Stop thinking about him, Anna. He's not for you.* She went to class, but before she entered the building, someone grabbed her.

"Hope you had a nice time last night. I did."

Anna said, "Dave, what are you doing here?"

"Nothing, just wanted to see you. Have a nice day." He walked off, and she stumbled up the stairs.

Jen came over after Dave had left. "Hey, are you okay?"

Anna said, "I'm fine—just clumsy."

"You're working a lot of hours," Jen said. "Do you have to work so much?"

Anna said, "Yes, I don't want to ask my parents for more money, and I pay for my car insurance and mostly everything besides school."

Jen said, "Well, we miss you at dinner."

Anna, puzzled, asked, "We?"

Jen said, "Well, I do for sure. I think Pete does because he keeps mentioning you. I think he likes you."

Anna said, "No, I'm sure he doesn't. I can come to dinner Thursday, but I work all the other nights."

Anna suddenly got a text. *Who could this be?* she thought. She looked at her phone and read the message: "Do you miss me yet? D." *Is that Dave? I never gave him my number, and he was just here.*

Jen said, "Anna, let's sit down. Class is starting."

Anna followed her and sat down. She wrote back. "How did you get this number?"

"I have my ways. Think of me in class."

Anna texted, "This is too distracting. I need to pay attention."

He texted, "Okay, I'll leave you alone for now."

Anna tried to focus on the professor and silenced her phone.

After a few weeks of Dave texting her on occasion, Anna wrote in her diary, *Why does Dave text me on and off? I'm not sure what he is doing. Does he like me or not? He gives mixed messages. I need to focus on school, and he is just distracting me. I will need to tell him to stop.*

The weekend came, and Dave texted her. "Sorry, Anna. I won't be able to see you this time, but next weekend for sure."

Anna texted, "You don't need to apologize. We are not together. We are just friends."

He texted, "With benefits?????"

Anna thought, *What does that mean? It can't be good.*

He wrote, "See you next weekend at my party."

She wrote, "Okay."

The next weekend came, and she went to Jen's to meet up before going to Dave's. Jen was excited and had already had a few beers when Anna came over. The music was loud, and Jen was dancing, and she pulled Anna into her house after she knocked and started to hip-check her to get her to dance. Anna smiled and shook her head a few times. She went to the couch and sat down.

Jen said, "Come on." Brooke came over, and they danced and sang.

Anna said, "Could I have a beer?"

Jen yelled, "It's in the fridge."

Anna went to get a beer and chugged it down next to the fridge, then opened another one. She watched the two girls and said, "Shouldn't we go now?"

Brooke laughed. "Relax, Anna. The party isn't going anywhere. You're not on a job interview."

Anna sat down and felt her head feel fuzzy and lighter. After half an hour, Jen said, "Well, let's go." The three of them walked to the party with Jen in the middle and Brooke talking with Jen. Anna thought, *Why doesn't Brooke like me? She ignores me.*

Jen said, "Anna, Pete's going to be there. He told Brooke that he does like you."

Anna stuttered and said, "I'm not interested in a relationship. I need to focus on school." *Now I really don't want to go to this party,* she thought.

Jen went first up the front steps and opened the door, and Anna looked around and saw almost twenty people there already. She followed

Jen to get a beer, and Pete quickly came over. "Hey, Anna. You look so nice. Do you want a beer?"

Before Anna could answer, Dave appeared and handed her one. "Of course she does."

Pete gave Dave a dirty look. Dave handed Jen and Brooke a beer as well. "Ladies, looking good. How's your evening so far?"

Looking toward Anna, Jen said, "Great so far. How's your father?"

Dave said, "You know, busy trying to make more money. Never has enough."

"How is Sue?" Jen asked.

"Why don't you call her?" he responded. "She misses you, I think." As the music got louder, Dave grabbed Anna's hand and said, "Let's go outside. I have to ask you something."

Anna's heart raced as she followed him. Pete shook his head. Dave said, "I'm so glad you came. I wasn't sure you would."

"I do want to hang out with my friends," Anna said.

"I hope I'm included in that group," he said. "I wanted to see if you wanted to go out with me—on a date."

Anna blushed. "I like you, but it's not going to work. I need to focus on my classes. I also think it would affect my friendship with Jen."

Dave looked puzzled. "Why's that?"

She shrugged.

Dave said, "Anna, we're just friends." He pulled her close and kissed her lips with such passion, she thought, *No one has ever wanted me like this before.* Anna kissed him back, but when she opened her eyes, she saw Jen staring at them from the hallway. Anna pulled away but felt compelled to say, "Dave, you need to stop."

Anna scurried over to Jen with her heart pounding out of her chest.

Brooke said, "What did Dave want? I saw you guys talking."

Before Anna could answer, Jen said, "Brooke, don't be so nosy."

Anna took a long sip of beer and said, "I like this music."

Pete said, "Thanks. It's my music list."

"Good taste," she complimented. She followed Dave with her eyes and saw a group of girls stop him. He started talking to them, and she could see the girls laugh—they were flirting with him. More people arrived, and she was crowded in the room, not able to see. "I'll be right back," she told her friends. She went to the bathroom, and when she came out, she saw Jeff far off in the other room. She went out the back door and walked to her dorm. She texted Jen, "Sorry I left. I wasn't feeling well. Have a good time."

She opened her journal and wrote, *Wow. What am I going to do? Dave has a power in him, and I don't think I can say no to him. That kiss makes me want him so badly. I'm nothing special, so why would he want me when he could get anyone, with those breathtaking eyes and body, and when he is so charming as well? I have to take it slow, and I don't want to jeopardize my friendship with Jen. I've never had a friend like her, so genuine. And I can't believe I saw Jeff. I still feel so badly about that. I have to go to bed.* She closed the book and went to find one of her mother's pills. *I have to calm down,* she thought.

Anna avoided Dave the next few weeks, and when he texted, she wrote, "Dave, I cannot see you." She waited for a reply, but there wasn't one.

Anna went to work and class with no communication from Dave. She wrote one night after work, *Dear Diary, I guess I was right all along. He never liked me and I was just another number to him. Why can't I get him out of my head? He overwhelms me, and I want him to grab me and kiss me. That kiss was like nothing I ever felt before. It is addictive or he is addictive. I need to go relax and forget about him.*

The day before she was leaving for her break, a knock came on her door. She said, "Lori, you don't have to knock," but when she opened the door, she felt limp, looking at Dave standing there with his gorgeous blue eyes piercing her with desire and self-assurance. He grabbed her and pulled her into her room. He started to kiss her while he closed the door behind him. Anna kissed him back, thinking, *Thank God he is here. I am someone. He does want me.*

He pressed her close to him, and she took him in. He pulled back from the kiss, and she asked, "What are you doing to me?"

He said, "I want you to think of that kiss over the break and decide if you want to be with me or not. I have waited too long now." He left, and his presence and smell lingered as she fell on her bed. *I cannot resist any longer.*

CHAPTER 6

Anna and Dave

nna took some cough medicine to help her sleep after noticing she did not have any more pills. She woke up and drove home the next day, thinking about Dave and how he had kissed her. She arrived at home and brought her bags into the house. Her father was in the kitchen. "Hi, Dad. How are you?" she greeted.

Dan looked up and asked, "Is it break time already?"

Anna fumbled with her bags. "Yes."

"Good," he said. "Your mother could use some help around here."

"Why?"

Dan said, "Ask her." He got up and left the kitchen.

Anna went to her room and saw her mother sleeping on her bed. She went to see if Luke was home, but he wasn't. She checked her phone and discovered she'd gotten a text from Lori. "Have a great break, Anna. I'll see you when we get back."

Luke came home a half hour later and came to Anna's room. He plopped down on her bed as she was laying down resting. "Hi, sis. How's everything?"

Anna said, "Okay, but I'm worried about Mom. Dad said he's glad I'm here to help her. Do you know what is wrong?"

Before Luke could say anything, Kathy walked into the room. "Anna, it's so good to see you," she greeted. "Your father is making too much of this, but I guess you should know."

Anna sat up in her bed, alert and fidgeting and waiting for her to continue.

"I had a biopsy for a lump they found in my breast. They don't think it's anything but wanted to make sure."

Anna jumped up from her bed. "Why wouldn't you call me and tell me? Why am I kept in the dark about everything? Are you okay? When will you know?"

Kathy paused and waited for Anna to calm down. "Anna. There's nothing you can do. I should know the results in a few days."

Anna sat down and stared at the floor. She thought, *I am a horrible daughter. I never call because she never calls me. I have to make it up to her.*

"Mom, go rest," she suggested. "I will make dinner and take care of things."

"Anna, I am fine," Kathy said. "I feel well and need to keep going to keep my mind off of it. It helps me to be busy, so I'm going to make dinner for my family tonight. I'm so happy to have you home."

She gave Anna a hug but longer this time, and Anna held her close and whispered, "I'm sorry I got upset. I guess I never have thought about losing you until this second."

After Kathy went downstairs and Luke went to the bathroom, Anna went to her mother's bathroom and closed the door. She opened her pill bottle and took a few. She swallowed one and put the others in her pocket and flushed the toilet before she came out.

Anna sat on her bed to write in her journal. *Dear Diary, My mother had a biopsy for a breast mass, and I have never been so scared. What if she has breast cancer? What if I actually lose my mother like Dave? I have never thought of this before, and now everything feels different. I am so scared.*

Kathy called her down to eat. Anna felt the next few days trickle by.

Anna was reading on the couch when the phone rang, and she quickly looked at it and saw it was the doctor's office. Kathy answered the phone. "Hello. Yes. I see. No further testing is needed, except a mammogram in six months. Great. Thank you."

Anna overheard the doctor and hung on every word.

Kathy said, "It's negative. See, you worried for nothing. That's why I didn't tell you."

Anna took a deep breath and said, "I'm going to lie down in my room. I'm so relieved."

The holiday went by slowly. Anna kept checking her phone, but there were no texts. *I have to get Dave out of my mind*, she thought. *Why can't I stop thinking about him?* She called Evan at work. "Hi, Evan. How was your holiday?"

"It was okay." He seemed a little surprised to be hearing from her.

"Do you need me tomorrow? I can come back early to help out."

"If you want to, I guess. I have a shipment coming in the morning and could use some help."

Anna, relieved to have something to do, said, "Great, I'll be there at ten."

She went to see her mother and said, "Mom, they need me at work, so I'm going to go back today."

"That's too bad," Kathy said. "Can I pack something for you?"

"No, Mom. I'm fine."

Anna packed quickly, and just as she was getting in the car, Luke came over. "You say you're worried about Mom, but you never stay here. You are always leaving."

"I just thought you were at Ted's house. Please, Luke, take care of Mom. I can't stand the tension when Dad is at home, and she is so lonely and sad when he is gone. I don't know what is worse—when he's here or when he's gone."

Luke said, "Now you know why I'm never home. It's unbearable. Go to school and enjoy yourself. I'll be off to school next year, and it can't come fast enough."

Anna saw a quick flash of her mother all alone for days on end. "Let me know where you are going. Maybe you can come to U of M."

Luke said, "No way. I'm going far away, and I'm joining the military to pay for it. I'll never have to feel like I owe that man anything. I'm going to do it all on my own."

"You sound like you hate him, Luke."

"It is what it is. I take him for who he is. Anna, don't ever get involved with someone like him. I read that patterns can repeat themselves if you're not aware."

Anna looked at him, puzzled. "Why would you ever think I would marry someone like Dad? You're ridiculous." She kissed him goodbye and said, "Come visit sometime." He nodded, but she wondered if he ever really would.

Anna arrived back in Ann Arbor, picked up dinner at the sub shop, and watched a movie on Netflix. She went to work the next day, which was the Sunday before school started back, and helped stock the shelves before the store opened at noon. By five, she was pretty tired. Evan said, "You have been here a while—why don't you finish up and head home?"

Anna rang up the last customer in her line and got ready to go. "Thanks, Evan. I'll let you know my new schedule tomorrow." She left and went to her room to find the door open.

She pushed the door back and saw Lori talking with Dave. Lori said, "Oh, hi, Anna. I came over to see you and look who I found knocking on your door."

"Hi, Lori. Hi, Dave, what are you doing here?"

"I was wondering if you'd like to get some coffee?"

"I have to go now anyway," Lori said. "I'll see you later, Anna."

Anna said, "Okay. We'll have to catch up."

Dave grabbed her hand and led her to his car before she could think of an answer. Anna's thoughts were racing as she bit her lip and fidgeted in the car as they drove to Starbucks. Dave was looking at his phone and ordered at the counter, two drinks and two scones. He said, "So, Anna. You are hard to get out of one's mind. I missed you over the break. Have you thought about us?"

Anna said, "I don't even really know you! How can there be an us?"

"Well, what do you want to know?"

Anna thought, *How odd. Am I interviewing him?* "I guess I'd like to know something personal that no one knows about you."

Dave put his phone down and pondered for a while. "This isn't a happy one, but here goes. Well, I remember when I was sixteen and my father bought me a new Cadillac truck. I totaled that car two weeks later. Some lady came out of nowhere and hit my truck after she blew a red light. She got a ticket, and the cops said I was lucky to be alive. When my father came to get me, the police told him that it wasn't my fault. But when we were driving home, he said, 'I wish you died in that accident.' Those words are always in the back of my mind."

Anna, shocked, said, "I'm so sorry."

Dave, looking directly in Anna's eyes, said, "I don't know why I just told you that. I haven't thought of that in a long time. I guess you make me feel comfortable." Then a quick change came over him, and his voice grew more intense. "I don't want you to pity me or feel sad for me. It actually made me a stronger person."

Anna held back tears for him. "Well, my father would have said the same thing."

"Now that is hard to believe!" Dave said.

"Well, he's a critical person. I don't remember him ever saying anything nice to me. I've never felt good enough. I could give you many examples, but I try to put it all out of my mind." As Anna talked, she noticed that Dave's gaze wandered briefly over to the girl behind the counter.

"Do you still feel like you're not good enough?" he asked, his eyes returning to hers.

"Do you know her?" Anna asked, nodding at the girl.

Dave shook his head as if he were in a daydream. "Know who?"

"Never mind," Anna said. *Maybe I'm imagining things.*

Dave's phone beeped, and he glanced down at the screen. "I'm sorry, but I need to go. I forgot to do something for work, and it's important."

Anna said, "Okay. I'm going to stay here a while. I'll walk back."

Without a thought, he got up. "I'll call you later." He grabbed her and kissed her lips. Anna felt her heart race and was aware that the women around them were staring at them. She couldn't help but think that they were jealous of her. After Dave left, she stayed for a couple minutes and then walked back to her dorm.

Anna found Lori in their room, crying on her bed. She put her hand on Lori's back and said, "What happened?"

"Carl broke up with me," Lori said. "I can't believe it. I thought we would get married."

"I'm sorry, Lori. Did you have a fight?"

Lori looked at Anna. "Worse. He found someone else. Is it okay if I move back in here? I don't have anywhere to go."

"Of course—this is your room, too. It would be nice to have an actual roommate. Have you told your parents?"

Lori said, "I should call them. I pushed them out of my life because of the lie I was living. I have a great dad. I need to talk to him."

She picked up the phone, and Anna went to the bathroom. When she got back, Lori said, "My dad is coming to pick me up so we can talk. I'm so happy and relieved to tell him what's been going on."

Anna thought, *Wow, there really are some dads out there who care.*

Anna went to bed but tossed and turned, thinking of her own father. She wondered why she couldn't put him out of her mind like she usually could. She finally took a shot of vodka from a bottle she had taken from Jen's apartment and lay back down after taking a deep breath. After half an hour and before Lori got back, Anna fell asleep.

The next day, Anna came back to her room after class and saw a dozen roses on the desk and Lori crying on the bed. "Are those from Carl?" she asked. "Why are you crying?"

Lori said, "For a moment, I thought they were from him, but they're for you."

Anna ran over to the desk and grabbed the card. "Sorry I ran out on you last night," she read. "You need to know you are more than enough. D." Anna sat on her bed and glanced at Lori. She felt badly that the flowers had given Lori false hope and upset her all over again, so she didn't say anything about who they were from. When Lori left to go the bathroom and wash her face, Anna reached for her journal. *Dear Diary, I just got a dozen roses. I can't believe how thoughtful and nice Dave is. He understands about my father and we have similar experiences, making us understanding of each other. Kissing him is the most amazing experience. I have made up my mind.*

Anna picked up the phone and called Dave. "Hi, Dave. Thank you so much for the flowers. They're beautiful."

"I'm glad you like them. Can you come over tonight around eight so we can hang out?"

"I'll be there after work. See you later." She hung up and thought, *I'm on top of the world.*

Anna went to work, and when Evan saw her, he said, "You're in a good mood today."

Anna smiled. "I'm going on a date after this."

"Oh, what's his name?"

"Dave." Anna started checking people out and watched the time trickle on.

Evan said, "You can leave early. You look like you've already checked out."

Anna laughed. "It's okay. He won't be ready till eight anyway. But thanks."

Anna got to Dave's apartment and knocked on the door. He opened it, looking casually handsome in a tight-fitting t-shirt and sweat pants, and Anna thought, *Why would this guy want to be with me?*

Dave moved to let her in, and she asked, "Where's Pete?"

Dave said, "I don't know. Out somewhere." He seemed distracted by text messages for the first few minutes after she arrived. Then he said, suddenly, "I'm sorry, Anna, but I have to take care of something for work."

Anna felt a wave of sadness and tried to hold back her tears as she said, "I thought we're going to hang out."

He got another text, and she said, "Okay, I guess." She looked at his face and breathed in his smell.

Dave grabbed her and kissed her and said, "Until tomorrow. I'll make it up to you."

The next night, Anna was in her room pacing the floor.

Lori said, "What's wrong?"

"Nothing." Lori looked at her in disbelief. "Okay, I'm waiting to hear from Dave."

"Oh, you must really like him," Lori said.

Anna said, "I didn't realize how much I do. There is something about him."

"Why don't you just call him?"

"I will in a little while," Anna said. "I'm going to study first."

She looked at the clock every few minutes until she finally she got a text: "Anna, I have a lot to study and won't be able to meet. Come over after work. What time do you get off?"

Lori said, "What's wrong? You look so sad."

"He can't make it," Anna said. "He has to study and wants to see each other tomorrow." She texted back, "Okay. I get off at eight."

He replied, "You're a doll. Can't wait to see you then. I'll make it up to you."

"Let's go catch a movie to take your mind off it," Lori suggested. "I need a break from my sadness anyway."

"How did your father react when you told him?"

Lori took a deep breath of relief. "He gave me a hug and said that he had suspected and was waiting for me to tell him. He told me he knew I would tell him when I was ready. He made me feel so much better, and he said I'd meet the right guy and to have patience and focus on my studies and meeting new people. He always says the right thing. I don't know what I'd do without him."

"I have no idea what that's like," Anna murmured under her breath.

"What?" Lori said. "I didn't hear you."

"Nothing," Anna said. "Let's go to the movies."

The next night was a Thursday, and Anna walked over to Dave's after work. She knocked and waited a few minutes till he opened the door.

"Hey," he said. He pulled her inside the house and kissed her. "I've been waiting to do that again. Come on up." She followed him to his room, where he had a couch and a flat-screen television on his wall.

"Nice room."

He lay back on his bed and said, "Come over. I won't bite—or at least not hard."

Anna's heart was beating out of her chest, and she thought, *Is this it? Will I feel him now?*

He pulled her onto the bed and stared at her. "You're really beautiful," he said as he stroked her face and hair.

"You make me nervous," she admitted.

He said, smirking, "Why would you be nervous with me?"

She said, "I've never met someone like you. You're so confident and sure of yourself."

"Well, I shared with you something no one really knows about. There's something so sweet about you that makes me want to be with you."

"What is it?" Anna asked.

"You are so innocent, it seems, and genuine. I can see you in my future."

Anna blushed and said, "How could you possibly know that?"

He stroked her face and down her arm and across her stomach and said, "You are special, and you don't even know it."

He started to kiss her face and neck as Anna was whisked away with his desire and self-assurance. He lifted up her shirt and motioned to her to sit up so he could get it off. She complied. He said, "I've wanted this ever since I met you in the cafeteria." He took his shirt off, and she felt his warm, soft skin against hers and thought, *I never want to leave.* He stroked her back and took his pants off, so she took hers off, too. He kissed her stomach, and she felt his penis on her leg, and he entered her and said, "Are you on the pill?"

Anna said, "No."

He quickly put on a condom and said, "We'll have to change that."

Anna heard her phone beep with an incoming text as they were making love.

He whispered, "Is there anything you really like?"

Anna said, "All of it." After he came and dropped down beside her on the bed, she looked at the clock. It was twelve.

"Why don't you sleep here tonight?" He turned off the light and fell fast asleep.

Anna lay there and felt wired. She watched him sleep and thought, *He's so attractive and confident. He's so different from Jeff. Why would he want me? He said he sees me in his future. Is that true? He doesn't even know me, really. I must get some sleep.* She tried to sleep but felt like she was in a twilight, never fully falling asleep.

She woke to see Dave coming in from the shower. He sat on the edge of the bed and kissed her. "You are something, Anna. Last night was amazing." He kissed her forehead and said, "I have a class to go to. Can I walk you out?"

Anna looked at the time and realized she was already late but said, "Sure," as if she didn't have a care in the world. Later, when she was walking back to her dorm, she remembered the text coming in the night before. She looked at her phone to see it had been from Lori. "Are you coming back tonight? I just wanted to make sure you are okay."

Anna felt bad and rushed back, but Lori was already gone. She texted her. "I'm fine, Lori. I'm sorry—I'm just reading this now. Let's meet for lunch at noon."

She looked at the clock and thought, *I've already missed half an hour. I'll go to the next class.* She opened her journal. *Dear Diary, You won't believe how great last night was. He is so intoxicating and charming. I felt like we were the only people in the entire world. I know it was soon to be intimate, but I feel like I've wanted him forever. I have my doubts that he would even want me. I'm so excited and can't wait to see him again. I have to go to class now. Bye for now.*

She grabbed her coat and went to class and thought, *What will Jen think of us dating?* She sat next to Jen, who had a smile on her face but looked concerned. Anna thought, *She can't possibly know.* "Hi, Jen," she said. "How are you?"

"I'm good, thanks."

"Could I see the notes from last class?" Anna asked.

"Sure. I hope it was worth it." Anna ignored the comment and focused on the teacher.

After class, Jen said, "Hey, aren't you coming to lunch?"

Anna was ahead of Jen, feeling bad about Lori. She said, "Oh, I was planning to meet Lori for lunch."

"I didn't think you saw her much."

"Well, her boyfriend broke up with her, and she moved back in."

"That's tough. I'm sure she's having a hard time."

They got to the cafeteria, and they spotted Lori sitting at a table. "Hi, guys."

"Lori, remember Jen?" Anna asked.

"Oh, yeah," Jen said. "At one of the parties." She sat down as Brooke and then Dave came over. Anna felt her heart race when she saw him, remembering some of what they'd been up to the night before.

"Hello, ladies," he said. He sat across from Anna, smiling at her.

"Dave, you have good taste in flowers," Lori said.

"Thanks. Only the best for Anna," he said.

After a while, Anna said, "Oh, I have to work. I'll catch up with you guys later."

Dave stood up and walked her to the door. "I can't wait to see you again. Tonight?"

Anna felt her hormones surge and said, "I'll text you later."

"I want to see you tonight."

"We'll see. I have some work to do."

But Dave had already left and was too far to hear her say anything. Anna thought, *Why does he want to see me again? Why do I hesitate some? What is wrong with me?*

She went to her dorm after work and found Lori on her bed studying. Lori said, "Hey, Anna. Your friend Jen is really nice, and Brooke, too. They invited me to hang out with them anytime."

Anna said, "That's nice."

"Are you going out tonight?"

"I have to write this article, and then I think I'll go over to Dave's."

Lori said, "Can I ask you something?"

"Of course."

"Well, Jen said that Dave isn't the best boyfriend. He has a sordid past with women."

"Look at him, Lori. Women throw themselves at him. Don't worry about me. I know what I'm doing."

"I just don't want you to go through what I did."

"Everyone is different. Not all men are like Carl. Dave is a great guy. I have to go now."

Anna knew she sounded confident, but she didn't feel that way. She thought about her mother and felt tears pool in her eyes. *If only I could call my mom or dad to get some advice*, she thought. She finished her coffee and walked over to Dave's.

Pete let her in and said, "Hi, Anna. He should be home in a little bit. Come have a beer if you want."

Anna said, "Thanks."

He handed her one and said, "Have a seat. I don't want you to be uncomfortable being here." Pete paused and looked at Anna somberly. Anna bit her lip. He said, "I know you probably think I'm saying this just because I wish you'd give me a shot instead of him, but Anna, be careful with Dave. He doesn't treat women well! You seem to be a nice person."

Anna drank down her beer quickly. Pete asked her if she wanted another one, and she nodded. She thought, *He's a nice guy. He's just saying all this because he wanted to go out with me.* He handed her another beer, and she asked, "Do you mind if I go to Dave's room to wait? I have some studying to do."

Pete's shoulders fell. "Sure. I didn't mean to make you uncomfortable. I just think you're a good person and, well, just think about what I said."

Anna went to Dave's room and sat at his desk to work on the article that was due for class. She instinctively started opening drawers but quickly closed them. She took a sip of her second beer and started reading a letter she found from someone named Tiffany. "Hi, Sexy. I am waiting for . . ."

Dave entered the room. "Hi, Anna. What are you doing?"

"I was just waiting for you and drinking a beer. Where have you been?"

Dave glanced behind her at the desk. "Are you looking through my stuff?" He took the letter and put it away. "That's nervy of you, Anna."

"I'm sorry," she said, "but I just want to know more."

"Anna, my past is my past. I've been with other women, but I'm with you now. It's better that you don't know about the other women. You'll come to know me in time. You'll know the type of guy I am as you spend more time with me. Just give it time."

He took her hand and brought her to his bed and started kissing her neck and lips. He took her clothes off and said, "Wow, you're gorgeous." Anna started kissing his stomach and felt his body. She looked up into his eyes and felt her heart race and an emotional pull to be overwhelmed by him. They fell on the bed and made love. Anna fell fast asleep after and woke the next morning when she heard Dave turn on the water in the shower.

After he finished, he came in and said, "Wow, Anna, you were amazing last night. I have to go to class, but I'll text you later."

Anna sat up in bed and went into the hallway after he left. Pete passed by her and said, "Will you be moving in?"

"Very funny," she said, blushing. She washed up in the sink and put on her clothes from the previous day then walked back to her dorm. She wondered why she felt so bad about something she had wanted to do.

Anna took a long, hot shower and got ready. She went to her class ten minutes late and smiled at Jen as she walked in. After class, Anna said, "Want to go to lunch?"

"Sure. I told Lori to meet at twelve thirty. Are you preparing for the test tomorrow?"

Anna said, "Oh, I need to do a lot of studying tonight. I'm going to do an errand, and I'll meet you at lunch."

But later when Anna was on her way to the cafeteria, her heart started racing and she became short of breath. She felt faint and started to sweat. She texted Jen: "I don't feel well. I am going to go lie down." She thought of going to the health center but decided to go to her dorm instead. She lay down, taking deep breaths. After another ten minutes, she called her mother.

Kathy answered. "Hello?"

Anna said, "Hi, Mom. How are you?"

Kathy said, "I'm fine. Are you okay?"

"Not really. I feel like my heart is racing and I may pass out."

"Take some deep breaths," Kathy said, "and try to take a nap if you have time. If you need a break from school, you can always come home. Your father is away for the weekend, if you want to keep me company."

Anna thought, *That sounds nice.* She immediately said, "Okay. I'll see you this weekend." Her heart slowed down, and she fell asleep.

The next two days went by the same way. She told Dave before they went to sleep Thursday night that she was going home for the weekend to see her mother.

"I was hoping to spend the weekend with you," he said.

Anna said, "My mother is alone this weekend and wants me to be with her."

"Well, I want to be with you, too." His voice was very cold and surprised her. He turned over in bed and said, "Just go to sleep."

Anna felt her nerves get worse. *Why is he acting like this? I just want to see my mother.* She went to the fridge after he was asleep, grabbed a beer, and drank it quickly. She went to the bathroom and then back to his room. She was finally able to fall asleep, and when she woke up, he had already left.

After Anna took the exam, she packed a small bag. As she was getting ready, Dave knocked on her room door. He came in and said, "I hope you have a nice time with your mother. Just give me more notice to get used to you going away. I need to meet your family soon also." He was giving her a passionate kiss when Lori came in.

"Oh, I'm sorry," she said.

Dave said, "No problem. I was just leaving. Goodbye, ladies."

"Are you going somewhere?" Lori asked Anna.

"I'm going home for the weekend. My father's away, and my mother asked me to keep her company."

"Oh, you're going to miss the party."

"What party?"

"Dave and Pete's party. I just got a text from Jen this morning. Last-minute planning, I guess."

"Oh, yeah. I guess I forgot about it since I was planning to leave anyway."

Anna drove home with her thoughts racing. *Did Dave plan the party after I told him I was leaving? Why didn't Jen text me about it?* She got home and went into the house using the back door. Her mother's car was in the driveway, but Anna didn't see her. She went upstairs and into her mother's room and found her sleeping. Anna looked at the clock and saw that it was two thirty in the afternoon. She went into her mother's bathroom and shut the door and took a few of her mother's pills and put a few in her pocket. She came out and decided to cook dinner for her mother and Luke. It was so quiet in the house.

At four, Anna went upstairs to wake her mother up. Kathy woke up groggy. Anna said, "Why are you so tired, Mom? You look much thinner, too. I made some dinner for us."

Kathy said, "I just took a nap and fell into a deep sleep. You didn't have to make dinner. Give me a minute, and I'll be down."

Anna went to make some tea. "Where's Luke?" she asked her mother. "Shouldn't he be home by now?"

Kathy, coming down the stairs, said, "I think he's at Ted's, or maybe he's working. He got a job to pay off the car he bought. He's very busy these days since he got his car and is trying to get a scholarship for school. He's not at home much."

Anna texted Luke: "I'm home and cooked dinner if you can come."

He texted, "Be home after eight. Working till then."

When they were eating dinner, Anna noticed her phone buzzing. She picked it up to see three texts and two missed calls from Dave. The last one read, "Anna, what's going on? When I try to reach you, you have to answer. Call me right away."

"Mom, I need to call someone," Anna said. "I'll be right back." She went to her bedroom and shut her door then called him.

Dave said coldly, "Yes."

"Hi, Dave. Is everything okay? What's so urgent? My phone must have been off because I just noticed your texts and calls."

"Anna, I need you to answer my calls. I'm so busy, and when I call you, I need you to answer."

"Okay."

"Where are you?"

"I told you—I came home for the weekend. I'm eating dinner with my mother. Can I call you back?"

"No, I'll be busy. I'll just call you tomorrow."

Anna thought about the party and felt like she was missing out but said, "Okay. Have a nice time."

Anna had not noticed, but Luke had come in and was listening in the hallway. When she ended the call and opened her door, she was startled to see him. "When did you get in? Mom said you're never at home. She seems completely depressed."

"Anna, we've talked about this so many times," he said, exasperated. "I can't help her. She doesn't listen to me and doesn't help herself. She has to *want* to get help. I can't do it for her. I have a lot going on, and I have to live my life. For example, I got early acceptance into Penn State."

"Wow, that's great. I'm happy for you. I had no idea you even applied. Let's go eat with Mom."

Luke pulled on her arm and said, "Let's hang out tonight."

"Can we hang out here with Mom? I'm worried about her. Let's watch a movie or play games like we used to."

"Okay, sure. But you're going to tell me more about that guy."

"He's just a friend," Anna said.

Anna texted Dave around eleven. "Hi, Dave. I'm sorry about earlier." She watched her phone, but he did not respond.

That night, Anna wrote in her journal. *Why can't I get Dave out of my mind? He wants to be with me. I feel so fortunate he wants to be with me. Why doesn't he respond to my texts? Is it something I did?* She put her journal away and went to sleep.

The next day, she texted Dave again. "I'm going to come back early to see you."

Dave texted, "No. Stay with your mother and take care of her. You already told her you'd spend time with her. See you tomorrow night."

Anna went back on Sunday night and went to her dorm first. Lori was studying on her bed, and Anna said, "Hi, Lori. How was your weekend?"

"Oh, they had a crazy party. So many drunk people."

"Was Dave drunk?"

Lori said, "I don't think so. He seems to keep control over things, but he does seem to know everyone."

"Well, it was his party."

Lori said, "How's your mother? Is she okay?"

Anna said, "Yes, thanks. I'm going to head over to Dave's."

"Okay," Lori said. "See you tomorrow."

A few months went by, and Anna spent most nights at Dave's place since Lori was in her room. Anna kept busy with work and school. Christmas came and went, and as spring break crept up, Dave told her, "Anna, this spring break, I'm going to Myrtle Beach with some guys from work. I'd like to take you, but it's only for guys. I'll plan something for us too one day soon."

"Okay," Anna said.

CHAPTER 7

Anna and Her Father

Anna was driving home for spring break when she suddenly felt her heart race and her palms start to sweat. She was overcome with a feeling of dread and pulled into a grocery store parking lot to take some breaths. She searched her purse for a possible misplaced pill but had no luck. Then she got out of the car and walked around for a minute, thinking, *Why am I like this? I have not seen my father since Christmas, and he wasn't even there much. He'll probably not be at home. Calm down, Anna.* She got back into the car and thought of Dave. She pulled into the driveway and saw that her father's car wasn't there. A wave of relief washed over her.

She went into the house and found her mother reading a book on the sofa. She went over and gave her a kiss. Anna said, "How are you?"

"Fine, of course. I'm into this new book."

"Where's Dad?"

"He went to work out and to the office, but I'm sure he'll be home later."

Luke came back from work and said, "Hey, Anna. Spring break already?" He gave her a hug. "Remember, you promised to go hang out this time with your little brother."

Anna said, "Oh, okay. Where do ya want to go?"

"We'll figure it out."

Dan came back around six as Anna was finishing up setting the table. Anna's muscles tensed up as he hung up his coat.

Dan came in and went to his office without stopping. "How's school going?" he asked.

Anna kept her eyes on the table. "Good."

Kathy pleaded to Dan, who was in the office, "Dan, dinner's ready. I'm so glad to have a family meal tonight."

"Sorry, I have a late dinner meeting tonight. Don't wait up." He grabbed a water bottle and headed up to take a shower.

"What a surprise," Luke said.

Anna said, "Mom, how do you put up with him?"

"Someday you will understand marital issues and adult responsibilities. Life is not always as you want it to be. Nothing is ever ideal, but you accept things that you cannot change. You'll understand as you get into your own relationships. Now, your father works hard for you two, and I want you to appreciate what he does."

Luke sat there and shook his head, whispering for only Anna's ears, "Hopeless."

Anna thought, *Luke is right. I need to change the subject.* "Well, thanks, Mom, for dinner. It looks great."

Tears were forming in Anna's eyes, and she got up to go to the study to get a tissue. She noticed her father's phone on the desk with a new message alert. Something came over her, and she picked it up and started to read. "Can't wait to see you at dinner, darling. I am looking forward to holding you tight and feeling you against me. Till I see you at Compari's. Love, E."

Anna put the phone down exactly as she'd found it and went to the bathroom. Her shortness of breath escalated her heart rate, and anger filled her as she thought, *How could he do this to Mom? She waits here for him night after night, and he is off screwing around. I have to calm down.*

Luke knocked on the door and said, "Come back to dinner. What're you doing?"

"I'll be out in a minute," Anna said. She waited in the bathroom until she heard her father come down and say goodbye. She then came out of the bathroom and ran up to her mother's bathroom to get a pill.

Once she finally got back to the table, Kathy asked, "Are you okay?"

Anna said, "Sorry, Mom. I just have a headache."

Kathy got up to clear some plates, and Anna whispered to Luke, "Dad is cheating on Mom. I just read a text from a woman waiting for him. I'm going to catch him. I know where they're meeting."

Anna was so nervous, she only picked at her food.

Kathy, watching Anna, suggested, "Why don't you go take some Advil and lay down?"

Anna started to take a few bites. "I'm just not as hungry as I thought. Actually, I have to go out for a while. I'll be back soon." She got her coat and shoes on, and Luke followed her out to her car.

"Anna, this isn't a good idea. Besides, Mom knows already."

But Anna couldn't let herself believe this. "She has no idea. He's an asshole."

"Is that news to you?" Luke asked.

Anna said, "I have to see for myself, whether you come or not."

Luke got into the car beside her and put his seat belt on. "I can't let you go by yourself."

She drove faster than usual to Plymouth Center and found a spot right in front of the restaurant. She said, "I never get that lucky."

Luke put his hand over hers and looked into her eyes. "Anna, are you sure you want to see this? It might be too painful."

"Luke, I have to see for myself. I need to know what our father is all about. This will explain a lot to me." Anna took her phone out of her purse and put it on camera mode. Her stomach started to heave, and she swallowed to calm down. She got out of the car, and Luke followed her to the window to look inside. They were not able to see from the window, so Anna decided to go into the busy restaurant. She could see her father's coat hanging up and went to the bar to get a better view.

Luke was behind her, saying, "What if he sees us?"

Anna could see her father in a booth holding hands with a stunning, large-breasted woman with a petite nose and long, flowing auburn hair. The woman was laughing. Anna felt strange looking at this woman with her father and quickly thought about her mother and could not remember a time that he made her laugh like that. She snapped her camera on her phone and took three shots. Her father had not taken his eyes off this woman. Anna hesitated and then said, "Let's get out of here, Luke."

They went back to the car, and Luke opened the door for her. He said, "I'll drive," as Anna started to cry. He drove off and said, "Anna, why are you so shocked? Mom and Dad haven't been happy for years."

"How can you be so unemotional, Luke?"

"I guess I'm like Mom. Nothing surprises me, and life is what it is. Crying won't help me and won't change anything."

Anna said, "I need a drink, Luke."

"Anna, please don't do what Mom does and medicate her problems away. You should deal with the issues and cope with them."

"I know, Luke. I don't drink all the time. I'd like one drink to just help me calm down."

They went to another sports bar down the street, and Anna went to the bathroom to take a pill and ordered a shot and a drink. She came back to the table after she grabbed her drink and took the shot and said, "Luke, it's hard for me to understand why Mom stays. I try to look at Dad to find the reason, but nothing comes to me."

Luke said, "Anna, don't think anything. She has to do what's right for her, and you need to live your life, too. Dad is an ass, but Mom isn't exactly a saint. Remember, everyone has their responsibility in how things evolve."

Anna thought, *Am I hearing him correctly?* She got up and paid the bill. "I want to go home now."

"Anna, please just don't make assumptions. Why don't you just talk with Mom? Maybe that'll help you."

"Maybe you're right."

Anna went home and saw her mother watching television. She grabbed the remote and turned the television off. "Mom, I love you. I need to tell you something. I followed Dad tonight and have pictures of him with another woman."

Anna opened up the pictures on her phone, but Kathy got up and, without looking, said, "Would you like some tea?" In the kitchen, she put the kettle on and said, "Anna, my sweet Anna. Your father has a lot of clients, and some are female. I don't need to look at any pictures for me to know anything. I have always understood your father. We all make choices in our lives based on what we believe to be true. Your father looks after you and me. If he had to wine and dine clients to do that, then that's okay with me."

"Mom, he is holding this woman's hands. Why won't you look at the pictures?"

"Please listen to what I'm saying, and maybe you can learn something from me. We all can find ourselves in a situation that we would not have thought we'd be in, and then we have choices to make. Every choice has consequences. I believe your father is working and working hard for his family. Now, let's end this conversation and feel good about how your father takes care of us. Good night, Anna." Kathy went up to bed and left Anna standing in the living room, thinking, *I don't believe this.* Anna tossed and turned all night.

The next day, Anna woke up after getting barely a few hours' sleep and heard her father downstairs. She stayed in her room and wrote in her journal, *How did my mother find herself in this situation? Why does she accept this horrible marriage? I would never let someone treat me that way. I'd rather be alone. Does she think so badly about herself that she allows her husband to cheat on her? I have so many unanswered questions. I don't know anything about my mother, and she will not open up to me.* She closed the journal and took a shower. She packed her bag for school and went downstairs. She looked in the study and saw her father on his computer.

Dan said, "Anna, come here."

Anna held her head high for the first time and came into the office and sat in front of him as she had so many times in her childhood.

Dan said, "I hear you have questions about your mother and me, and I'll only say this once: what happens between us is our business. Things are more complex than you may know, and you need to focus on school."

Anna watched her father talk and kept quiet. She remembered how he held that woman's hand and how enamored she was and wondered if she knew he was married. With tears in her eyes, she got up to leave. She turned to look at him and said, "I cannot and will not accept what you are doing."

She left before she allowed him to have a comeback, grabbing her bag and a bottle of rum from the liquor cabinet on her way out the door. She said, "Mom, I'm going to school. I forgot I have to work. I'll call you later." Before Kathy could reply, Anna was in her car, thinking, *I cannot wait to leave. This place is too much.*

Anna got to school and lay on her bed. Her phone rang, and she answered, "Hi, Dave. How are you?"

"You sound awful," Dave said. "What's wrong?"

Anna said, "I'll tell you when I see you."

"I'll be back on Saturday. We'll go out to eat and talk then."

Dave knocked on her dorm room on Saturday. She opened the door, and he grabbed her around the waist and kissed her. "Wow, you taste so good." He shut the door behind him and started to undress her. "Is Lori gone?" he asked.

Anna wanted to say wait, but she was overcome with emotions. She felt unable to breathe and let him talk her into it. They made love and afterward lay on her bed.

"I've been wanting you all week," Dave said.

Anna slowly got dressed and said, "I missed you, too."

He watched her getting dressed and said, "I never realized you had a birthmark on your hip. I like it."

Anna blushed. "Well, it's always been there."

He said, "I'm starving. Want to go to that Seva Restaurant, or would you prefer Chinese?"

"I don't really care. I'm just glad we're together."

Dave said, "Okay, then let's go get Chinese." They left and arrived at the restaurant and ordered. Anna thought, *When will he ask about how I was feeling the other day? I want to see if he remembered.*

Anna finally asked, "So how was your trip? You haven't told me anything."

"There isn't much to say. We had beautiful weather and lots of late nights. It was good, I guess."

"When are you going to ask me about the other day? You said I sounded awful—do you remember?"

"Oh, right. What was with you the other day?"

Anna took a deep breath. "Well, last weekend, I found my father's phone and saw a text from a woman. He was meeting her at a restaurant, and I decided to follow them. He's actually having an affair on my mother. It's all just too much to cope with."

"I think it's more common than we know," Dave said. "Does your mother know?"

"Both my mother and brother know, and they seem to accept it. I don't understand how she can accept it. He's never home, and he treats her horribly."

She was waiting for Dave to respond, but he started to eat. "Why aren't you eating?" he asked.

"I lost my appetite."

"Anna, I've learned that we never know everything about people, and I try to embrace that. Maybe your brother understands that it's your mother's life. You should be grateful you have both your parents."

Anna thought, *He's not listening to me.*

"Anna, if they have all accepted it, then you need to as well. I don't even have my mother."

Anna wondered if he was going to open up about that now. After some time passed, she finally said, "Do you think of your mother often? What was she like?"

Dave said, "Not now, Anna."

They slept in her dorm room for the first time, since Lori wasn't back yet. Anna woke up in his arms and thought, *This feels so right.* Lori came in around eleven the next morning, just as they were getting back from brunch.

Dave said, "Hi, Lori. Anna, I'm going back now. I'll call you later."

"Okay," Anna said.

Lori asked, "So, how was your break?"

Anna said, "It was okay, and how was yours?"

"I'm so glad I told my parents the truth," Lori said. "I feel we're getting closer, you know? Like we're all adults now."

"That's good, Lori. Have you even heard from Carl?"

Lori said, "Not a word. It's better that way, though. Time does actually heal. I think differently about relationships and him now. I'm actually glad we broke up. He did me a favor. He was so controlling and jealous. You know he never wanted me to talk to other guys. I never even slept in my own dorm. I felt I was brainwashed, and now I can see things clearer. I have my own thoughts again, and my time is what I decide to do, not what he wants to do. I'm so much happier. Want to go to dinner tonight with me, Jen, and the others?"

"When did she get back?"

Lori said, "Oh, I saw her over the break. We live close to each other."

Anna thought, *Why didn't they call me?* But she said, "I have to work at five thirty, so can we go early?"

"Sure," Lori said.

They walked to the cafeteria and sat down with their food. Jen walked in with Dave and Pete. Anna had eaten by then, so she took a few minutes to catch up with Jen. Dave grabbed some food and sat next to Anna.

"Oh, I thought you were working?" he said.

She said, "You never called me. I have to go in a little bit."

"Come over after."

Anna nodded. She noticed Jen and Lori were laughing at a private joke. Then she looked at her watch: it was five ten. She got up and said, "I'll see you guys later."

They said, "Okay." She looked back through the glass after she'd left and saw that they were all laughing and talking, and she thought, *I don't belong there. I don't belong in my own house. Where do I belong?*

Anna went to work, class, clinical practicum, and to Dave's most nights for the next few months. One evening, before they went to dinner, Lori asked Anna, "Could we talk before we go to dinner?"

Anna was occupied with putting her hair up. "Of course."

"I'm a little concerned about you," Lori said. "I noticed that you've been drinking a lot lately. You don't seem like yourself."

Anna paused and thought, *I had no idea she was watching me.* "I guess I've been drinking to help me sleep, but you don't need to worry about it."

"Has Dave talked to you about this?"

"Why would he? Did you mention this to him?"

"I'm sorry—I did talk to Dave about it, but I should've just come to you first." After a long pause, Lori said, "What are you going to do next year? Jen asked me to live with her and Brooke, and we want you to come as well."

Anna paced the floor and felt her anger swell inside her. "It's nice to be the last one asked." She went to the bathroom and splashed water on her face. She looked in the mirror and thought, *Anna, calm down. Why is everyone talking about me? Why didn't Dave tell me about this? He probably just didn't agree with her.*

Lori suddenly appeared and said, "Anna, are you okay? Jen told me she thought maybe you and Dave would be living together. I told her I didn't think so. I'd like you to live with us next year."

Anna took some deep breaths and said, "Could you guys stop talking about me and talk *to* me instead? I know you both have become better friends."

"You're just so busy with work, school, and Dave. You're never even here to spend time with. It's strange how the roles have reversed. Life is full of surprises. I've never wanted you to feel left out. It's hard to talk to you, though. You become so defensive all the time."

Anna sat down as tears streamed down her face. "I'm sorry, Lori. I have to work a lot because I don't have parents like yours. I envy that about you. I don't want to ask my parents, so I have to work. I also know you guys don't approve of Dave and me, and I guess I avoid you guys a little bit."

Lori said, "Why would you need anyone's approval anyway? But as far as me, I just want you to be happy. I have just heard some bad things about him, but I'll try not to judge him. I guess I think of him like Carl and don't want him to hurt you like I was. I know he is not Carl, though. Do whatever feels right to you."

"Thanks, Lori. I'm okay, and I know you're a good friend. I guess I'm going through a lot. I'd like to live with you guys, too, depending on the cost."

"Let's go to dinner."

"I don't really feel like it right now," Anna said. "I'm going to lie down for a while."

Lori pleaded, "Oh, Anna, please come. I don't want you to be upset."

"Really, I'm okay. I haven't been feeling that well anyway." Anna gave Lori a hug and said, "You're a good friend. Go to dinner—really."

Lori said, "Okay. Can I bring you something back?"

"No, it's okay."

After Lori left, Anna opened her bottle of pills, took one, and then found a bottle of wine and drank a few sips. She lay down, took out her journal, and wrote, *Dear Diary, I'm feeling so confused. Do I have a problem? Why is Lori worried about me? I have to concentrate on my finals so I improve my grades and my father won't be disappointed in me.*

Her phone pinged, and she looked at the text: "Anna, where are you? Why aren't you at dinner?"

Anna replied, "I'm lying down, resting. I'll see you tomorrow night."

Dave texted back, "Come over at eleven. I want to see you."

Anna's heart jumped up with the thought of seeing him. "I'm tired. Can I come earlier?"

"No, I'm studying."

"Okay."

Anna fell asleep for a while and woke when Lori opened the door. "Hey, Anna. I brought you a cheeseburger and a salad."

Anna rubbed her eyes and said, "Oh, thanks so much, Lori. I'm feeling better now."

While she sat on her bed and ate her dinner, Lori said, "Anna, I have a confession to make about Dave. I didn't tell you earlier because I didn't want you to be mad. When I met him at the coffee shop, a girl came over and yelled at him. She said, 'You're such a jerk!' and then she looked at me and said, 'Stay away from him. He'll break your heart.' She walked away, and he apologized. He said he knew her a long time ago and that she was more serious about him than he was about her."

Anna said, "That doesn't seem odd. A lot of women want to be with him."

"No, it was more intense than that. I don't trust him, Anna. Just be careful."

Anna got up and put her jacket on. "I'll see you later. I'm going to go over to Dave's after the library."

As she started out into the hallway, she thought, *I need to get out of here before I say something I'll regret.* She went to the coffee shop and sat with her computer, trying to study, but she kept thinking of Dave and had so many questions.

She finally looked at the time—ten in the evening. She packed up and went to Dave's early.

When she rang the doorbell, Pete answered. "Hey, Dave's upstairs."

Anna went up and said, "Dave, I thought you were studying."

"Oh, I got back a little bit ago," he said. "Come here." He started kissing her neck.

Anna thought, *I need to talk to him, but I don't want to argue.* And she fell into his arms.

On Saturday, Anna was getting ready to move back to her parents' house for the summer. She was packing in her dorm room when Lori's parents arrived. Lori gave them both a long hug. "I'm so excited to come home and spend time with you guys."

Her father hugged her for a while and said, "I'm so glad to have you back. It's so quiet at home without you." He looked at Anna and said, "Well, you survived another year. Thanks for looking out for her. Do you need some help packing your car?"

Anna said, "No, thanks, I'm fine. I'm waiting for my mother. I'll call you soon, Lori. I'm going to go to Dave's for a while."

"Oh, please let us help you, Anna." She grabbed a bag and put in on the dolly her father brought. He joined in, and before Anna knew it, her car was all packed up.

Lori winked at Anna. "Now you can just spend time with your mother."

Lori gave her a hug and kiss on the cheek. "Have a wonderful summer. Can't wait to live in an actual house with you next year."

Anna almost felt sick to her stomach and ran to the bathroom. *Why on earth would I lie about my mom coming? I wish I had parents like hers.* Anna left the back door and walked around for a while and came back just in time to see Lori drive away with her parents. *She is a good friend. She understood that my mother isn't coming, but she kept it quiet.* She then got in her car and texted Dave. "Hey, I'm leaving early. I'll talk to you later."

CHAPTER 8

Anna's Summer

Anna arrived back home and parked on the street. For a while, she stayed in the car, looking at her house and thinking about all the memories it contained. She watched her bedroom window and wondered how many times she looked out that window checking the driveway for her father's car. She finally came into the kitchen as Kathy was coming out with some plants. "Hi, Anna. I'm so glad you're home. I'll be out gardening if you want to help."

Anna said, "I'm going to unpack first." She watched Kathy from the window for a moment. *She looks happy in the garden.*

When she went downstairs, Luke came in and gave her a hug. He said, "Hey, I'm glad you're back."

Anna said, "I can't believe this is your last summer before college."

"Yeah, I think I want to be a lawyer. I joined the army, so I have to leave in July for boot camp."

"You're going to leave me here alone?" Anna said.

"Welcome to my world. I've been here without you for two years. You know, I was thinking maybe you should work the evening shift at the hospital. That way you won't run into Dad much."

Anna said, "That's good idea, but he is never home anyway."

Dan came in after six and sat down to eat. He was reading a text message and didn't notice that everyone was staring at him. Finally, he looked up and said, "I'm glad you're back, Anna. Your mother could use more help around here." Then he checked the time on his phone and said, "Oh, I have to go."

Anna swallowed hard, and before she knew it, these words came out of her mouth: "Another late-night meeting with a client, Dad?"

Dan looked at Anna and said, "Do you have something to say to me, Anna?"

She said, "Have a nice evening. Think of us, here at home."

Kathy gave her daughter a warning look. "Anna."

Dan got up and left. Anna looked at her mother, thinking, *The sadness is overwhelming.*

That evening, Lori texted Anna and said, "Hey, there. Hope you're good. FYI the monthly rent is $2,800 a month, so with four of us, it comes to $800 a month. I know it's high but it's the going rate in Ann Arbor. I hope it's okay."

Anna felt like throwing up. *My father will never pay that*, she thought.

She went to get some water, and Kathy said, "What's wrong? You're pale as a ghost."

"Lori and some girls wanted to rent a house for next year. The rent for the house is eight hundred a month plus utilities. Dad won't pay for that."

Kathy said, "I'll deal with it and make sure you have it. I'm so glad you have met some friends. I've never wanted you to be an introvert like me."

"Mom, you can still meet some friends. It's never too late." Anna looked over at Luke, who was shaking his head as if she could read his mind, so she just left it alone.

Anna arranged her schedule with Debbie, her boss to work evenings. Luke came in as she hung up the phone. "You were right about working nights, Luke—it is going to take a lot of pressure off me when I don't have to see much of Dad this summer." Her phone rang, and she saw Dave's name pop up. "Luke, I have to get this. We'll talk later." She pushed him out of her room before he could say anything.

She sat on her bed and answered, "Hi, Dave. How're you?"

"I'm fine. I was thinking Sundays would be the best day to see each other. My father and his girlfriend usually go out that day, and you can come here."

Anna said, "I didn't know your father had a girlfriend."

"He has for a while now. Will that work for you? I'd like to see you more, but I'm working long hours and taking a class."

Anna said, "I guess so."

"It's only for the summer."

"I know. It'll be okay. I have to work all summer too to save for my rent. I don't want my mother to have to find the money. Oh, I forgot to tell you that I'm living with Lori, Jen, and Brooke."

Dave said, "I know. That's great."

"How do you know?"

"Remember, I know everything." He laughed, but something about his comment made Anna uneasy. "They are my friends, and I see them all the time."

Anna said, "Will you see Jen over the summer?"

"Jen and I are good friends. She lives a few blocks away. Why are you questioning me about this? You are going to have to trust me, Anna. I'm a busy person and have many goals. You need to understand this about me, or this won't work."

Anna suddenly had a horrible feeling. She said, "Dave, why are you so upset? I just asked you a question."

"No, you didn't. You implied some negativity in my actions, and I have many women as friends and clients. You have to learn to be secure in us and to trust in me. I really like you, Anna, and I want this to work, but you need to understand my lifestyle, because it won't change."

Anna had tears in her eyes now and an empty pit in her stomach that she felt was familiar, though she couldn't say why. "I'm sorry, Dave. I do trust you. It's the other women I don't trust."

"All you have to do is trust me. I'll text you my address so you can come on Sunday at one."

"Okay."

"Okay, talk later."

Before she could say goodbye, he was gone.

Luke came back in right away. "Who is Dave, and why have you not told me you have a boyfriend?"

"Take it easy, Luke. He just graduated with a degree in business and is working with his father. He's going to graduate school next year, for his MBA. We've been dating for about six months, I guess."

"When can I meet him?"

"One of these days."

"How about next Sunday?"

Anna said, "Not good. I'll let you know."

"I hope he's like Jeff. He was a nice guy."

Anna opened her journal after Luke left. *Dear Diary, What just happened with Dave? I felt lost and empty when he was talking about this relationship not working. He's never done anything like that before. I know he is busy and has a lot going on. Maybe that is all it is. My stomach just felt so sick. Maybe I love him and the thought of breaking up kills me. Wow, do I love him? I can't wait to see him.*

On Sunday morning, Anna drove to Dave's house in the upscale town of Birmingham. She found the address and entered the driveway, thinking, *This can't be it.* She drove around a bend and saw a massive castle-like house emerge from behind the trees. She inched forward, thinking, *Wow. He never told me how rich he is.* She pulled up around a huge fountain and parked then went to the door and rang the bell.

A man opened it and said, "Welcome. You must be Anna. Come in, please. He'll be down in a minute." He handed her a bottle of water, and she followed him into the three-story living room. "My name is Harold. You can sit and make yourself comfortable. Can I get you anything else?"

Anna said, "No, thanks, Harold." He smiled at her, and she smiled back until he was so far down the hall she could no longer see him.

Anna texted Dave, "I'm here. Where are you?"

Dave appeared from behind another door and grabbed her. "I've missed you."

He started to kiss her on the couch, but Anna stopped him. "Harold is here."

"He's the butler. He knows not to come in here unless I call for him."

"You never told me how rich your father was."

"I thought I did. Come see my bedroom." She followed him up the stairs, amazed at the house. They finally got to his room, and he closed the door.

"Dave, you could have any girl. Why are you with me?"

"I guess it's the sex," he joked.

"I mean it—why?"

"Do we have to go through this again, Anna? You need to be more confident in yourself. You're beautiful inside and out. That's why." He kissed her back, and then she was lost in the moment of being in his arms.

The summer went by quickly, with Anna working and taking three classes. She made a point of spending some time with Luke, though she reserved her Sundays for Dave. Luke left home the last week of July, leaving Anna alone at home with her mother, except during the rare times that Dan was around the house.

One Monday night in August, Dan left a note on the kitchen table. "I'm taking you both to dinner on Saturday night. Be ready at seven."

Anna stared at the note. She couldn't remember a time when her father had suggested something like this.

Kathy came into the kitchen and said, "What're you looking at?"

"A note Dad left. He wants to take us to dinner." Anna showed her the note.

"That's nice. I wonder what I should wear?"

Anna saw her mother's demeanor change in a way she'd never seen before. She wrote in her journal, *I have tried to put what my father is doing behind me. Everyone seems to think that it's not a big thing. Maybe I am wrong and he was just working with his client. Maybe now that we are all getting older, he will relate differently to us. Can there be another side to my father that I am unaware of? My mother married him, so there has to be something there.* She closed her journal and took a shower.

Saturday evening came, and Anna sat in her mother's room, watching her try on different dresses she had never seen before. "Mom, I like the black one the best. It's very sexy."

Kathy blushed and said, "Okay, I'll wear that one. I wonder what your father has in mind. He used to surprise me all the time when we were dating."

"What else did he do? What was he like?" Anna asked.

"He's a good man, Anna. Life just gets busy with family and work. You'll understand when you start a family of your own someday. Don't rush it, though." Kathy entered the hallway once she got dressed.

Anna said, "Wow, Mom. You look amazing." She got dressed and came into the kitchen just as a car pulled into the driveway. Anna and Kathy looked and saw a town car. Anna noticed Kathy's demeanor change again; she looked disheartened.

"What's wrong?"

"Nothing. I was just hoping we would all go together."

The driver got out of the car and knocked on the door. "Good evening. I'm Sam, and I'm here to escort you to dinner."

Kathy said, "Thank you."

Anna followed her mother into the car. "I wish Luke was here for this."

They arrived at Andiamo's, an Italian restaurant, shortly after seven. The driver opened the door, and Anna got out, feeling embarrassed. *I could have driven here*, she thought, as people stared at them. They walked into the restaurant, and the chauffeur asked the greeter to take them to their table.

Dan was waiting with champagne. "Hello, Anna, Kathy. Come and sit down."

"What's the occasion?" Kathy asked.

"Have some champagne first."

After they ordered, Dan said, "I'm sure you're wondering what this is all about. You all know how hard I've been working, and it is finally paying off. I've been promoted and will soon be traveling overseas once a month. But here's the best part—I've received a large bonus, and I decided to buy a house in Destin, Florida. Right on the water."

Kathy's smile went to a frown. Anna held her hand and kept quiet.

"Well. I thought you'd be ecstatic. You're all so unappreciative of what I do for you." He slammed his fist on the table then got up to leave.

Kathy blurted out, "You're right. Thank you, Dan."

"Dad, maybe Mom is upset that you bought a house without her input. That's a big decision."

"No, it's okay," Kathy said. "We can all have somewhere to vacation together."

Dan sat back down.

"Dad, I'm worried about Mom," Anna said. "You'll be gone *more* often now? With Luke gone and me in college, she'll be alone all the time."

"Anna, a promotion means more responsibility. This is a good thing," Dan said. "Your mother is a big girl, and I won't be told what to do by my own daughter! Kathy, you have spoiled these kids too much."

Kathy got up and ran to the bathroom, and Anna followed.

"Anna," Kathy said, pushing her away, "I need a minute. I'll be fine."

Anna paused and waited outside the women's room, watching her father talk to the waitress, smiling and laughing like nothing just happened. *How can he not even care! He has not changed at all.* Kathy came out, and Anna walked with her back to their seat.

"Let's eat before it gets cold," Dan said. Anna forced herself to eat since she no longer had an appetite. "So," he said, "the house is gorgeous. The ocean view is incredible. Here, look at these pictures." He started to hand over his phone to show them but then seemed to think better of it. Instead, he said, "There are some pictures on the counter at home for you to see."

Kathy said, "Can you take me there?" Anna was shocked that her mother had actually asked him to do something for her.

"Why don't you and Anna go next week?" he suggested.

Anna said, "Dad, I'm moving back to school and am working every day till then. I think it would be great for *you* to take her."

Dan seemed to think about this. "We'll see."

Anna asked the waitress to box up her dinner. Dan said, "Well, I hope you enjoyed the dinner. I have to meet some clients for drinks." He got up and left, just like that.

Anna had left her phone back at the house by accident. When she was finally able to take a look at it, she saw that she'd missed two calls from Dave. She suddenly ran to the bathroom and threw up, and then she quietly went up to her mother's bathroom and took a pill. Later, she wrote in her journal, *I am devastated and angry with myself for thinking my father would surprise me, and he has not changed a bit. Everything is all about him. My poor mother—what is she going to do now? I have that same sinking feeling in the pit of my stomach for my mother. Should I just move home and commute?*

Anna put the journal down and felt the pill kick in. She grabbed her phone and saw that Dave hadn't left a message. She texted him, "Hi, Dave. I went to dinner with my parents. Long story. I left my phone at home. Can I talk to you tomorrow? I'm tired and need to rest. Have a good night." She did not get a text back and fell asleep.

The next day, Anna came downstairs to find her mother having coffee and looking at the pictures of the house. She poured some coffee and said, "Good morning. So, do you like the house?"

"This can't be our house. What kind of money does your father make? This house is right on the water and is six bedrooms with a pool and a Jacuzzi. I can't see myself ever owning something like this."

Anna wanted to ignore the pictures, but her curiosity got the best of her. *Wow. How much money does my father make? I feel like I don't even know anything about him.*

CHAPTER 9

Anna's Junior Year

The following Sunday morning fell on Labor Day weekend, and it was time for Anna to pack her car and head back to school. "Mom, I'm always here to talk," she said, standing next to her car. "Please call me."

"My kids are growing up, and I'm happy for you. You don't need to worry about me. I might just have plans of my own," Kathy said with a wink.

Anna felt excitement for her mother and gave her a hug. "I'll call you soon. I love you."

She drove to Ann Arbor, and as she looked at the address she had written down, she realized that she'd never even seen the house she had agreed to rent. She saved up half of the money and her mother had somehow had the rest, which she never asked her about. She texted Lori that she was on her way, and Lori texted back that she was already there.

Anna knocked on the door, since she did not have a key yet, and was surprised when Dave opened the door.

She stepped back for a second, and Dave said, "Surprise!"

Before Anna could speak, she heard Lori say, "Hey, Dave. Who's at the door?"

"Anna."

Lori ran to the door. "Well, can't you help her move in? Why are you both just standing there? Silly."

Anna felt distant and awkward. Dave grabbed the bag she was carrying and said, "Lori was thinking the bedroom in the back would be good for you. Come see it."

Anna followed him up the stairs, and Lori said, "I'm so glad you decided to live with us. We're going to have a great year."

She smiled and looked into the room. It was all right, but she wondered if she had other options. "Could I see the other rooms?"

Lori said, "Well, Jen and Brooke already picked the rooms they wanted, but if you would really like one of them, let me know."

Anna looked at the other ones. A room in front had better light and she would have preferred it, but it felt too late to say anything now. "It's okay. I'll take the room in the back."

Dave put the bag in there and said, "I rented my own apartment this year, so you won't be here much anyway." He smiled. Once again, Dave already had decided for her.

Lori came in and said, "Are you sure you're okay in here?"

"I'm sure," Anna said.

"Okay, then let's unpack your car."

"I can do it. It's fine."

"I have to go to a meeting, but I'll help you later if you want." He kissed her cheek and said, "Bye."

Anna unpacked her car and was setting up her room when Jen came in and said, "So, how are things going with Dave?"

Anna kept putting her clothes away as she said, "They're good. Why do you ask?"

Jen plopped herself on the bed. When she tipped her head to the side, her long, wavy auburn hair hung down so low it nearly touched the bed. "You know, he has never had a girlfriend for this long before. I'm sure you're aware that he has had many girls, and most of them were short lived because they left him."

"Why? I thought he left them."

Jen said, "Well, I used to think that until I met a few of them. Please don't let this get back to him, but they told me he quickly became controlling like he did with me."

Anna started to throw her clothes in the drawers, angry, and thought, *Why is she telling me this? I have to change the subject.* "By the way," she said, "you said that your parents used to be friends. Why'd your father have a falling out with Dave's father?"

Jen got up and walked to the door. Then she turned around and said, "A lot happened when Katrina died. I'd rather let Dave be the one to talk to you about that. Let me know if you need anything."

Anna thought, *Controlling after just a few weeks? I'm glad he's not like that with me.* She sat at her desk and looked over her schedule for the semester.

Lori knocked on her door and sat on the bed. She said, "I am so excited for this year and to be out of the dorms. My parents said hi to you. They're glad we're living together again."

Anna saw Lori's curly blond hair in her eyes and said, "I'm so glad we're roommates again. Sorry about not keeping in touch over the summer. With my classes in the daytime and working, I didn't have much time."

"When did you see Dave, then?"

"On Sundays, mostly."

Jen yelled from the kitchen, "Come down when you guys are finished. We'll make our first dinner together."

Anna grabbed her phone after it pinged with a new text. It was from Dave. "Hi, Anna. Can you come over? I cancelled my meeting and need to see you."

Anna thought about Jen and Lori and how fun it would be to cook together, but she replied, "Okay."

He sent her the address to his new apartment, and she went downstairs to break the news to her friends. Except she couldn't bring herself to tell the whole truth. "Hey, guys. I have to go to work for a bit. You guys have dinner without me tonight."

Jen was pouring a box of spaghetti into the pot of boiling water. "Should we wait for you tonight, or are you staying over at Dave's?"

"I'm not sure yet. Don't wait for me. See you later."

As she slowly closed the door on her way out, she heard Jen say, "I hope she understands what she's getting into. Dave has more skeletons in his closet than anyone I know."

Anna called Luke as she was driving over to Dave's. "Hi, Luke. How are you?"

"Hey, sis. I'm great. I've never been so fit in my life. The ladies are digging it. Ha-ha. I'm glad training is over. It was rough, but I made it through. Some people didn't. Dad actually helped me because the thought of failing and needing him made me work harder. I'm now in the dorm, and classes just started. How are you?"

"I'm so glad to hear you're doing well. I'm good. Have you talked to Mom?"

"Once. I called her to let her know I made it here. As usual, she didn't say much."

Anna pulled up to the apartment. "I'm glad to hear your voice. I'll check up on you soon. Bye."

When she stepped through the door, Dave grabbed her and carried her into the bedroom. His shirt was already off, and he only had boxers on. His muscles flexed as he picked her up and carried her to his bedroom.

Dave pleased her and then himself and fell onto the bed, exhausted. "I'm so glad you're here with me, Anna." He turned to her. "I'm going to be working a lot and taking classes. I want you to know that I'm working for us. I need you to know this and be patient with our limited time together."

Anna heard, *You are my future. I am working hard for us.* She took a breath, and tears streamed down her face.

"Why are you crying?"

"Do you think of me in your future?"

"You're the first person I've seen in this way. I do have pursuits for us. I need you to be understanding, though."

"I do understand."

He kissed her and said, "I need a nap."

Months passed, and Anna called her brother. "Hi, Luke. Are you going home for Thanksgiving? I'd like to see you."

"Actually, I'm staying in Pennsylvania. I have boot camp, so I'm going to a friend's house for Thanksgiving. I'd like to have seen you, too. How are you?"

"I've been good, but I wanted to see you." She waited for a moment, wondering if it was wise to keep pressing him, and dug in. "You know, you can't just *forget* you have a family."

"What makes you think I've forgotten? I'm building a life and have to go to boot camp to pay for my school. Don't make assumptions, Anna."

"I'm sorry, Luke. I just can't face Mom and Dad alone."

"Then don't go. You can come here."

"No, I have to see Mom. I can't just turn away from her. Who does she have?"

Luke said, "She's made her life what she wants it to be. I'll be back for Christmas for a few days. Have a nice Thanksgiving, and I'll call Mom then. Take care of yourself, Anna. Talk soon."

Anna started to pace in her room and thought, *I need a drink, but I don't want them to think I have a problem.* She put her coat on and said, "Jen, I'm going over to Dave's."

Jen's face fell. "Hang out with us, Anna. He's busy anyway."

"I'm going to get some studying done, too."

"Okay." Anna noticed Jen rolling her eyes to Lori, and she slammed the door harder than she should have. She went over to Dave's apartment and let herself in with her key. She looked in the fridge for some beer or a drink and poured herself a mixed drink. She then texted Dave. "Hey, will you be back soon?"

Dave texted back, "I'm in Birmingham at the office. Something has come up, so I won't be back. See you tomorrow."

Anna had another drink and thought about going back to her house, but the thought of Jen's rolling eyes made her stay where she was. She watched a movie and fell asleep on the couch.

She woke the next morning to Dave patting her shoulder. He said, "Anna, what are you doing here? I told you I wouldn't be back."

She had a horrible headache. "Oh, well, when I texted you, I was here to surprise you, and I started watching a movie and fell asleep."

"I'm sorry I didn't get back, but I told you to be patient. Want to get some lunch?"

"What time is it?"

"Eleven thirty."

"No, I have to work at twelve," she said. She grabbed her stuff and gave him a kiss then went back to her house to clean up and go to work.

Anna texted Dave from work and said, "Hi, Dave. Thanksgiving is in a week, and I'd like you to come to my parents' for dinner. Is that okay with you?"

"We will talk tonight."

Anna got off work at six and went home to take a shower. Dave was already there, hanging out with Jen and Lori. He barely noticed her as they were laughing at him and listening intently to him.

"Want to order a pizza?" Dave asked.

"Actually, let's go out to eat so we can talk," Anna suggested. "We've not seen each other."

Jen said, "Weren't you together last night?"

Anna didn't feel like getting into the details of what had happened. "Oh, okay, let's order pizza."

"No, it's okay. Let's go out." Dave got up and said, "I'll be in the car. Good night, ladies." Anna quickly brushed her teeth and ran out the door after him.

At dinner, Anna said, "So, what do you think about Thanksgiving? You never answered me."

"Well, only if we can make it for my family dinner, too. You should meet them officially. We've been together a while now."

"I'll call my mother and tell her around one for an early dinner. Will that work? What time does your family usually eat?"

"We usually sit down around six, so we can make it if we leave your place around four."

"Okay, I'll check with my mother."

As they ate dinner, Anna said, "I'm nervous about meeting each other's families."

"Oh, you'll also meet Sue, my dad's girlfriend. No need to worry about them. Most people like her."

"Do they know about me? Every time I went over last summer, they were never around."

Dave hesitated then said, "I think so. My dad and I mostly talk about work and not personal things. We're not like that in my family. My father's very private. All I know is he has a girlfriend who lives in her own place but comes over most of the time."

"I'm worried about my father meeting you. He's not so easy to talk to. I really want him to like you."

Dave grabbed her hand and said, "Remember, I'm likable. I know how to conduct myself. You don't need to worry about that."

Anna couldn't help but blurt something that she'd been wondering about. "Do you want children?"

Dave looked at her in surprise. "Yes, of course, but at the right time. I want to spend more time with my children than my father did with me. I want to be successful and financially sound. I want to give you the life you deserve, Anna. I will take care of you."

Anna took a sip of her wine and felt a wave of relief come over her. "I love you, Dave," she said. He kissed her, but she wanted to hear it back and felt deflated somehow.

Anna woke that night in his bed after tossing and turning. She got up and got her journal out of her bag and went into the living room. *Dear Diary, I am really letting myself fall in love. I trust he loves me and wants to take care of me. I will keep the memory of tonight in my head always. He wants what I want, a family.*

CHAPTER 10

Anna's Thanksgiving

They left for Anna's house around eleven on Thanksgiving and got there a little before noon. They came in through the front door, and Dave held out a bottle of wine and twelve white roses for Kathy. Kathy came over, and Anna said, "Mom, this is Dave. Dave, this is my mom."

He took her hand as she said, "Call me Kathy."

"Pleasure to meet you. Anna resembles you. I thank you for having me over."

"Where is Dad?"

Kathy said, "He'll be home in a while."

"I'm sorry that we're not staying too long. Since my mother has passed, I feel I should be with my father at holidays."

Kathy looked at Anna in surprise. "I didn't know. I'm so sorry for your loss. Do you mind me asking if she was sick?"

"She suffered from depression for a long time. But she died from a head bleed from taking a fall." Dave paused and then said, "It's difficult to talk about."

Kathy tried to change the subject. "Well, I made something light for us to eat since you'll be having a big dinner there."

"Didn't you cook a turkey?" Anna asked. "You love to cook turkey on Thanksgiving."

"Not this year. Since you kids wouldn't be here, it took a lot off my plate not to have to make a big dinner." As Kathy was talking, Anna heard her father come in from the garage. Dave followed her into the kitchen, and she said, "Hi, Dad. This is Dave."

Dan looked at Dave and said, "Is that your ride outside?"

"That's my baby."

"I like you already. Want a drink?"

Dave said, "Sure."

"Follow me."

Anna and Kathy stood speechless in the kitchen. Kathy finally said, "Well, your father doesn't like many people. You're lucky he took a liking to him right away."

Anna said, "No, he took a liking to his ride."

Anna heard her father and Dave laughing in the study. When she looked in the room, Dave winked at her. "The food is ready," she said.

"Excuse me, Dan." Dave went to the bathroom and then to the kitchen.

"Kathy, is there anything I can help with?"

Kathy blushed. "Oh, goodness, no. Sit down and relax."

He saw the salad on the counter and brought it to the table. Dan shook his head and said, "Dave, you don't have to impress Kathy. The women can handle the food."

Anna felt her face get instantly hot and went to pour herself some wine. "Asshole," she said under her breath.

As he put some food on his plate, Dave said, "It's nice to give good first impressions, don't you think?" He paused and added, "Do you work out, Dan?"

"Of course. I work out almost every day. It does help a lot and keeps me productive."

They ate some salad and sandwiches as Dave and Dan carried on a conversation. Kathy and Anna kept quiet. Dan turned to Dave. "I feel full now, so come into the study, Dave."

He got up, and Dave gave Kathy a warm smile. "Thanks so much for the delicious food."

When they left, Anna started to clean up before she joined them in the study. She stepped quickly into the hall to drain her drink so that they would not see it. When she came into the room, she said, "Dad, do you know Dave's father is a businessman, too?"

Dan laughed and said, "I think she wants me to like you."

"Well, I hope you approve of me. I really like your daughter, sir."

"So far, so good. Now, if you'll excuse me, I have to step out to a client's invitation."

Anna said, "You're leaving Mom alone on Thanksgiving?"

Dave grabbed her hand as if to quiet her. "These are the kinds of sacrifices that make one successful." He looked to Dan as Dan nodded in agreement.

"Well said," Dan said, smiling at Dave. "Have a nice rest of your day."

Dave got up and held out his hand to Dan. Dan gave him a strong handshake. "It was nice to meet you."

Dan said, "I look forward to seeing you again." He looked out the door and said, "Again, nice ride."

Kathy waited for Dan to leave before she said, "Please, sit down. Anna can get you some coffee or tea."

"Not for me, thanks. Anna, we do need to get going. I have had a nice time, Kathy. Thanks for the lovely company."

Anna kissed her mother and said, "Will you be okay?"

"Of course, honey. Besides, your father will be back soon."

Anna thought, *I know better. He won't be back till tomorrow.*

As they drove away, Dave said, "Your parents are really nice, Anna. Do you think I won their approval?"

"My mother likes everyone. She sees the good in everyone, even my father."

Dave said, "He's not so bad, Anna. He works hard. He—"

Anna cut him off. "He's a cheater and a liar. I saw him with another woman at dinner. They were close, and he was holding her hand."

Dave pulled over and with a strange look on his face said, "Anna, I won't have you cutting me off or yelling at me. I know you have issues with your father, but I don't have to see things the way you do."

Anna's voice became faster and louder, not hearing Dave. "Are you seriously defending him? He leaves my mother alone on Thanksgiving to see his lover, not his client. You don't know everything."

Dave looked her in the eyes. "If there is one thing I won't tolerate, it's disrespect. This is a deal breaker for me. Your parents have their reasons for being together. You're an adult now and need to focus on us." He got out of the car and took some breaths, and Anna felt her heart drop.

"I'm so sorry, Dave. Please get in the car."

She waited as he texted someone. He finally got in the car and held her hand and said, "I care for you deeply. But if you do that again, we'll be done."

Anna nodded her head and thought, *He would leave me. All those other girls he left. I do know that I was wrong. I never want to feel alone like that again. I would feel so bad if he actually left. I won't ever do that again.*

They drove in silence the rest of the way to his house, and Anna put her hand over his as a comfort to her. Dave said, "Anna, I'm not sure this is a good idea anymore. You have put a lot of doubts in my mind about us."

Anna bit her lip and immediately had tears rolling down her cheeks. "How can I make it up to you? We all make mistakes, Dave. I'm so sorry. It won't happen again."

Dave said, "Well, they already know about you, but you'd better stop fidgeting and let's just go inside." Anna walked slightly behind him and tried to put her hand in his, but he quickly got up to the house and put his hand on the handle. She thought, *I have been here so many times before, but no one was home. I hope they like me or his father likes me.* Harold opened the door before Dave turned the knob. Dave said, "Hey, Harold."

Anna said, "Nice to see you again, Harold." He was so tall that she had to look up to meet his gaze. Though she found his size intimidating, she saw warmth in his eyes.

Harold gave a warm smile. "Good evening, Anna. May I take your coat?" She handed it to him.

A man came around the corner and said, "You must be Anna. I'm Jake. Come in. Come, make yourself at home, please." He was tall, slender, slightly graying, but distinguished, and Anna noticed that his blue eyes were just like Dave's.

A woman wearing a beautiful dress and high heels soon joined him. "Hello, Anna. I'm Suzanna, but call me Sue. Would you care for a drink?" She had short brown hair that curled around her ears and large breasts squeezed into her dress.

"Some wine would be nice," Anna said.

Harold left the room to fetch Anna's drink, and Sue said, "Come. Let's go sit down."

Anna looked at Dave's father and said, "You have a beautiful home. How long have you lived here?"

"We moved here ten years ago, I think."

Anna's heart raced as she was trying to think of something to say, but instead she took a deep breath to try to relax. Dave whispered, "You're fidgeting again."

Sue said, "Let me show you around. Come."

Anna thought, *They have no idea I've been here all summer. I guess I should play along.*

Sue showed her around the first floor and said, "It must be nerve-racking to meet us. How long have you known Dave?"

Anna said, "About a year now."

Sue stepped back and said, "I see."

Anna said, "You know I've been here before?"

Sue said, "Yes. I wanted to take you on a tour to help calm you down. I know how Jake can be or meeting a new family can be."

They entered the dining room, and four people stood to greet her.

"Anna," said Sue, "this is Dave's brother, Tom, and his wife, Laura. And this is Jake's sister, Clara, and son, Mike."

"Nice to meet everyone," Anna said. "Happy Thanksgiving."

Tom broke the ice. "How on earth would a nice girl like you get mixed up with a guy like my brother?"

Anna smiled. Laura said, "Oh, Tom. Stop joking around. Hi, Anna, it's so nice to finally meet you."

Dave said, "Let's sit."

Anna sat in between Dave and Sue and squeezed Dave's hand under the table. Jake was at the head of the table and held up a glass of wine. "I'm so very grateful for my family to be with me on another Thanksgiving dinner. My boys are coming along and learning how to be as ruthless as I am, and the business is doing better than ever. I'm blessed. May this next year be even better." They all clinked glasses, and Anna drank down her wine quickly as she made sure no one was staring at her.

Anna felt Jake's eyes on her throughout the dinner. She took a sip of her wine when he looked away, and Dave said, "Anna, stop playing with your food. Relax already."

Like usual, Dave's critical comments only made her more self-conscious. Suddenly, she noticed everyone staring at her and realized someone had asked a question that she hadn't heard. She said, "Excuse me. Could you repeat that?"

Jake said, "What are you studying?"

"I told you, Dad—she's going to be a nurse like her mother."

"I wasn't talking to you. Let her speak for herself." Jake turned back to Anna. "So you want to take care of people. Why?"

Anna's heart raced, and she said, "I like helping others. I find it rewarding."

"Thank god there are people like you out there. She's a keeper in case I ever get sick."

After dinner, Jake said, "Well, let's let the ladies catch up because there is some football to be watched." The four guys left while the women went into the family room, where coffee was being served.

Laura asked Anna, "So where are you from?"

"Northville," Anna said.

"Are you from a wealthy family?"

Sue slapped Laura's hand playfully. "Laura, that's kind of personal and inappropriate."

"Well, she may not be used to this type of environment. I'm just trying to help."

Sue looked at Anna and said, "Never mind her. It's great that you are going to be a nurse. Are you living on campus?"

"No, I live with some roommates—Dave is friends with them, too."

Sue said, "Oh, would that be Jen and Brooke?"

Anna said, "Yes. Actually."

Laura interrupted and said, "You know, I'm expecting."

Sue and Clara bit their lips. "That's great," Clara said. "How do Tom and Jake feel about it?"

"Well, I haven't told them yet. I'm not due till April."

"Why haven't you told them yet?" Sue asked.

"Please don't say anything, but I'm waiting until they close on this deal they're working on. I don't want to distract them from their work. They say it will wrap up by the end of next week, and then I'll tell them," Laura said.

"How can you keep that from your husband for so long? I don't think I could do that."

"In this family, it's business first," Laura said.

Clara said, "Not necessarily. My son is not like that."

"Where are Dave and the guys?" Anna asked. "I would like to watch football with them."

"Well, they're in the third room on the left, in the study, but it won't be much fun."

Anna walked down the hall and slowly opened the glass door to hear them cheering. Dave saw her looking in and came out to the hallway.

"What's going on?"

Anna said, "I wanted to watch the game with you."

"We're talking business in between the plays. Women aren't really invited to business talk. We won't be much longer."

"Okay. But I want to be with you."

"I'll make it up to you later."

As he opened the door to go back into the room, Anna overheard Jake say, "She sure is self-assured and rude, son. Are you sure she'll fit in this family?"

Anna gasped as she slowly walked down the hallway and entered the living room.

"Let me guess," Clara said. "You're not invited?"

"No, I guess not."

"You'll get used to it if you want to be in this family," Laura said. "The men are pretty busy. I hardly see Tom."

"What about when the baby comes?" Anna asked.

"That won't change anything. I'll have to get a nanny."

"Anna, how did you meet Dave?" Sue asked.

Anna said, "Through Jen, actually. I met Jen in class and started going to dinner with them."

Sue said, "I like Jen a lot. She comes over sometimes to hang out here. Well, you probably know Alicia and Pam, too, then."

Anna shook her head. "No, I don't know them."

"Well, with Dave's good looks, he gets a lot of attention from women," Laura said.

"He also has a lot of friends, too," Sue said. "So, Anna, how much longer do you have until you graduate?"

"I'm a junior, but I am trying to finish a semester early."

Dave came out then and said, "Anna, let's get going."

Startled by the rush but grateful to finally have his attention and escape the house, she stood up and said, "Thank you for your hospitality. It was nice to meet you."

Jake came out and put his hand out to shake Anna's. "Nice to meet you, Anna. I wish you well in your studies and nursing career."

Anna thought, *It feels like I won't ever see him again.*

Anna noticed he was looking at Sue when he was talking to her. She said, "Thanks for inviting me."

Dave said, "I'll see you tomorrow, Dad."

Anna kept silent on their way back to his apartment, lost in her thoughts. Halfway back, Dave said, "So, why did you feel you needed to come watch the game with us?"

"What do you mean?" she asked. "I wanted to be with you."

"I know it may seem strange, but in my family, the men always have some private time to relax and discuss business. The women like to have time to gossip or talk about whatever they do."

"Did you know that Laura is pregnant? She said that her own husband doesn't know and she'd tell him after the business deal is over."

Dave said, "Were you supposed to tell me that?"

"I don't think so, but I don't have secrets from you. It's very strange. Would you be like that, Dave?"

Dave arrived at the apartment and parked the car. "Anna, this is my family, and you won't be able to change the dynamics. I'm starting to think that you may not fit into the family, and if you can't accept this, we won't have a future together. I won't be put in the middle between you and my father. I work with him, and I'm grateful for the opportunities I have. This is who I am. I am willing to work with you if you are willing to work with my family. I hope this does not change your mind about being together."

Anna bolted from the car and ran to the nearest trashcan to throw up. He shook his head and said, "Come on. Let's get inside."

Anna went to the bathroom and locked the door, starting to cry.

"Anna, crying is not going to help. I need you to be strong and support me so we can have a life together."

Anna thought, *I couldn't be without him. I need him. I'm jeopardizing my chances with him, and he's pushing me away. I have to stop crying and be strong. He's right.* She came out of the bathroom and wrapped her arms around him. "Okay. You're right. We're in this together."

Dave held her for a minute. "Anna, I need this to hold. I can't have you go back and forth when something happens that you don't like. I need to trust you understand that my work is for us, but it's a priority. I don't want to talk about this again."

"I understand," she said.

As the semester progressed, Anna worked hard at school and work and saw Dave sparingly, maybe once during the week and once or twice on the weekends. Dave was at school but would often go home on

Fridays to work at the office. He had dinners scheduled almost every evening, and he was at least forty-five minutes away.

One day, Anna called her mother and asked, "How are you, Mom?"

"I'm good. You will be happy to know I got a little part-time job at the florist's shop, helping to make arrangements."

"Mom, that's so great. What does Dad think about it?"

"He doesn't know. He's so busy, I don't think he's noticed. It's only a few hours a day during the week."

"Well, I'm happy for you."

"I went to see that house in Florida. You should try to go at some point. You can go any time."

"Did you go with Dad?"

"No. He bought me a ticket and left it on the desk. I wasn't going to go, but then I decided I might as well go see it at least. It is so luxurious that it doesn't feel right to me."

Anna felt furious when she thought of her mother traveling all that way by herself, but she didn't let it show. "Maybe I will."

"How are things going with Dave?"

"Well, good. He has to work in Birmingham with his father, so he's very busy. And between school and work for me, we don't see each other as much as I'd like. I have my roommates to keep me company and hang out with too."

"It'll get easier when you're out of school. He reminds me of your father a little."

Anna suddenly felt nauseated. "Mom, I have to go now. I just wanted to check in with you. I'll talk to you soon." She hung up, went to the fridge, and drank a beer to calm down.

Anna got a text from Dave that Friday night. "Hi, I'm not going to be back tonight. I'll see you tomorrow afternoon."

She came out of her room and saw Jen and Lori getting ready to go out.

"Hey, Anna—you haven't come out with us this semester. You're going to come to the club with us tonight. I won't take no for an answer."

"Okay," Anna said.

"Really? You're really coming?"

"Why are you so surprised? Dave is working, and I'd like to come."

Jen said, "Well, some others from our class will be there, too."

"Good. Do I know them?"

"Well, Cheryl and Ty and a few others," Jen said. "Brooke is meeting us there. She met someone and wants to finally introduce us."

Anna looked at Lori, who was smiling at her awkwardly, and said, "Lori, why are you smiling like that?"

"I'm just so happy to be going out with you. I hate that you just work and study. We're only this age once, and I've wanted to hang out with you more."

"Okay, okay. Maybe you guys are right. I need to get out more. I'm going to go get dressed."

They arrived at the bar and went straight to the counter. Jen said, "Three Miller Lites, please." She handed beers to Anna and Lori. "Well, ladies. Here's to roommates."

They clinked glasses, and Anna drank a large sip. "This is nice. I'm glad I'm out."

Jen said, "Hey Anna, Brooke is bringing a male date with her. I was shocked when she told me."

Anna squinted her eyes as she responded, "Yeah, I thought she liked women." Jen shrugged her shoulders and motioned to Anna to look at the door.

Anna drank her beer as she turned around to look and saw Brooke.

"Hi, everyone. This is Jeff." Anna couldn't believe her eyes. She felt faint and grabbed ahold of the barstool she was leaning on.

Jen looked and saw Jeff. "Anna, I had no idea it was Jeff. I guess Brooke had no idea, either."

"What's going on?" Brooke asked.

Jeff smiled at Anna. "Hi, Anna. It's good to see you," he greeted.

Before Anna could respond, Lori gasped and said, "Hi, Jeff. Anna, why don't you come to the bathroom with me?"

Brooke turned to Anna. "What did I miss?" Anna remained frozen and felt so many emotions that confused her.

Lori turned to Brooke and whispered, "Jeff is Anna's ex. She dated him for over a year."

The strange tension from the silence filled the circle, then Jeff said, "It's okay, everyone. Relax. Would anyone like a drink? Brooke, what can I get for you?"

Brooke hesitated and finally said, "I'll have a beer."

He said, "Anyone else?"

Everyone shook their heads as he walked to the bar.

Ty and Cheryl from their anatomy class came over, and Ty said, "Oh, Anna. I didn't know you were coming out tonight. How are you?"

Anna took a big sip of her drink and realized Ty was waiting for a response as she was staring in Jeff's direction. "Oh, good, thanks. I'll be right back."

She walked over to where Jeff was at the bar, not knowing what to say. Jeff turned and bumped into her arm, spilling the beer a little bit. "Oh, I'm sorry, Anna."

Anna said, "It's really nice to see you, Jeff." *I really miss him*, she thought. *He is so accepting and compassionate and nice.*

Jeff put his hand on her shoulder. "It's so nice to see you, too, Anna. How have you been?"

"Good, thanks," she answered. "I'm busy with school, but it's going by fast. How have you been?"

Jeff said, "I'm good. Luke must be in college now. How is all that adjustment going for your mother?"

Anna thought, *How does he remember all this? He cares so much.*

Before she responded, Brooke came over and took her beer, and Jeff said, "Oh, I'm sorry, Brooke. We're just catching up a bit."

Brooke turned to Anna and asked, "Is Dave coming tonight?" She turned to Jeff and said, "She's dating a friend of ours—Dave. We don't get to see her often."

Jeff finished his beer. "That's good, Anna. I have always wished you well."

She chugged down her beer and said, "Thanks, Jeff, I have always wanted you to be happy."

"Let's go, Jeff," Brooke urged. "I'm hungry."

Jeff, realizing Brooke was uncomfortable, paused and said as they all walked over to the group, "Nice to meet everyone. Have a great night." He then turned to Anna and winked at her. "Good night."

After they left, Jen said, "Wow, that must've been weird."

Anna felt saddened. "It would have been if I wasn't with Dave, I guess." Just then, she received a text from Dave and said, "Excuse me."

She went to the bathroom and read, "Why are you out tonight? I thought you were studying."

She replied, "I needed a break tonight. I decided to hang with the nursing students and roommates. How did you know I was out?"

Instead of texting back, Dave called her. "Jen told me you guys went out. I thought we talked about this at Thanksgiving."

"Talked about what?"

"Do I have to repeat it? This is not supporting me. How can I meet with clients when I'm worried about you?"

"I'm okay, Dave. I'm out with the girls. I'd rather be with you, but I understand that you have to work."

"Maybe I was right before. You're not ready for this relationship. We'll talk later." He hung up, and Anna turned around as a wave of nausea crept over her.

Anna was washing her hands when Jen came in. "I thought you fell in. You've been in here a long time. Are you okay?"

"Well, actually I was just feeling sick," Anna said. "I think I need to go home. Maybe it was something I ate."

"Or too many too fast. I'll walk you home."

Anna said, "I just need some air. I'll be right back."

Anna went outside and saw Jeff again walking to the entrance alone. "What are you doing back?" she asked.

"Brooke left her sweater here," Jeff said. "But now that I see you, I have to tell you I've missed you, Anna. I thought maybe I would have heard from you or seen you, but it never happened."

"I know. I'm sorry for the way everything happened. I wasn't ready."

"I do understand, more than you know. I'm glad you have someone now. I really hope you're happy in your life. I'll always care for you."

Anna looked over and saw Dave and Brooke coming up on them on the sidewalk. She felt like she might throw up again. "Dave, what are you doing here?" Dave gave Jeff a dirty look, ignoring her question. "Dave, this is Jeff," she introduced.

Brooke quickly interrupted. "Dave, this is my date, Jeff. He and Anna go way back, apparently."

Jeff reached out his hand to shake Dave's and said, "Hey, man, nice to meet you."

Dave stared at Anna and didn't offer his hand to Jeff. "Anna, let's go." He took her arm and led her down the sidewalk to his car.

Anna looked back at Jeff and mouthed, "Goodbye."

They got in the car, and she said, "Pull over—I need to throw up."

Dave pulled over to the curb, and Anna opened the door and vomited on the grass in front of a house. After she'd caught her breath, they continued on to his apartment in complete silence. She followed Dave into his apartment after he parked the car, and she went straight to the bathroom. When she came back from the bathroom, she found Dave on his phone.

"Yeah, I know, I'm sorry I left so abruptly," he was saying. "Something came up. I'll see you tomorrow. Have a good night."

"Who was that?"

"I hope you're happy, because my client sure isn't. Get some sleep, and we'll talk in the morning."

"Dave, I'm sorry, but there was no need to come and get me."

"Obviously you can't handle yourself, and I can't have my girlfriend going to bars and getting drunk and talking to men. How does that reflect on me? How can I trust you, Anna? Just go to bed."

Anna finally fell asleep after an hour, and when she woke up the next morning, there was a note on the counter. "Anna, I had to leave, but we will talk later."

She put on the clothes she was wearing the night before and realized she didn't have a car to get back home. She called Jen. "Hey, Jen. Could you pick me up?"

Jen said, "What time is it?"

"It's ten. I'm sorry I woke you up, but I have to work soon."

She said, "Where is . . . Oh, never mind. I'll be there in half an hour."

"Thanks so much."

Anna sat on the stoop of the building waiting and saw Brooke pull up. She said, "Get in." Anna did, and Brooke said, "Jen's hangover is pretty bad, so I told her I'd get you. Are you okay?"

"Yes. Dave went to work early and didn't think about the fact I didn't have my car."

"Are you okay with Jeff and me?" Brooke asked.

Anna said, "It's okay."

Brooke stopped at a red light. "I was trying to figure out what is wrong with him since you dumped him."

"I think the timing just wasn't right for me," Anna said. "He was my first boyfriend."

"Oh, that's too bad for you."

Anna thought, *He's too nice for you*, and then said, surprising herself, "Actually, Brooke, I was surprised to see you with him because I thought you might be gay?"

Brooke, not seeming upset, said, "Well, I'm actually bisexual. I love all people."

Anna suddenly felt uncomfortable and was glad to get back to the house.

She walked in feeling dizzy and sick and hung over. She said to Jen and Lori, who were sitting in the family room, "I hate feeling like this. It's not worth it." She thought of Jeff and Dave and started crying and ran to her room.

Lori ran after her, and as Anna fell onto her bed, she put her hand on her shoulder. "Is there anything I can do, Anna?"

"My head is just pounding, and I need to take a nap. I drank too much."

Lori rubbed her back a little. "I'll get you some ibuprofen and water. Maybe that will help."

When she got back, Anna had calmed down. "Lori, do you think I'm making a mistake? I mean with Dave?"

Lori, puzzled, said, "Only you can make that decision. I don't know him well enough. I'll be your friend no matter what. Why don't you get some rest and we'll talk later?"

Anna took the pills and a deep breath and thought, *She is a good friend.* "Thanks, Lori. I really appreciate your help."

Dave came over to pick her up Sunday morning. He said, "Good morning, ladies. Anna, are you ready?"

"Aren't you coming to breakfast with us?" Lori asked.

Dave said, "No, I'm taking Anna out."

Anna came out and barely looked at him. "Let's go," she said.

They barely talked in the car. Dave pulled into the parking lot of IHOP and said, "Anna, I'm sorry I came on so strong the other night. It's just that my feelings for you are so strong, and I can't even think of you being with another guy or out drunk somewhere when I'm not with you." He grabbed her close and kissed her.

Anna finally felt her shoulders relax, and she kissed him back. "Dave, I'm not a child. You have to know how I feel about you."

"When I saw you look at that other guy, I certainly didn't feel that you loved me."

"He's my ex, and I haven't seen him since we broke up. He's dating Brooke now." Anna was fidgeting. *I know I must have looked like I still liked him. What can I do? I don't want to lose him over this.*

Anna put her arms around him. "I think we need to get away. My father bought a house in Florida and told us to use it anytime. Can we go over the winter break?"

Dave got out of the car. "We'll see. Let's go eat."

They sat down, and he ordered before he said, "Anna, where is the house? I'll get some tickets for three days."

Anna thought, *That's so short. I want to stay longer, but I don't want to argue.* "Okay. It's in Sarasota and on the Gulf Coast, so I think we should fly into Tampa because my mother said it's more expensive to fly into Sarasota."

Dave said, "No worries. I'll take care of it."

At the restaurant, Anna ate her breakfast and started to feel calmer. She took a deep breath and thought, *Once school is over, we'll be together, and things will be better.*

CHAPTER 11

Anna's Christmas Break

When Anna's grades came back after her last final, Dave came over to her house. "Anna, I'm taking you out to dinner to celebrate. We haven't seen each other, and I know you've been studying hard."

Anna quickly got dressed after she kissed him. She kept quiet in the car as she thought, *I have so much to say, but I never know how he'll take it. What has he been doing with all his time? We haven't seen each other for almost two weeks. I just don't want to argue. I'll wait to see what he says.*

They sat down in the restaurant. "I wanted to give you a gift for Christmas," Dave said. He handed over a long box and a card.

"I thought we weren't going to exchange gifts because of our trip," Anna said.

"Let me worry about the money. I wanted to get this for you. Please open it."

Anna opened the box. Inside was a diamond bracelet, along with their tickets to Florida. "No, I can't accept this gift. This is way too much."

"Anna, I work hard to be able to do things like this. Please put it on. It suits you well."

Anna was shaking so much she couldn't open the clasp. Dave took it from her and helped her put it on. "Why are you so nervous?" he said. "That is what I love about you. You don't know how special you are."

Anna hugged him across the table and said, "Thank you. It's really too much, though. I'm just a college student. I don't deserve this."

"A college student dating a wealthy businessman. You are going to have to get used to this lifestyle. I can't wait to go away with you."

Anna thought, *He's been working hard for us. That's what he's been doing.*

The next day, Anna was driving home for winter break, listening to Elton John and singing to the music. She arrived at the house around three in the afternoon with her small suitcase. Kathy was in the kitchen and came to the door to pick up the bag from Anna. She gave Anna a long, close hug and said, "It's so nice to see you, Anna."

Kathy wasn't usually so affectionate, and this worried Anna. "What's wrong, Mom? Is it your health?"

"No, honey." Kathy laughed. "I just want to give you a hug. I haven't shown you much affection, and I just want you to know that I love you."

Anna reciprocated the hug as tears streamed down her face.

"I'm sorry I haven't been the mother you wanted me to be."

"Mom, what are you talking about?"

"Well," Kathy said, "my doctor has been trying to get me into therapy for a long time, and at my last visit, I guess I broke down. She gave me the number to a therapist she thinks highly about who has helped her other patients and actually watched me make the appointment to be sure I'd follow through. It's helped me a great deal."

"I'm so happy for you, Mom. You've been so unhappy for so long."

"Well, it's hard work and a process that I'm learning about. But enough about me—tell me what's going on with you and what you'd like for dinner."

Anna and Kathy were making pasta and meatballs and listening to Beethoven when Dan came home. He came into the kitchen and picked up the mail.

"Hi, Dan. How was your day?" When Dan didn't say anything, Kathy said, "Dan, when I talk to you, I'd appreciate you responding to me. Do you see your daughter is here as well for the winter break?"

Dan looked up and said, "Oh. Hi, Anna. Good to see you." He kept his eyes on the mail and then said, "Oh, Anna. Is Dave going to be coming for Christmas, or did you mess that relationship up?"

"Dan," Kathy said, her voice calm but stronger than Anna had heard before. "Please don't talk like that to her."

"That's okay, Mom. I'm still dating him, yes, but he won't be coming here for the holiday."

"That's too bad. I enjoyed talking with him the other night. He seems to have a good head on his shoulders. I hope you don't mess it up."

As he was walking up the stairs, Kathy looked at Anna as if she wanted to say something, but she held her tongue.

"When is Luke coming home?" Anna asked.

"I think tomorrow. And he's bringing someone with him."

Anna said, "Oh, wow. I thought he swore off any relationships."

"I'm excited to meet her. I just want you kids to be happy."

I'm actually enjoying my time here with my mother, Anna thought with surprise. *I feel happy here for the first time. She doesn't seem so sad.*

Anna went out for a jog in the bitter cold the next morning around ten. When she got back, she saw Luke's car in the driveway. She sped up and was completely out of breath by the time she came in the back door. Luke was sitting at the table with Kathy and another girl.

"Hi!" she said, but when Luke got up to hug her, she put out her hand and laughed. "You probably don't want to get close to me yet."

Luke smiled and said, "This is Alia. Alia, this is my sister Anna."

Anna waved to her and said, "It is so nice to meet you, Alia. Let me take a quick shower, and then we can chat." She went up to her room and heard some laughter in the house. The sound was such a welcome surprise.

When Anna came downstairs, she heard her phone go off. She went into her room and noticed she'd missed a message from Dave: "Anna, call me right away when you get this."

She called him, but the call went to his voicemail. She said, "Sorry, I was on a run and in the shower. Hope you're okay." She went downstairs, bringing her phone with her.

Alia came up to her and gave her a hug. "I've wanted to meet you all for a long time. I've heard a lot about you, but only when I pry it out of Luke."

"Yes, that sounds about right. I hate to say it, but he hasn't told us about you. Typical! But I like you already."

"Well, we met the first week of school. It's hard to believe we've been dating for four months now."

"Oh, wow." She looked at Luke and said, "Really, Luke? You couldn't call to tell me at some point over the last four months?"

Luke smiled. "Let's see—when did you call me to tell me you were dating Dave?"

Anna laughed. "Okay, you're forgiven."

Anna noticed that Alia had short wavy hair just long enough to pull up. She was petite and had a beautiful smile that lit up the room. *I really like her*, she thought. *There's something about her that makes you feel at ease.*

As they were talking, Dan came into the room and said, "Oh, hello. I'm Dan, Luke's father."

Alia glowed with a smile and stood up to hold her hand out. "So nice to meet you. I hope it's okay that I'm here."

"Will you be joining us for Christmas?"

"Well, unless Luke decides to break up with me by then." She smiled.

But Dan didn't seem to get the humor. "That would be a bad decision. I'm going out for dinner. I'll see you all tomorrow."

Kathy tried to stop him. "It would be nice if we actually have a family dinner tonight, Dan, don't you think? We haven't all been together in months, and this is our chance to get to know Alia."

Dan looked at her in surprise. It was the second time she had questioned him that day, and he clearly didn't like it. "What's going on with you? You know I'm busy. I'll see you later."

Luke looked over at Anna and mouthed, "Did that just happen?"

"Yes," Anna said with a smile. "There have been a few changes around here." When Kathy's back was turned, she whispered, "Mom's in therapy." Luke's eyes widened.

"Luke, your family is awesome. I had to plead with him to come," she said, looking at Anna.

Luke said, "I was just protecting her from you guys." Laughing, he said, "Right, honey?" while looking at Alia.

Anna started to laugh with her mother and said, "I've never heard that word come out of your mouth, honey. You must be in love." Her phone rang as she was talking. She stepped away to answer it.

"Hello?"

Anna's smile turned quickly to a frown. "Hi, didn't you get my message?"

Dave said, "Anna, we'll have to talk some more when we go away."

"But, Dave, you can't expect me to have my phone with me every second of the day, when I'm taking a run or a shower."

"My father just came in, so I'll have to talk to you later. Did you clear our trip with your parents?"

Anna said, "Yes, it's fine." *I'll check with my mother later, but I can't let him know that.*

"Good. I'll call you later."

Anna came back into the kitchen and saw Alia holding Luke's hand. She was talking to Kathy. "I'm a family kind of person. I'm so close with my own parents, and I have one brother and one sister. We love to get together and play games and stuff. Luke has been coming over for a while now. I think they like him." She turned to Anna. "Oh, hey. Is everything okay?"

"Fine, thanks," Anna said.

"Do you like to play cards or games?" Alia asked.

"Well, I never really have."

Alia said, "Well, if you want, I can teach you some card games tonight."

Anna smiled. "Okay, sounds like fun."

Luke said, "So, where is Dave? I thought I'd get a chance to finally meet him."

"Well, we decided to spend Christmas with our own families this year. We're going away in a few days together."

"Anna, was that him on the phone?"

"Yes."

"You do realize you don't seem happy to talk to him, right?"

"I just miss him, Luke. I wish he was here."

Alia seemed to sense this was a private conversation, and she left the table and went into the kitchen. "Kathy, let me help you."

The four of them were eating dinner when Dan came in around six. Kathy said, "Oh, I thought you had a dinner?"

"Well, we decided to cancel since it's Christmas Eve. I'm hungry."

"I'm so glad you can join us. Maybe you can play some card games with us, too?" Alia said innocently.

Dan shook his head, puzzled, and said, "So, Alia, tell me about your family."

Alia repeated the things she had told the others earlier.

"What does your father do?" Dan asked, zeroing in on the only topic that mattered to him.

"He's an electrician. He works so hard for all of us. There were times we hardly saw him, but now he has his own business and has people working for him so he's home more often."

Dan said, "Nice he's a businessman now."

"My mother also runs a small daycare out of our home. She loves kids and has done that since I was small. She doesn't seem happy unless there're kids in the house, and there's a lot of noise."

"Wow, I'm just the opposite," Kathy said. "I've always liked the house to be quiet."

After dinner, Dan excused himself and went to his office while everyone else cleaned up the dishes. When he came out, they were playing games at the kitchen table. Anna thought, *This is really nice. I wish Dave were here.*

"Mr. Lawrence, would you like to come play with us? It's a tradition in my family to have a game night," Alia asked, looking at him with a pleasant smile.

"Thank you for offering, but I'll pass for now."

Anna gave Luke a puzzled but optimistic smile, thinking, *Things are changing here right before my eyes.*

The next day was Christmas morning. Anna overheard Luke and Alia arguing. Alia said, "I'd like to stay a little longer, Luke. I really like your family."

"No, we need to see your family. Your parents are waiting for us."

Alia said, "They understand that we need to spend time with your family as well."

"It's really okay for us to leave. We don't do anything on Christmas anyway."

Anna came into the kitchen, and they broke off their argument. "Hi, guys," she said. "I hope you slept well."

"Yes, I did. Thanks so much for letting me sleep with you in your bed."

Anna said, "Anytime."

"We're going to eat and take off," Luke said.

"Oh, it would be nice to spend the day with you guys," Anna said, "but I know you have other commitments."

"It doesn't seem like we just met," Alia said. "Can I have your number, Anna?"

"Why do you need that?" Luke asked, suspicious.

Alia said, "I'd like to be able to call her, nosy."

They exchanged numbers, and Alia gave Anna a big hug. Kathy came into the kitchen, and Luke said, "We have to go, Mom. I'll talk to you later."

Kathy paused to absorb the disappointing news then went over and gave Luke a warm embrace. "Please be careful and drive safely. I love you."

"I'm not dying, Mom," Luke said. "We'll be fine."

Anna stayed at the house until Wednesday and then went back to school. Before she left, she asked her mother about the key to the Florida house, saying, "I forgot to ask you and Dad, but Dave and I have plane tickets to Florida."

Kathy got up and went to the closet, getting some keys and handing them to her. "Anytime, Anna. I hope you love it there. Remember, it's a big house. Just remember to lock it up after." She put her arms around Anna and added, "Have a lovely time."

Anna arrived back at school on Wednesday morning and was packing her bag for the trip Thursday. When she thought about how this would be her first trip with Dave, she felt butterflies in her stomach. She decided to call him.

"Hi, Anna."

"I'm back from home and was wondering when I would see you."

"I won't be back until the morning. I'll be there around nine to come and get you and go to the airport."

"Oh," Anna said. "I was looking forward to seeing you tonight, like we planned."

"I told you I need your support. I'll see you in the morning. Remember, we'll be spending four days together. I have stuff to do for work."

"Okay, I am really looking forward to the trip."

Jen came into the house and said, "Hi, how was your holiday?"

Anna said, "I actually had a nice time. My brother brought his girlfriend home with him, and I really liked her. The whole mood of the house was much better."

"What do you mean?" Jen asked. "Is the mood bad generally?"

"Oh, well," Anna said, backtracking as she realized she shouldn't reveal too much, "I mean, there isn't much going on, and it's so quiet. How was your holiday?"

Jen said, "It was nice. We missed you Sunday night, but I guess you were spending quality time with your family?"

Anna took a deep breath, thinking, *What did they do without me now?* "Oh, what did you do?"

"We were at Dave's house. He said you were busy. He had some people over."

"Oh, right," Anna said, her thoughts beginning to race. "I *was* busy. I just forgot. Was it fun?"

Jen said, "His parties are *always* fun."

Anna got up, thinking, *I want to have a beer so bad.* "I have to finish packing. Excuse me." She went to her room and closed the door. Tears streamed down her face, and she grabbed a pill and took it. She wrote in her journal, *Why is it every time I get excited, I find out something to destroy it? He has to know I would find out about the party—he didn't even invite me. How can all my roommates have gone and I didn't even know about it? Maybe he has a good excuse? I don't want to ruin our Florida trip. Maybe I'll keep this to myself until after the trip.* She thought about her trip and went to the kitchen to get a beer when she noticed no one was around.

She was almost finished when Jen came in and said, "Lori will be here soon. Maybe we can get a movie and hang out? You must be getting ready for the Florida trip."

Anna said, "It'll be nice to have time alone."

"That does sound nice. I hope you have fun. I'm jealous you get to be in the sun."

Lori came in the door and said, "Hey, guys. I'm so glad to be back. I need a break from my parents who won't let me have any space." She put her stuff away and came back.

"Hey, Anna," Lori said, "I texted you when I was at the party. Did you get it?"

"No, I don't think so."

"Dave's house is huge, and his father is very personable. You must like hanging out there."

Anna shrugged. "Yes, it's nice."

"Lori," Jen said, "do you want to watch a movie?"

"I have a movie in my car. I'll go get it."

"I'll make the popcorn," Jen said. "Is Brooke coming?" Lori looked at Anna and just shook her head no.

Anna watched with them for a little while but then went to bed early. "I have to get up early, so I'm heading to bed. Good night."

Lori and Jen, still watching the movie, said, "Good night."

The next morning, Anna woke up early and could not fall back asleep. She got up and took a shower, and it was still only seven in the morning. She made some eggs for herself and texted Dave.

"Hi, I woke up early. When are you coming over? I'm so excited."

Dave didn't respond. She started to read and got a text a while later.

"I'm on my way now. See you soon." Anna noticed it was now nine, and she started pacing the floor.

Jen came out and said, "What's wrong? Is he late?"

"Yes."

Just then Dave arrived at the door, and Jen let him in. He gave her a hug and then came over and gave Anna a hug. "Are you ready? Bye, guys—see you in a few days."

As they drove to the airport, Anna couldn't restrain herself. "I heard you had a party Sunday night. How come you didn't invite me?"

"It was last minute, and I knew you were with your family, so I didn't want to interrupt you. It wasn't a big deal."

"I don't understand. All my friends came, and they didn't invite me, assuming you would have."

"Anna," Dave said, "I'm not going to argue with you. I told you I didn't mean anything by it. Let it go."

Anna thought, *I knew I should not have said anything.*

They arrived in Sarasota after a three-hour flight and went to pick up the car Dave had rented.

As they were driving and Dave put the address in the GPS, Anna thought, *Why isn't he talking to me? I feel like he's punishing me for talking to him. I shouldn't have said anything. I knew better, and I knew what would happen. And it did.*

"Dave, are you okay? Why are you so quiet?" she asked.

Dave rolled his eyes. "Anna, you need to relax and not worry so much."

He turned the corner into a neighborhood and stopped at a gate. "Did you know this was gated, Anna?"

She said, "Oh right. My mother wrote down the code." After the gate opened, they drove through and saw enormous houses, all of them overlooking the ocean. "This cannot be it."

"Your father has good taste." They drove to the fifth house up and pulled into a circular driveway with a large fountain in the middle. He pulled in front of the house, and Anna sat in the car just staring at this house as she felt her heart racing. She tried to take a deep breath as she thought, *I feel so angry. Where does he get off buying this without my mother and does he actually make that much?*

Dave put his arm around her waist and led her up the walkway where she noticed how the stairs were wide and then narrowed as she took each step. She started searching for the keys and the paper with the alarm code but found her hands trembling as Dave said, "Here, let me get that for you."

Dave opened the door, and Anna stood at the front and saw a two-story foyer and large living room. She saw some French patio doors that opened onto a huge deck and noticed crystal blue water sparkling as the sun beamed through the glass.

Anna said, "Wow." After her shock ran through her, she went over to the doors and out to the deck. Dave went to the bathroom, so she sat on the lounger to stare out at the vast ocean. *This is incredible. I guess I can be happy my mom can enjoy this.*

Anna and Dave were on their way to look at the bedrooms when Anna heard a voice and saw her father come out of the master bedroom with the same woman she had seen in the restaurant. Now the woman was wearing just a robe. Anna ran down the stairs into the kitchen to splash water on her face and saw a bottle of bourbon on the drink cart. She poured herself a glass as Dave put his hand on her shoulder.

"Anna, stay calm. Let's see what he has to say."

"I don't care," Anna said. "There's nothing he could say to explain this."

Dan came down the stairs, poured himself some water, and sat on the couch. "Anna, why didn't you ask me about coming?" Anna paced the floor and then stared at him without responding. "I never wanted you to find out about this," he said. "Now that you know, it is really none of your business. I don't expect you to understand."

Anna was standing but swaying back and forth. She said, "I already knew you were cheating on Mom. I'm not stupid. Don't pretend your family are idiots. I saw you with her a year ago. I think you're just a selfish jerk. I have no idea why she stays with you. I wish you weren't my father."

"I understand you're mad," Dan said, "so I'll excuse what you just said to me. I'm going to leave, and I want you to have the house for the weekend to enjoy and calm down." Then he looked over to Dave and said, "It's nice to see you again, Dave. Sorry for the circumstances."

Anna watched them shake hands. She was furious but kept quiet and went out on the deck with her phone. When she turned her phone on, she noticed she had missed a text from her mother. It said, "Anna, I think your father may be going to Florida for the weekend for work at the last minute. I wanted to let you know so you weren't surprised when you saw him. Maybe you can have some time to bond. Have fun. Love, Mom."

Anna felt strange, and her eyes moved to the upstairs window. Her father's mistress was staring down at her with tears running down her face. Anna thought she looked familiar but couldn't understand why. *Why on earth would **she** be crying?* Anna thought. *It's not as if she didn't know he had a family.* After a few moments, the woman suddenly pushed back away from the window but then leaned forward, and Anna thought she saw her lips say sorry before she moved back away.

Dave came out onto the balcony and put his arm around Anna.

Anna pushed back away and turned to him and said, "How could you shake his hand? He just betrayed me and my family, and you shake his hand."

"Anna, he really just betrayed your mother," Dave said. "This is between them. I know you're hurt, but he's still your father, and I have to respect him for that."

"Dave, I want to go back. I can't stay in this house where he takes his whores."

"Anna, there's nothing we can do. We need to spend time together, and I want to be with you. You already knew what he was doing, so why was this such a surprise to you? Can't we have a nice weekend? Look at this view. Besides, I never get time away."

Anna took her shoes off and stepped onto the sand. At the water's edge, she put her feet in the ocean.

"Let's take a walk and clear our heads," Dave said, coming up behind her. "Maybe I can get your mind off what just happened." He took her hand, and they walked along the water for a long while in silence.

Anna looked at him and admired how the light hit his face. She remembered how mesmerized she'd been by his looks when they'd first met. She still found herself strongly attracted to him, despite everything. "I love that you are here with me." He grabbed her face and kissed her with such a passion that she forgot everything for a moment.

They went out for lunch. Anna wanted a drink and had Dave order one for him and give it to her.

"You know, Anna," Dave said, "you don't know much about your parents' marriage. Didn't you say they have never slept in the same room? Don't get mad, but maybe some of this is your mother's fault?"

Anna felt her face instantly get hot. She took a deep breath and bit down on her lip then finished another beer. "I don't want to talk about it, please. Let's just have a nice time together. I'll have to deal with that later."

When they got back to the house, Dave started to kiss her neck, but visions of her father having sex with that woman ran through her head.

"I'm so sorry, but I can't do this here. Can we just go to a hotel?"

"That's ridiculous, Anna. Let's just take an early flight and go back if you are going to be like this."

"Please, Dave, can we just go to a hotel?" But he was already on the phone with the airline, changing their reservations so that they could fly out sooner. As usual, once Dave had made up his mind, he forged ahead without discussion. *I have no say. He never listens to me. What am I doing? I'm so mad at myself for pushing it.*

On the plane, Anna was fishing in her purse for her lip balm when she pulled out a piece of paper. She looked over to see that Dave was still sleeping and unfolded the note. "Anna, I'm very sorry about the situation with your father. I never wanted to hurt your family. E." She quickly tore the note up and went to the bathroom to throw it away, but she hesitated and put the ripped pieces in her pocket.

When they got back to Michigan, Anna and Dave fell into their routine of school and trying to find time to spend together. Anna called her mother one afternoon, and Kathy said, "Hi, hon."

"Are you okay? You sound so down."

"I'm just tired."

"I was thinking of coming over this Saturday for the night," Anna said.

"That would be lovely."

"Have you spoken to Luke?"

"No. He did send me a birthday card, though."

Anna felt her heart sink. "Oh, Mom—I forgot your birthday. I'll come home and make it up to you. We'll go out to dinner."

"You know I don't like a fuss on that day. It's just another day."

"I'll take you out anyway. I'll see you then."

Anna drove back to Northville through the mid-February flurries and realized it was already four in the afternoon and she had not yet spoken to Dave. She felt her heart race and thought, *Now I have to deal with him getting mad at me again. Why didn't I ask him before? I have to get this over with.* She sent him a text. "I'm so sorry, Dave, but I forgot to tell you that I am going to spend the night with my mother. I have been so busy that I missed her birthday."

Dave texted back, "I thought we were going to go to the movies?"

"I'm sorry," Anna wrote, "but when I was talking to her, she sounded so lonely, and I feel bad about her birthday." Waiting for his negative response, she felt herself shaking.

"Okay, then. I'll talk to you tomorrow. I have a lot to do tomorrow so that won't work."

Anna thought, *That wasn't so bad. See, Anna, he is a nice guy or maybe he is getting better. Or maybe he has something else better to do like going to a party without me.* She drove up and sat in her car in the driveway for a while, watching her mother through the kitchen window. She thought, *I feel so sorry for her.*

Kathy saw her and waved her in. In the kitchen, she said, "What are you doing out there?"

"Oh, I was just texting someone."

Kathy gave her a hug, and Anna said, "Let's go to P.F. Chang's for dinner?"

"That sounds nice, but we could just eat in if you want."

"Mom, it's okay to be important. I feel so badly that I missed your birthday."

Kathy said, "Let's stop talking about it and go out. I'm actually hungry already."

At the restaurant, Anna was thinking about her father and debating if she should tell her about Florida. They sat down and ordered some wine and some food. Anna asked, "Where's Dad?"

"He's on a trip. Since he took that promotion, he actually travels much more now. I'm getting used to not having him around."

"Mom, when you texted me in Florida, you knew he was there, right?"

"Yes," Kathy said, "that's why I texted you. Did you two or three actually bond?"

"No, I mean with another woman."

Kathy's face darkened. For a moment, she was quiet. Finally, she said, "I know you don't understand why I tolerate it, but we haven't been close for a long time now. He's your father, and you don't need to know everything about us."

"You can talk to me, Mom. I'm an adult now. You could get a divorce. We're both out of the house now, and you don't need to stay for the kids. Luke and I want you to be happy."

"I'm working on some things in my own way and at my own pace. I'm getting stronger in therapy and with work. I'll do what is right when the time is right. You'll understand one day when you're older. Life is not always what it seems. Remember, there're consequences of any choice we make in life, and you must try to understand those consequences as much as possible before you choose. Also, you should have the coping skills and tools available to help you with those consequences. Now, let's eat and talk about you."

Anna thought, *I want to know more, but she has said a lot, and I don't want to push it.* She said, "Everything is good with me. Oh, I'm on track to graduate early, next December. That will help with the rent, which I appreciate you taking care of."

"Why are you rushing things? You should have more fun and spend time with your friends. I would've done things differently if I could go back. I don't want you to be a grownup too fast. There is plenty of time for that. Learn from my mistakes."

Anna said, "Mom, I want to be self-sufficient. I want to be able to take care of myself. I want to pay Dad back for the tuition."

"Oh, I understand now. You're thinking like Luke does. Even though your father is tough, it doesn't mean he's not reasonable. Take your time, Anna. It'll go by so fast anyway."

Anna said, "Mom, the decision is already made. Dave is so happy that I'll be finished soon."

Kathy looked concerned. "Don't get married too fast, either, Anna. Take your time. You're only young once."

Anna suddenly got a text from Lori: "Hey, Anna. We're headed to Dave's apartment to hang out, but he said you're with your parents. Just checking if everything is okay?"

Anna shook her head, thinking, *I knew it. I knew he was up to something.* "Sorry, Mom." She then texted, "I missed my mother's birthday so I wanted to come home. Have fun. Sorry I didn't let you know."

Jen texted, "No problem, have a nice time, and say hi to her for me and happy birthday."

Anna then tried to focus on their conversation but thought, *I know she is looking out for me, but my life is different from hers. I won't make her mistakes.*

CHAPTER 12

Anna's Last Summer in College

Anna called Luke one day before she left for the summer, thinking, *I haven't called Alia after she left me a message a month ago. I feel badly now.* "Hi, Luke. How's Alia doing?"

"I'm doing well, thanks. Alia is doing great, too. She changed her major and now wants to be a dentist. She is ambitious. I thought she told you all this?"

"I guess we've both been too busy lately to catch up. We're on such different schedules. I do feel bad, though, that I never got back to her when she called a while back. Can you tell her that? Also I wanted to know what you're doing for the summer."

"I'll let you tell her that. I rented a room for the summer to stay here and work, and I have a lot of training to go to anyway. I'll visit you, though, and maybe you can come down. You do realize that I'll never move back there, not even for the summer or a break."

"I guess, then, spending time with Mom is all on me! Luke, what about me and Mom? We want to be with you, too."

Ignoring the comment, Luke said, "I'd like to finally meet Dave one of these days."

Anna said, "Dad met him and they got along. But how can you meet him if you're not here?"

"We'll find some time to come this summer."

Anna moved back home. As she got settled in her old room, she looked up her work schedule online, thinking, *Another summer working every evening and taking classes. I'm glad this is the last one.*

Just then, Dave called. "I haven't seen your parents in a while. Why don't we take them out for dinner?"

"I don't really want to go out with my dad. I barely even see him, and when he's here, I avoid him."

"Anna, he's your father. If your mother can live with him, I don't see why you can't find something good in him."

"Why can't you understand me and stop trying to make me think differently? You didn't grow up here."

Dave said, "Remember, Anna, I have gone through losing a parent. I may have more to say about this."

"You're right—I'm sorry. I know you've been through a lot. What about next Saturday night?"

Dave came all dressed up on Saturday. He knocked on the front door, and Kathy answered it and said, "Oh, wow. I didn't know this is a formal event. Those flowers are beautiful. Thanks. Come in, please."

"Hi, how are you?" Anna reached over to hug him, and he kissed her cheek.

Dave said, "Mrs. Lawrence, the house looks so nice."

"Please, call me Kathy. Thanks. Did you like the beach house?"

"Very impressive. How many times have you been there now?" Anna couldn't believe he would ask that question after what they had walked in on down in Florida. It almost felt like he was trying to embarrass her mom.

"Well, actually, only once, at the end of last summer. It's a little overwhelming to me. I'm not used to a house that big."

"I'm sure you deserve more than that! Is Mr. Lawrence coming home soon?"

"To be honest, I'm not sure. I never know what he's doing."

"Didn't Anna ask you and your husband to have dinner with us tonight?"

"Oh, well. She mentioned you were coming and that you wanted to take us out, but we never know if or when Dan is coming home, so I made dinner."

As she was talking, Dan drove up in the driveway. Anna thought, *I never thought I would be glad that my father was home.*

Dan came in the back door with a smile on his face. "Hi, Dave. I was glad to see your car out there. It's been a while. Let's catch up."

Anna thought, *Does he even know I exist?*

They went into the study, and Anna noticed Dave close the door behind him. Anna looked at her mother and said, "This doesn't seem right." She watched her mother try to think of something to say, but she stayed silent.

After a half hour, Dan came out and said, "Kathy, get ready to go out for dinner."

"But I have dinner all set."

Dan said, "Save it. We're going out."

"I appreciate that you made something," Dave said, "and I'm sure it's amazing, but now you have dinner for tomorrow. I don't think you should have to work so hard."

Kathy said, "Well, let me get ready."

When they got to the restaurant, Dave opened the car door for Kathy.

"Thank you," she said.

The restaurant had a table waiting for them, and Dave ordered a bottle of port wine. "Dan, can you taste this? I hope it's to your liking."

They spoke for a while as Kathy and Anna talked about school and Anna's plans for after graduation. Kathy said, "It's your birthday in September. It's hard to believe you'll be twenty-one."

Anna said, "I know. I'm excited to start working and feel like I'm making a difference."

"I'd like to have a party for your birthday," Dave told her.

"No, please. I hate parties and being the center of attention. Can we just go away for the weekend?"

Dan said, "Tell me when you want to go to Florida, and I can make sure the house is available."

Anna said, "Available!"

Dave interrupted her. "I think that would be nice. What about the week before you go back to school?"

"I'm never going back there," Anna said. She stood up. "I'm going to the bathroom."

Kathy followed her and said, "Anna, remember—this is between your father and me. Don't let this come between the two of you."

"There have to be some consequence for his actions, Mom. Like you said before, his choices also have consequences. I don't have to be part of it all."

Anna went into the stall and took a pill. When she headed back to the table, she saw the two men laughing. She thought, *I feel so nauseous.* She sat down and listened. They were talking about the possibilities for business partnerships in the future. *We're not even married yet.*

The rest of dinner, no one mentioned anything about her getting upset. Anna fell silent for the rest of dinner.

After dinner, they went back to the house, and Anna and her mother changed and went to relax as the men continued to talk in the study. Dave came out after a while and said, "Hey, Anna. I'm going to go now, but let's go out to dinner by ourselves tomorrow."

"I'm working tomorrow evening and every night for the rest of the week."

"Well, I'm going to buy some plane tickets for the last week of August for Florida."

Anna said, "I told you I'm not going back there. Let's just go up north."

"I'll see what I can do, but you are going to have to get over this."

Anna went to shut the door, but Dave grabbed her and kissed her first. "I want you to take one Wednesday off, just call in sick so we can go out to dinner." Before she could respond, he was walking down the walkway.

Anna thought, *How can I be so angry but then have it dissolve when he kisses me?*

The weeks went by, and eventually Anna convinced Dave that they should go to northern Michigan instead of Florida. One night, Anna was in her room packing when Kathy came in. "Anna, I'm not sure I should tell you this, but Dave is pretty serious about you. How do you feel about him?"

Anna said, "Well, I love him, of course."

Kathy seemed to gather her thoughts, and when she spoke, she chose her words carefully. "I want to tell you something about me. When I first started dating your father, he seemed like the greatest thing on earth to me. I was vulnerable and had a need to be needed and taken care of. I felt like a knight had come into my life, and I was the luckiest and happiest person on earth."

Anna smiled. "I feel that way sometimes, too."

But Kathy shook her head. "Well, that feeling didn't last long after we got serious. I started to feel like nothing I did was enough to make him happy. I kept trying to change to become the person he wanted me to be. I worked harder and harder trying to satisfy him. But it was never enough. I feel it's my responsibility to help you understand that marriage is difficult. You really need to see your partner for who he really is and go into the relationship with your eyes wide open."

"What are you talking about marriage for? You don't like Dave? I'm so happy, and you are telling me not to be with him. He's not Dad, you know. They're different people."

"I'm only saying this because I love you, and I want you to benefit from what I've gone through. Just think about what I'm saying. Are you really seeing him clearly? Sometimes our emotions and our past experiences can sugarcoat or mask the reality of the person in front of you. I don't want that to happen to you."

"I understand, and I do know who I am with," Anna said. "Now, please let me pack because he'll be here soon."

"One more thing. You also may want his approval because he has similarities to your own father because you never felt any approval from your own father. Please, don't respond, but just think of what I'm saying. I will support whatever you do."

Anna felt sick to her stomach when her mother left the room. Just as she finished zipping up her bag, she heard Dave come in the back door and talk to Kathy in the kitchen.

"Hi, Kathy. You look nice."

"Please take care of my baby girl," Kathy said, her voice cold. "You know she is sweet and innocent and vulnerable. I want someone to protect her, not use her vulnerabilities for their own agenda."

"Are you accusing me of manipulating Anna?" Dave said.

"I don't know your true intentions, and I'm trusting that they are good ones."

Anna cringed. Dave, she knew, did not respond well to anything he perceived as criticism. "Well, we will all have to wait and see," he said. "I am offended by the accusation."

"I'm not accusing you, but I'm no longer innocent, and my eyes are open. Please don't hurt my little Anna."

Anna came into the room. "Are you ready?"

"Very."

Anna kissed her mother. "Have fun," Kathy said. "I'll see you soon."

They got into the car, and Dave grabbed her hand and said, "I'm really looking forward to this trip."

"Is everything okay between you and my mother?"

"Fine," Dave said. "I think she has big problems with your father, though. Let's not think of anything but us."

They had been driving for about three hours when she asked, "Where are we going?"

"It's a surprise, but it's in Traverse City." They made their way through the beautiful coastal town, full of restaurants and quaint cottages. Soon, Anna saw an enormous log cabin appear with a view of Lake Michigan behind it. The crystal blue water sparkled as the sun penetrated through the vast clouds. She felt her problems melt away as she took some deep breaths, and he said, "Come, let me show you the best part of the house." Before they went into the house, they went to the private back deck, and she noticed he had a small bag on his arm. He said, "Anna, isn't this like heaven?"

She said, "Yes, it's beautiful here."

"I'm glad you think so, too," Dave said. He reached into his bag and pulled out a small jewelry box.

She said, "I thought we said no gifts!"

He knelt down in front of her and said, "Anna, will you marry me?"

Her heart began to race. Dave continued, "Anna, I think we can make a nice life together, and I don't believe in waiting anymore. I know what I want, and this is it."

Tears ran down Anna's face as her mother's words came back to her. She said, "Dave, I want to marry you one day, but could we wait a while? There's no rush, right?"

Dave bolted to his feet and blurted out, "No, if you're not sure now, then it's not meant to be. I want to have a wedding when you're done with school. I can't wait. I love you. If you're not ready for this, then you'll never be ready, and we should just end it."

Anna felt like her world was crashing down in front of her and understood that he was serious. "Yes. I'll marry you," she said. If she had to choose between now or not at all, she would choose now.

He grabbed her hand and put the ring on her finger; the beautiful diamond sparkled in sun, nearly blinding her. He kissed her and started to take her clothes off. "I've always wanted to have sex out here," he said. Anna felt the wind rush over her naked skin, and as he pushed his way inside her, an overwhelming feeling of euphoria came over her, and she started to cry.

Afterward, he brought her to the bedroom, and they took a nap. When Anna woke, she said, "I'm so hungry."

"Let's get dressed and get some dinner," Dave said. They drove to a restaurant down the street that was right on the water. At the table, he sent some texts, and Anna nursed her drink and thought about who she wanted to tell. She sent a text to her mom.

"Mom, Dave proposed to me. Did you know he was going to do that?" She paused a minute and bit her lip and ended the text with, "I said yes."

She then sent a text to Alia. Dave grabbed the phone from her and checked her text messages. He said, "Already telling the world. That makes me happy."

Anna smiled, but she felt uneasy, too. Why did he always have to control everything? Her mom texted back a few times, but Anna only glanced at them, uncertain what to say. It was clear to her now that her mom had doubts about Dave, and the tension made her feel conflicted.

She fell asleep on the drive back and woke up when he pulled into the driveway. "I'm the luckiest girl in the world, Dave. Aren't you coming in? I want to tell my parents with you."

"They already know. I have to get back, but we'll celebrate soon." He gave her a quick kiss and drove away.

Anna came into the house and right away showed her mother her ring. Kathy barely looked at the ring and said, "Why didn't you answer my texts? I was so worried when you didn't respond after you texted me."

"Oh, I'm sorry. The connection was bad, and I turned off my phone."

"I'm concerned you're rushing things, honey. You're so young. Are you *sure* about this?"

Anna paused, thinking, *He'll leave me if I say no. My mother knows me so I can't show any doubts.* "I'm so happy, Mom. Of course I'm sure. Did you know about it already? I mean, with the talk about marriage before."

Kathy said, "Yes, they talked about it that night we went out to dinner."

Wow, he was preparing and respecting my parents, Anna thought.

Kathy said, "Luke and Alia are on their way over."

"Oh, I'm so excited. I wanted to see them before I go back to school." Anna went to take a shower and change. She texted Dave, "Can you come back for dinner? My brother is coming with his girlfriend, and I really want them to meet you."

Dave wrote back, "I'll see what I can do."

They arrived, and Anna ran outside to give Alia a hug first. She said, "Hi, guys. You must be tired from the drive." She went in the kitchen as Kathy was chopping and preparing to grill for the evening.

Alia gave Kathy a hug and said, "I'm so happy to see you. Please tell me what I can do to help?" Kathy had a great big smile when she saw Alia and Luke.

Anna received a text from Dave, saying, "I can be there by seven. Go ahead and eat without me."

Luke came over. "So, where is Dave?"

"He can't get back here until around seven."

"Are you sure about this?" Luke said, peering at her. "You are only twenty-one years old."

"I've never been happier, Luke," Anna said, projecting a confidence she wasn't sure she felt.

Alia, Anna, and Kathy were all in the kitchen enjoying conversation and making dinner together when Dan came home.

"Nice to see you again, Alia," he said.

Alia smiled. "Thanks so much. You must be so happy about Anna and Dave."

Dan turned to look at Anna's hand. "Congratulations, Anna. You're making a good decision."

Anna attempted to hold in her emotions by looking to the ceiling like she did as a child and thought, *He is finally proud of me for something.* "Thanks. That means a lot to me. He's coming over soon." She saw Luke staring at her and shaking his head with a look of disbelief and pity.

"Well, I guess I should cancel my meeting, then." He went to his office and shut the door. Anna could hardly believe it—in her entire childhood, her father had never canceled a meeting.

Dinner was over and the women were in the kitchen cleaning up when Dave drove up. Anna watched him get out of his BMW and thought, *Wow, he wants to marry me.* She opened the door before he knocked and tried to hug him, but he grabbed her hand and looked for her father.

"Hi, Dan." The men shook hands, and Dave walked into the kitchen with Anna trailing behind him. "Good evening, everyone. You must be Luke." He reached out to shake Luke's hand.

Luke stood up from the table and shook Dave's hand. "Nice to meet you, too."

Next, Dave stepped over to Alia and handed her some flowers. "Anna has said some nice things about you, Alia, is it?" Anna looked at Alia, who was staring at Dave with the same look most woman gave when they saw him for the first time, making Anna feel special that this great-looking guy was her fiancé.

Alia said, "She has said some nice things about you, too."

Dan said, "Let's go have a drink."

Dave followed him into the study and turned to say, "Luke, want to have a drink?"

Luke, in the hallway, and said, "No, thanks."

Dave leaned on the door by the study. "You're in the service, right?" Luke nodded. "What branch?"

Luke came over to the entrance to the study as Anna was eavesdropping from the kitchen. "In the ROTC. I'm going to be an attorney for the army. Congratulations, by the way. You're marrying a great girl, but I guess you figured that one out and don't want someone else to snatch her up."

"I'm not sure what you mean by that, but Anna is a great girl. Do you play golf?"

Dan started to laugh. "Luke, golf? I don't think so."

Luke, ignoring his father, said, "Well, I mean Anna is so young and hasn't even graduated or started her career."

Anna felt the tension rise and quickly came over and said, "Do you guys want dessert?"

Dave shook his head no and put his arm around her. "It's just that when I see something that I want, why wait?"

Anna stepped on Luke's foot and said, "Luke, Alia told me you started to play golf. Is that true?"

Luke took the cue and said, "I haven't played much, but I'm learning. My girlfriend's brother has gone out with me. He had to be patient with me, but I've gotten better. The problem now is just finding the time, with school and training."

"Are we going to have a drink or stand in the hallway all night?" Dan asked.

After Dan and Dave had their drink alone together in Dan's study, everyone went to the dining room and sat around the table. Anna looked around and thought, *This is so strange.*

Dan poured some port wine and held up his glass. "To the engaged couple." They clinked their glasses, and Dan said, "So what are the plans for the wedding?"

Anna opened her mouth to say that they hadn't talked about the plans yet, but Dave spoke over her. "Well, we'll get married at the country club. A large wedding, most likely in the spring, since Anna will be finished with school by then."

Kathy looked at Anna, who had tears in her eyes. Anna stood up and said, "Excuse me."

She excused herself to the bathroom to try to calm down. *I can't believe he made all these decisions without even asking me first.*

Alia knocked on the door. "Are you okay, Anna?"

Anna wiped her eyes and took her deep breaths as she found a Xanax pill in her pocket and swallowed it down. "I'm okay. It's just all overwhelming. I'll be out in a minute." She came out and looked in the dining room and thought, *It will all be okay. Look at everyone together. It's so nice.*

Around eleven, Dave said, "Well, it was so nice to see everyone, but I really must go."

Anna walked him out, still angry. "Dave, we've never even discussed the wedding plans—why did you tell my father all that?"

He said, "I assumed you would know where it would be and that the sooner we can do it, the better. I don't want a long engagement. It will all be fine." He tried to kiss her, but she turned her face away, and his lips landed on her cheek. "Don't play games with me, Anna. I'll talk with you tomorrow. I won't be coming over until the end of the week." She watched him walk away, and he turned to wink at her.

Anna returned to the table, and Alia said, "Wow, that is so soon to get married. I understand you're so overwhelmed. Let me know if I can help in any way?"

"Married," Anna said. "I know. It's so strange."

"You don't look so happy," Alia said. "Are you okay? You don't have to rush it, you know."

"I'm just tired. I'm fine," Anna said. "I'm going to bed. Good night."

"We're taking off early, so I hope to see you for breakfast in the morning."

Anna tossed and turned and couldn't sleep, so she turned the reading light on to write. *Am I making a mistake? He has all of this planned out already, and I'm just a person that fits in a box. Does my opinion matter at all to him? Why do I have so many doubts and questions? I feel so sick to my stomach.* She went to the kitchen to get a glass of water and saw Luke sitting at the table.

"You couldn't sleep, either?"

"No," he said. "I'm worried about you. Don't take this the wrong way, but there is something I don't like about Dave. I don't like how he talks over you and never lets you speak. He reminds me of Dad. I have always wanted us both to be happy, Anna. Especially you. I don't want to make you upset, but I have to tell you this. I will support you no matter what, though."

She said, "He's fine, Luke. I'm so happy with him. I know he has a strong personality, but that is what I love about him." Even as she heard the words coming out of her mouth, she knew she didn't completely believe them. Something *was* wrong, but acknowledging it felt so dangerous. It seemed better to keep pressing on. Maybe she could convince herself to believe what she was saying about Dave.

Luke said, "Anna, I've read about this. Some people seek out a partner who is similar to people in their lives, just because it feels familiar and because they think it's an opportunity to change the script. But you cannot change Dave, just like you could not change Dad. I'm worried that because Dad never gave you his approval you are going to start seeking the same thing from Dave, since he has a similar personality. But you don't have to live like that."

Anna felt her guard go up and her defenses kick in. "Luke, you never seemed to care before, and you don't know anything about me now. You just met him. You never give anyone a chance. I'm marrying him, and you have to let it go."

Luke got up to leave, and Anna grabbed his arm. "I know you care in your own way, but I can take care of myself."

"You also don't know much about me, either," Luke said. "I'm going back to bed. I said what I had to, but you will only hear what you want to hear. I love you, Anna. You're my only sister. Please just think about what I'm saying?"

The next day, on Sunday, Anna drove back to the rented house in Ann Arbor for her final semester. When she arrived, Jen was already there. She gave Anna a big hug and said, "Congratulations, Anna. I'm so happy for you and Dave. Can I see your ring?"

"Oh, you already know?" Anna asked.

"Before you guys left, Dave told me what he had planned. I actually helped him pick out the ring. Oh, it's so beautiful on you. I hope you don't mind that I helped him. He wanted a female's opinion."

Anna thought, *What else don't I know about? She seems to know so much about Dave.* She took a deep breath and said, "Jen, you know a lot more about his family than I do. Can you tell me about them, especially his father?"

"Well, I can only tell you my take on things. Dave has never been close to his father. He always felt his dad thought he was just in the way because he was not as good at things as his brother was. Jake likes to joke around and sometimes be hurtful in a way, but you can't take it to heart. You have to be around him and gain some trust from him. He doesn't trust people easily. He's been easier on Dave since their mother died, but Dave is not sure how long that will last. I know the family dynamic is different, but just keep going over there and you will eventually be accepted. Sue will be a good person to befriend as well. She can be cynical, though, at times."

Anna tried to absorb all this information, and her face must have shown her concern because Jen said, "Anna, you need to relax if you are really going to be part of that family. Not to concern you, but there are many secrets in the family. Maybe you are rushing too fast."

"I'm fine, really. I'd like to know about his mother, Katrina? Did you know her well?"

"That is a huge Pandora's box for Dave," Jen said. "She was so beautiful and kind and treated Dave like he was a king. I liked her. She was warm and caring. There was always something odd between her and Jake, though."

"What do you mean?" Anna asked.

"I don't remember if they ever talked to each other when I was there. I felt tension when they were around each other. It's hard to describe."

Anna then said, "Jen, would you be my maid of honor?"

"Really? I'm so flattered, but why me?" After a pause, she added, "I mean, I am really flattered."

"Well, you know Dave so well, and we have been roommates for a while now, and I feel close to you."

"Have you asked Dave yet?" Jen said carefully.

"No, I was just thinking about it, and you are friends with both of us. This is my decision anyway, right?"

Jen nodded, though she looked uncertain. "I would like that. Now, let's go get your stuff and move you in."

That evening, Anna's phone rang, and before she could even say hello, Dave barked, "Why would you ask Jen about my family? What are you trying to do?"

Anna instantly thought, *What did I do?* She felt paralyzed and kept quiet.

"Anna, I'm talking to you."

"I'm sorry, Dave."

They were both silent for a moment. Then Dave said, "Please, if you want to know something about me, ask me. Okay? I thought that was clear before."

Anna said, "Okay."

"Did you ask Jen to be your maid of honor?"

"Yes. I was talking to her and thought, since she was my friend and yours, she would be a great maid of honor. Dave, why does she know so much about you that I don't know? Why won't you talk to me?"

"I don't open up to people. You will learn about me over time. My family and I have known Jen and her family for a long time. That is how she knows me."

"Well, then, I guess I need to spend more time with your family, too," Anna said.

"We have to focus on finishing school and planning the wedding. We'll have a lot of time for that after the wedding."

Anna looked out the window and saw Brooke pulling up with another car behind her. "Okay. When will I see you?"

"Tomorrow night. We'll talk more then. Good night."

Anna hung up, and her heart raced as she saw Jeff come through the front door, carrying Brooke's suitcases. Anna dashed into her bedroom and took one of her mother's pills. When she felt a little calmer, she came out and pretended to be surprised to see them. "Oh, hi! How was your break?"

"It was nice, thanks," Brooke said.

Jeff came over to Anna, and she felt him stare at her with sadness. He asked, "How are you?"

Jen popped out of her room and blurted out Anna's news. "She's engaged!"

Jeff's face fell, but he quickly recovered. "Sorry, I wasn't expecting that one. Well, congratulations."

"Thanks," Anna said. "It seems like you two lovebirds had a nice summer, too."

Brooke said, "Oh, no—I mean, we did have fun, but we actually decided to just be friends."

"Oh," Anna said, flustered, "I didn't mean anything by that."

Brooke said, "Let me see your ring." She studied it then said, "Nice."

Anna thought about how safe she had felt with Jeff and how caring he had been. She'd never felt that kind of security with Dave. The stress of the past few days began to overwhelm her. "Well, it has been great catching up. I'm sorry to run, but I was just headed to take a nap. See you guys later."

Anna went to her room and closed the door. Tears started falling down her cheeks. She sat down on her bed and opened her journal. *I'm so confused. Jeff is such a nice guy. Why is he here causing me to feel bad? Why do I feel so bad?*

A knock on the door came, and Jeff said, "Anna, can I talk to you a minute?"

Anna wiped her face and closed her journal. She opened the door and said, "Come in."

Jeff came in and closed the door behind him. He sat on the chair, and she sat on the bed. "Anna, I'm not sure why I am telling you this, but to be honest, I still have feelings for you. I guess I hoped that, over time, you would want to come back to me. I'm a fool, I guess. I'm going to go and stay away from you because it's not healthy for me. I just wanted to say I hope you have found your happiness in life. You are a very special person."

He came over to where Anna was sitting and put his arms around her. *I don't want him to stop*, she thought.

"I will always love you," he whispered. "Take care of yourself." He went to the door with his head hanging low and closed the door behind him as Anna sat there, frozen and confused.

One Sunday evening a month later, Anna and Dave were at a restaurant. Dave said, "I was thinking, Anna, that in December you should move in with me after you graduate. I think we can start our lives and plan the wedding better. What do you think?"

All Anna could think was, *I won't ever have to live with my father again.* "Yes," she said, "I would like that."

Dave said, "I will have one more semester of school, and when I'm done, we can find a house in Birmingham or Bloomfield Hills."

"Or we could move to the Northville area," Anna ventured, "to be closer to my mother."

Dave said, "But Birmingham or Bloomfield are only a half hour away. It shouldn't be a problem."

Anna could tell he wasn't going to compromise on that. "Okay. I want to start working, though, in January, and I don't want to move jobs."

"Well, after we're married, you won't have to work."

"Dave, I want to work. I'm doing all of this to work. That is not something I will compromise on."

"Well, work in Ann Arbor for now, and after we get married, we can figure it out."

They went back to his apartment, and Anna noticed Dave texting with someone back and forth. She thought, *This couldn't be work related on a Sunday night. But if I ask, then he'll just get mad, and I don't want to deal with that tonight.*

After three more texts, though, she couldn't restrain herself. "Who is that you're texting? On a Sunday night?"

"Do we have to go through this again?" Dave asked. "I have to be available to my clients."

After that, Dave went to watch television, but Anna followed him to the couch and sat down next to him so their legs were touching. "Why are you so distant?"

Dave got up and paced the floor in front of her. "Every time you question me, I wonder if I'm making the right choice about this marriage."

Anna said, "Dave, I have to be able to ask you questions."

"If you don't trust me, then we don't have a relationship. I'm going to be working on weekends, too."

Anna grabbed his hand in desperation as he walked to the right of her and stopped him. "I'm sorry. You're right. I understand, and I support you. Please sit down, Dave." He took a deep breath and went to the kitchen to get a drink and came back to finally sit down.

She sat next to him, but she could still feel the tension for a while. Dave finally put his arm around her after at least half an hour, which felt like a decade to Anna, and said, "I think it would be good if you moved in here after the semester is over."

Anna felt a wave of relief and thought, *I'm so happy he isn't going to end this relationship. I have to trust him that he isn't going to hurt me, but he's helping us.*

Dave ran his hand over her shirt and her breasts as she was abruptly startled away from her thoughts. He said, "Let's go to bed."

The next Saturday, Lori came into the family room, put her sandwich down on the coffee table, and looked over Anna's shoulder. "Hi, Anna, what are you doing?"

Anna looked up from her laptop at Lori looking down at her screen. "I'm looking at houses for fun. After Dave graduates, we'll buy a house together." She closed her laptop and sat up facing Lori, who was now sitting and eating her sandwich. "Lori, I wanted to let you know that I'm going to move in with Dave at the end of this semester."

Lori said, "That is too bad, but I'm happy for you. I guess I'll have to tell Jen and Brooke we'll need to find another roommate."

"I'll miss you," Anna said. "We've been roommates a long time now."

"It's still hard to believe I know someone who's getting married. I can't imagine I would ever be ready for that right now. We are all so different."

Anna said, "I haven't really thought about it. It seems when you find the right person, you don't want to lose him."

Lori said, "Don't you think that there is probably more than one right person? It seems like timing, career, and a lot of other factors besides just love matter in making a marriage last. I have seen from my own parents that love is not enough. They separated, you know, for a few years when I was young."

"Wow, I'd never have guessed that based on the way they are with each other. They seem to be so happy together."

"Yes, they are, now. That's what I mean—hard times and other factors played a role, and they had to separate to figure it out. I'm so glad they ended up back together. They're much happier now after they separated and went to counseling to work on the relationship. It seems like relationships are so much work, and I have figured out that I'm not ready now for that type of commitment. I'm actually glad now that Carl broke up with me."

Anna thought, *Is she trying to make me change my mind? What is she getting at? She must be just saying that because she didn't want Carl to leave her.* She said, "I am glad for you, but we're all different. If he hadn't broken up with you, maybe you would be engaged and happy to be, like I am."

Lori shook her head. "But that's what I'm trying to tell you—I wouldn't have been happy in the long run with Carl. He wasn't ready to be committed to me, and neither was I. I need some time to figure my life out, and if we got together and didn't listen to the signs, then we may have gotten married and been unhappy. I have learned a lot by the breakup and by my parents' problems."

Anna gave Lori a firm look. "Like I said, we're not all the same, Lori. You never would know how it would end up because you broke up. I know many people who got married early and it works out. I know there will be ups and downs, but that is life and true for everything."

Anna got up and briskly walked to the bathroom. "Excuse me."

She shut the door and splashed water on her face and looked in the mirror to see her face all red and flushed. *I need to calm down. Why is she pushing me away from getting married? I need to focus and just get good grades and spend time with Dave.*

Jen came into the room after Anna came back to get her laptop and said, "Are you ready, Lori? We're going to a party if you want to come."

Anna looked at them and thought of Dave and said, "No, thanks. You guys go have fun."

Lori got up and looked at Anna. "Is everything okay, Anna? We were just chatting. I wasn't talking about you but about me. I wish nothing but the best for you."

Anna said, "I'm fine, Lori. Go and have fun. I forgot to ask you if you could be my bridesmaid?"

Lori grabbed Anna's hands and looked in her eyes. "I would love to do that for you."

She went back into her room but left the door open. As they were getting ready, Anna overheard Lori say to Jen, "I feel so sad for her. She seems so conflicted and confused. I wish she would just take her time instead of rushing into things."

"I know," Jen said, "but she has to figure it out for herself. That's the one thing I know. You can't help someone when they don't want the help. We've given her enough information about Dave for her to make up her mind. He's the one who is rushing things so fast. I know Dave, and he's manipulating things his way. I wish she would pay attention to the red flags waving in her face."

Anna was short of breath and her heart raced. She opened her journal and wrote, *Lori and Jen think I am making a big mistake marrying Dave. Are they right or are they just jealous that they don't have anyone? Many people get married young. I think they are jealous of me and are reacting to that. Why do I feel so confused? What are the red flags Jen is talking about?*

As she was writing, Dave called her. "Hi, Anna. I won't be able to see you tonight."

"When we live together, will you be at home with me every night?"

"What a question. Of course. Why are you asking?"

"Because you don't spend much time here."

"That's because you're not there. I have to go, but I'll see you tomorrow. Oh, and tell your parents that my father is going to pay for the wedding. They don't have to worry about that. Goodbye."

Anna stared down in her phone and heard the silence before she got to respond. *What is he talking about? The bride's family usually pays for the wedding. Well, at least I won't owe my father anything. Like Luke said, no strings attached.*

She immediately went to the kitchen and made a rum and Coke, with a third Coke and two-thirds rum. She drank half of it and felt her overwhelming anxiety calm down. She got into her pajamas and turned on the television after she made a second drink. She flipped through the channels, kept trying to find something that interested her, but eventually just turned the TV off. After her third drink, she picked up the phone and called Alia.

"Hi, Anna. It's so nice to hear from you." Alia started to laugh and said, "I'm sorry, Anna, but your brother has decided to tickle me. He's so bad. Luke, stop it—your sister is on the phone."

"Hey, sis," Luke yelled in the background.

Alia said, "Are you okay? You sound kind of down."

"No, I'm fine," Anna said, "just tired." She wanted to ask her a question but said, "I'm just checking in to see how you guys are. I'll catch you later."

Anna overheard Alia say, "Luke, let me focus on your sister. Can you get me a Diet Coke?"

Luke said, "Oh, okay. I'll get you later, then."

Alia said, "Sorry, Anna. Please tell me what's going on?"

"I guess I'm just nervous about getting married so young," Anna said. "I just hope I'm doing the right thing, you know? What do you think?"

Anna waited in anticipation and took a few more big sips of her drink, yawning more now. Alia said, "Only you can make that decision, Anna. I'm too far removed to see what you two are like together. You know I'll be here no matter what happens."

Anna listened and just thought, *I feel worse now, not better. She can't answer me.* "Okay, then. I'm feeling really tired now and need to get an early night. I'll talk to you soon."

Alia said, "Anna, just remember to ask yourself the question, 'Can I live with his faults?' The negative things about your partner are the ones that will be the future problems, not the good stuff. My intuitive mother has told me that in the past, and I never understood it until I got a little more mature and in a relationship. I always ask myself if I can live with Luke's faults, and it now makes sense to me. I hope that helps you. Take care and hope to see you soon. Bye."

Anna felt like the bottom dropped out. She took another sip of her drink and thought, *I am going to look at the good stuff. We all have bad stuff, but it's the good stuff that makes the bad things better. She doesn't know everything.*

Anna picked up her journal and wrote, *I'm so happy for my brother. He seems so happy with Alia, and she is so good for him. Dave is good for me, too. He is investing his time to bring me and us stability for our future. I love him and want to be with him. It will all work out fine.* She put her journal down and took her last sip of her fourth drink as she thought, *Why don't I feel it will all work out fine?* She thought of Luke and Alia. *They seem so in love, as though they really enjoy being together. Does Dave even like me? Do I really like Dave?*

Dave came over Saturday morning, and they went out to breakfast. Anna said, "So, I meant to ask you about the wedding. I really don't want a big wedding, Dave. I would just like family and close friends only. What do you think?"

"I don't think we have control over that," Dave said. "My father is paying, and he wants to use this event to build up more business. Inviting clients makes them feel like they're more than just clients, which brings in more business."

"But Dave, this is *our* wedding. Maybe I can get my father to pay, and then we won't have all that pressure. I don't want our wedding to be a business meeting."

"I can't do that to my father. Anna, this is for our future, too. This only helps our financial picture when we have kids."

"That won't be for a long while, Dave," she said. "I'm not ready to have children."

Dave said, "I know, but we'll have them eventually."

"How many do you want?"

"With you, at least a dozen."

Anna said, "Very funny. I was thinking maybe three."

"I wanted six. Let's compromise and go with four."

Anna said, "We'll see."

It was a Sunday when Anna felt compelled to call her mother. When her mother answered the phone, she blurted out, "Hi, Mom. How are you? I know this may be hard to hear, but I'm going to move in with Dave in December. I won't be moving home."

Kathy just breathed in the phone and, after a pause, said, "Okay, Anna, maybe that is a good thing."

"What's wrong?" Anna said. "You sound so down."

Kathy said, "Oh, nothing. Well, Luke called this morning and said he isn't coming home for Christmas. He has to go to training and doesn't have time to come home. I just miss him and Alia. I enjoy them being around."

Anna said, "I'll be with you. Do you want me to come see you next weekend?"

"No, you're so busy, and I'm okay. I'm glad you're living together before you get married. If you live together first, then you can see if you want to marry him."

"Mom, I *am* marrying him. Oh, and tell Dad that Dave's father Jake is going to pay for the wedding. He has it all taken care of."

Kathy said, "I'm not sure if he'll like that, Anna. Your father is proud and would like to pay for the wedding."

"He'll be fine," Anna said. "I really don't want him to pay, anyway. Because with him there are always strings attached. I will come home soon, Mom. I have to run. Goodbye."

Anna immediately called Alia. "Hi, Alia, my mother is so upset. Is Luke there?"

"What's going on?" Alia asked.

"Luke called her and told her he wouldn't see her over the holiday."

Alia said, "Oh, I know. I was upset at him, but he does have this commitment and doesn't have the time. I'll call her because I'm going to come and visit with her myself when he's out of town."

"Oh, Alia, that would really cheer her up. We can hang out as well."

"How are the wedding plans going?"

"Fine," Anna said. "We're going to have a bigger wedding than I wanted, but it'll still be nice."

"Everyone wants to see that amazing good-looking couple tie the knot. Are your doubts still there?"

"Actually, I haven't thought about them lately." Anna thought, *Why am I lying?*

"That's good. You can talk to me anytime, if you want."

Anna got up and looked at a picture she had of Luke and Alia. "I know. I hope you and Luke never break up. If you do, we have to remain friends."

"It's a deal," Alia said.

A little while later, Anna got a text message from her father, which was a first for her, and she didn't recognize the number. "Hi, Anna. Can I have Dave's phone number? Dad." Anna thought, *I didn't even know he had* my *number.* She texted him the number and wrote, "What is this about?" She waited for a response that never came. Dave was in the living room when she heard his phone ring. She listened as best she could.

"Hi, Dan. How are you?" Anna tried to listen but was unable to hear her father. "Okay, but my father has a lot of clients he's inviting. You want to have a list for yourself. Okay. I'll talk with him about splitting the cost, but he's pretty much planning the whole event. Okay." As she waited for the response, Anna bit her lip with anticipation. "It will be elegant and classy, I promise. If my father has something to do with it, it will be perfect." Anna was staring at Dave. "Okay, sounds good. I'll let you know."

Anna came into the room and casually asked, "Was that my father? What did he say?"

Dave smiled at Anna as if he knew she was listening in and said, "He has a list of people he wants to invite as well and will only feel comfortable if he pays for half the wedding at least. As long as they are splitting it, and my father can plan it, it shouldn't be an issue."

"I'd actually like to be involved, you know. I'd like to pick the cake and flowers and other things, especially since I cannot pick the guest list and the facility."

Jen and Lori quietly entered the kitchen and were listening in. Anna could see Lori rolling her eyes to Jen. Dave said, "I'll plan a day that you come over the house, and we'll have the wedding planner over."

Anna said, "Great."

For the next few weeks, Anna was busy with school and writing papers. She called Dave when she was on her way to the bookstore one day, and Dave said, "Anna, why are you still working there? You should quit that job."

"It's my spending money, Dave."

"I'll give you spending money now, Anna. Give your notice today. You have a lot going on and could use more time."

Anna started to fidget and thought, *I like my independence, and I like working there.* But she said, "I'll see. I don't like to rely on anyone."

"I'm your fiancé, Anna. We're together now, and I don't want you to worry about money."

Anna thought, *I don't want to lose this job, but this isn't a battle I want to have. Maybe he's right and I can use more time to plan the wedding and study.* She said, "Okay. I'll talk with Evan."

At the store, Evan was busy with customers. Anna said, "When you have time, I need to talk with you." She thought about not coming to work there anymore as she was unpacking some boxes. *I have had this job since I started school. I feel sad to move on. I met Jeff here.*

She was stacking some books when Evan came over and said, "So what do you need to talk about?"

As Anna opened her mouth to reply, he noticed the sparkling diamond on her hand. He looked at her with wide eyes, and she smiled. "Yes, I'm getting married. I'm also giving my notice today."

"Oh, no. You have been my best employee, and a friend. I really wish that wasn't happening, but I guess I have no choice but to understand. If you change your mind, I'll be here."

"Thanks," Anna said. But his expression worried her. "You don't seem happy for me, though."

"I'm sorry," Evan said. "I guess I'm more shocked, that's all. I'm happy for you—if this is what you want." He paused a minute and said, "Stop by in a week, and I'll write a letter of recommendation for you."

"Don't I need to give you a two-week notice?" Anna asked.

"Only if you need the money. Actually, Dave was here one day and gave me a heads-up that you were getting married and would be too busy to keep on working."

Anna tried to keep the shock from her face. She was blindsided, but her gut told her she shouldn't let it show. She knew she had to get out of the store. "Thank you for giving me a chance to work here," she said, plastering a smile on her face. "I appreciate it. Can you mail me the letter, please?" She felt compelled to give Evan a hug and looked to the ceiling to hold in her tears. "Take care, Evan, and thanks for everything." She left the store without looking at Evan or she knew she wouldn't be able to hold it in.

Anna sat in her car and put her head on the steering wheel and let herself cry. *Why is he always taking over? What is wrong with me? Or I mean him? He puts me in such a bad place. Does he think he's helping me or does he want to control me, like Jen says? I have to give him the benefit of the doubt. He did ask me to quit, and Evan was just prepared. Everything will be okay.*

CHAPTER 13

Anna and Dave Move In

Anna took her final exams the week before she went home for the holiday. This was the end of her academic career, the culmination of all her hard work, but it felt so anticlimactic. On Saturday morning, she was in her room packing and feeling overwhelmed with sadness. Lori came into the room and sat on her bed, watching her.

"I'll miss living with you. We've known each other for three-and-a-half years now. A lot has happened."

"I know, Lori," Anna said. "I feel sad, too, but I remind myself that we'll still see each other all the time."

Jen joined them. "You're just moving around the corner." She paused and then said, "Maybe this will cheer you up: I was wondering where you would like your bachelorette party? I was thinking of getting a limousine and going to Motor City and having a late night out in Detroit. I wish we could do something bigger, but we are just college students with no money."

Anna said, "Oh, I don't think that's necessary. I really don't want a party."

"But that's the whole point of having a maid of honor," Lori said.

"Can I think about it?"

"Anna, let your friends do something for you. We want to."

"Okay," Anna said, "but let me think about what I want to do."

Jen said, "Okay, but let me know in the next few days—I want to get planning!"

Anna finished packing and gave Jen and Lori quick hugs. She was starting to feel emotional again and wanted to get the goodbye over with. She'd be staying at her parents' house. "By the way," she asked, "did you find another roommate?"

"Oh, Dave didn't tell you?" Jen said. "He's going to pay for your rent for the rest of the year so we don't need to get someone else."

Anna felt deflated. *Of course he is.*

"Well, of course, if you guys have a fight, you can come back. Haha," Lori said. "Or if Dave is traveling, you can come hang out and spend the night."

"Oh, right," Anna said. "I forgot he told me that a while ago. Well, have a nice holiday, you guys, and I'll let you know soon about the party."

Anna selected her mother's number from her contact list, thinking about how this would be the last time she would have to stay under the same roof with her dad.

Kathy answered. "Hi, Anna."

"Why are you out of breath—are you okay?"

"I was wrapping some gifts to mail out today before it is too late and ran to the phone."

"You don't have to do that, Mom. Alia is going to come by herself for a few days."

"These are for your brother, and I mail out some gifts for the troops overseas. Did I tell you I'm volunteering for a group that helps them?"

"That's great, Mom. It always makes me happy to see you getting involved in things. Did Dad give you the list of guests for the wedding yet?"

"No," Kathy said. "I didn't know he was going to give it to me."

"And what about from your side, Mom? Do you have any family you'd like to invite? There must be someone who can represent your side of the family."

"Well, your second cousin, Tom."

Anna briskly cut her off. "No not him, ever." Silence filled the air. "Sorry but he is too weird. Just think about it and I'll see you soon."

When Anna arrived at the house, she came in through the back door and gave Kathy a hug. "Mom, now that I'm getting married and I'm an adult, I need to know about your family."

Kathy looked to the floor and sat down, weak in the knees. "Anna, my dear, I've spent my whole life trying to forget my past. I know it seems unfair of me to keep all that from you, and you have a right to know. But I don't want to talk about it. If you promise not to talk to me about it, I have a box of journals and pictures that I put away, never to open again. I kept them for exactly this reason, because I knew someday you would have questions. I have a sister, Eve. We haven't spoken for years, and that was my choice. You'll learn a lot from the journals, but you have to promise not to ask me any questions. It's too hard for me."

Anna's heart raced. *I have an aunt out there. What could be so bad that she won't even say the words? What is she running away from? Maybe now I will finally be able to understand my mother.*

"Okay, Mom. I promise. I'm so sorry it is so hard for you."

Kathy and Anna ate dinner alone, and they didn't talk much. Anna was beginning to understand the depths of her mother's sadness, a sadness that had always been there, despite the ways in which Anna had tried to avoid it. Anna started to fidget, so eager to see those journals and start to put the puzzle pieces together.

Kathy could sense her anticipation and finally got up from the table. "I'll try to find that box for you. I think it's in the attic."

"Let me help you." She followed her mother. "I didn't even know we had an attic!" she said.

Kathy went upstairs in her walk-in closet and pulled down a latch with a set of stairs that came down. Anna followed her up and pulled the string connected to a light to turn it on. She started to cough with the amount of dust that was being stirred up. She saw at least ten boxes a few feet away. "I think it is the one in the back." She moved some of the mildewed boxes around. Finally, she found the one she'd been looking for, but it was so heavy she struggled to pick it up.

"Let me help you," Anna said. She saw a look of dread in her mother's eyes. Tears began to stream down Kathy's face. Anna held onto her shoulders and said, "Mom, go. I'll take care of it. You go and relax downstairs." She didn't allow her mother to leave first before she ripped open the box that read "Kathy's box."

"I know I probably can't stop your curiosity at this point, Anna, but all I can say is that sometimes it's better not to know. Ignorance can be bliss."

"I thought," Anna said gently, "that you were in therapy and dealing with some of your past, Mom."

"I'm taking it slow, Anna. It takes a lot of time. I never looked at myself as a survivor before from my past traumatic experiences. I am learning so much about my life and how I have made my decisions based on my past. It is overwhelming at times to understand myself. Just focus on your life in the present and your future. Enjoy this time in your life, honey. You never know where your journey will bring you." She paused and said, "Please remember not to make decisions based on your childhood with me and your father. I really hope we didn't mess you up too much. I'm going to go lie down and take a rest. I'll leave you to it."

Anna paused for a moment, looking at the box in front of her, and thought, *What is she talking about? What is wrong with her and me? Why do I have an eerie feeling? Should I open this or leave it alone? How can I leave it alone when I have wanted to understand my mother for so long?* But with the answers so close, she just couldn't resist. She picked up the first book and dusted it off.

Dear Diary, I am thirteen years old and I have a fourteen-year-old sister, Eve. I decided to write this journal so I can write down what happens and never think of it again. If I put what happens on paper, I can pretend it never happened. My mom and dad are fighting again. I want to run away with Eve when they fight. I cannot remember a time when they did not fight. The fights seem to be getting worse, and Eve tries to protect me by putting headphones on, or we take walks at night. We never knew if he would hit her or just scream at her and us. I have a bad feeling, though, lately. My father's drinking is worse, and his temper is worse. I will write later.

Dear Diary, My mom was taken to the hospital. My father was drunk when he got home from work and started yelling, but this time he picked up an iron and threw it at my mother, but she ducked and yelled, "Girls, get out of the house." I ran to the woods in back of the house, but I was alone. I did not see Eve. I heard screams from the house. I ran to my neighbors' house which was a repeated thing and told them my father was throwing things at my mother. They called the police and would not let me leave. When the police got there, they called the ambulance. My neighbors took me to the hospital, and the policeman told me my mother died. My father went to jail. I asked where Eve was, and they did not know. When I told them, the guy called the house. He told her to look for another girl, Eve.

I sat down, waiting. I heard the doctor at the desk say to the policeman that she was hit so hard in the head she died instantly. How can this happen? How can someone do that? But the officer just shook his head over and over. I always thought the adults were in charge, but even they can't seem to explain it to me.

Anna stopped reading and noticed that her body was shaking and she had sweat rolling down her face. She realized she was sitting in the attic and the dust was all around. She closed the journal and brought the box down the stairs and to her room and closed the door. Anna reread that phrase over and over again, *hit so hard in the head*. She felt she finally understood why her mother would never talk about those days. Anna hesitated to read more but thought that the story couldn't get worse, and she was aching to know what had happened to her aunt. She took a deep breath and went to get one of her mother's pills but could not find the bottle that was always there. In its place was a bottle of citalopram, and she opened it up and took one. *Maybe this will help*, she told herself.

Back in the room with the box, she continued to read the journal. *Eve was found in her closet. The police took her to the hospital, and Eve would not talk or look at me. We went to a back room, and the lady from the state took us home with her for the night.*

Dear Diary, today we went to court to find out where my sister and I are going to live. I want to stay with our neighbors, but the courts told us we had to go to blood relatives. Today, I am moving in with my mother's sister and her son, Tom. They told us that even though I never met them, they wanted us to go live with them. I am glad to meet some relatives. Maybe she looks like my mom because I miss her terribly.

Dear Diary, It has been a week now and we moved in. My aunt put an extra bed in the room with Tom so we would have a place to sleep, but the bed is too small. My sister and I took turns using it at first, but then my sister told me she'd rather sleep on the couch.

I started a new school, and I like my teacher, but the kids are not friendly at all. I hope it gets better. Tom, our cousin, is quiet and just stares at Eve and me. He is a few years older than Eve. I don't like it when he stares. My aunt is okay. She does not say much but feeds us and combs my hair sometimes. Eve still won't talk to me about what happened to Mom. She barely talks to me at all anymore. I feel sort of alone.

Anna took another deep breath and felt like she might throw up. She thought, *Why isn't that pill kicking in yet? What did I take?* She put these thoughts out of her head to read some more.

Dear Diary, You're my only friend. Kids are being mean to me at school, and Eve ignores me. I am trying to make friends, but they call me names instead. My other school was so much better. I just go walk around by myself. Middle school is horrible. After school, I go to this big tree house I discovered at the end of the street, and I am here writing now. I wonder whose it is and why they left it there. I am sure glad I have somewhere to go. I am feeling afraid of Tom. He tries to watch me shower and stuff. He is so creepy, but I don't feel I can tell my aunt or sister.

Anna ran to the bathroom and threw up. She put cold water on her face then turned the cold shower on and jumped in with her clothes on. The cold water shocked her, and she sat down in the tub and cried. After a while, she felt exhausted. *I don't know if I can read any more, but I need to know.* She dried herself off and went back in her room. She looked out the window and saw that her mother's car was gone and wondered why she didn't hear her leave. She continued to read. Compelled to read more but resistant to read, Anna could not stop herself.

Dear Diary, A week has gone by and my aunt took another job to support us. I heard her talking on the phone to someone and heard her say, "No, there is no money. They told me there was money to take care of the girls, but they lied. I have four mouths to feed, and I may have to send them back. I was hoping to move and have a better life. I don't know how much longer this can last." That was all I heard. I hope she does not get rid of us. Where will Eve and I go? Maybe I'll help out more around the house and make things better for her. Then she won't want me to leave. Maybe I have to get a job, too. I am so scared.

Dear Diary, I don't know what happened, but last night that cousin Tom came into my room and started touching me all over, even between my legs on the inside. I don't know what he was doing, but he put his hand over my mouth and said that they would throw me out of the house if I told anyone, and I would have no food or place to live. I let him do it. I then started to bleed and got up after he left to clean my sheets. I can't let my aunt know my sheets were dirty. She may get rid of me.

Dear Diary, Tom comes into my bed every night now, and I cannot sleep. I am afraid when I fall asleep he will wake me up and do it again. I feel like I disappear somewhere else when it is happening. I try to get Eve to sleep with me, but some nights she won't. Last night, he was on top of me and my sister came into the room and saw us. Eve walked out of the room, and Tom had a smirk on his face that seemed evil, and then he just continued.

Anna dropped the book and fell on the bed, her heart pounding, and had a vision of Tom on top of her. She tried to breathe but was not able to get a full breath. She looked out the window to see that her mother was still gone. She picked up the phone and called 911. "I think I am having a heart attack," she said when the operator answered.

The ambulance rushed over, and as they arrived, so did her mother. The paramedics came into the house and took Anna's blood pressure.

They put an oxygen mask on her face, and she started to feel slightly better. Kathy rushed over by her side and saw the journal she had been avoiding lying open-faced on the floor. She said to the paramedic, "I think she is having a panic attack. I have them, and I know what it looks like."

Kathy went out of the room and came back in. She snuck over to Anna and whispered so the paramedic couldn't hear, "Here, Anna. Put this under your tongue. It will help you to relax."

The paramedic said, "I think we should bring her in."

"I really appreciate your concern, but I think she'll be okay now," Kathy replied.

He looked at Anna and said, "I want to take you to the emergency room to have further testing. Is that okay with you?"

Anna looked at Kathy and then at the paramedic and shook her head. "No, I'll be okay." She felt her heart slow down, and as the paramedics went outside to their vehicle after she signed her name stating she was denying treatment to be brought in, she said, "Mom, Tom raped me, too."

Kathy went pale. She took the bottle of pills out and took two. "I had no idea, Anna."

"How could you bring that monster into our house?"

Kathy went to get some water and splashed it on her face then turned to Anna and said, "I knew it wasn't a good idea to let you read that." She paused and sat next to Anna, who was feeling slightly better. "When Eve saw us and didn't help me, I thought this was normal. At some level, I felt I wanted his attention, and it was so confusing. I now know in therapy that I blamed it all on me and thought there was something wrong with me. I felt I caused it all, and until now, I blamed myself. When he called out of the blue years ago, it never dawned on me there was something wrong with him." Kathy stared at the wall as she was talking. *I am understanding my mother now*, Anna thought.

When they left, Anna felt a wave of exhaustion come over her. "I need to get some rest, Mom." Kathy stroked her hair as she fell asleep.

Anna woke up at eleven the next morning and thought, *I have not heard from Dave.* She got up and felt dizzy and had to sit back down. She looked to the floor and saw her mother's journal where she'd left it. She picked it up and closed it.

Anna went downstairs to get some coffee after she heard her father leave for work. Kathy had slept in as well and came down around noon. Anna said, "Mom, I hope you don't mind, but I want to meet Eve."

"I understand, but I won't have anything to do with it," Kathy said. "I'll give you her number and address."

Anna's phone rang, and she answered it.

"Hello, my fiancée, I had a great night. We had dinner with an overseas client, and they want to do business with us."

"Oh," Anna said.

"Did you get the guest list from your parents? My father is on my case."

"Not yet, but I will soon. I decided to stay here the week, Dave. I am spending a lot of time with my mother, and I am studying, too. I hope you don't mind?"

There was a pause, and Anna felt more tense every second that passed. "I guess so but only because I am so busy this week, too. I will call you later, then."

Anna kept looking at her mother's journal but did not pick it up or open it for the rest of the week. She was still reeling from everything she had learned. It felt like the past was clawing its way into the present. She was learning how her mother's past had influenced her present, and Anna had a feeling of dread that the same thing might be true in her own case. But she just wasn't ready to accept it.

Alia called Anna and said, "Hi, Anna. I am going to come Thursday night and stay till Saturday or Sunday."

"Okay," Anna said. "I'm so glad you're coming. We could use some good company."

Alia said, "How are you?"

Anna, impatient to hang up the phone, said, "Good, thanks. Drive safely." And hung up.

Wednesday afternoon, Anna packed a bag and went to the apartment to wait for Dave to surprise him. She went on the computer and looked at the address and number of Eve Ward that her mother had given her. As she was staring at the number, her phone rang, and she jumped, startled, before answering it. "Hi, Dave."

"What are you doing?" he asked.

"I am waiting for you. Where are you? I came for a night to surprise you."

Dave said, "I haven't been there all week since you weren't there. I can't come tonight."

"That's okay. I'll see you later." Distracted by the new knowledge about her mother's past, Anna was relieved Dave was not coming now. She needed time to contact Eve and to process everything she was learning.

Anna dialed the number. After two rings, she was ready to hang up but heard, "Hello."

"Hi," Anna said, her voice shaky, "I am looking for Eve Ward."

"Yes, this is Eve."

"This may sound strange, but do you have a sister named Kathy?" Anna asked.

"Yes, I do. Is she okay? Did something happen to her?"

"No, she is fine. I am her daughter, Anna. She gave me your name because I have been asking her to help me learn something about my extended family."

Eve said, "Oh, wow. So Kathy knows you're calling?"

"She has an idea I might. I have been asking her to tell me for years whether I have more family, but she ignored me till now. I am engaged now, so I guess she finally gave in."

"It is so nice to hear your voice, Anna. You were such a beautiful baby."

"You saw me?"

"Didn't your mother tell you?"

"Not really. Just that she had a sister. How long did you know me?"

"Anna, I don't feel right about telling you things. Your mother and I have had a difficult past, and as you probably assume correctly, she does not want anything to do with me. I respect her choice, and you need to go to her if you want to know about the past. I need to respect her wishes."

"But she gave me your name, and she knows I'll try to contact you. Could we just meet somewhere? I really want to meet you." *Why did I say that?*

Eve said, "Let me think about it for a while. Congratulations on your engagement. You know you're the same age as your mother was when she got engaged." She took a deep, worrisome breath. "I have missed you and thought about you every day, Anna. I wish you well."

Before Anna could say anything in response, Eve hung up.

Anna tried to take deep breaths to calm her panic and went to her purse to grab the bottle of pills she had taken from her mother. She poured some wine and drank a few glasses as she wrote in her own journal. *Dear Diary, I just spoke to my long-lost aunt. She knows who I am, and I know nothing about her. I feel my mother has given me a puzzle to put back together. I have a journal of pain from my mother. I can't believe she lived through having her own mother killed by her father. I understand why she wanted to protect me, but why from my aunt? What happened that she dissociated from her own sister? The more I know, the more I want to know. I hope my aunt calls me. I understand the void I have had for my whole life now. I am finally getting sleepy and will write later.*

She woke in the middle of the night with a hand on her breast that was exploring her body. She instantly kicked Dave in the gut and jumped out of bed.

He said, "Ow! What did you do that for?"

She turned on the light and said, "I'm sorry. You really scared me. I guess I was in a deep sleep and you startled me."

"Who did you think I was?" He went to the bathroom and shut the door. Anna looked over at the clock. It said 1:32. She went to the kitchen and drank some water then went to the bathroom and came back to bed. Dave was already in bed with the lights off. Feeling guilty, she moved her hand over his underwear, but he put his hand out to stop her.

"Go to sleep, Anna."

Anna turned over in bed with an emptiness in her stomach, thinking, *Why doesn't he ask me what I am thinking and why I reacted the way I did? He never asks me about anything. "Just go to sleep Anna, it's late. We'll talk in the morning." That's all he ever says.* She tossed and turned the rest of the night, finally going to sleep on the couch with the television on.

Anna woke early and went to the kitchen to make some breakfast before Dave woke up. She had the eggs and toast ready and was pouring the coffee as he made his way into the kitchen.

"Morning. I thought we could have some breakfast together."

"Thanks," he said as he reached for his iPad to read the Detroit news. He kept reading as they sat down together.

"Dave, could you put that away?"

"Anna, give me a minute."

She sat at the table and waited, watching him. *I am going to be married to him,* she thought. *Will it be like this?*

He looked over at her. "What is it?"

"You said you weren't coming last night."

He said, "Obviously I changed my mind when I knew you were here."

"Well, I found out I have an aunt. My mother told me, and I called her yesterday." He waited, and she continued. "She won't talk to me, though. I have so many questions, Dave, and no one will tell me what happened."

Anna stared at him, waiting for a response as if her life depended on it, and he finally took the cue and said, "I'm sure there is a good reason they want to keep you out of it. Could you tell me why you kicked me when I came into bed last night?"

Anna had forgotten about that and quickly thought, *I can't tell him about Tom.* She said, "You startled me. I'm not used to living with you yet, I guess. I'll have to get used to you coming home late and waking me up like that."

He nodded and said, "Yes, you will. I like waking you up like that."

She tried to change the subject. "Will you come for Christmas Eve, on Thursday?"

He said, "I'll be able to come around eight. We should go to my father's first and then to your parents' house."

Anna, thinking of Alia, said, "I would like to hang out at my house because Alia will be there without Luke."

"We are family now. What about my family?"

She said, "You're right. I can hang out with her on Friday. We'll go to both."

He kissed her and said, "I'll call you later." Then he headed off to work.

Anna put the dishes away and took a shower. As she turned off her shower, she heard a text come in. She dried herself off quickly and read it. "Hi, could you meet me at Starbucks today at noon? Eve."

Anna thought of what Dave had said, but quickly her curiosity to know the past overcame her, and she wrote, "Yes, I would like that. What do you look like?"

"I know what you look like. I'll find you. See you soon."

So many questions flooded Anna's mind as she tried to get dressed. She tried to study for her nursing certification test, but her thoughts raced back to her questions. *Why did she change her mind? What is she going to say?* Time seemed to stand still as she waited for noon to come.

She finally left and went to the Starbucks at eleven. She arrived and scoped out the best seat for watching people come in the door and for privacy. She got some water, not wanting caffeine to stimulate her any more than she already was. She played a game on her phone to calm her. She felt an urge to call Jeff, which seemed strange to her. After a while, she froze as she saw her father's mistress come in the shop. She wanted to disappear and tried to hide, but this person was walking right to her. Her anger led to confusion and then to disbelief.

"Anna," the woman said as she sat down at the table. "I am your aunt Eve."

Anna felt hatred for the first time in her life. She would have liked to punch Eve, but instead she ran out the door and kept running until she felt exhausted. She had just made it back to the apartment when her phone rang. It was Eve. *Should I give her a chance?* she wondered. Finally, she picked up.

"Anna, thank you for picking up the phone. I know you are confused and angry, but I'd like a chance to explain."

"You don't deserve that," Anna said. "I don't want to know you. Please don't call me again."

She hung up, and tears spilled from her eyes as she thought of her mom. *How do you do that to your own sister? My mother is her only family. Maybe I'll understand better as I read.*

Dave called then. "Hi, Anna. I know you've been wanting more involvement in the wedding planning, so I made arrangements for us to meet with the wedding planner. Next Saturday at ten, okay?"

Anna, caught off guard, said, "Oh, well, I think that will work."

Dave seemed irked that she wasn't more grateful. "I thought you would be happier about it."

"I'm just studying and feeling overwhelmed with all the material," she said.

"Okay, take a break and get some food. Are you going to your parents' tonight?"

She looked at the time and said, "Yes, I'm going to study for the certification exam and go to my parents'. Alia is coming later today. I'll see you tomorrow. What time is the dinner?"

"Six, sharp."

Anna went home to find that Alia had canceled her visit. Anna called her, and Alia said, "Hi, Anna. I guess you heard. I started driving and my car—well, it's old, and the transmission or something went. Luke already left, so I don't have a car. I don't have the money for a rental, and now I have to get it fixed. I feel awful."

"I'm so sorry, Alia," Anna said. But secretly she was relieved because now she would be able to talk to her mother about everything that had happened with Eve. "We'll see you soon. Just get your car fixed and spend time with your family."

"Thanks for understanding. Your mother insisted she pay for a rental, but I refused it. I don't feel it's right. She is so sweet."

"She misses you. So do I. Merry Christmas, and I'll see you soon." Alia started to talk, but Anna pretended she couldn't hear her and hung up. She then opened her mother's journal, but she felt sick. She started to cough and sneeze and then a few hours later she came down with a fever.

Anna drove to her parents' and barely made it to the house. Kathy came out and helped her up to bed before taking her temperature; it was 103 degrees. Anna took some Nyquil and passed out. She woke the next day, and Kathy called Dave to tell him she was sick. Anna then took the phone. "Hi. I'm sorry, but I don't want to get everyone sick. I feel horrible. Say hi to your family."

"I'll check in with you later, then. I'm really disappointed, you know. This doesn't look good for you, not to come."

"Would you rather me come like this, sick as a dog?"

"No, we can't afford to get sick. Just get some rest."

Anna hung up and felt some relief. *I'm glad I don't have to get all dressed up and try to fit in and talk about nothing. I do feel horrible.* Her shakes got worse as she started to vomit. Kathy took her to the emergency room, and it was packed.

"I'm sorry, Mom. This is the worst Christmas Eve."

"No," Kathy said. "I have my little girl. That is all I need. Now, we have to get you better. You have worn yourself out."

Later, Anna wrote in her journal, *Dear Journal, I have not written in a while and so much has happened. I decided not to do anything with Eve or my father's mistress. I won't tell my mother. I don't want to hurt her anymore. She has been through so much. I wonder if she knows that I know. I still wonder so much. I hate my father. How does one do that to his own wife? I wondered why she seemed so familiar. She wrote me that note. There is something so wrong with my family. I feel so tense and anxious all the time. I will try to focus on getting married and the happy things happening. I hear about being mindful and living for the now. I will try to do that.*

CHAPTER 14

Anna's Wedding Planning

Anna spent the next week studying and looking for jobs. She had an interview set up on the following Friday, a day after she took the nursing board exam. She purposefully left the journal at her mother's so she would not be enticed to read more and lose focus.

One afternoon, Anna was studying material on liver function, but her mind kept wandering. *Why can't I stop thinking of my mother? Does she know about her sister? How could Eve think she can justify what she is doing to me? I need to focus. I have to stop allowing these thoughts to consume me.* The phone rang, and she answered, relieved to get out of her own head.

"Hi, Dave. How are you?"

"I noticed that you have an interview at U of M this Friday. I think you should cancel it. You have a lot of planning to do for the wedding, and we'll be moving soon to West Bloomfield."

"Dave, can we talk about this later? I am studying and want to stay on track."

"Just tell me that you'll cancel it. That will take your mind off of that stress."

Anna thought, *He won't let this go until he gets the answer he wants.* She said, "I may go just to get some practice with interviewing. I'll see."

"I can help you build those skills. You don't need to waste everyone's time over there."

Anna sighed. *I don't want to fight, and he is not giving in.* "Okay, I'll cancel it."

"Okay, good luck on your studying. Also, Saturday morning is the day you need to come over and meet with the wedding planner. She'll go into all the details with you. Her name is Rachel."

"Okay, Dave," Anna said. "I'll talk to you later."

She hung up the phone then called her mother. "Hi, Mom."

"Hi," Kathy said.

"Could I come to see you this Saturday night?"

Kathy sounded surprised but happy about the idea. "Anytime. You know that, silly."

"Okay," Anna said. "I have to go to Dave's house in the morning to meet with the wedding planner, and I'll come in the afternoon."

Kathy said, "Great. Good luck on your exam and interview. I am so excited for you. You are fulfilling the things I wanted to do but never did. I always wanted to work for U of M. I'm so proud of you."

Anna said, "Thanks, Mom. I'll talk to you later." *I can't tell her I cancelled it.*

On Thursday, Anna took the certification exam at a computer. She was nervous but tried to stay calm by breathing and focusing on her mother and how great it would feel to make her proud. When she finished, the proctor said, "You'll have the results tomorrow, online."

Anna exhaled. "Thanks. I'm glad that is over."

On the way home, she called Jen. "Hey, are you busy? Can I stop by?"

"Come over in an hour. I'd love to see you."

Anna went home and had a glass of wine. She picked up the phone to cancel the interview but put it down before she dialed. *Maybe I'll go through with it after all, but just not say anything.*

She went to her old house and saw both Jen and Lori. Lori said, "I miss you. How are you?"

Lori and Jen sat next to each other, and Anna thought, *They look like best friends. I feel so weird here with them.* "I'm okay," she said. "I'm meeting with the wedding planner Saturday."

"What about your bachelorette party? Have you decided?" Jen asked.

"I've been distracted by taking my board exam. I'm sorry."

"Oh, right!" Jen said. "How did that go? You'll be my guide when I have to take them."

Anna said, "I did okay. It took four hours for me. I felt they asked some ridiculous questions, but I heard they have some test questions for the future that don't count. I hope that was those. My biggest worry now is about the wedding and how many people Dave's father is inviting."

"I will be there, too, remember," Jen said. "And your other friends. We will help you through it."

"Thanks so much," Anna said. "You're both such great friends. Here's my brother's girlfriend's number, before I forget. Her name is Alia, and I want her to come to the party."

Jen said, "I am happy to call her. Can you let me and Lori just surprise you?"

Dave can't say anything if I had nothing to do with planning it, she thought and said, "That actually would be great. I wish I could hang out longer, but I need to head out. I'll see you guys later."

Saturday morning, Anna drove to Dave's house, speeding in order to get there on time. But despite her rush, she slowed down as she walked up to the door, mesmerized by the vast openness of the front staircase and enormous iron-gated door, and rang the bell. She hoped Jake wasn't there. Ever since Jen had confided all the family details to Anna, she had been nervous about seeing her future father-in-law again.

Harold opened the door, reminding her of a smaller, nicer Frankenstein, with his pale face, enormous hands and feet, and intimidating size. But he had a pleasant face and a kind smile. In fact, she realized with a start, out of everyone in Dave's family, it was Harold who was nicest to her.

"Good morning, Anna. It's nice to see you. Please follow me." She felt calmed by his presence and gladly followed him, looking at the magnificent wooden ceiling and the dark, ominous artwork she'd missed the last time she was there. In the dining room, the table was covered with books. Harold said, "Can I bring you something to drink?"

"No," Anna said, smiling at him. "Thanks."

He said, smiling, "I'll bring you some tea, then."

Anna sat and waited, looking around the room as if she were in a museum. A woman shouted, "I'll be right there."

That's weird, Anna thought. Before she could respond, a woman in her mid-thirties with a tight dress and high heels on, stunning by all accounts, said, "Oh, you must be the bride, Anna. I am Rachel, and I have lots to show you. Please feel free to look over these suggestions."

Anna said, "It's nice to meet you."

"Okay, well, there's a lot to get through. Let's start with the flowers." She opened a book to a page already marked. "Here are a few pictures of the approved flowers. Which one would you like?"

"Can I look at the other pages?"

"I was instructed to stay on the pages marked," Rachel said.

Marked by whom? Anna wondered.

"There are so many choices. We've narrowed it down to make it easier. Believe me—it's helpful."

Anna thought about asking, *Who is we?* But she decided, *I already know who that is.* "I was picturing yellow flowers," she said.

"Oh, I'm sorry, but that color is not approved. Why don't we move on to the cake?"

Anna held back tears as she thought, *I'm not involved in choosing anything for my own wedding.* Rachel was organized and moved quickly through every detail of the event.

"There just are not many options to choose from. Who approved this list?"

"Jake—I mean, Mr. Lawrence—has approved these things. Do you have your dress yet?"

"I don't, but I'm excited to go shopping with my mother."

Rachel opened up a book of dresses. "Pick out a few that you like from here." Noticing Anna was shifting in her chair, she added, "If you don't like any, then let me know. I will work with you. This really will be a magnificent event, even if it might not be what you pictured for your wedding." Anna looked at Rachel, who had a sympathetic look on her face.

Dave finally entered the room and came over to where Anna was sitting. "There are so many things to do. How is the bride and the planning going?"

Rachel said, "We already went through the list, and she has great ideas."

But Anna couldn't pretend to be happy. She paused and thought, *Dave, none of these ideas are mine. I'm picking from a list your father made? This is not what we talked about. I can't say any of that or he'll cancel the wedding.* She took a sip of the tea that had appeared seemingly from nowhere and said, "I wish I had more to choose from, Dave."

Dave put his hands on her shoulders and looked at her. "It will all work out and look fabulous. Would you ladies like some lunch?"

Anna wanted to leave. Feeling nervous, she said, "I made some plans to visit with my mother since it's on the way home. Will you be home tonight?"

"I'll leave you two alone," Rachel said. "Anna, here is my card, and please let me know about the dresses. Congratulations again, and you'll make a lovely bride."

When she left the room, Dave turned to Anna. "Everyone is working so hard for us, and I wish you were more grateful. You need to see what you have, Anna."

Anna left the room to find the bathroom and saw Sue and Rachel talking quietly. They both waved Anna over, and Rachel said, "Anna, this is a stressful time for every couple. Please be patient. I have known Dave for a long time, and he is under a lot of pressure."

"I know you are trying to help, but I need a minute," Anna replied. She went to the bathroom and heard them talking but could not make out what they were saying. She really wanted a drink. She finished up in the bathroom and came out.

"Hi, Anna. Could you sit down with me and chat for a minute?" Sue asked.

Anna nodded and followed her, feeling calmed by her presence. Maybe another woman would understand where she was coming from. After all, Sue had once been new to this family, too. She said, "Chamomile tea with lemon and honey. I love the smell and then the taste, and it's so calming. Do you ever practice yoga?" Anna shook her head no. "Now, I can imagine you have just finished school, taken your boards, moved in with Dave, and are planning a wedding. Do I have that right?"

Anna nodded, knowing her anxiety showed on her face.

"Wow, not to mention you're only twenty-one, right?" Anna nodded. "You have a lot going for you. You are a beautiful young girl and educated now. I'm sure everyone thinks you're crazy for getting married so young, but I do understand. It's not your age. But you *are* afraid Dave will leave you if you don't get married. Aren't you?"

Anna felt a surge of tense energy. *That is quite harsh. Why would she say that?*

"Well, if you really do want to be with him, you need to make it easy on yourself. Jake is a powerful person in the business community. He knows a lot of people and has influence that is shared and will be passed down to Dave and Tom. There are good things about being in the family, but you'll have to sacrifice a lot, too. Laura has understood that, and she and Tom have a good marriage. You are a smart girl, and I'm sure you're catching on."

Anna thought for a moment and said, "What you're saying is that I have to accept that Jake is planning the whole wedding and go along with it?"

Sue said, "Unless you want to make life difficult for yourself. The other option is to break up now. That is still an option for you. Although, from the look on your face, it isn't anymore."

Anna wanted to ask more questions but didn't want to know the answers. She shook her head no then got up and said, "Thanks, Sue, for the talk and the tea. I need to go see my mother now."

Sue got up and hugged her. Anna went in the dining room where Rachel and Dave were still talking over the plans, and she said, "Sorry about that outburst. I've just been stressed about my boards and moving and the wedding. Rachel, could you just pick out the details? I trust you have great taste."

Rachel said, "Are you sure about that? I would like your input."

"Well, why don't you show me the dresses?" Rachel gave her a choice of ten dresses, and Anna chose one at random. "Could I try that one on?"

Dave said, "That's my girl." He picked Anna up and twirled her around and said, "I can't wait to dance with you at the wedding."

Sue stood in the corner of the room, watching, and Anna noticed that her smile was very odd. Anna thought, *Is Sue envious of me that I am marrying into the family or that she had escaped a life tied to the Lawrence family? I can't figure her out!*

Anna drove up to her parents' house and watched her mother washing dishes through the kitchen window. She noticed her mother had dark wrinkles on the sides of her eyes and her frown lines. She saw that her hair had grown grayer. Kathy wasn't dyeing it anymore like she used to. Anna suddenly felt a deep love for her mother. *I need to finish reading the journals,* she thought. *Does my mother know Eve is still with my father? Why does she stay with him? Why do I feel strange about the way Sue was talking? Should I listen to everyone and leave Dave because I am so young?*

Kathy hugged her when she came in and said, "I saw you sitting in your car. What were you doing out there?"

"Watching you and thinking. Mom, please sit down. I wanted to talk to you about something." Kathy poured some water for them both and sat down with her undivided attention. Anna took a sip and said, "I went to meet with Eve. At first she didn't want to meet with me, but then she texted me and said she'd changed her mind. I know you probably don't want to hear this, but I need to tell someone. The woman I saw with Dad in Florida and in the restaurant—well, it was Eve. I'm so confused that Dad would have an affair for years with his own sister-in-law. I feel I don't know anything. I'm so sorry to tell you this."

Kathy sat down, and her eyes dropped to the floor. Her hair fell forward, like a curtain covering her face. Anna could not tell whether she was shocked by the news. Finally, Kathy looked Anna in the eyes and said, "Anna, life can get complicated, and I'm working on myself now, finally. I didn't know what you told me, but I have known he has had affairs, and I knew years ago that he had one with Eve but I didn't know it was still going on. To be honest, I don't blame him because I chose not to have sex with him. We have not slept together since your brother was two years old. As you are reading my journal, you must realize that I have a lot of demons I'm working through. I should've done this a long time ago, but as my therapist tells me, I wasn't ready or open at that time. One has to be ready to cope with harsh realities and be strong enough to learn. I'm learning that my journey is not over and that I continue to have choices to make. I understand why I have made my past decisions, and that helps me to not beat myself up over them. I have a lot of guilt over leaving my sister in that house to watch what happened to my mother alone. We were always together, and even though Eve told me to run, I felt I should've stayed with her. I'm learning that I was only a frightened, abused little child, and I don't have to punish myself the rest of my life for that. I now see me as a survivor of abuse and that I just adapted to things happening without any guidance and did the best I could. That is how I allowed or accepted your father in my life. I was just used to a bad situation and accepted it because my self-esteem was so poor." Kathy stood up and started to stretch and then relax and paused for a minute. The tension in the air came down, and she then continued.

"I also know Eve is really messed up. Maybe she's punishing me in a way because I left her alone, scared. I may never know.

"Now that I know what happened to you with my cousin, I think maybe it would be good for you to go to therapy and deal with your past, instead of waiting till you're my age. I don't want you to continue to make the same mistakes over and over because you haven't dealt with your past, and I know now there is a consequence to how your father treated you and Luke. My main regret now is how your childhood affected you both."

Anna got up and poured herself a glass of wine. "I know you're right. I will after the wedding. I don't think I'm ready right now."

Kathy said, "Don't you see what I'm trying to tell you? You need to go *before* you make the decision to marry him."

"Mom, I'm not you. Dave is not Dad. I have decided and feel good about this decision. I'm so glad you are figuring it out for yourself. I love Dave, and he loves me. I know I'm young, but the choice not to marry him doesn't seem to be a choice for me."

Kathy said, "Doesn't that worry you?" She shook her head. "Well, promise me after you get married you will go."

"I promise. I think I'm going to go take a nap. This conversation has made me feel so exhausted. I know why you take so many naps now."

Anna gave Kathy a big hug and went to her room to write. *Could there be any more skeletons in my family's closet? Does everyone have this kind of past, but no one knows about it? What are the skeletons in Dave's family? Could I be marrying Dave because of some unresolved issues from my past? When I think of breaking up, it makes me feel so sick, so I must be doing the right thing.* She put the book down and finished her third glass of wine from a bottle she had hidden in her closet. A few minutes later, she fell asleep.

Her phone woke her up an hour later. Dave said, "Hi, Anna. I'm sorry that my father has most of the wedding already planned. I feel I'm in the middle. He pulls me into his way of thinking. After we get married, it will be you and me. We will make our own decisions once we're married."

"I love you," Anna said.

"Did I wake you?"

"Yes, I was taking a nap."

Dave said, "I'll meet you back at our apartment."

Anna thought, *I want to stay here, and I hope he doesn't argue with me. What can I say to make this go smooth?* "Dave, if you wouldn't mind, I'm tired, and my mother sort of needs some company with my father being gone. Can we catch up tomorrow? I'd really appreciate it."

Dave paused, and Anna could feel some tension but waited until he said, "Okay, I'll see you tomorrow. But you need to make this up to me."

The next morning, Anna came to the kitchen and smelled bacon and eggs and found her mother humming. She watched her glide through the kitchen, a sight she hadn't seen since she was a young girl.

Kathy saw Anna and gave her a hug. "Good morning, Anna. I hope you're hungry. I love having you here. I was thinking that I'd like to come to see your apartment next week sometime and maybe go dress shopping?"

Anna's mood immediately deflated as she thought, *I wanted this experience to shop for dresses. How can I let her down easy?* "Mom, I have met with the wedding planner and chosen a dress already."

Kathy seemed puzzled. "You tried this dress on already?"

Anna said, "No, I guess she's going to get one for me so I can try it on. In that case, there is no reason we can't go for the fun of it. Who knows? Maybe I'd like a different dress better. Hold on, Mom. I just remembered that the exam scores are probably up now." She logged on to the website. "Thank God. I passed my exam, Mom!"

Kathy kissed her forehead with warmth that made Anna feel safe. She had that feeling so seldom these days. "Of course you did, silly. I never had a doubt in my mind that you would."

She quickly texted Dave her news, but he didn't respond. "He must be in a meeting," Anna said.

Dan came in and put his coat up and his bag in the laundry room and grabbed a water bottle. Kathy said, "Hi, Dan. How was your trip?"

Dan looked up from his phone and said, "It was fine."

Kathy said, "Anna is here, if you didn't see her."

Anna just felt anger with his presence and could only think of him and Eve together and how nice he treated her in the restaurant.

Kathy pressed on with the discussion even though it was apparent that Dan had no interest. "Oh Dan, Anna passed her nursing board exam."

Anna gave him a moment to respond, and when he didn't, she blurted out, "Dad, are you going to go out with Eve tonight?" He choked on his water, and Kathy stumbled on her feet.

Dan looked to the window and, with no eye contact or any acknowledgment of what Anna had said, responded, "I'll be home late." He walked out, holding his coat in his hand.

Anna helped her mother up from the floor and said, "I'm sorry, Mom. It just came out."

Kathy put her hands on her shoulders and said, "Anna, sit down. I'm working on this in therapy, and when I'm ready, I'll make a change. You need to have patience with the process and remember this is my choice and marriage. Can you do that for me?"

Anna shook her head and said, "I'm sorry, Mom. I'm just so angry with him for what he's done to all of us." She paused and said, "Well, mostly to you, Mom."

"Another reason for you to go to therapy," Kathy said. "You have a lot to figure out so that your childhood traumas don't play a role in your decisions in a negative way."

Anna poured some wine, and Kathy watched her, as it was nine a.m. She took the glass out of Anna's hands and threw it down the drain. "I need you to know something about Tom. In therapy, I realized I buried those memories to cope, and when he came that night, I must have buried them so deeply they didn't even come up for me when I saw him. Do you remember I slept on the couch? I didn't even take a sleeping pill, which was the first time in a long time. Somewhere I was either protecting you or me. I have beat myself up that I somehow fell asleep when that monster came into your room. I'm trying to work on forgiving myself because it's in the past, but I do need your forgiveness. My mind can't even think of it."

Anna put her hand on her mother's cheek and brushed her hair away from her face. "I know, Mom. I don't blame you. We can even learn from bad things in our lives. I was angry with you, but now I understand a little more."

Kathy put her arm around Anna. "I wanted to protect you from the bad things of the world. I never wanted you to see any abuse. I think I stayed with your father because he never physically hurt me. I always said I would leave if he laid a finger on you or me. I didn't understand that the emotional abuse was just as bad. I always avoided giving him something to be angry at to prevent an argument or escalation, which is something my mother never did. And look what happened to her."

"Mom, I'm understanding more now," Anna said. "I would not say there was no physical abuse, though."

"Anna, what I experienced as a child—well, let's just say I know your childhood was better," Kathy said. "There's one thing before you get married that I want you to ask yourself. Family patterns tend to repeat, I'm learning, and I don't want you to repeat my mistakes. Ask yourself, 'Can I live with the negative aspects of Dave?' Take a long, hard look at his faults, because they're not going anywhere, and see if they are something that you can live with for the rest of your life. I wish I had done that, but I had no one to guide or support me. The warning signs were in front of my face, but I had no one and was in a bad state when I met your father. I was happy someone even wanted to be with me. I was so broken, and he knew how vulnerable I was and used that to his advantage to manipulate me. Maybe it was not intentional because he also has his messed-up childhood, and past muscle memories making his decisions."

Anna suddenly felt sick with the panic she had felt before and wanted to leave the house. She gave Kathy a big hug and said, "Thanks, Mom. I will. I have to go now. I'll call you to make plans for you to come later." She grabbed her bag with her mother's journal in it and went home.

Anna arrived at the apartment and checked her phone. There was a text message from Dave. "Congratulations, Anna. I had no doubt." Anna was happy to see this.

Next, she checked her email and noticed one from U of M. "You missed your interview on Friday. I am not sure what happened, but I was looking forward to it. I have to assume this means you found another position. Good luck to you in the future. I enjoyed our brief conversation."

Anna's heart sank. *I cannot believe I forgot to cancel the interview. What is wrong with me? You never want to burn your bridges.* She wrote back, "Dear Elizabeth, I am sorry about my oversight. I thought I had canceled the interview, but I see that I never got word to you. I am getting married, and we decided to move to West Bloomfield. I need to look for jobs closer to our new home. I am so sorry I missed the opportunity to meet you. Maybe our paths will cross again in the future. Sincerely, Anna." She felt humiliated.

She closed her tablet, grabbed a beer, and jumped on the couch with her mother's journal. She was actually glad she didn't have to plan a wedding. There was so much pressure to make all the perfect choices that would please Dave and his father. Letting them take the lead was a relief. She opened up the journal to read.

Dear Diary, Last night I was home alone. Tom came into my room, and I forgot to put up my cardboard box by the door I use to wake me up if someone comes into the room. I am so angry with myself. He caught me sleeping and pushed himself into me and it hurt so much. I screamed so loud that our neighbor walking past the house heard and came running into the house that was unlocked and into my bedroom. He grabbed Tom and threw him against the wall. Tom ran out the front door so fast. Ted screamed, "You better never come back here." The police came over and asked me all sorts of personal questions. I lied to them so they would not take me out of my aunt's home. Where would I go?

Just then, Dave came into Anna's room. "Hey, surprise! I came back early and got some dinner for you passing your test."

Anna jumped to her feet. "You startled me, thanks."

Dave put a box on the counter. "The hall had a cancellation, so we moved the wedding to April fourteenth. Since we have everything already planned, I didn't think it would matter. We asked your father already."

Anna knew there was no point in arguing with him once he made a decision, but she couldn't help but say, "But it's already February twelfth."

"Well, the sooner the better," Dave said. "What's wrong? I thought you'd be excited."

Anna thought, *Why is he in such a rush? I feel so out of control. Is this a negative aspect of Dave that my mother told me to look at and see if I can live with it?*

She looked at him as he was pacing the room and becoming impatient as she said, "I am. It's all just going so fast."

He looked at the journal and tried to read the front cover. "What are you reading?"

Anna dropped the journal then stooped to pick it up. *If he knew how messed up my family and I really are,* she thought, *he'd never marry me.* "Just a book my mother gave me," she said. She set the book on the couch upside down and put her arms around him, distracting him. "I can't wait for you to call me Anna Faye Lawrence."

He kissed her lips and said, "That does sound nice."

She then got a text. Dave picked up her phone and read it. "Hi, Anna. Since your date moved up, I arranged a dinner for Feb. 30. I checked with Alia and she was good with that date. The rest is a surprise. Jen."

Anna, feeling a little violated that he'd taken the liberty of reading her texts, said, "She seems to know things before I do."

Dave went to get a beer. "You know we're friends, and she'll always know our family. She swung by when my father was making the changes. She goes by the house when I'm not there. She always has since our parents—well, mothers—were close." He took a sip and stared at the floor with his sandy brown hair glistening in the sun coming through the window. His lips curled under as if he was about to cry. *He looks so sad,* Anna thought. He looked deep in thought and said, "You better get used to having her around. She is your friend, too. Besides, she's a reminder of how we met."

I wonder what he's thinking about, Anna thought. *I can't wait to know what is inside that beautiful mind.*

"Let's eat," Dave said, shaking off the dark thoughts. "By the way, we need to think about our honeymoon as well. I also brought in some pictures of houses for you to look at. I have a realtor, and we went over some houses in the West Bloomfield area. I'd like to be on a lake if possible and also near my father. It would make things easier for work."

Anna felt hot all of a sudden and lost her appetite. Her heart beat sped up instantly as he was talking. *What is he talking about? Is he going to plan my whole life and I have no involvement except to just be present?* "Dave, you have to involve me when you are talking to a realtor. It feels like I am just along for the ride and not involved in my own life."

"Anna, look at the pictures. I'm involving you now. I haven't decided on anything. You can't be so sensitive. We've already decided where, so now we just need to pick out a house. Amanda, the realtor, will be calling you to set up an appointment." As he walked toward the bathroom, she heard his phone ping with a text.

Anna opened the folder he'd left on the table to see magnificent brick and stone houses with double front doors and four-car garages. Dave yelled from the bathroom, "Oh, and if we don't like any of those, we can also build a house."

He came out and saw Anna's face. "Dave, what happened to the idea of a starter home? How can we, I mean you, afford a house like this?"

He put his hand over hers. "Anna, from now on, you let me worry about the money. Anything you want is yours. I told you that working hard pays off."

Anna looked down at one of the houses and said, "I think we need to start off with a much smaller house. I'm only twenty-one, and I don't want the responsibility of a house like this."

"I saw that list of hospitals and jobs you had written down," he said. "We have too much going on for you to work now. Wait till we get settled down, honey. I don't want to move and move again. We will have help to take care of the house, too. Let me take care of you. We'll have more time together once I'm closer to work." He kissed her forehead and then her lips and said, "Why don't you clean the dishes and we can watch a movie before we go to bed?"

The next day, Anna woke to find that Dave was already gone. Rachel called her. "Hi, Anna, can you come over to Jake's house to try on the dresses today?"

Anna quickly thought about how she had been planning to spend time sending out her resume. But now that Dave was insisting she not work, the efforts felt pointless. "Okay. I'm going to see if my mother can come, though."

"Would it be better for me to come there?" Rachel asked.

"Yes, please, that would be great."

"Okay, then, about one?"

"Great." Anna quickly called her mother. "Hi, Mom. Can you come over today so we can go have some lunch? Rachel is coming over with some dresses for me to try on, and I'd like you to be here."

"Okay," Kathy said. "I do have to leave about four, though. I have some plans tonight."

Anna put the folder down. "Oh."

She said, "Well, I'm finally making some friends now. Your father is in Florida, so I am working on having more support and started a class and met some classmates."

Anna saw another call coming in. "That's wonderful, Mom. I can't wait to hear about it. See you at eleven thirty." She picked up the other line. "Hello?"

"Hi, this is Amanda Callaway. I'm the realtor working for you, and I wanted to set up a time this week to go see these houses with you. Would tomorrow work?"

I guess he didn't listen that I want a starter home. Anna's heart began to race. *Things are moving too fast*, she thought. But she couldn't bring herself to speak up. "Okay," she said, without looking at her calendar.

"Great. I'll meet you at my office around ten, and we can go from there."

Anna sat down and remembered her text from Jen. Instead of texting back, she decided to call her. "Hi, Jen. I just wanted to say thanks for organizing all that with Alia. It sounds nice."

"What's going on?" Jen asked. "You sound upset."

Should I be telling her anything? It seems to always get back to Dave, she thought. "Everything is moving so fast. I feel I can't keep up. It's all good things but a lot of changes."

Jen said, "Oh, but those houses are beautiful. Once Dave knows what he wants, he is impatient. I guess I could see how overwhelming it all may be."

Anna thought, *I bet she even saw the houses herself.* "Well, I'll be okay. Just venting a little. Isn't Alia nice?"

"She sounds really nice. I can't wait for the dinner. We'll have a great time. I'm sure you have a lot to do, so I'll catch you later."

Anna hung up and thought, *I can't tell her anything that I don't want Dave to know. I can't trust her now.* She went to shower and took her time, enjoying the feel of the hot water on her back. When she was brushing her teeth, she heard the doorbell. She quickly dried her mouth and opened the door. When she saw her mother, she started to cry hysterically.

Kathy came in and shut the door and held her. "Honey, what's wrong?" She led her to the couch, and they sat as she embraced her daughter and let her cry.

After ten minutes, Anna finally settled down, and for the first time, she felt her mother understood without telling her. Kathy stroked Anna's hair and said, "Tell me how I can help you."

Anna said, "You already have. I'm nervous about how fast everything is moving." She showed her mom the house pictures and the invitation with the new date on it.

Kathy said, "Anna, you need to remember you have a big part in what happens. If you want to wait, then you should let him know. If he loves you, he will understand and be patient. There is no rush."

Anna quickly remembered what Dave had told her about breaking up if she wasn't ready to get married now. It was now or never, and he would not compromise, she knew. She said, "No, I'm sure this is what I want."

Anna felt her mother examining her face differently, and she wanted her mother to believe her even though she doubted herself. Kathy said, "Anna, I have learned so much in therapy. I never spoke up in my marriage. I have to own my own complacency and allowing him to control things. Please learn from my mistakes. The earlier in the relationship you speak up, the better. You have a voice, too, and he is establishing the patterns in your marriage and taking over. If you don't communicate your thoughts and feelings, then you are allowing the pattern to emerge as well. I have learned I need to teach people how I want to be treated. Relationships are complex, and you both bring a whole different perspective and experience to the marriage. I'm learning, even though it is late, that I can teach even your father how I want to be treated. I need to have clear thoughts on what I want and what will make me happy. After all, I am responsible for my happiness, and you are responsible for yours."

Anna exhaled as if she had been holding her breath for the entire time her mother was talking. "It's so difficult. He seems to always have a response that I cannot counter. He makes sense at the time, and I end up agreeing with him. I do think he means well, Mom." Anna, realizing her mother knew her too well, thought, *I guess I can no longer talk to her about Dave.*

Kathy walked over and helped Anna to stand up. "Here follow me and let's focus on our muscles and let's reach to the sky and stretch. Feel the burn in your arms and legs and back. Focus on your breath. Pause Anna. You are safe. How do you feel?" Anna allowed herself to relax and said, "Really calm actually. I am surprised."

Kathy went to the kitchen and got a water bottle. She looked out the window as she said, "Anna, it's okay. I'm always here, and you need to learn from your own journey. I was reminded not to assume that our experiences are the same, and you need to learn from your own mistakes unless you are open to learning from mine. Please, don't shut me out. Let's eat something; I'm hungry."

Kathy was enjoying her food and lightheartedly muttered, "Anna, did you know that when we notice our bodies, they tell us what our emotions are doing? When we are tense, our stress hormones like cortisol levels are activated and we feel on guard. We exert energy being tense when there is no reason to be. That is why I asked you to stretch; that brings down our cortisol levels, and we feel calmer and our thoughts become clearer, and we stop reacting and start deciding cognitively. I think that is so cool, and it helps me so much."

Anna paused and allowed her muscles to relax; then she looked at the clock and tensed up.

"Oh, we're late."

Kathy said, "Relax and stay calm. Just text Rachel that we'll be a few minutes late. See, problem solved. No stress."

They arrived back at the apartment after lunch, and she saw Rachel waiting in her blue BMW talking on her phone. Anna waved to her to come inside, and she opened the door, holding the dresses. Anna, empathizing with her heavy load, went over to help. "Thanks so much for coming over here."

"I like it out this way," Rachel said. "I'm happy to come. I have ten dresses and my book in case you don't like any of them. I did bring the one you picked out, too." Anna helped her carry them in, and they hung up the dresses in her closet.

Kathy came out of the bathroom, and Anna said, "Rachel, this is my mother, Kathy."

Rachel shook her hand in a nurturing, comforting way. "So nice to meet the mother of the bride. You are as lovely as the bride."

Anna saw her mother blush and allow the handshake to go on for a few extra seconds. "So nice to meet you as well. Are you planning the whole wedding?"

Rachel said, "Well, I know the family's taste. I planned his other son's wedding, and my mother planned Jake and Katrina's." She looked at Anna and said, "Should we try on the one you chose first or last?"

Anna said, "How about I go into the other room and pick one out?"

Rachel followed her, and Anna said, "It's okay. I can get this. I'll let you know if I need help."

"My independent daughter," Kathy said.

"How refreshing," Rachel said.

Anna pulled one of the dresses over her head but struggled a little with the collar. She finally wiggled into the dress and called out, "Mom, could you come zip me up?"

Kathy went into the room to help. As she came out, Rachel said, "Wow. You are stunning."

Anna looked in the long mirror hanging in the foyer and imagined how she might style her tousled, shoulder-length hair and accentuate her full lips. She imagined what it would be like to walk down the aisle in this dress. "Well, is this a maybe?"

Kathy said, "That's a beautiful dress. How much is something like that with all the glitter and sequins down the sides?"

Rachel smiled. "I'm not supposed to tell you the cost. I do love that dress." She followed Anna into the bedroom and said, "Let me un-zip this one, at least."

While Anna was picking out the next dress, she overheard Rachel ask Kathy, "So do you have any other children?"

"Yes, I have a son who is a few years younger than Anna." She sipped her coffee. "Can I get you something to drink?"

Rachel said, "No, thank you. So your only daughter is getting married."

Kathy said, "Don't remind me. They grow up so fast. One day you are blowing their noses and the next you are picking out a wedding dress."

"I'm sure that it's difficult to let go," Rachel said. "My mother was friends with Katrina, Dave's mother." Tears filled Rachel's dark brown eyes as Anna came out wearing the second dress, "Oh, wow, you are so beautiful."

Anna tried to twirl around in the dress and said, "Did you know her, Dave's mother?"

Rachel got up and fixed the dress at the bottom. "I didn't know her well, just that my mother was close to her. I do remember she was so beautiful and she could really turn some heads when she entered the room." She was fixing Anna's hair to flow with the dress.

Anna said, "Dave really misses his mother. I wish I could've had a chance to meet her. I feel sad about that."

Rachel said, "How do you like this one?"

"I don't feel comfortable in this dress. It's too low cut for me." She went to take it off.

Anna then put five dresses aside that she didn't like the look of on her bed. She found the one she picked in the magazine and put it on. *This doesn't look as nice on me as it did on the model in the magazine*, she thought. She quickly put the first dress she tried back on and thought, *Dave will love this. I can't believe I'm actually getting married, and I feel so excited now.*

Anna walked back out and overheard Rachel say, "I've always had a bad feeling about what happened to Katrina because my mother fell into a deep depression after she died." She noticed Anna and got up and said, "What about the other dresses?"

Anna said, "I tried on the one I picked in the magazine, but I didn't like it on me. I would like you guys to tell me honestly about this dress."

Kathy got up and put her hands on Anna's cheek. "Yes, this is the dress. It's perfect on you."

Anna said, "Rachel, I overheard about your mother. Is she okay?"

Rachel helped unzip Anna and said, "I'm sorry to bring that up. This is your day, and you're a beautiful bride. Let's focus on your wedding and happy things."

"I'd really like to know," Anna said.

Rachel looked at her watch. "I actually have another meeting that I have to get back to. We'll talk later." She went to the bedroom to gather up all the dresses as Anna came in to help.

Rachel put her hand on her arm. "You are so sweet, Anna, and helpful. I didn't mean to bring my mother up." Anna just looked at her in concern as she continued, "Well, my mother hasn't been the same. Just between us, there was something strange about the whole thing, and my mother won't discuss it. I am at a loss."

Rachel sat on the bed, and Anna handed her a tissue and put her arm on her shoulder. "I'm so sorry for your mother. Maybe you can get her some help with a specialist?"

Anna went to the kitchen and asked her mother for her therapist's number, and Kathy gave her a card.

Rachel was in the living room, putting all the dresses in their bags.

Anna handed her the business card for the therapist. "Here. She has helped my mother a lot. Maybe she can help yours."

Rachel put the card in her pocket without looking at it. She grabbed the dresses and went to the door. "Thanks so much for listening to me. You will make a beautiful bride, Anna. I'll be in touch about the fittings and other things that need to be planned."

Anna looked at her mother and said, "Something was strange about that."

"We shouldn't push things, Anna," Kathy said. "Allow people to ask for help when they are ready. There is obviously something unresolved there." She looked at her watch. "I have to go as well, honey. I'll call you later."

Anna said, "Mom, thanks for coming and being here for me. I'm so glad you're getting better."

She kissed Anna and said, "It seems you were my little angel, and now you're so grown up. It went by so fast." Tears came to her eyes. "I love you. I'll see you later."

Anna closed the door, and so many thoughts flooded her mind. She tried to calm her heart down by drinking some wine and sat down to read more of her mother's journal.

Dear Diary, It has been a while since I wrote. Eve has not really spoken to me since it all happened. She is keeping me out of her life. Just hi and stuff. I feel different from other kids. Not sure if anyone knows about me. Teachers seem to feel bad for me, and I hate that. I don't think of the past, just of the future. Not much more to say now.

Anna closed the journal and quickly hid it before she took a nap, feeling emotionally exhausted. She awakened to the sound of Dave opening the front door. "Hi, Anna, did you go shopping today?"

"No, sorry, my mother was here and Rachel came over."

Dave, annoyed, said, "We need some food in the house. Can't you at least do that? I've been working all day."

Seeing Anna's face marred with tears, he said, "It's okay. You can go when I'm working tonight. I have some things to do. Did you pick out a dress?"

Anna, eager to get away from him, said, "Yes, I did." She put her coat on. "I'll go now and bring back some dinner."

Anna kept her phone close as she was out grabbing groceries. She came back as Dave was on the computer. He didn't even look up as she struggled to carry the bags into the kitchen. *Thanks for the help*, she thought. She thought of her mother and said, "Dave, could you help me?"

"Give me a minute."

She had already put everything away by the time he came into the kitchen. "What's for dinner?" he asked.

"I got Chinese," Anna said. She was already counting the hours until she could go to sleep.

The next day, Anna woke up alone as Dave had already left for work. She went to the real estate agent's office at the address Dave had written down for her. In the waiting room, she saw a young, extremely petite woman with short blond hair and bright blue, inviting eyes.

"Hello, you must be Anna," she greeted. "I'm Amanda. We have a lot to cover today, and Dave mentioned he'd meet up with us when he can. But he wanted us to get started without him."

Anna thought, *Why is everyone Dave knows so attractive?* She said, "I was wondering if you have any houses that are, well, in a neighborhood that is more for middle-class people?"

Amanda stopped walking down the hall and turned to Anna. "I'm puzzled. I assumed you and Dave, or Mr. Lawrence, already agreed on the houses I'm showing you today! He said he already showed you the listings?"

Anna hesitated and said, "Never mind. It's okay. We did agree, but I, well, my taste just runs a little more modest than his."

Amanda smiled. "You'll quickly adjust, I'm sure. He needs to be able to entertain his clients, and I'm sure they expect something more glamorous."

I don't want to entertain guests in my home, Anna thought as her heart rate sped up. She grabbed a pill she had in her pocket ready for a time like this.

Anna walked into the first house. "Wow, this is a grand entrance."

Just then, Dave texted her. "Sorry, I won't be able to meet up with you both. I'm hoping you like the third house the best. Talk later."

As Anna looked around, she thought, *I don't belong here. This is too much.* When they were done, she said, "Could we just go to the one on the Lake next?" Anna thought, *Dave wants the third house on the lake, so I might as well just go see that one and not waste time.*

Amanda said, "Sure. I know that's the one Dave likes best."

"Has he seen it in person?" Anna asked.

"Yes, I took him a few weeks ago when he had a free moment."

"Of course. By chance, did he already put in an offer?"

"Well, no," said Amanda, "but he would like to today, if you agree. It will go fast. He saw it before it even came on the market. It will go on tomorrow if he doesn't put in an offer."

They arrived in the neighborhood, and Amanda said, "Anna, let me show you a park that you can walk to from this house." She drove past the house and parked on the side of the road. Anna saw a swing set, a big sandbox, a few slides, and some climbing gyms on the water. "I do like this, and it's a short walk here. There is a walking path around the lake if you like to take walks. I can tell this is all a little overwhelming for you. It would be for me, too."

Anna nodded her head as she felt Amada understood for a moment.

Anna asked, "Where is the closest hospital?"

Amanda laughed. "I don't think that's something you need to worry too much about at your age."

"No, I'm a nurse and want to get started working. I just graduated."

"Oh," Amanda said. "I had no idea. Well, I'll have to look into that, but you may have more than you can handle right here." She pressed the buttons on the security system, and a large wrought-iron gate swung slowly open. They drove around a few large trees and saw a house made of stone and brick. "There is something here for you, too, Anna."

"It's strange that there is a gate when the neighbors' houses are so close."

"Yes, I hear that complaint sometimes," Amanda said, "but when something is on the water, the land is much more expensive and the lots are smaller. I guess the idea is to fit in as many mansions as possible."

When they went inside, Amanda said, "I hope you had a chance to see the pictures on the virtual tour. This house is so beautiful. This one has a pool and clubhouse in the back, which is so quaint and is like a small house in itself."

Anna walked around, feeling dizzy. "Well, it's beautiful and magnificent. How could anyone complain?"

Amanda got a phone call. She spoke for a minute and then said, "Anna, Dave would like to put an offer in, if you're okay with that."

Well, I don't think I have a choice. He's made up his mind, Anna thought and just nodded to Amanda.

Dave texted her. "We're going to have a wonderful life there. I love you."

Anna got home with a renewed determination not to give up her goal of working as a nurse. She turned the computer on to research hospitals near Quarton Lake, Birmingham, and sent her resume to Beaumont Hospital in Royal Oak and Providence Medical Center. Anna opened her journal and wrote.

Dear Diary, It is now just a few months until my wedding. I have a dress, and now I have a house, rather a mansion, to live in. I am learning so much about my family and trying to understand what has happened, and I feel so much for my mother and what she has gone through. I am starting to think that maybe I don't say anything because I don't have much of an opinion or I don't really know myself well. I am going to start to pay attention to what I want and learn to communicate better.

Anna heard the door open, and she jumped up and put her journal under the couch cushion. "Hi, how was your day?"

"We got the house," Dave said. He picked Anna up and said, "I'm so excited. It's hard to believe we will be married and living the dream."

Anna calmly said, "It is amazing, Dave. But can you tell me exactly what your salary is? How can you pay for that without me working yet?"

Dave quickly dropped her on the couch and walked toward the kitchen. "Anna, I told you that I don't want you to worry about the money. That is my business."

Anna swallowed hard as she went to the kitchen and pouring her wine. *Don't back down. Just relax and ask again.* "Dave, honey, we are a team and a couple, and I want to be involved with the finances." Her muscles were tensing more as she was speaking.

He rolled his eyes and said, "Okay, after the wedding is over, we'll sit down and go over all the finances. It's complicated. Right now I want us to focus on the wedding and honeymoon." He put some papers on the counter. Anna looked down and saw pictures and airline tickets to Hawaii.

"I saw you one day looking at a travel book to Hawaii, and I wanted to surprise you. Actually, Tom bought this for us as our gift. His client has a house there, and he goes once a year and arranged for us to have a romantic week on the sandy beach."

Anna couldn't remember when she would have been looking at a book about Hawaii. She said, "I don't remember that, but it is a beautiful place."

She saw some catalogs of furniture he'd brought home. "Look through those, too. We have a lot of furniture to buy. I'm going to take a shower after I take a run."

Anna thought, *He did it again. Another day and I still don't have any answers to my questions.*

CHAPTER 15

The Bachelorette Dinner

The next morning, Anna worked out and, after she showered, saw a text she'd missed. "Hey, we are at your parents' and cannot wait to see you later. Alia."

Anna looked at her calendar. It was Friday, and it said "bachelorette dinner."

"Dave," Anna said, "they are picking me up at six in a limousine, I think. Do you know where you're going for your bachelor party tonight?"

"Yes, they are. I forgot to tell you—I'm going to Las Vegas for my bachelor party. Scott and a few of the guys plus my brother are going. I just found out yesterday, but we're leaving tomorrow late afternoon."

Anna felt herself tense up and thought, *I won't let him notice I am so angry. I don't want to be in a bad mood tonight.* As she turned away, she knew he watched her facial expression closely as if he was studying her. Dave then tried to move around to be able to see her face, but she put her face down and her hair fell at an angle that covered it.

Finally he said, "I hope you don't drink too much tonight."

Anna felt her anger swell. *I have to say something now so I don't allow him to do what my father did to my mother.*

Anna felt her anger take over and reacted. "Dave, you're going to go to Vegas, and you're worried about me drinking too much at a restaurant? I have let you and your father make all the decisions about the wedding and where we're going to live. I feel I don't get a say in anything, and you don't even ask me about Vegas and our honeymoon. *When*, Dave, will we have a discussion about our lives? A discussion—*not* you telling me how things are going to be. I have opinions of my own, and you should discuss things before they happen. I need to be a part of my own life and have a say." Immediately, Anna had regrets.

Anna saw Dave's face turning red, and he looked as if he was holding his breath as he put his coat on and turned to her before walking out the door. "Anna," he said, "you need to think about whether you want to marry me. I thought this was all worked out between us, and now I have serious reservations. If you don't accept and appreciate the lifestyle I will provide for you, then don't marry me. There are many women out there who would appreciate me. If you do not understand this, then I will not marry you. You need to decide."

He slammed the door as he left, and Anna ran to the bathroom to throw up. She started to feel the same way she had when she read her mother's journal for the first time. She started to focus on her breathing and needed to calm her stomach down in order to be able to take a pill to help her. By the time she was finally able to swallow it, she looked at the clock to see it was five, and her friends would be there at six.

Anna opened her journal to write, *What came over me with Dave? Why did I let my anger and emotions tell him how I felt? Am I wrong? Is my mother wrong? I don't want to live without him. I feel so sick that he may not want to marry me. My mother told me I need to work on having my own voice in the marriage. I am responsible for teaching Dave how I want to be treated. What if he doesn't agree and leaves me? What if telling him how I want him to treat me pushes him away? Dave is what I want to be happy. I am pushing him away. He wants to give me a nice life so that I don't have to worry about things.* Anna looked at the clock and saw was five twenty. She texted Dave, "I am sorry. I love you and I do trust you." She waited, sitting there, for a reply. Her anxiety started to overwhelm her, and she felt a need for reassurance from Dave. She started to pace, and then she heard a knock on the door.

She opened the door and saw Alia, who immediately came in and grabbed her with an enveloping hug. "I have missed you, Anna. I can't believe your bachelorette party is here already."

Anna started to cry as she looked up and saw Jen and Lori staring at her, and Jen put her hand on her back. Anna noticed her hair was professionally done—she was a knockout, and Anna wasn't even dressed yet. Alia pulled back and said, "Are you okay? What's happened?"

Before Anna could respond, Jen said, "Hey, girl. Come on. We'll get you ready in no time."

Anna looked at Alia and wanted to be alone with her, but she allowed Jen to take her hand and lead her to the bedroom. Jen looked through the closet and pulled out a black dress and whispered, "It'll be okay. I spoke to Dave."

Anna froze and felt a wave swoop down on her. *I am so glad. I need to know more. Why does Jen know about our intimate problems? I can't ask her.* Anna heard her phone ping. She grabbed it and read the text from Dave. "I know you are under a lot of stress, but I won't keep doing this." Anna took a huge breath. *It will be okay.*

Jen leaned over and read the text and said, "Okay, now. Put this on. We'll fix your hair and makeup and enjoy ourselves."

Jen called to Lori and Alia. "Go wait in the limo with Brooke. We'll be out in a few."

Lori said, "Okay. Come on, Alia."

Alia paused and looked over to the bathroom, calling, "Anna, is everything okay?"

Anna said, "Yes. Go to the limo. We'll be out soon."

Lori and Alia were in the limo when Anna came down, and the driver opened the door for her. "Good evening," he said.

Lori was blasting the music and drinking beer as Brooke and Alia were talking. Anna sat down and quickly drank down a beer and felt the relaxation kick in. She tried to talk to Alia, but it was difficult to hear anything. Alia's presence made her feel safe as Alia put her arm around Anna, and Anna allowed her fears to dissipate and focused on trying to enjoy being in the moment.

Anna looked out the window and saw Detroit and all its lights. "Okay, where are we going?"

Jen said, "You are our captive now. You just relax and have fun."

She looked out the window as the limo slowed to a stop and saw the sign for Motor City Casino. At dinner, Jen took Anna's fourth drink from her and said, "You need to slow down and eat dinner. We don't want you getting sick now."

Alia watched this interaction and saw that Anna was slurring her words. She gave her a glass of water. "Here, drink this."

After dinner, they went to play the slots and blackjack. Jen came over and said, "We're going to the disco now. Get ready to dance your ass off." She grabbed Anna's arm, and they walked over, laughing, to the dance floor. She put a bridal headband on Anna's head and gave her a drink. They were dancing on a crowded floor when a guy started dirty dancing with Anna. Anna started to reciprocate and dance with this stranger, and then his friend came over and she had a guy on the front and back for a while. Alia noticed someone push through the crowd. He grabbed Anna and pulled her away as he pushed the two guys down.

He practically carried her out of the crowd as other people fell onto each other. They went out of the disco, and Alia followed.

"Dave, what's going on?" Alia yelled.

He looked back and calmly said, "Don't worry, Alia. I have her."

Anna then ran over to the bathroom, throwing up on the floor before she got to the toilet. Alia followed her and pulled her hair back and helped her to the toilet.

Lori and Brooke followed close behind, and Brooke said, "I guess it's time to leave already. This wasn't predictable!"

"No," Alia said. "I'll take her home and send the limo back. I'll stay with her. No reason why we all have to leave." They walked out of the bathroom, and Dave was on his phone when Alia said, "Dave, I'll take her home."

"No, no. I will take her home and you go with Luke. He's on his way. I told him about what happened."

Alia, puzzled, said, "Please take care of her. You know she wasn't doing anything. She was just dancing and those guys came over."

"I know what happened, Alia. You don't have to stick up for her." Before she could say goodbye, they were down the hall.

Anna woke up the next morning and tried to open her eyes, but the light streaming in the room felt like daggers. *I think my head is going to explode,* she thought. She peeled herself out of the bed and went into the bathroom. She looked in the mirror and saw that her eyes were puffy and her hair was matted down. She heard Dave in the kitchen and thought, *I cannot let him see me like this. I look awful. What happened?* The room started to spin as she ran to the toilet, putting her head between her knees.

Dave knocked on the door. "Anna, we have to talk. Can you come out?"

"I don't really feel good. Can we talk later?"

"We have a meeting with the priest in a few hours. We have to get going."

Anna said, "There is no way I can go meet with a priest right now. You never told me about that."

"A hangover is not a reason to cancel a meeting," Dave said. "Just get dressed and drink some water and take this ibuprofen. I'm going to the store, so be ready when I get back."

Anna heard the front door shut and went to her room to get dressed but lay down on the bed instead.

When Dave came back, she had fallen asleep again. "Are you ready?" he called. He came into the bedroom and sighed when he saw her. "Maybe you forgot, but this is the only time to meet the priest. He's busy. I really wish you didn't drink yourself silly. You could have gotten hurt if I wasn't there. I'm losing trust in you, Anna."

Anna had so many questions, but her head was pounding and she was just trying not to throw up again. She took a shower and left with her hair still wet. She grabbed a bucket before she followed him to the car; her head still felt like it was going to explode.

Dave said, "Are you serious? You better never drink like that again. You have an image to uphold now." She held her head up with her hands and thought, *I don't have the energy to argue with him.* He added, "I hope you brought some makeup because you really look awful. What will my family think?"

Anna finally felt the medicine kick in, and her headache started to ease. She took out her little bag of makeup and pulled down the mirror. She looked into the mirror. *Oh my God, I look awful with those bags under my eyes and so pale.* She put some base makeup on, which gave her some color, and added some blush. As she was putting on her eyeliner, she started to dry-heave and threw up in the bucket.

They arrived at the house, and he stopped the car. "I leave at four for Vegas," he said. "That's why we took your car. You can go home after." He paused and turned to her and looked at her sternly. "I hope that's the end of it. Anna, my mother was an alcoholic and look where that got her. I don't want to see you like that again."

No one told me that before. Is that true? Now I feel bad for him.

He got out of the car and opened her door. "I know you don't feel good, but you brought this on yourself. You can lie down on my bed until he gets here."

She took a deep breath and took a mint out of her purse. She got out of the car and walked behind Dave to the front door as the Harold opened the door, as if he had been waiting for them. "Good day, Mr. Lawrence and Miss Anna."

Anna could barely mumble with her dry mouth but mustered up a hello.

Dave said, "I'll be in the study."

Anna went straight to the bathroom and drank some water from the faucet, wet the hand towel, and put it on her face. Sue came over as she was leaving the bathroom and said, "You don't look very good. Can I get you something? What happened?"

"I drank a little too much last night."

Dave came in and said, "Anna, Father Mick is already here in the dining room."

All I want to do is lay down, she thought.

She followed Dave, and as she entered the room, she saw a middle-aged man wearing the traditional white collar. He had a warm smile and comforting presence and came over to greet them. Dave said, "Father Mick, this is my fiancée Anna."

He gently shook her hand, and she could sense he had a slight tremor, as if he was nervous. "Hello, Anna. It's so nice to finally meet you. Come, sit down."

She sat down next to him and felt safe in his presence.

He drank some water and closed his eyes, as if the water provided a spiritual experience he enjoyed. "My dear children," he said, "marriage is a difficult endeavor in this day and age. Lots of pressure and certain expectations can divide two people who love each other. You both need to understand the sacrament you are undertaking and the commitment you are making to each other. And the love that makes it all worth it."

Anna looked over at Dave, who was staring at his watch, and she kicked his chair to get him to pay attention.

"Anna, why do you want to get married? Why do you want to marry Dave?"

Before she could say anything, Dave said, "Father, I know that I love Anna and want to make a life with her. We both know we want children and will both have different roles and responsibilities. Anna understands who I am, and she has a way about her that captured me. She is quiet and reflective and is not impulsive like me. We complement each other."

"Thank you for those thoughts, Dave. I would like to hear from Anna now. Also, remember to listen and hear your partner. I can see you can be impulsive and not wait till I ask you!" Dave attempted to not roll his eyes, although Anna could see that struggle within him.

Anna felt the ibuprofen wearing off, and her head began to pound again. "Well, when I hear 'spouse,' I think of safety, friendship, support, understanding, and equal partner. I think of someone who thinks of your needs and wants and compromises because you love each other. I want someone to go through the ups and downs of life with me."

Father Mick put his arm around her and said, "Why are you crying, my dear?"

Dave got up and paced. "She's overwhelmed and gets emotional. She also doesn't feel well."

Father Mick got up and put his arm on Dave's shoulder and said, "Come, sit. Dave, you must learn to step back and listen to Anna. Allow her to express herself and be patient with her."

Anna looked at Dave, who appeared restless and irritated, but felt the priest was witnessing this with her. She said, "I do have a bad headache, Father. I'm sorry."

Father Mick said, "You are both coming together as a unit and need to listen to each other, even on days that have been stressful. Love is the reason you are forming this union. Love has to be the driving force of a union if it is to be able to make it through the difficult times."

Dave said, "Could we discuss the ceremony now?"

Father Mick looked uneasy. "It is customary for us to meet at least three or four times before the ceremony. Marriage is a big undertaking and—"

Dave interrupted. "We don't have time for that. I thought my father and I explained that to you and paid the congregation well. Besides, Anna and I love each other and understand what we are doing."

The priest looked at Anna and then at Dave. Anna said, "Dave, maybe we should make time for this, time for us."

"Anna, I wish we had time to meet with him, believe me. Maybe he can give us some worksheets to do on our own."

Sue came in the dining room. "Oh, I'm sorry. I didn't know you were still meeting."

Dave said, "It's okay, Sue, we're wrapping up now. Thanks, Father, for everything. I'll be in touch to meet once again for the vows and details."

Anna said, "I'll walk you out."

Father Mick folded up his papers and slowly rose from his chair, shaking his head in dismay. "Dave, my son, you need to slow down and enjoy this life. Don't miss out on the small parts of a day, looking and searching for the next thing. Take time to enjoy each other. She seems to be a lovely girl."

He took out a few booklets. "You must complete this and hand it in to me before the wedding. Spend some time really answering the questions, and share your answers with each other so that you can learn what is really in your hearts."

Anna, wanting some time alone with the priest, said, "We will. Thank you, Father. Please, follow me."

When they came to the door, he said, "My dear, take care of yourself. Here is my card if you ever want to call me or need me for anything at all." He placed his hand on her shoulder, and she took a breath and felt such warmth and unconditional understanding.

She put the card in her pocket and said, "Thank you."

Sue came over as Anna closed the door and said, "Come with me. You should go lie down. I understand you had a difficult night."

Anna followed her, but she really just wanted to go home. She sat on Dave's bed, and Sue stroked her hair like a mother would for a daughter. Anna said, "Dave told you I was sick."

"No, Jen called to make sure you were okay. She said you were pretty drunk and threw up when Dave came and got you."

Anna rolled her eyes and said, "Sue, why didn't Jen and Dave ever get together? They seem to be so close. She is close to all of you."

Sue hesitated, like she was trying to find the right words. "I can understand why you are asking me this question, but I wasn't involved so much until a few years ago. I don't have all the history behind that relationship. As far as I know, they have always been as close as Dave allows. I don't think she likes him that way. I'm not sure why, though." Anna lay down thinking, *She is not helpful at all,* and closed her eyes as Sue left and fell fast asleep.

The Wedding

Luke and Alia pulled up in the driveway of the family home on Friday afternoon. Alia ran out of the car and greeted Anna with a great big hug. "I'm so glad to see you. Your big day is here!" Anna stepped back, startled by the affection, and then allowed her body to relax in Alia's presence. Alia said, "I have to change. Can we go to your room?"

Luke took Anna's hand and said, "My sister, getting married. Wow. I am always here for you!"

Alia wiped tears from her eyes and embraced them in her arms. As she released, she guided Anna away and said, "I'm so excited to give this to you."

Anna took the small box Alia gave her. "You shouldn't have done this."

Alia was practically bouncing on the bed, waiting for her to open it. Inside was a locket. She parted the two halves to see a picture of her and Dave. The back of the locket was inscribed with *April 14, 2017, Anna and Dave, Love Alia & Luke.*

Anna broke into tears. "This is so nice. I don't know what to say?"

"Your response says it all. You are like my sister."

Anna brushed her tears from her eyes. "I'm so happy Luke found you," she said.

They both came downstairs, ready to go to the rehearsal dinner. Kathy descended the stairs next wearing a stunning pale yellow dress.

"Wow," Luke said, "what beautiful women I have surrounding me."

Dan came into the room and said, "Hi, Alia. It's nice for you to come all this way for the wedding."

"I wouldn't miss it for the world." Alia said.

Anna thought, *My father can be nice. Why is he only nice for certain people? It makes me so angry.*

They piled into two cars. Anna walked into the church surrounded by the distant family she had as Dave saw her from in front of the church and put his finger out to say, *One minute.* He came over to her after it seemed like half an hour but was more like ten minutes. He hugged Anna, and she thought, *He hasn't greeted me like that in a long time.* "I'm so excited. Hi, everyone." He shook Dan and Luke's hands and kissed Kathy and Alia on the cheek. Then he said, "Excuse us for a minute."

He took Anna away to the back of the church and said, "I'm so excited this day is here."

"Did you get that paperwork done for the priest?" Anna asked. "We never went over it together the way he asked us to."

"Anna, I think it's a little late for that. We have a lifetime to do that. And anyway, what does a priest even know about marriage?" He kissed her and said, "Come on, let's rehearse." Anna watched him go up the aisle to the front of the church.

Father Mick came over and said, "Hi, my dear Anna. How are you?"

She pretended she didn't notice the tone in his voice and the look of concern on his face. "I'm great," she said, trying to convince herself. "I have those papers for you, by the way."

Father Mick said, "Maybe you should give them to Dave and go over them. Remember to call me anytime. I'm here even after you are married. Marriage can be a big adjustment the first year." Anna nodded her head in agreement.

Anna went to the dinner and noticed her family was on one side and Dave's on the other with the fathers at the ends of the table. Anna felt comforted by Sue sitting in front of her as she was talking to her mother and Alia and winked at her.

Anna kept quiet and noticed Lori and Jen down the other end of the table. She watched and thought, *They are all here for us and supporting this marriage. I am so lucky to be here getting married to this great guy and he chose me. I need to enjoy this moment.*

Anna waved the waiter holding the wine bottle over to her for her fourth glass as Dave seamlessly took the glass out of her hand and waved the waiter on. Anna thought, *Maybe he's right. I'll let it go for now.* She felt her anxiety spike as she looked around, watching his family, and then she went to the bathroom, grabbing a beer from behind a bar. She thought, *What is wrong with me? I feel so out of place. Am I making a mistake? What am I doing?*

Sue came in as she was washing her hands and put her arm on her back. "It will be okay, Anna. Wedding jitters."

Anna woke up the next day, holding onto her pounding head. In the bathroom, she noticed her eyes were puffy. She heard Alia in the hall and pulled her into the bathroom. "Look at me."

Alia said, "I'll be right back." She came back with some sliced cucumbers and coffee grounds and closed the door. She turned the shower on hot and said, "The steam will take care of this." She put the cucumbers on Anna's eyes and rubbed her temples.

Anna said, "I should have known not to drink so much last night. It just calms my nerves."

Alia said, "It's okay."

Kathy then came in and said, "Alia, can we have a moment?"

Alia left, and Anna thought, *What will she say? She keeps looking at me worried, and I hate that.*

Kathy stroked her hair, and as she brushed it with such tenderness, Anna started to relax her muscles and felt at ease with her mother's aura and energy. Kathy waited at least five minutes, just allowing her presence to set in. "Anna, I want you to know no matter what, you can talk to me. The one wish I have is you do not go through problems in quiet darkness all alone in shame. I lived in such shame and blamed myself for everything, and the weight of the world was on me. I took that weight off and feel like a successful survivor now. I want you to come to me when you are in that corner, scared and alone. I am with you always." Anna had no response.

The doorbell rang, and she heard Rachel come in with the hairdresser and makeup artist. Rachel was carrying the dress with her, too. *They will make it right*, Anna thought.

Anna entered the church by the side door and went into the dressing room. She looked out into the church. The people who were filling the pews were all complete strangers. She turned to her mother and asked, "Is this even my wedding?"

Kathy said, "It will be fine, honey. Just focus on Dave at the end of the aisle."

Taking a long, deep breath, Anna imagined her honeymoon and her new life with Dave. The procession was starting, and her mother was walking down the aisle with her escort to the front, then Alia and Luke, then Jen and Tom.

Her father turned to her. "Anna, please look at me. I know you do not think I've been a good father, but seeing you marry Dave makes me understand that I did my job well. You made a good decision for the first time, and he will take care of you."

What is he saying? He has never talked to me like this. Anna was speechless. All she could do was nod.

Wagner's "Bridal Chorus" began to play, and Rachel came over. "Okay, you two—you are up."

They walked down the aisle, and Dan placed Anna's hand in Dave's. They said their vows and, before she knew it, Dave was grabbing her and kissing her in front of the altar as the priest pronounced them man and wife.

Dave said, "Let's start our lives together. You are finally mine."

Anna's heart was pounding, and she walked down the aisle and out of the church into the limo. They took a few more pictures in the limo and then drove to the reception hall where the photographer took pictures of them getting out of the limo. Dave waved to her as she came out. "You have to shake everyone's hand and thank them for coming."

The band started playing, and everyone sat at his or her table in the reception hall. A voice on the PA system announced, "Welcome, Mr. and Mrs. Dave and Anna Lawrence." Dave grabbed her hand and whisked her onto the dance floor. After the dance was over, the father-daughter dance began, something Anna had been dreading.

Dan led, of course. "Anna, let Dave lead the way. He is able to take care of you."

Anna thought of her mother and his treatment of her and said, "Where is Eve?"

"This is not the time for that. You know there are two sides to every story. One day, if you are open and want to know, I will tell you mine."

Anna looked at the ceiling, trying not to cry. She heard someone say, "That is so sweet—she is crying." *If they only knew*, she thought.

After the dance, they took their seats, and Tom got up to give a toast. "To Anna and Dave. May you both find happiness in each other! Welcome to the family, Anna. I know you will support the family name and make us proud." The audience clapped.

Anna drank two glasses of champagne in just a few minutes, and Dave grasped her arm a little more roughly than he should have. "Anna," he said, "you won't be getting drunk today, at our wedding, in front of all these people." He took her glass from her and told the waiter, "No more for her." Anna bit her lip and looked to the floor as shame filled her.

Everyone was dancing and having a good time, and Anna danced while trying to keep an eye on Dave. He came over when a slow dance came on, but when it ended, he would leave her again to talk with the guests. Anna tried to hold back her tears as Sue came over and took her hand. "Come with me," she said.

They went to the balcony, and she handed Anna a glass of wine. "Here, Anna, take a deep breath."

"Thank you. This is all so overwhelming."

"I want you to know I'm here to talk if you ever need to. I have not had a chance to talk more with you about the family, though of course this is not the time. Dave has to mingle and make the clients feel special. It's part of the game. You have really made a perfect bride for Dave. Don't conform too much to what he wants. You have to remember your own needs." Sue gave her a hug. "Now, go and enjoy your special day."

Anna took an extra minute to enjoy the fresh air. She looked at the party through the window and saw her father sitting at his table, texting, and her mother talking to Suzanna. *I am glad they are all here, even though everything feels so messed up.* She looked at Alia and Luke dancing and staring at each other with a gaze she understood deep down that had never happened between her and Dave. Anna noticed her mother then staring at her and thought, *Why does my mother seem to look at me with pity? She seems so sad on my wedding day.*

On the way inside, she turned the corner and saw Brooke and Lori smoking. She stepped back behind a post and overheard Brooke say, "How long do you think the marriage will last?"

Lori blurted out, "As long as they are both alive. Brooke, you are so negative. Why don't you just wish them well?"

Silence filled the air, then Brooke said, "I guess you haven't known Dave that long. I wish them well, but I'm realistic."

Anna quickly took a pill she had hidden in her dress for an emergency and went inside, not wanting to hear anymore. She walked close to the dance floor as Lori and Alia grabbed her to dance in the center, and Dave grabbed her hand and danced around her.

After they said goodbye to everyone, they got in the limo, which took them to Ann Arbor. Dave closed the partition between them and the driver and started pulling her dress up. He grabbed at her underwear. Anna put her hand on his and stopped his hand. She kissed his mouth and whispered, "Wait. It'll be worth it."

The next day, the alarm went off, and Anna jumped out of bed. She heard Dave in the shower. She jumped in the shower with him. "Good morning, Mr. Lawrence," she said.

"We have to hurry. I hope you're packed." Anna watched him dry himself off, staring at his muscles glistening with the water. She was getting dressed when she heard a knock on the door.

"I'm here to drive you to the airport," the driver announced.

It was seven, and they had a nine o'clock flight. He took their luggage, and Anna said, "I'll be right there."

They flew first class to Honolulu, Hawaii, and Anna was just waking from a pleasant nap when they landed. Dave said, "Looks like first class suits you."

Anna smiled at Dave, "I guess I could get used to this."

"Let's go. We have a car waiting to bring us to the Kahala resort. You'll love it there."

"Have you been here before?" Anna asked.

Dave hesitated then said, "Well, a long time ago."

Anna wanted more information but didn't push Dave to say more.

They arrived, and Anna ran into the private room. She saw a huge bed open to the deck with a private Jacuzzi and pool right onto the water. She took her shoes off and opened the doors to feel the sand on her feet, the hot sun, and the breeze. She turned to look at Dave, who paid the staff and ordered some food. She said, "This is amazing. I may never want to leave."

"Well, this will be our place when we need a break and time alone. Go jump naked into the Jacuzzi. I'll be right there."

Once Anna was in the Jacuzzi, she wondered if he had been there before. She looked around and saw him texting someone. Then he answered the door, and a man brought in a tray of food. Dave came over and put some champagne with fruit next to her. He poured some in her glass and took his clothes off. With a glass in his hand, he started to kiss her neck and touch her breasts. Soon he was pressing against her and she felt him slide inside her under the hot water. Anna kissed him back and moved on top of him. She tried to look into his eyes, but they were closed. *I want him to look at me like Luke and Alia look at each other*, she thought, but she knew he never would.

They spent a week there on the private beach to relax. Anna thought about wanting to leave and explore the island, but they stayed in the resort and went to shows on the beach and dinner. She held his hand as they walked and thought that they were becoming much closer. They got back to Michigan, and the car that picked them up seemed to be driving away from Ann Arbor instead of toward it.

Anna looked at him. "Where are we going?"

"I have a surprise for you. I wanted to come back and return to our new lives in our new house." They drove to Quarton Lake in Birmingham, to the new house. Dave had arranged the entire move to take place while they were gone.

CHAPTER 17

The Married Couple

Anna looked at the house, still feeling it must belong to someone else. When she entered the massive double doors, the first thing she noticed was furniture everywhere. She went into the family room and slowly walked around, noticing the drapes and the televisions on the wall. Dave watched her intently with a smile on his face, looking for her reaction and assuming she would be excited. He truly didn't understand her or what she was about. Anna thought, *I hate this. I just want a starter home like normal newlyweds.*

She turned to him and said, "Who chose all this? Who unpacked everything? How did you get the whole house decorated in such a short amount of time?"

"I didn't want you to have to do this, Anna. I wanted to surprise you and have everything done so that we can focus on beginning our life together."

"I understand, but I would like to know who you worked with. Was it Amanda?"

He said, "No, actually Jen volunteered as a gift. She did work with Amanda, and Amanda had a moving company work fast to have it completed by the time we got back."

Anna thought, *Remember, Anna, he will get angry and leave if you don't just give in and say you like it.* She mustered up some positive feedback and said, "It's beautiful, Dave."

He ordered some food and said, "Here, follow me." He carried her bag up the winding staircase and down the hall into the bedroom. He put the bag down, and she followed him into the bathroom with two adjoining closets. "This is your closet, Anna. I had them put all your clothes in here, and Jen added a few more. I hope you love living here, Anna. I think we'll be so happy here."

Anna wanted to scream, *Did Jen go through all my stuff? I feel so violated. Did she read my journal? Where is my journal? Where is my mother's journal?*

Anna composed her emotional state and looked to the floor to also allow her hair to cover her face when she said, with a quivering voice, "Dave, it's nice. Please from now on, though, I want the two of us to make the decisions around here together. Okay?"

Dave said, "Okay. I know you're tired from the trip. We'll have to christen this bed tomorrow."

Anna said, "That's fine. Are you working tomorrow?"

"Yes. Someone has to pay for all of this. Maybe you can get some groceries and get your bearings with this new environment. I should be home early."

He went to the bathroom, and she scrambled to look in a few boxes on the floor that were not unpacked but open. Her journal was on the top. She picked it up and examined it to see if someone might have opened it to read it, but since she didn't have a lock on it, she couldn't tell. *I'll have to assume no one would read someone's journal, right?*

Anna felt tired but not comfortable in this house. They went to bed, and Dave put his arms around her. "Good night, Anna. I'm so glad to be here with you. I know it will take some time, but we'll get used to living here in our home together." Anna fell silent and closed her eyes until she could hear Dave fall into a deep sleep as she then squirmed her way out of his arms and looked around the room at her new surroundings.

She walked around this enormous house and opened up her journal.

Dear Journal, I'm not sure what has happened in the last few weeks, but I am married now and living in a mansion. I feel like I'm living someone else's life. Will I adjust to this place? How can I make this place my own? I feel I have no identity. I will have to figure it out. I'm so tired, but I cannot sleep. I will need to give it some time. Good night.

Over the next few weeks, Anna spent time setting up some interviews for herself at Henry Ford in West Bloomfield and Beaumont Hospital in Royal Oak. She went to see her mother as well but waited until she had these interviews set up. She went over and sat with her mother, who looked different to Anna, like her mood had lifted.

"Mom, you seem so happy!"

Kathy sat down and looked into Anna's eyes. "Well, I spoke to your father about a divorce, Anna. I wanted to wait till after your wedding. I saw a lawyer before I talked to him. I've had to take my time to feel strong enough to make that choice. I've learned so much in therapy, and I'm in a good place, but when I asked for a divorce, he said he wants to actually go to counseling now with me."

Anna sat back in her chair and was shocked she felt saddened when she heard the word *divorce*. She looked around the kitchen, and memories of her childhood started flooding her mind.

"Are you okay? You haven't said anything."

"Do you still want to be married to him?" Anna asked. "I'm confused as to why you would go to counseling."

Kathy got up to stretch her arms and move around and poured some more tea she had simmering.

"What you haven't seen is that since I'm having a life for myself and doing things and feeling more confident, your father has been home more often. I think he noticed I wasn't home, and he started to care or get scared. He started asking me to do things with him. I was angry at first but have been working on that in therapy. I think that he hated that I was so passive and accepting. I'm not sure of his angle right now, but I'm curious. I figure that it can't hurt to go to therapy, if not to save the marriage, maybe help to end it. I'm not hoping for anything, really."

Kathy got up and looked out the window. "Actually, Anna, I hope this time helps me to learn more about myself. I don't really have much left for him, and to be honest, I believe he is worried about his finances in the divorce. I am realistic that people don't really change that much, and even if he did, our history will always be with me. I'll never forget what he has done."

Kathy turned to Anna and held her hand with such intensity. "I hope you can learn from this to always keep your identity and be aware of how you are changing in the marriage with Dave. By the way, that's enough about me. How is the job search going?"

"I have two interviews next week," Anna said. "I'm excited about them."

Kathy looked relieved. "Well, maybe I'll be working with you." Anna stared at her as she continued. "I've been taking a review class to get my license back. I'm taking the test in a few months."

Anna jumped up and gave her a hug. "I'm so happy for you, Mom. You've wanted to be a nurse for such a long time."

She said, "We'll see if I can pass. I really want this. I'm studying all the time, but I really am enjoying it. I know how you felt now."

Anna said, "I just took that test, and I can help you study. Please let me help you?"

Kathy said, "The new me accepts your help. I would like that."

I am so happy I can help my mother, Anna thought. "That makes me so happy, Mom."

Back at the new house, Anna started to prepare dinner for her and Dave. She was excited to tell him the good news. He came home that night almost two hours later than he told her, but she was too happy to have that affect her mood. He came in and went straight to the shower, which she noticed was his routine. "I'll be there in a minute. Just want to take a quick shower."

Anna sat at the table. He had left his phone on the counter, and she heard it ping. She went over to it and saw a text from Jen. "Sorry, I can't come on Thursday. I'll see you probably Sunday."

She heard the bathroom door open, and she quickly sat back down as if she had been doing something wrong. She said, "I made your favorite lemon chicken. I also went to Costco and did a big shop for the house." He smiled at her. "So, how was work?" she asked.

"The usual. We have a deal going through, so I'll need more time at work."

"I'm waiting to hear from some nurse recruiters, but I have a few interviews lined up," she said.

Dave looked at her with a penetrating stare. "I thought you were going to wait a while to give yourself some time to adjust."

"Time for what, Dave? You have done everything. The whole house is filled, and I had nothing to do with it. You haven't left anything for me to do. I am grateful, but now I want to get my career going."

Dave, seemingly annoyed, finished one more bite of chicken and said, "I'm going out to get a beer with my brother. I'll see you when I get back. I'll only be gone a while." He kissed her on the cheek and left out the garage door as Anna was left at the kitchen table alone in this huge house.

She woke that night after taking a sleeping pill to Dave rubbing up against her and pulling her underwear off. Anna turned around and he was on top of her and started to penetrate her. Anna suddenly saw Tom on top of her and his hand on her mouth, and she froze. Panic struck her, and she threw him off her and screamed and locked the bathroom.

Dave stormed to the door and yelled, "What the hell, Anna? What is wrong with you? I'm just going to go to bed."

Anna laid on the floor shaking and crying, trying to calm herself down, thinking, *What is wrong with me?*

Anna woke the next morning to an empty bed and a note in the kitchen: "I hope that never happens again. I'll be home early." She thought, *What does early mean?* She tried to find things to do and took a walk around the neighborhood, which seemed barren and empty with only an expensive Porche or Mercedes passing by her on an occasion. *I don't fit in here.*

Dave came that night around seven. Anna had no appetite, and her anxiety was high. She was pacing the kitchen as he walked in. "Hi, Dave. How was your day? I made some enchiladas for you."

Dave barely looked at her as he sat at the table, texting on his phone as he mumbled, "Oh, thanks, but I had an early dinner." He looked at her. "So what was that about last night?"

Anna said, "You just startled me, Dave. I was having a nightmare, and you woke me up and I felt so frightened. I am sorry I did that, but I did it in my sleep."

Dave shook his head and said, "I hope that never happens again. I am going to take a shower and watch a game."

Anna looked to the floor and felt this wave of emptiness, darkness, and extreme aloneness and thought, *Now I know what my mother was talking about.*

A month later, Anna spent her day alone but excited she got a call from the nurse administrator. She woke the next morning to an empty bed. Looking in the guest room, she found Dave and woke him. "Why didn't you sleep with me?"

"I didn't want to wake you. I'll be home earlier tonight to have dinner with you."

Dave got up and went to the bathroom as Anna followed him anxiously and stood by the door, seemingly reluctant to tell him the news. Finally, she blurted out, "I was finally offered a job, in the labor and delivery department in West Bloomfield at the Henry Ford Hospital."

Dave didn't respond right away. When he spoke, he said, "I hope you didn't answer before you talked to me?"

Anna felt her heart race now. "No. Of course not, but it's sort of my dream job. I'm so excited about it, Dave."

Dave said, "Can we talk about this tonight, Anna? I don't have the time to discuss this now, but I have some reservations."

Anna thought, *Of course he does. He doesn't want me to work. He's not going to control this.*

He got out of the shower and dried himself and got ready. He came over and kissed her forehead. "Have a nice day."

After he left, Anna ran to the bathroom and threw up. She sat on the floor, wiping her mouth, and thought, *Did he make me that upset?* Thinking of other possibilities, she thought, *Crap, I haven't had a period since, let's see, has it been six weeks?* She got dressed and went to the CVS Pharmacy and bought a home pregnancy test and came right home. She sat on the toilet and peed on the stick and left it on the counter. She started to pace back and forth, and a million thoughts ran through her head. When she picked the stick up, she saw a cross. *Positive.*

Suddenly she wanted to take a pill and a drink to calm down and bit her lip as she paced the floor. *I am pregnant. I can't drink anymore. Would one pill or one drink hurt the baby? Is this really happening? How did this happen? I was on the pill and maybe only forgot it once or twice. Was that on my honeymoon? Have I not had my period in two and half months? How is Dave going to react to this? He's going to be so angry. He won't want me to work now.*

Anna distracted her thoughts by making a nice dinner and had it ready at six. She sat at the table, waiting. She poured a glass of wine then remembered, but she took one large gulp and poured it down the drain.

Finally, Dave came in. "How was your day?" she asked.

He went to change without responding to her. When he came back, he said, "Fine. I made plans with my father and Sue to go to dinner tomorrow night. He wants to get to know you better."

Anna didn't hear what he'd said, lost in her own thoughts. Her heart was racing and her breathing was shallow, the muscles in her neck stiffening; she knew she had to tell him soon, but when was the right time?

Dave got up from the table before he ate and said, "I'll be right back."

Anna stiffened. *Oh shit, I left the test on the counter. I am such an idiot.* She rose to go after him, but before she could get to the bathroom, he stormed out.

"Pregnant. How could you be so stupid, Anna? We never discussed this yet. This is not the right time for a baby."

Anna stood there, paralyzed, and remembered her mother's words. *Don't let him treat you badly. You need to teach him how you want to be treated.* "Dave, don't talk to me like that. I'm not a child. I'm your wife. This is a shock to me as well. I didn't plan this."

She saw his posture grow stiffer, his shoulders hunched high, and his face reddening with anger. He pushed Anna against the wall, and she hit her eye on the edge of the cabinet. She felt a surge of pain, and his demeanor suddenly changed as he watched her face. He went to the kitchen, and Anna ran for the bathroom and slammed the door and locked it. *Oh damn, I forgot my phone.*

She heard his footsteps come to the door and his breathing as he tried to open the door. "Anna, open the door." She heard a strange calm in his voice, something unfamiliar in his voice, and she felt terrified. *Is he going to really hurt me? Is he abusive? What is happening?*

Dave said, "I have a wet cloth for your face. You shouldn't have turned your head or you wouldn't have gotten hurt." *Is he blaming this on me?* Anna unlocked the door hesitantly, and he quickly turned the knob before she was able to lock it again and jerked the door open.

He had a bag of ice inside the cloth and handed it to her. "We'll get through this. It's not the right time, but we're married. Now you will stay at home with the baby. You won't be working now."

He was already thinking about how to use the news of the baby to his advantage, to force me to do what he wanted. Anna looked around the house. *This is not my life. It's all Dave's stuff. My mother told me to keep communicating. My mother knew, but I would not listen.*

Anna tried to look Dave in the eyes, but her heart raced, and she looked at the floor. "You scared me just now. I saw your anger, Dave, and you scared me."

Dave cut her off. "Do you know how far along you are?"

"No, I haven't gone to the doctor yet." *I need to get out of here. I need to breathe.* "I'd like to see my mother after dinner."

"No, that's not a good idea tonight. You can see her in a few days. Keep this on your eye. I don't understand how you hit your eye like that. You need to rest tonight."

Anna went to the bathroom again and looked at the Xanax she desperately wanted to take and thought about the beer or mixed drink she couldn't have. She needed to take something but looked down at her stomach and thought of having a small baby in her arms. Wow. She came out of the bathroom and went over to Dave on the couch.

What did I do? Does he hear anything I say about his anger? Should I do what I want and go see my mother or should I stay?

Dave said, "Anna, come over here. Sit here and put your feet up."

"I'm going to clean up the kitchen first," Anna said with relief, not wanting to be near him.

Tears ran down her cheeks as she finally got the dishes put away and picked up the phone and called her mother. "Hi, Mom. Are you busy?"

"Wait a minute, honey." Anna heard her moving. "Sure, Anna, are you okay?" Kathy said.

"I'm pregnant," Anna blurted. She was left with silence on the other side of the phone. "Mom, did you hear me?"

She finally heard her mother breathe. "I'm sorry, Anna. I don't know what to say. How do you feel about this?"

"I don't really know. We weren't planning on this. I'm so confused." Hearing Dave moving around, she lowered her voice. "Can we meet in a few days to talk?"

"Of course," Kathy said. "I love you, Anna. No matter what, it will be okay." After a pause, she said, "Can you do me a favor and stand up and stretch? All your muscles as well as you can? I know it might sound weird but just hear me."

What is she talking about? She put the phone down and brought her arms up and did a long big stretch and twisted her torso. She also stretched her legs and put her arms down and picked up the phone. "Thanks, Mom. I do feel better."

Kathy said, "Isn't it amazing when we have stress or tension we can stretch it out?"

Anna heard Dave calling for her and quickly tensed up again and whispered, "I have to go. Talk soon."

The next night, Dave was in the bedroom picking out something for her to wear. As she came into the closet, he said, "I think this will work. We have dinner with my father, remember?"

"I look horrible with my eye," Anna said.

"Can't makeup fix that?" He grabbed some base and concealer and started to apply it. Anna let him. *How on earth does he know how to apply makeup? I don't think I want to know.*

He said, "There. Now you can barely see it. Make sure you bring this with you so you can reapply it."

They drove to the restaurant in silence, and when they arrived, the waiter walked them to the table. Sue gave Anna a big hug. "Hi, newlyweds," she said.

She looked closer at Anna but didn't say anything.

Jake didn't get up but shook his son's hand and patted Anna's arm. "Nice to see you both tonight. Seems like we have a lot to talk about." He gave Anna a disturbing smirk.

Anna thought, *Did he really tell him already? I thought or assumed we would wait a while.*

The waitress came over, and Jake ordered a bottle of wine and some appetizers.

He looked at Anna as the waitress left, "Well, Anna, I hope you understand that Dave won't be around much. He has many more clients and more responsibility at work now. He's a full partner now, and a lot is expected, but I'm sure you two had these discussions already. Now that there is a baby in the picture, you will have to take on more at home. You know what success takes in this business, but it looks like you are enjoying the perks of living this lifestyle."

Anna looked at Dave, waiting for him to say something, but nothing happened.

Sue grabbed Jake's hand tightly and said, "Don't make her feel uncomfortable. Having a baby is good news. Anna, let's go get some air at the bar." She grabbed her hand and led her to the bar stools. Sue ordered a spritzer for Anna and a cosmopolitan for herself. "Anna, here—take one sip. It won't harm the baby." Anna listened and took a big sip of the cosmopolitan.

"Thanks, I needed that."

Sue put her hand on Anna's shoulder, and Anna noticed how thin Sue really was. She said, "I have known Jake and this family for ten years." Sue took a few sips of her drink. "I knew I was one of many affairs of Jake's, but that was okay to me because I never wanted to get married. I liked our relationship as it was. Over time, though, I began to understand that he was controlling and manipulative. I did try to end it a year before, well, before Katrina died. I knew her, Katrina, a little bit. I was her personal trainer before I met Jake. I stopped, of course, when the affair started. He was very persistent and persuasive."

"Excuse me," Anna said, "but why are you telling me all of this? Just because Jake cheated doesn't mean Dave will."

"Dave is a product of his parents, especially of his father, and that is the example he had growing up of what a relationship should be like. Of course he learned from them. Please don't be that naïve, or you will get hurt. I can see now that Dave chose you very carefully."

Anna's face turned bright red, and she got up to go, but before she could leave, Sue put her hand on her arm. "I'm sorry, Anna, for that remark. You really seem like a genuine person, and I want to help you. This family is dangerous."

"Why on earth, if this family is so dangerous, do you stay with Jake?" Anna asked.

"Please sit down." Anna slumped back onto the stool. She ordered a beer but hid it behind the drink menu. Sue said, "Jake actually asked me to marry him on several occasions. I haven't even considered it once, but I haven't told him that. As long as we aren't married, I have the leverage. I can leave at any time. As long as I keep my distance and let him do what he wants, he treats me well and I don't feel pressured. You see, once you get hooked, it is like a drug. I know Dave does not always treat you well, and that black eye says it all." Anna squirmed in the seat and had to take a deep breath. She stretched her shoulder to help her.

Sue continued, "You overlook it, and you justify his behavior because if you didn't you would have to leave. As long as you justify the abusive and manipulative ways of the men, you don't have to make the impossible choice to leave. You see, I refused to believe all of the rumors going around about how controlling and manipulative he was to Katrina, but I was so focused on denying that, I lost sight that he was doing the same thing to me. By then, it was too late. A life without Jake was frightening to me, so I justified and rationalized his behavior until Katrina turned up dead."

"What are you saying?"

"There was an investigation, but Jake was never charged with anything. It's difficult to prove someone was pushed down the stairs with no eyewitnesses."

Anna looked over at Dave and wanted to run out the door. He saw her and came over. His face darkened when he saw her drink. "What are you doing? You're pregnant." He grabbed the beer from her and said, "We ordered dinner already. Come sit down." He waited for her and followed behind, leaving Sue at the bar.

Anna sat at the table and said, "I'm sorry about being so defensive."

Jake said, "Anna, Dave should have explained to you that work is his priority. There will be times when he won't be home, and you will need to accept and support him. I hope we have an understanding. I blame Dave for not explaining that to you. Our family is probably different from other families, but you do have many advantages, like your lifestyle, that are benefits."

"Jake, to be honest with you, I don't care about the material possessions. What is important to me is the time spent with Dave and being together and building a life together. I never had that growing up."

Jake's eyebrows rose as he said, "Then you were not being fair to my son. You must have known who Dave is, and you chose to marry him. You'll have to find a way to accept the situation. Maybe you can spend more time with Laura, Tom's wife. Yes, I think that will help."

The waitress came over and said, "Oh, hello, ladies. These gentlemen ordered for you. I was impressed with their choices." She was laughing and shrugging her shoulders in a flirtatious way.

Sue whispered to Anna, "See? She's already addicted to them in just five minutes." She started eating her salad and said, "Good choice, Jake."

After dinner, Anna said to Dave, "I'm pretty tired and need some rest."

Jake overheard and said, "Sue, why don't you take her home? Dave and I have some more to discuss tonight."

"That's a great idea."

I don't want her to take me home, but I can maybe get some rest alone, if she just drops me off.

Anna got up and said, "Thanks for dinner."

Dave walked her to the front door. "We'll talk tomorrow about this. Go home and get some rest. Please, don't listen to what Sue has to say. She has a different perspective, and I don't really trust her intentions. I will see you later."

What does he mean by that? What have I gotten myself into?

They arrived at the house, and Anna sat on the couch. Sue went to the bathroom and got a cold cloth and put it on her head. She said, "I'm sorry for tonight. I may have gone too far in telling you all that history. You just got married. I guess you remind me of myself when I was younger and, well, I like you."

Anna tried to relax. "No, Sue, I'd like to know more. I want to know why you think Jake had something to do with Katrina's death."

"Anna, it's best you stay out of it and don't know any more. It's a curse."

"I won't discuss it with Dave," Anna said. "But don't you think I have a right to know, now that I'm married into an abusive family?"

Sue didn't seem to hesitate. She said, "Katrina called me a week before she died and told me she was going to file for a divorce and that I could have him. She told me she wanted to leave him for years, but he threatened to kill her if she tried, and she was afraid to leave. She had become so unhappy she didn't care what happened to her. I never told Jake about that conversation, but he kept tabs on her. He knew she was going to file. He had a private detective following her. She died from head trauma, from a fall, the very next day."

Anna got up. "I need a break. You are telling me such horrible things about a family I just married into and now am having a baby."

Sue got up and put her coat on. "I'm going to go now. I'm sorry if I overwhelmed you, Anna. I haven't told anyone this, and I guess I feel I can trust you. These are my thoughts. I don't have proof, and maybe somewhere I don't want to believe it. I am still with him. I guess not being married to him and not having the financial implication, I think I can't be hurt."

She came over to Anna and gave her a hug. "Go, get some rest. Take care of yourself."

Anna walked her out and went up to the bedroom to lie down. She pushed all of Sue's words out of her mind so that she could finally fall asleep. *It's all so surreal, it can't be real*, she thought.

Anna woke to some banging in the kitchen, and she put her robe on and fixed her hair in the mirror. She looked at her face and thought her eye seemed more swollen and bruised than the day before. She walked down the hall and saw Dave making eggs. The smell of bacon made her run to the bathroom again to throw up. She walked downstairs when she felt she could, and Dave came over and said, "You didn't eat much last night, and we need to move past yesterday and look to this pregnancy as a good thing. You now need to focus on being healthy."

Anna said, "I know you're right, but I'm so nauseated. I don't think I can hold the food down."

"Well, we need to go see a doctor, then. Do you have one?"

Anna said, "No, I'll call tomorrow for an appointment at Henry Ford. I think it's the closest."

He made her a protein smoothie and said, "Try to get this down, and drink lots of water. I'm going to go for a run."

Anna nodded in acknowledgment.

Dave came over to Anna and looked straight into her eyes. "By the way, I know Sue told you something about my parents. He cheated on her, my mom, but he also took care of her. You see, my mother wasn't mentally well." He took a long pause and continued looking out the window. "Their relationship was complex, like most people's—look at your own parents. Please, consider the source. Sue was jealous of my mother and wanted to take her place. My father still won't marry her, and he certainly would never have hurt my mother. My mother, well, she was so depressed for years, and we believe she took her own life."

He left out the garage door without saying any more, and Anna got up to go lie down from her pounding headache. *What on earth is going on? He had no emotion at all telling me that horrible thing.*

CHAPTER 18

The Pregnancy

Anna called the OB-GYN office the next morning and spoke with the secretary. "Hi, I recently became pregnant and need to schedule an appointment soon. I've been throwing up and hardly eating."

The receptionist said, "Okay, Dr. Price has an opening in a few days."

She heard her cellphone ring as she was making the appointment. She looked at her phone and saw "Missed call: Alia." She called her right back. "Hi, how are you?"

Alia said, "I'm okay. How are you?"

Anna sat on the couch. "I was just making an appointment."

"I called because Luke and I have been arguing," Alia said. "He has been pushing me away, and I'm scared."

Anna said, "Alia, he loves you so much. I've never seen him this happy. But you know we had a rough childhood. Trust is an issue for both of us. Maybe you need to give him some time. Be patient with him."

Alia took a deep breath. "Maybe I push too hard, too. You're right—I need to give him some space and let him think about things and come to me. I always think the worst when someone pushes me away, and I blame myself. I try to do more, and maybe that's not what he needs. Thank you for talking to me, Anna. How are the newlyweds?"

Anna said, "We're okay but just trying to get over the shock of living in this enormous house." She paused a moment, and tears poured down her face. "And now I'm pregnant. We were not planning this at all."

Alia said, "What did you say?"

Anna got up and started to pace the kitchen floor. "I don't really want to talk about it now. I'm not feeling well and need to go lie down. I'll call you later in the week. I hope things are okay with you and Luke." Before Alia could say goodbye, the phone was dead.

Anna arrived at her doctor's appointment on Thursday morning at ten. She was waiting on the table in her gown when the doctor came in.

"Hi, Anna. I'm Dr. Price. Is this your first baby?"

Anna said, "Yes. It was a surprise. I just got married, and we were planning on waiting."

Dr. Price smiled. "Oh, a honeymoon baby. Well, let's see how far along you are. When was your last period?"

Anna said, "I really can't remember. I'm sorry."

"Well, let's do the exam and ultrasound." Dr. Price put the gel on her stomach and moved the Doppler around. "Now, Anna, relax! Do you hear the heartbeat? It's so strong." Anna felt cold and uncomfortable with the Doppler moving all around. "Now, see," Dr. Price pointed. "There's the baby. When was your honeymoon?"

Anna said, "Eight weeks ago."

Dr. Price said, "It looks like you're about seven or eight weeks now. That would put you at January 20th as due date and conception at around end of April. Does that seem correct?"

Anna shrugged her shoulders in agreement. "Dr. Price, I need to ask you or tell you that I was drinking heavily then, and I was taking Xanax on occasion for anxiety problems. Did I hurt the baby?"

Dr. Price said, "It seems everything is developing well right now. Is there a problem that we need to address? You do need to quit everything."

Anna felt sick and ran out of the room but didn't make it and vomited in the hallway. The nurse ran over and helped her to the bathroom. When she was done throwing up, the nurse gave her a shot. "This will help. Come lie down and rest a minute. It'll make you drowsy."

Anna woke to Dave and the nurse in her room, talking. "Well, she woke up. How do you feel? Can I take you home?"

Dr. Price came in and handed her some water. "Here, please drink this."

"She is actually seven or eight weeks along with a due date at the end of January," Dr. Price said. "She is pretty sick now and will need fluids and lots of rest. Some women don't have a nice, easy pregnancy, and it seems Anna is having a difficult time and will need support."

Dave nodded as an acknowledgment, but Anna didn't have much confidence that he would provide what the doctor was asking for.

As they drove home, Anna started to cry. "I'll ask my mother to stay with us."

"No need, Anna," Dave said. "I hired someone to take care of the house and you. She came over earlier in the week, but you didn't answer the door."

Anna said, "Please, Dave, I want my mother, not a stranger. I don't like when you make these decisions without me."

Dave said, "Can you just meet her? She'll be at the house when we get there."

Anna felt too sick to argue.

They walked in, and Anna sat down on the couch. A few minutes later, she heard Dave listening to the voice messages. "Hi, Anna, this is Linda from Henry Ford, Labor and Delivery Department. We sent you a formal job contract, but I haven't heard if you are taking the job or not. Could you call me as soon as you can? Or I will have to hire the other person."

Dave deleted the message right away and said, "Well, I guess you won't be working now."

"Did you just delete that message?"

"Yes. No need to look into that now. You heard the doctor—you need to rest and take care of yourself."

Before Anna could say anything, the doorbell rang. "Oh, here she is," Dave said. He opened the door. "Hi, Sophie. It's so nice you can do this for us. Come in."

Sophie came over to Anna lying on the couch and said, "Hi, I'm Sophie. It is so nice to meet you. Congratulations also." Anna saw a perky, upbeat girl with mid-length blond hair, a strange crooked smile, and white teeth, and she seemed almost so pleasant, it was sickening. She had on tight jogging clothes that were almost inappropriate for a job interview.

Anna heard her cell phone ring and said, "Excuse me for a moment."

Sophie went to grab her arm and said, "Let me help you."

"No need—thanks," she said, answering the phone. "Hi, Mom. What are you doing?"

Kathy said, "I'm taking a class, and I have good news that I passed the exam. I am so happy to be doing this. Oh, I'm coming over tomorrow. We need to talk. How are you feeling?"

Anna, knowing her mother would quit her class to help if she told her what was going on, said, "I'm feeling okay. I'll tell you more tomorrow at lunch then."

Anna, feeling defeated again, said, "Thanks for coming, Sophie. How did Dave find you?"

"Oh, my family and his have been friends for years. I'm happy to help out. Whatever you need for as long as you need it. I'm sorry you feel so sick."

Anna rolled her eyes. *Another friend of the family.* "Well, I don't really need much help, but maybe a few hours a day to help with the house would be okay."

Dave overheard her. "Nonsense. We have to make it worth her while, Anna. Please come from nine to six every day."

Anna looked at Dave, shaking her head. "I don't need that much care. My mother can help out also."

Dave, trying to compromise, said, "Okay, nine to four, then. I'll leave a list for you of things to do in the morning."

Sophie came over to Anna and said, "Thanks. I can use the work, and I would love to be able to help."

Anna nodded. "See you tomorrow."

Anna woke at ten the next day and came out of her room to see Sophie carrying her laundry downstairs. She had her hair in a ponytail and seemed to bounce down the stairs in an energetic way. Anna made her way downstairs, and when Sophie came out of the laundry room, she said, "Oh, good morning, Mrs. Lawrence."

"Please call me Anna. I can't believe I slept so long. Did Dave let you in?"

"No, he left a key for me in case you were asleep. I let myself in. I hope you don't mind."

Anna said, "No, of course not."

"Can I make you some toast and eggs or something else to eat?"

"I'm not used to someone helping me. I'd like to make my own food. I'm going to take a nausea pill first, though." Sophie grabbed the pill bottle and brought it to Anna with a glass of water. Anna said, "Thank you."

"I really want to be helpful to you. Please allow me to feel I'm working for a living."

Anna said, "We'll have to get used to each other. How do you know my husband's family?"

Sophie bit her lip as if she wasn't supposed to say anything. "Well, my mother worked for Mrs. Lawrence, or Katrina, for years. She was so nice to us, a very kind person. I can see you are similar to her. I will go and get some toast and eggs. Relax and let that pill work."

Anna said, "Okay, but my mother is coming at eleven thirty, and you can go and take a break before she comes, okay?"

Sophie nodded. "You don't want her to know I'm here?"

"If she knew I needed help, she'd want to come herself, and I don't want her to give up her classes and what she is doing now."

"Understood," Sophie said.

Anna fell asleep on the couch after she ate a little bit and woke to the doorbell. She got up and looked around but didn't see anyone. She opened the door to find her mother. Kathy gave her a big hug and said, "Hi, honey." Anna felt her tears flow freely as if she had never cried before.

Kathy shut the door and brought her over to the sofa and stroked her hair slowly and allowed Anna to cry in silence.

Kathy put her hair back and looked at Anna. "What happened to your eye? It's yellow and green and puffy."

Anna looked down and saw her pajamas on. *I forgot about the eye. I didn't have a chance to put on my makeup.*

She stumbled over her words as she tried to explain. "I ran into the door. It's nothing. I am so overwhelmed, Mom. I'm not ready to be a mother."

Anna suddenly bolted to the bathroom to throw up. Kathy followed and held Anna's hair away from the toilet seat as she retched. "I'm here. I didn't realize you were this sick."

"I need to take another pill for the nausea."

Kathy went to the kitchen to find the bottle and brought it back to her. "I'm going to come to help you."

"No need, Mom," Anna said. "Dave hired someone to help. He doesn't want me here alone."

Kathy looked disappointed, but Anna tried to reassure her. "Mom, I don't want you to stop what you are doing. I'm so excited for you to get your license back and do what you have always wanted. I'll be fine. Why don't you have some lunch? I'll give you the tour when I feel a little better."

They ate at the kitchen table, and Anna said, "I'm sorry, Mom. I know you didn't want me to get pregnant right away. Dave insists I don't work now. I don't think he ever wanted me to work. Now he is getting what he wants."

Kathy hesitated for a response and said, "Maybe that is not true, Anna. I just hope you are you speaking up for yourself and making sure your voice is heard? Are you teaching him how to treat you, like I talked about before? Well, I know now that is what happened to me. I allowed your father to dictate and manipulate or abuse me. I was just happy that someone wanted me because I had no confidence or self-esteem."

Kathy got up to stretch, and her energy came down as Anna felt safer when her mother was more relaxed. "I am a survivor of trauma and abuse and adapted on my own to survive. I realize so much and part of the treatment is to self-regulate when I have a trigger and stretch and allow myself not to relive the past. You see in a trigger your past memory takes over and you react to a situation and relive past events in the present. I have been tense all the time and reacting to life. Now I can recognize my body reactions and regulate them, and then I am pausing and deciding my action intentionally and that is building my confidence and self-esteem. You can do this, too, Anna." Kathy held Anna in her arms. "My dear, you are a victim of abuse as well. I am so sorry I stayed with your father and let the abuse happen. I never wanted that for my own kids. I just justified that you didn't have it as bad as me so I normalized our life. I am just so sorry, Anna."

Anna felt a wave of emotions come over her. Kathy said, "Anna, please do some stretching with me to help."

Anna went to the fridge and poured some wine and drank it down. She looked at her mother and said, "Thanks, Mom. Now what am I going to do?"

Kathy's eyes filled with tears. "I have let you down, Anna. I think that by staying with your father, I taught you that it was okay not to take care of yourself and that the way he treated me was normal or okay. I made so many excuses to stay and avoided the reasons to leave. I taught you and your brother that it is okay to allow someone to minimize you and, well . . . "

Anna said, "Mom, you need to stop thinking about the past. You're trying to help me now. The past is the past."

"I know," Kathy said. "My therapist keeps telling me that I'm a different person now and not that young, insecure little girl who chose to stay. She keeps telling me I did the best I could with who I was back then, but I have grown and I'm a stronger person today." Kathy then laid on the floor and stretched her back and her arms and allowed her muscles to relax. She said, "Cooked spaghetti. I am becoming so relaxed to let my frontal lobe come on and think clearer and more cognitively intentional."

Anna decided to copy her mother and laid on the floor and also was able to become relaxed. "Wow, Mom. This really works. I feel so much better."

Kathy got up and sat back on the couch with Anna. "Anna, this is so hard. When I look at you and Luke, it's so hard not to beat myself up. I loved you two more than anything in the world, but I was so young and, well, repeated some of my childhood problems."

"Isn't that inevitable, Mom? You were and are a great mother. Never think anything different. Look at what you are doing now. I am always learning from you."

"It's hard to believe I'm now finally teaching your father what I will and will not put up with, and I am thinking and doing what I have always wanted to do. He always made me feel I was so stupid and couldn't do anything. Well, I already thought there was something so wrong with me. I lived my life thinking no one would want someone so messed up. I was so happy your father wanted damaged goods that I never paid attention to all the red flags. I no longer think that way, but it has taken so long, and the journey is so hard. I won't enable him to treat me poorly anymore. He can't believe it. I now know why he never wanted me to go to therapy. He never wanted me to become healthier. He wanted control over me." She took some deep breaths and another big stretch.

Anna hugged her mother. "I know. It will be okay, Mom."

Suddenly, Sophie came out from the laundry room. Anna, stunned, said, "I thought you had left."

Sophie said, "I'm sorry. I was in the laundry room when your mother got here, and I didn't want, well, you know."

Anna felt violated but tried to hide it. "Mom, this is Sophie. She is going to be here a while to help me."

Kathy got up and said, "Nice to meet you. I'd like to give you my number so you can call me if she needs me."

Sophie took the card and nodded her head.

Kathy said, "Anna, I have to meet someone at the library. Will you be okay?"

"Of course. I will see you soon."

"I love you more than anything," Kathy said.

Anna looked at Sophie as she busied herself cooking a meal for Anna and Dave. "I'm going to go lie down. I'd appreciate if you kept whatever you heard between us. Okay?"

Sophie nodded her head. "I didn't hear anything." She looked at the ground.

Anna paid attention to the non-verbal communication and tension from Sophie. *I know she heard it all, and now she will tell Dave.*

Anna said, "Are you close with your mother, Sophie?"

"My mother is, well, the opposite of yours," Sophie answered. "She was so positive and such a good mother as I grew up, but as she got older, she lost that drive, especially after Mrs. Lawrence died. Many people were never the same after she died. Anyway, you need to rest now. I will finish the dinner and leave it for you and Mr. Lawrence."

Anna shook her head. "Thanks, Sophie."

CHAPTER 19

Sara

Anna woke with a stabbing pain in her abdomen on November 10th, the day of her baby shower and a few weeks before her due date. She went into the bathroom and sat on the bench to steady herself as she waited for the abdominal pain to pass.

Anna went downstairs, holding onto the railing. "Dave, I don't know why you insisted on a baby shower. I really don't like to be the center of attention, and we can afford to buy all of the baby stuff ourselves."

"You know many people want to come and share this with you," he said.

"Dave, something is wrong," she said. "I have a horrible pain that doesn't seem normal." She bent over and pressed her hand where the pressure was.

Sophie came in, noticed Anna, and ran to her. "We need to get you to a doctor. Mr. Lawrence, you should call and let them know we're coming."

"She has to go to the shower," Dave said. "I have some important clients coming today to celebrate with us."

Sophie shook her head. "This is serious. Let's get her there now, and if the doctor says she's okay, we can go to the shower from there."

Dave appeared annoyed, but when Anna screamed out in pain, he relented. He called Dr. Price's office, but since it was a Saturday, the physician on call told them to meet him at the emergency department. As they were leaving, Anna said, "I would like Sophie to come, too."

Dave said, "There's no need, Anna. I'll call her if I need to."

As they pulled out of the driveway, Anna saw that Sophie was following behind them in her own car. Knowing she would be with them made Anna feel a little less afraid. She was coming to understand who she could count on and who would fail her time and again.

Dave pulled up, and an attendant met them outside with a wheelchair. Anna said, "The pain is getting worse."

The attendant brought her into a room right away, and she looked up and saw Dr. Price.

"Anna, tell me what happened as I examine you."

Anna said, "I thought your partner was on call."

"I'm here with you now. Don't worry," she said.

As Anna tried to explain where the pain was coming from, Dr. Price performed a vaginal exam and then an ultrasound.

Anna said, "Where is Sophie?"

The nurse came back and had Sophie and Dave with her. Anna grabbed Sophie's hand and said, "Call my mother."

"I already did. She's on her way."

Dr. Price said, "Anna, Dave, the baby is breech, and Anna is eight centimeters dilated. The baby is in distress, and we need to do an emergency C-section. I'm sorry, but I need your consent."

Anna nodded, and Dave was taken away to sign some papers. "Please, do everything you can."

Anna felt herself become drowsy as anesthesia kicked in. Everything was happening so quickly.

Anna woke up and looked around the room to see Kathy holding her hand. Kathy rubbed her head and said, "It's okay. Everything is okay. You delivered a baby girl, and she is healthy and doing well."

"Thank god," Anna said. She began to cry. "Where is she? I need to see her." She looked around to get her bearings.

"You're in the recovery room. You can see her when you are stable and can go back to your room. She's so beautiful, Anna, just like you when you were born."

"Where's Dave?"

Kathy said, "I'm sorry, but he went to work for a few hours. Sophie has been here the whole time, but she went home to take a shower and get some rest. Also, your father is here, in the waiting room."

Anna said, "Really? He's actually here?"

"Yes. He came here right after I called him."

The nurse came over. "So, Mrs. Lawrence, how are you feeling?" She took Anna's blood pressure, and Anna tried to sit up but the pain kicked in as she held her breath.

"I'm in a lot of pain, but I really need to go to my room so I can see my daughter."

The nurse said, "Can you sit up? I'll give you some pain medication first."

Anna said, "No, I don't want to be too drowsy when I see her."

"Okay, but don't let the pain get out of control," the nurse said. "I will bring you some extra strength ibuprofen." Anna gladly took it and waited impatiently.

The nurse came in, and Anna felt the pain continue to worsen. "Would you want something else for the pain?" the nurse asked. Anna nodded, and she came to give Anna a shot. She then had the attendant come to push her to her room. She was in her bed and felt the medication kick in as she fell asleep again.

Anna woke to see her father holding a baby. Her mother was stroking her head.

Dan said, "She is waking up, Kathy. Are you okay, Anna?"

Anna felt dizzy. The room was spinning some. She attempted to sit up and noticed Dave was still not there.

Kathy smiled and said, "I am so happy to give your daughter to you, Sara."

Dan came over and placed the baby in Anna's arms. "Sara Katrina Lawrence."

Sara looked up into Anna's eyes, and Anna felt tears run down her cheeks. "My love. Mom, is there any other greater love than this?"

Kathy said, "I still feel that way about you."

Dan was looking from the corner of the room, and Anna kept her distance.

He hesitated and then said, "I'll wait in the waiting room. The nurse wants to help you feed her."

Anna pulled her gown down and felt the warmth of Sara's body against her own. It was so comforting. The nurse tried to help Anna position the baby to nurse.

"I'm Linda," she said. "Now, put her to the side and you need to try to have her mouth open wide and take the whole nipple in so it is not painful for you."

Anna helped Sara, and it took three tries, but Sara took to her breast well, and Anna felt comforted, though her nipples were tender and the process hurt more than she'd expected.

Linda said, "Wow. You're both naturals. How is your pain?"

"It's coming back, but I don't want to fall asleep on her."

Linda said, "I'll get you something that's not as strong." She came back and said, "Take this. You should switch sides now, about ten minutes each side."

Anna tried to wake Sara, and Linda said, "Can I ask you a question?" Anna nodded. "Did you apply for a job here about nine months ago?"

Oh my god, I never called that lady back. What is wrong with me? Anna started to fidget in her bed, and Linda said, "Oh my gosh, I'm so sorry. That was not right of me. You need to rest."

She moved to the door, and Anna said, "Yes. I had a job offer, and then I got pregnant and was so sick, I didn't even respond. I'm sorry. That was so wrong."

Linda walked back over to Anna and put her hand over Anna's and said, "I really do understand. Maybe the time wasn't right then, but things could change. Call me when you're back on your feet if you're ever interested."

Anna said, "Thanks, Linda. I really appreciate that." Kathy came back in, and after half an hour, Dave joined them in the room. He went over and touched Sara's face.

Dave curtly said as he stared at his newborn daughter, "Hi, Kathy. Thanks for staying, but you can go now. I'll take it from here."

Anna thought, *He is so rude to my mom.* She said, "Mom, where's Dad?"

Dave cut in, "Dan was here? You didn't tell me he came over, Anna."

Kathy said, "He left a while ago. He went to work. We'll talk later. Get some rest and enjoy this beautiful baby in your life. I'll be back tomorrow." She looked at Dave. "Congratulations, Dave. You have a beautiful daughter. Take care of both your girls."

Dave walked Kathy out, and Anna heard him say, "No need to come tomorrow. We'll be going home then." Anna felt angry but distracted herself staring at this new baby. *Is she really here? This all seems to be a dream. How did this happen so fast?*

After twenty minutes went by, the door opened and she saw Sue and Jake come in. *Oh my God, I don't want to see them now. I'm a wreck.*

Sue came over and gave her a big hug. "Oh my gosh. She's so beautiful." She whispered, "Don't worry. We're just stopping over for a minute."

Anna took a big breath as her heart raced.

Jake said, "She looks like you, Dave. What's her name?"

Anna looked at Jake and said, "Her name is Sara Katrina Lawrence, after your late wife. I believe she looks like her as well."

Jake turned his head in puzzlement and annoyance and turned to Dave. "Yes, Dave looks like his mother as well."

Jake put his hand on Sara's little hand and said, "Hope you all rest well. We'll see you later."

The next morning, Anna awoke to Sophie holding Sara in the corner of the room. "Hello, Anna. She is so sweet. I am so happy for you."

Anna felt comfort around her that happened over time, "Hi, Sophie. I'm glad you're here, but I have the nurses to help me now."

Sophie said, "Dave thought it would be good if I came to help out. He wants me to move in a while as you recover. I hope that is okay with you?"

He did it again, she thought. "Anna, he wanted me to get used to the baby and help you while you're in the hospital," Sophie added. Anna felt a sharp pain in her incision and bent over in the bed as Sophie put Sara down and rushed out to tell the nurses.

Dr. Price was on the floor and came in to see Anna. "Hi, Anna. Can I see the sutures?" Anna tried to lay back but needed to bend over to help the pain. She laid back again the best she could as Dr. Price examined her abdomen. "I think you'll have to stay another few days. I want you to be able to have less pain in order to take care of Sara, too. It's not infected, but you're healing slowly. You'll be okay. I'll make sure you get some medication so you can get up and around some, too."

Dave had come in and overheard the conversation. "Dr. Price, we will have some help at home, so can she go home tomorrow?"

Dr. Price said, "Maybe in two days. I want her to be stronger."

Dave shook his head. "I have an important meetings today and tonight. Sophie is going to stay with you two. I'll be back tomorrow."

He kissed Sara's head as she slept. A different nurse came in and gave her some medication, and Anna suddenly felt calm and fell asleep.

Anna felt the whole next few days were a blur. She finally got out of bed the next afternoon and tried to walk around when Kathy was there to help. After Kathy left, Anna was walking around the nurse's station with Sophie holding her hand and noticed Dave talking with Dr. Price.

Sophie helped Anna back to her room and went out to talk to Dave. Then she came back in and sat on the bed. "I'm sorry, Anna. I'm just bothered that Dave wants you to go home today and he sort of ordered the doctor to discharge you."

Anna felt confused but stayed quiet. Sophie said, "I know it's none of my business, but why do you always listen to him? You are like, well, like his mother Katrina. She was so nice and sweet, and I just hate what happened to her."

Anna said, "I'm not sure what you're talking about. What happened?"

Sophie took a minute as Dave came into the room. "Anna, I think it will be better if you come home today," he announced. "All those pills are making you sick, and Sophie can help at home in your own bed. We'll get a nurse if we need to as well."

Anna thought, *I actually want to go home, and if I argue, he will just push it.* "Okay."

She signed the paperwork as the nurse was giving her last-minute instructions and made a follow-up appointment in a week. Anna looked around, and Dave wasn't there.

"Sophie, where is Dave? Getting the car?"

Sophie stuttered, saying, "No, I'll be driving you home. I hope that is okay with you?"

Anna looked at her phone to send a text and wrote, "Dave, where are you? Aren't you driving me home?" Before she sent it, she deleted the message. "It's fine, Sophie. Let's go home, little Sara."

When they arrived at her house, she saw Luke's car in the driveway. Sophie said, "Surprise!"

Alia and Luke were waiting in their car, and Alia jumped out and ran over. "I need to see the baby. How are you, Anna? I've missed you so much."

"I'm glad you're here. No one told me you guys were coming."

Luke gave her a hug. "That's what a surprise is, silly. I wouldn't want to miss seeing my niece. Wow, she is so small."

Sophie opened the door for Anna, and she had to brace her abdomen to help her out of the car. Alia said, "I'll bring Sara in, if that's okay." Anna nodded.

Alia took the car seat out of the back seat and carried her to the front door. "Anna, this house is amazing. I'm so happy for you. Where is Dave anyway?" Luke was waiting for the answer as well, staring at Anna.

Anna avoided the question, and Sophie said, "He'll be here soon." Anna looked at Sophie and thought, *She can read my mind. I'm glad to have her.*

Kathy and Dan then pulled in the driveway as they were walking in the front door.

Luke stared at his father as Dan carried a few bags of groceries from the car.

Luke looked at Anna in disbelief, and she shrugged her shoulders, whispering, "I don't know. We'll talk later."

When they were all in the house eating dinner, Anna thought, *I feel so disconnected from this family. This is not the family I know.* She was lying on the couch and watching them all talk and laugh together when she heard the garage door open, and Dave came in.

"Well. I hope everyone is enjoying my house. Thank you all for coming, but I think you guys should get ready to go. Anna and Sara need their rest."

Why is he being so rude? I want them to stay. He hasn't been here all day and now he wants to order people around, she thought. "Dave, it's okay if they stay here. I want them here. I've been resting on the couch, and Sara is sleeping in her crib."

Luke looked at Dave and said, "Congratulations, Dave. You have a beautiful daughter. I'm a little concerned that Anna wasn't ready to come home from the hospital."

"She has Sophie, and now I'm here. It is better to recuperate in your own bed."

Alia, feeling the tension, said, "Either way is good, but she's home now. I'll help get her to bed tonight, and we'll be back in the morning to see them before we leave town."

Anna said, "Thanks, Alia."

Anna spent the next few days in bed. She didn't want to do anything. Sophie brought Sara to her room every few hours. "Anna, it's time to feed her." Anna would roll over, let Sara eat, and then say, "Okay, Sophie, she's done. Come and get her."

Sophie came into the bedroom with the phone. "Hi, Anna. Your mom is on the phone again for the fifth time. Please talk to her."

Anna shook her head, and she heard Sophie say, "I don't know. She doesn't come out of the room, and she barely eats. She has not showered in days and just sleeps all day. She even missed her doctor's appointment and refused to go." Sophie then left the room.

Anna woke to Kathy pulling on her shoulder. "Anna, wake up. I'm taking you to the doctor. You need to get out of bed and put some clothes on." Anna just shook her head no.

Sophie came into the room, and Kathy said, "Sophie, can you get her sweatpants and a shirt?"

"What is wrong with her?" Sophie asked.

Kathy whispered, "She has postpartum depression. It can be pretty severe, and I had it, too." She rolled Anna over, and a stench of stale, bad breath filled the room. "Now, Anna. Sara needs you to go to the doctor and get some help. She needs her mother to take care of her."

Anna said, "She's fine. Sophie is taking care of her."

Sophie started to talk, but Kathy put her finger up to her as if to say wait a minute. "Sophie is going to help you get dressed, Anna. I'll be right back," she said.

Kathy came back, and Sophie only had Anna's bra and shirt on her now. "This is impossible. She won't wake up."

Kathy said, "Honey, you have an appointment with Dr. Price. You need to help us get you ready."

Anna was so difficult to wake up, and Kathy looked in her dresser drawer and saw a pill bottle for Xanax with Kathy's name on it, plus a small empty flask of vodka. She shook Anna some more, and Anna said, "Mom, I just need to sleep."

"How many of these did you take?" Kathy demanded. She slapped Anna's face as she drifted off and became unarousable. "Call 911, Sophie," she ordered.

Kathy got a cold cloth and put it on Anna's face. "Wake up now," she said sternly. "Sara needs you. Remember when I told you that I was down after I had you, and my sister had to come help? Well, that can run in the family, and now you are going through it. We will get you feeling better, but you have to stay with us."

Anna woke in the emergency room with her mother holding her.

"Mom, what is going on? What happened?"

"Anna, get some rest," Kathy said. "You tried to kill yourself with your pills and alcohol."

Anna held her head up. "I just wanted to sleep, Mom."

Someone came around the corner and, looking at a clipboard, said, "So, Anna, how are you feeling now?"

"I just wanted to get some sleep. That's all," Anna said.

"I am Dr. Reddy. I am a psychiatrist and want to talk about what you did to yourself today. Were you trying to hurt yourself, Anna?" He looked at her in an inquisitive way.

Anna said, "I don't know. I am so tired and just really wanted to sleep."

"Do you feel like that now?" Anna looked up at her mother, who was now in tears. The psychiatrist said, "I know this is hard, but could you maybe let me talk with her alone?"

Kathy got up and slowly let go of Anna's hand. "I love you, Anna."

"How long have you felt depressed?"

Anna shook her head. "I'm just tired."

Dr. Reddy took some breaths and wrote some things on the notepad then looked up. "Anna, you took ten Xanax with a whole pint of vodka. You can die from that, so we call that a suicide attempt. We're going to have to keep you here."

Anna said, "No, I need to get home to my daughter. I didn't know that I could kill myself." She calmed herself down as she cried, and she took a breath.

"Doctor, I have had thoughts that life is so difficult that I'd like to just go off to sleep and things would be easier, but I honestly didn't have a plan to hurt myself. Please let me go home with my mother. She'll watch over me."

Kathy came back in and said, "I'll take care of her. We'll get an appointment with my therapist and with her doctor. I won't let her out of my sight."

Dr. Reddy wrote down more notes and said, "If you will sign this form to take responsibility for your daughter, then we'll let her go in a few hours. She is physically stable now. Where is your husband?"

Anna said, "I guess he's at work now. I'd rather him not find out about this. He doesn't quite understand."

Kathy looked to the psychiatrist and said, "I will let him know what has happened, but I'll sign the form to take responsibility."

Dr. Reddy said, "I need to ask some more questions. Anna, do you want to hurt yourself? Do you feel down and depressed? Do you have no motivation? Are you sleeping at night?"

Anna shook her head no to these questions. She thought, *He is now just covering his tracks so he doesn't get sued. I just need to go home before Dave gets there, and I want to see Sara.*

Anna signed the discharge papers with the nurse as Kathy was getting off the phone. "All right, we have an appointment in an hour to see Dr. Price."

The nurse wrote down the information about the appointment and said, "Okay, you're free to go. Do you want a wheelchair?"

"No thanks. I'll be okay," Anna said.

Dr. Price came in the room and said, "Anna, from the emergency notes, it looks like you have postpartum depression. I would like you to start these pills and next week to start counseling. We will get you feeling better again, but you must take these every day."

Anna nodded and thought, *Will those pills hurt Sara? Then again, the alcohol must be.*

"I'll see you in two weeks, and your mother said she has a good therapist you can see next week. Call me if anything changes."

Kathy said, "I'll be with her."

They got home around five after stopping at Kathy's house so she could pack a bag for herself. Anna headed for her bedroom without even checking on Sara. The doorbell rang just as Anna went to lie down on the couch, not being able to find the energy to reach her own bed.

Anna saw Kathy answer the door. "Oh, hi, Jen and Lori. Anna is actually sleeping at the moment. It would have been better if you'd called first."

Jen said, "I've been texting and calling Anna, but she won't pick up. Dave finally told me to just come around."

"Would you like to see Sara, the baby?" Kathy asked.

They came in, and Sophie said, "I'll make some coffee."

Jen saw Anna and came over to her. "Hi, Anna. You haven't answered my texts. I've been worried about you."

Anna stared out the window as she said, "Sorry."

"Anna has had a rough start," Kathy said. "The C-section was hard, and the unexpected early delivery has taken a toll."

"We have all the gifts from the shower in the car," Lori said. "Can we bring them in and put them somewhere? Maybe that'll cheer her up."

Sophie said, "Oh, I would be glad to bring them in."

"It's so nice, Sophie, that you're able to help Anna and Dave," Jen said.

Dave finally came home, and Anna looked at the clock. It was five forty-five. She thought, *So much earlier than usual. He must have known that Jen was here.* He said, "Well, hello, everyone. What a nice surprise."

"Dave, could we speak in private for a moment?" Kathy asked.

He gave her an irritated look. "I guess so."

"Anna, is it okay if I hold Sara?" Jen asked.

Sophie came back in the room and picked up Sara and said, "Here, Jen. Let me hand her to you?"

Anna watched Jen hold her and smell her head as Sara then started to cry. She thought, *Her cry is so irritating.* "Sophie, can you get her to stop crying?" she asked.

Jen handed the baby to Sophie and put her arm on Anna's shoulder. "I'm here for you if you need me."

Lori then came over. "I'm sorry this transition is so hard for you, Anna. Please let us know what we can do to help."

Anna said, "I just need to go to sleep now."

They got up as Dave and Kathy came back into the room.

Dave said, "Okay. But I want you to know I don't believe in medication for depression. It never did help my mother."

Jen and Lori looked at each other then at Anna and said, "We'll come by another time soon, Anna."

Dave walked them out and then came back and packed a bag for himself. Anna saw him come down with the bag, and he came over to her. "Anna, your mother and Sophie will take care of you and Sara. I have to go on a business trip. I'll call you later."

Anna just nodded without any emotion.

He said to Kathy, "She'll be better when I get back in a few weeks, right? I can't have another depressed woman in my life now. I was raised by one."

CHAPTER 20

Therapy

The next week, Anna woke the morning of her appointment and thought, *I feel a little better. Where is Sara?* She went to Sara's room and looked around. The room was spotless, and everything was in its place. Anna put her robe on and went downstairs to see Sophie singing to Sara, who was in her swing.

Sophie said, "Oh, your mom is here. You are so lucky, Miss Sara, to have your mother. We're so glad to see you," she said to Anna. "Are you feeling better?"

"A little better today," Anna said. "Is my mother driving me?"

"She ran out to get some groceries, but she'll be back here soon. Can I make you some breakfast?"

"That's okay. I'll just have some cereal after I get ready. Did Dave say when he'd be home?"

Sophie shook her head no.

Kathy came in with a few bags. "Hello, how are my two girls today? I need to hold my favorite baby girl before we leave." She held Sara tightly in her arms. "Anna looks better today."

Kathy and Anna drove over to the office in Novi, and on the way, she said, "Anna, I know I've been telling you what I have been learning in therapy. I want you to focus on your journey because I know your marriage and personality are different from mine."

Anna said, "Mom, I'm only going until I feel better and I can take care of Sara."

Kathy said, "I've been working on a quality of life that I feel good about. What is wrong with wanting the same for my lovely daughter?"

Anna remained quiet. *She is making me not want to go*, she thought.

They arrived and checked in at the desk. Anna was filling out the paperwork as the therapist came out. "Anna Lawrence?"

Anna stood up and shook the therapist's hand. "Hi, nice to meet you."

"Please call me Lynn," she said as they walked together back to her office. "And make yourself comfortable."

Anna sat down and noticed that Lynn was a thin older woman with light wrinkles around her eyes and mouth, as if she frowned a lot. She sat with her feet on the floor in a relaxed posture that made it clear she was at ease in this space and with her work. Lynn took out a notepad and said, "I sometimes jot down notes as we go along, Anna, but I want you to know that everything we say in here is confidential. It is up to you to share what you are comfortable with."

"I feel you already know about me from my mother," Anna said.

Lynn said, "I believe you have your own perspective and thoughts on your own life, so I am focused on you, not what someone else has told me. If you would like another therapist, I can recommend someone."

Anna said, "No, you seem to have helped my mother quite a bit, so I'm okay with this."

"Can you tell me what brought you here?" Lynn asked.

"Don't you know?"

Lynn said, "I would like to hear what you have to say about it."

Anna shook her head. "Well, my doctor said I have postpartum depression. I had a daughter, and I only recently got married, last year. I was married when I got pregnant, but we were not trying for a baby yet. Everyone thought I was too young to even get married."

Lynn said, "Do *you* think you were too young?"

"I don't know. Now I have a daughter and a husband. I guess it's a lot, but I have Sophie. She lives with us and pretty much does what I should be doing."

"It sounds like you have some guilt that you are not doing what you should," Lynn said.

Anna paused then said, "My husband, Dave, well, he decided without me that we would have Sophie come and live with us. I guess he didn't think I could handle anything."

"Did you communicate with him about what you wanted?"

"Yes, I tried. But I also wondered, when he didn't think I could take care of things, whether maybe he was right. I have my own doubts about my abilities, and he is so convincing that I find it really difficult to argue with him. I did have a C-section and was in a lot of pain. It was hard to get around. I did need some help. You see? He was right, and he was looking out for me."

"It sounds like you don't trust your own opinion."

"Well, I guess I started to doubt myself. I work on communicating and allowing my voice to be heard, but since the baby or rather since I said yes to getting married, I just don't have the energy to argue. I guess that's why I just lie in bed. Sophie is so great with Sara, and she sings to her and bathes her and keeps the house so neat and clean. There is nothing for me to do."

Lynn put her pad down and put her hand over Anna's. "Anna, I'm so glad you have been talking and are open to this. It takes a lot of courage to open up. I would like to ask if you're feeling helpless?"

Anna thought about her question. "I guess I'm overwhelmed, and Sophie does a better job than I could. I never wanted this big house, and I wasn't trying to have a baby. I wanted to start to work and just enjoy being married and having a career. We don't have the normal struggles of a newlywed couple because he comes from money and has money."

Lynn sat back and seemed to be processing the information. "I understand," she said. "Your vision in your mind of what marriage looked like is not what it actually is." Anna nodded. "We actually harm ourselves with these preconceived notions of what things will be like and actually can grieve when life turns out differently than we expected. However, learning to accept our actual reality can help us to appreciate it and work within it. No matter what, there are struggles in your life, but maybe not the ones you envisioned."

Lynn took a moment before continuing. "Also, Anna, remember—you just had a baby, too, and postpartum depression is common. It's a chemical or hormonal event that happens alongside this exhausting and life-transforming experience of having a baby. It changes everything, including your marriage and other relationships. You have to allow yourself some time to adapt and adjust, especially since you are so young." Then she said, "Anna, tell me what you want to happen with Sophie and your future."

"I would like her to not stay the night and only come when I need her. I have to learn on my own how to take care of things. I do want to go back to work and have Sophie watch Sara when I'm at work—when I actually need her."

"Do you feel strong enough to make this change right now? Does talking about what you want make you feel less depressed?"

"I believe if I had to take care of Sara, I would feel less depressed," Anna said. "I want to do it now."

"Do you feel you can discuss this with Dave?" Lynn asked.

Anna hesitated. "I don't know about that. I know he doesn't think of me as strong, and whenever I do speak up, he discounts me or puts off any sort of discussion or we just fight. I never seem to be able to get through to him what I am thinking." Anna paused then said, "Do you know my mother has been doing therapy with me since she has been in treatment with you? She doesn't know that I know she is doing this. I try to allow her to think she is helping me. I do want to thank you for helping her. She is much happier."

"You are too kind, Anna," Lynn said. "I like to believe the people who really want to change will start to see things differently and make those changes to help themselves. Remember, changing perceptions and coping mechanisms is very difficult and can change the relationships in your lives dramatically and in ways you cannot predict and may not want. When you rewrite the roles, people around you resist because it is natural to resist change."

Anna said, "Like my mother leaving my father, and now my father is trying to change so she won't leave. She didn't see that coming."

"You seemed to have changed the subject away from Dave. Is there a reason for that?" Lynn asked.

"No. I have actually tried to talk to Dave, on the advice of my mother, to get him to hear my side of things, but he is pretty dominant and sure of himself. It's hard for me to get him to listen, and usually he gets his way." Lynn allowed her some more time. Anna said, "I guess I did marry someone like my own father."

"Is there another example of this besides Sophie?"

"Lots of them. I told him I wanted a smaller house, but he bought the house he wanted and even furnished it without discussing it with me first. He made it seem like it was a surprise and a gift. When I bring it up, he has a way of brushing me off and making me seem ungrateful and spoiled or something."

"Oh, I see," Lynn said. "How do you think you can get your voice heard?"

"Just when I feel I make some progress, it backfires on me. My mother thinks I am reliving her life, and I try to explain to her that I am not her and Dave is not my father. He does have similar traits to him, though, I must admit."

"Sometimes we can subconsciously make decisions that are similar to our upbringing for different reasons," Lynn said. "At times, we want to repair things that happened in our childhood or gain some approval we may not have received. Sometimes we are more comfortable with a negative environment because it is familiar and what we believe we deserve. Do you think you have done this?"

Anna started crying. "I hope not, because now I have a daughter and she will be in a childhood hell that I grew up in. Why would I ever do that?" She got up and took some tissues from the box on the side table.

Lynn said, "Anna can you take a moment in your emotional state to pay attention to your muscles and your body as you are reacting to these emotions? Now try to relax them by stretching them out and then allowing them to just hang."

Anna listened and said, "I see my mother do this and she says it helps lower cortisol levels and stress and make you calmer." Anna stood there stretching and feeling less emotional.

Lynn gestured to a basket of water bottles. "Please, take one."

Anna drank some water and noticed a picture on the wall of Rachel, her wedding planner, Sue, and Lynn standing together with their arms around each other. "Lynn, do you know Rachel and Sue?"

Lynn got up and gracefully put her hand on Anna's shoulder. "They are my daughters."

Anna thought, *What is going on? Rachel told me that her mother was friends with Katrina and that she has never been the same since her death. Sue and Rachel are sisters? I'm so confused.* She looked at Lynn and said, "You knew Katrina, my mother-in-law?"

Lynn sat down. "Yes, I did. Very well." Anna grabbed her coat, and Lynn said, "Please, Anna, can we discuss this?"

"You knew that I am her daughter-in-law and didn't tell me that you knew the family?"

"I'm sorry, Anna. I should have disclosed that, but my only intention is to help you." Lynn got up and turned to the window in a solemn way. "I loved Katrina. She was my patient for years, and we became close, so we chose to be friends instead of having a professional relationship. That is the only time I have ever done something like that. She was such a good person."

Anna said, "So you know what happened to her?"

Lynn, puzzled, said, "What do you mean? She fell and died of a complete cervical fracture. It was so awful."

"No, I mean was there foul play with Jake or Mr. Lawrence?"

Lynn stood up and stood over Anna now. "I'm not sure where you got that idea. I mean, everyone knows that Katrina and Jake had their problems, but we should not jump to conspiracy theories. Besides, there was a thorough investigation, and it was dropped."

Anna got up, feeling uncomfortable, and started to pace.

Lynn said, "Anna, I am sorry that this has gotten off topic, but we should refocus on other ways of communicating with Dave. Our time is up, but I would like you to work on that for our next session."

Anna said, "There won't be another session. By the way, does my mother know all this?" Lynn shook her head. Anna left the office, and Kathy set down the magazine she'd been reading and followed her into the hall.

Anna put her head down in the car. "Mom, Lynn is Rachel and Sue's mother. Rachel and Sue are sisters."

Kathy said, "Oh, really."

"I don't think you are making the connection. Lynn was a good friend with Katrina, my mother-in-law. Her daughter was Jake's mistress when Katrina was alive."

"You seem upset by this."

"I think Lynn should have told me."

Kathy said, "Anna, she works with a lot of people. I'm not sure why there's a problem."

"Mom, she knows Dave's parents well. That means she knows Dave."

"I can only see that that would benefit you and not hurt you."

Anna thought, *Did Dave arrange this? Was Lynn reporting back to Sue or to Dave? Why does the whole world seem to be getting smaller and smaller?*

Kathy pulled up in the driveway, and Anna said, "Mom, I'm okay. I need some time to think. I'll call you."

"Anna, I understand. I know you have a lot on your mind, but there's something I need to tell you. Your father, well, he moved out of the house. We are separated for now and going to marriage counseling. He asked me to go. I decided to go to ahead with the divorce and not to get back together."

"Mom, I wish you did that a long time ago," Anna said. "It's a little too late to have helped me or Luke." Kathy's face registered hurt at this remark, but Anna was too angry with Lynn and Dave to care. "I'm going to see Sara now."

Anna went in the house and straight to the nursery. She picked up Sara, who was sleeping, and held her close. She thought, *Who can I trust? Can I trust Sophie? Dave pays her, and she could be spying on me and telling him what is going on. Did Rachel spy on Sue or me?*

Sophie came in and said, "Are you okay? I just got her down."

Anna nodded. "Why don't you go home now? We'll be fine."

Sophie said, "Dave thinks I should stay here."

"You'll still get paid whatever he agreed to, but I don't need you to stay the night anymore. I'll talk to him."

"I put some chicken in the oven for dinner," Sophie said, "so don't forget to take it out in about twenty minutes. All the laundry is put away. I am glad you're feeling better now. Will I see you in the morning?"

"Yes," Anna said. "Please come at ten."

Anna put Sara down and opened her journal. *Hello, I have not written in a long time. Life is all happening so fast. I have a beautiful daughter and am in a questionable marriage. I found out my parents are separated. I feel so angry because I wanted her to leave so long ago, and now that I am not living at home, she leaves him. Why now? I want her to be happy, but now I'm in a marriage I may not have been in if she had left a long time ago. I feel so tired and run down, but I cannot rest or relax. Every time I let my guard down, something happens to ruin it. What should I think of my husband? Was Sue right in what she told me or does she have another agenda? There are so many mixed messages. What should I make of Sue and Rachel being sisters and Lynn being their mother and Katrina's friend?* She heard the garage door open and put her journal away.

Dave came in as Anna was closing the door to Sara's room behind her. "She's sleeping."

"Why did you send Sophie home?"

"Let's go talk in the kitchen," Anna said.

Dave first went to change his clothes then grabbed a beer and checked his phone. He was in no hurry to join her. When he finally sat down across from Anna, she said, "So. Dave, I think I was depressed because she took over and I didn't have to do anything. I think I can take care of things at night. I am having her come in the daytime, but I think a few hours a day will be good for now."

Dave put his hand on her arm. "I hope you can handle everything here. I did all this for you. I expect you to keep up with everything."

Anna allowed herself to stretch her arms and legs and focused on breathing and felt her tension in her body come down as well as her emotions settle.

"Dave, remember when I got my nursing license and wanted to work?"

Dave squeezed harder on her arm. "Anna, you are a mother now, and you will not work."

Anna interrupted him and said, "Dave, I have my own needs and desires. You know I have wanted to be a nurse and have a profession of my own. I have never hid that. It is important to me. I'll only work a few days a week. That is all I want, a small part-time job. I appreciate your hard work and dedication to our family."

Dave let go of her arm and slammed his fist on the table. "I don't like this, Anna. If it takes anything away from Sara or me, you will quit. I also know you saw a therapist and she is putting all of this in your head. You are fine, and I don't want you to go again."

Anna thought, *You mean you don't like it when I have a voice*, but she chose not to pick another battle at this time.

CHAPTER 21

The Investigation

Anna wrote in her journal one day in January, *Dear Diary, I decided to wait until Sara was three months old to get a job. I think that Prozac medication that Dr. Price gave me is really helping me, and I am feeling stronger and much healthier. I need to stay away from the alcohol and Xanax. I need to cope better without looking for something to make me feel better or self-medicate from my emotions. I think that those things bring me down and make me weaker and not as motivated. I now need to be strong for Sara and myself. I think that I understand Dave a little better and his need to control everything. I think he likes when I am not strong. I am going to use some of my time to find out what I can about Katrina. People liked her, and so many people seem to have doubts about her death. Maybe finding out about what really happened to her will help me.*

Anna put her journal down and held Sara, who was making cooing noises. She smelled her head and took a deep breath. "You make me so happy. I won't make the same mistakes my mother made with me." She went downstairs to see Sophie in the kitchen. "Hi, Sophie. I have some errands to do today, and I'd like to go without Sara."

Sophie came over and took Sara from Anna. "Of course. I love time with her. She is such a good baby." She went to the baby swing and looked over. "What errands are you doing today?"

Anna thought, *That is strange for her to ask.* Stumbling with her words, she said, "I have an appointment and just a few stores I want to browse in. I'll be home in about three hours."

Anna drove to the library to use the computer, knowing Dave wouldn't be able to find out what she was doing if she did her work there. She looked up "Katrina Lawrence" in the newspaper and found both her obituary and an article from the police about her death.

"Birmingham Wife and Mother Gravely Injured from a Fall at Home," the headline read. Anna read the short article about Katrina's "terrible accident" in the home she shared with Jake and two boys, which led to a cervical fracture that caused paralysis and coma. After three days, the family decided to stop life support, and she died a few hours later. The police investigated the circumstances of the fall to determine whether it really was an accident. Cervical fractures of this severity, Anna knew from her studies of anatomy, usually involved significant force to the neck. At the time the article ran, the investigation was still ongoing.

Anna sat back in the library chair with her mouth hanging open. Thoughts were racing about Jake and Dave and Tom. *What really happened? Did Jake push Katrina down the stairs? Did Dave know about any of this? Why is Dave so secretive about Sue, and why doesn't he ever talk about his own mother? How can I find out without Dave knowing? How did he know I saw Lynn? I just have more questions than answers!*

Another week went by, and Anna asked Sophie again to watch Sara for the day. Anna felt her heart jump in her chest as she walked into the Birmingham police station. She walked up to the front desk. The police officer sitting there, a woman with a long ponytail and a deep frown, was busy writing something, and she coughed to get her attention. The officer looked up and said, "Yes?"

"I would like to request some public information on an old investigation," Anna said.

"Okay, sit over there and someone will help you in a moment." The officer made a phone call, and Anna felt her chest pound. *What am I doing here?*

A few minutes later, an older gentleman came over to Anna. "Come with me, please," he said, and she followed him to his office and sat down. "So, what can I help you with?"

Anna said, "I would like to know about what happened to a death investigation a few years ago. The woman's name was Katrina Lawrence. She was killed—I mean, died—from a cervical fracture from a fall."

The officer started entering some information into the computer. "Can I ask why you want this information?"

Anna felt her breathing speed up and said, "Curiosity."

"I am Officer Lott, and you're lucky because I was on the case, but I never did meet you."

"I married Dave Lawrence, one of Katrina's sons. My name is Anna. This is confidential, right?"

The officer pushed the screen to the side so that he could see her better. "Mrs. Lawrence. Are you afraid, or are you in an abusive situation?"

Anna plastered a shocked look on her face but quickly dropped her shoulders and relaxed her muscles as much as she could to lower her tension. Her thoughts became clearer and easier to communicate. "No. Why would you ask that?" she said. "It's just that no one in the family talks about it, and I have heard some rumors and want to know for myself what happened. You see, I have a baby now as well."

The officer said, "I see. I can tell you that when people have money, investigations are short."

Anna peered at him. "What does *that* mean? Why was there an investigation in the first place?"

"It is standard practice to investigate a death like this. You see, the life insurance company wants to know. Also, there was an anonymous tip in this case. However, there was not enough evidence to support a conclusion of foul play, so the matter was dropped after only a week."

Anna shook her head. The officer sat back in his chair and tapped his pen on the side of the table and added, "I remember the husband. One thing I remember very clearly is that Mr. Lawrence was quite cold and unemotional about his wife's death. That always seemed suspicious to me, but as I said, my hands were tied."

"Thank you for your time," Anna said. She walked out of the building and noticed Jeff, of all people, in one of the back rooms. Just as she saw him, he looked up and met her eyes, his mouth falling open in surprise. But before he could make his way to her, she ran to the car and pulled away. Jeff stood in the entrance to the building, calling after her and waving his arm, but she didn't stop.

Anna let a few months go by before she took any further action. She just wasn't sure what to do with the information she was learning. Finally, one day, she called Lynn. "Hi, Lynn, it's Anna Lawrence."

"Hi, Anna. I am so glad you called."

Anna said, "I don't really want an appointment, but I'd like to meet with you to talk about Katrina."

Lynn paused. "How have you been? How has your mood been?"

"I am feeling better now. I have been trying to understand Dave through his mother, and you knew her the best. I'm sure it's difficult to talk about her, but I'd really appreciate it, as a friend, not a therapist."

Anna bit her nails as she waited for what felt like forever for a response. "Okay," Lynn said, "but only once, Anna. I miss her terribly, and it's difficult to talk about."

"Thank you."

A few days later, Sophie came in, and Anna said, "I have so many errands today. Thanks for coming."

Anna met Lynn at the library, in a private room in the back. "Hi, Anna. Why did you want to meet here?"

"It's just quiet, and there are some papers here that I wanted to show you."

Lynn looked down and saw the old newspaper articles and the police report. "What are you doing?"

"I'm trying to find out what happened to her."

Lynn shook her head and started to walk away.

"Please don't go," Anna said. "If you really cared about Katrina, you'd want to know the truth. I need to know so I can trust my husband."

"Anna, this isn't a good idea. The past is the past. We need to learn how to live our present life and allow the past to be."

Anna thought, *That is not what she really thinks. I know she is hiding something, but I need to be careful that she doesn't leave.* "I know you are still grieving. Rachel said you've never been the same since her death. It was almost like she'd lost her own mother."

Lynn sat down and looked squarely into Anna's eyes. "Anna, Jake is not well. I believe he has narcissistic personality traits or disorder, and because of that, Katrina paid the ultimate sacrifice. I went to the police, but nothing happened, and my story, Katrina's story, wasn't heard. Jake made sure of that, and I have lived in fear of him since that day. Ask yourself, if you figure this out, what then? What will it matter?"

"I need to know if Dave knows what happened," Anna said.

"You mustn't go to the police, okay?" Anna nodded. "Katrina grew up naïve to the world and married Jake in her early twenties. She had Tom and Dave early as well. She loved those boys, more than anything. Jake became extremely emotionally abuse, and the demeaning negative comments were ongoing. His affairs were obvious and many. Katrina saw me in confidence. He didn't know about our sessions." Anna patiently waited and held onto her million questions in her head as Lynn took a sip of water.

Lynn seemed to relax a bit by sitting down in a chair and tipped her head to the right. "Katrina was becoming stronger and had a much better sense of her own identity. We decided to end our professional relationship. We started spending time together as friends, and she started to go back to school and had a life other than being the wife of Jake Lawrence. She started telling me that things were improving, but I was becoming overwhelmingly scared for her. I had my doubts, but she was convincing. She didn't want to leave those boys and didn't want Jake to get custody. She started to spend less time with me and stopped telling me what was going on. I worried for her, and she always reassured me that she was doing well. She put a letter under my mat at home a few days before she died. She knew I kept a key there, but I didn't find it until a few months after the investigation was over."

Anna said, "Did you give it to the police or do you still have it?"

"I only read some of it because it was too difficult at the time," Lynn said. "I did give it to that Officer Lott, the one on the investigation, but he told me the case was closed after he took the letter. I never did see it again, and when I approached the detective, he told me that the letter had disappeared. He wouldn't tell me any more except that he was sorry. I didn't believe him, but I knew then to leave it alone."

"Can you tell me what the letter said?"

"I just remember her warning me that she was filing for divorce and if something happened to her that it was Jake who hurt her." Lynn started to sob, and Anna put her hand on her shoulder.

"It's so difficult because I helped her to become well, and sometimes the consequences of a woman making that kind of change are unpredictable and too painful to bear. I quit counseling for a while and went to counseling myself. I decided that the benefits of helping people outweigh everything else. I have come to believe that Katrina had some happiness and peace with her journey in the end. She found some happiness in a miserable existence, and without that, she would have died inside. I'm always leery of the outcome of change, but it's always worth it if someone finds their happiness for themselves. For example, with your mother."

"Was there anything about Dave in the letter?"

Lynn said, "No, not in the letter. Katrina told me Dave was in desperate need of his father's love and affection, and Katrina could see that she had lost him to his father as he got older. She had hope for Dave because they were so close as he was growing up, but slowly Jake chipped away at that relationship by telling him negative things about her. However, she lived for the moments when Dave would find her and sit with her as she stroked his hair. I think that happened up until she died. That certainly leaves me with some hope for him emotionally."

"I really appreciate you sharing this with me. I know there is nothing I can do. You know that Sue has talked to me. You just verified what she has told me. Maybe, just maybe, the police would listen now."

"Anna, even with the evidence of the letter, there is no proof of her being pushed or of him even being home when it happened."

Anna said, "I found out that Katrina had a life insurance policy, and when Jake claimed it after her death, it triggered an investigation."

"You know he refused an autopsy on her as well, don't you? Except the hospital report noted a high level of benzodiazepines in her system, which I know she would not take." Lynn paused and looked out the door. "Anna, I cannot talk about this anymore. I have tried to put this in the past, and I need to do that for myself."

I have a million questions, but I need to leave it alone for now, Anna thought. "I appreciate you talking to me."

Lynn put her hand on Anna's. "Please be careful, Anna. Dave has some traits of his father's. I think you know that."

Anna immediately went home, wanting to hold Sara. In the nursery, she picked up Sara and hugged her closely. "Thanks, Sophie."

"Where did you go?" Sophie asked. She looked at Anna with concern. "Is everything okay?"

Anna didn't want to say anything just yet, even to someone she trusted as much as she trusted Sophie. Dave seemed to have eyes and ears everywhere. "I'm fine. I'll see you tomorrow."

Dave came in an hour later and kissed Sara. "Anna, I'm going out tonight to meet some clients. By the way, where did you go today?"

Anna fumbled with what to say and said, "The library. Why?"

He shook his head. "We need to talk when I get home!"

As Anna bathed Sara and got her ready for bed, she wondered what could possibly have angered Dave about her going to the library. Anna thought about how they had not spent much time together, but just as she was feeling better, the thoughts of Jake, Sue, and Lynn all came flooding back. She grabbed a few beers and started to drink one but then thought, *That makes me weak, and I need to be strong and in my healthy head.* She poured the rest down the drain as she thought of Lynn and how Katrina had medications in her system that Lynn was sure she would not have willingly taken. Would Dave ever do something like that to her? The fact that she even had to ask that question made her feel more frightened than she'd ever been.

She sat in the rocker and looked down at Sara, admiring her beauty. Her big, blue eyes shined. Anna loved her cute, petite nose and long fingers, but she couldn't help but notice that Sara looked more like Dave than her. Sara stared into her mother's eyes as if there was an understanding between them, and Anna felt a fierce protectiveness come over her. If they had to make it on their own, Anna would find a way.

"I won't allow your father to hurt you like my father hurt me. You will only have unconditional love from me and a home where you don't have to walk on pins and needles every time your father comes home. I love you more than anything in the world, Ms. Sara." She kissed her forehead and put her in her crib. She watched her as she dosed off to sleep, looking so serene and peaceful. Anna felt a great sense of satisfaction knowing that, at least for the moment, she was protecting her daughter.

Anna distracted herself by sending out a few resumes over email and noticed a message from the West Bloomfield hospital where she had delivered Sara.

"Hi, Anna, I am writing to see if you are interested in a job in the labor and delivery unit where you delivered your lovely baby. I had an opening and had not heard from you, so I thought I would check first with you. Please let me know your thoughts and availability for an interview. Sincerely, Linda Corset, Unit Manager."

Anna felt a pull of longing to reclaim her old dream. She immediately wrote back, "Dear Linda, I sincerely appreciate you thinking of me for this opening. I would really like to come for an interview. I would like to share that I am looking for part-time work at this time. I could come any morning in the next few weeks. Sincerely, Anna Lawrence."

As Anna was finishing the message, she heard the garage door open and felt her heart jump a beat. Dave came into the room and barely looked at her, which was unusual. Anna went over to him and put her arms around his shoulders, but he shook her off.

"Dave, what is happening? You said we needed to talk—what is this about?"

Dave took a deep breath but looked stern and defensive. "Sit down, Anna. Do you want to tell me what you have been up to?"

Anna's thoughts raced as she shook her head. "I'm not sure what you mean."

He grabbed Anna's arms, which were leaning on the table, and held them down. Then he looked into her eyes. "I mean the investigation into my mother's death. Do you think you can go to the police and talk to people without my father finding out? Do you know how influential my father is? Haven't you figured that out yet? I've told you time and time again to ask me if you have any questions, but you actually went to the police."

Anna felt she might throw up. *How does he know?* "Dave, your family is so secretive, and Sue told me things I knew you wouldn't talk to me about. Why won't you tell me what happened to your mother?" She twisted her arms to get out of his grasp, and he let her go.

Anna thought, *I need to go get Sara and leave before things get too bad. I have to be strong for her, not like my mother was with Luke and me.*

Anna said, "I think I hear Sara. I'll be right back." She left and felt a surge of adrenaline and allowed herself to stretch and relax to calm her nervous system down and think rationally before she picked Sara up. She brought her down. Dave was sitting at the kitchen table texting someone and looked up at her, shaking his head in disbelief. Sara was crying now as Anna bounced her up and down. "Dave, I think she is sick. I'm going to take her to the emergency room. She feels warm to me."

Dave got up and said, "I'm going, too."

She quickly put Sara in the car seat and got into the car as Dave was texting on his phone in the mud room. She started the car and rolled the window down. "It's okay. I'll call you after we see the doctor."

As she drove through the front gate, she saw Jake driving past her car and into the driveway and thought, *What is he doing here? I'm so glad I got away. Where do I go now? Who can I trust? It seems everyone is involved.*

Anna found herself outside the police station again and felt safe there. She saw it was six at night and brought Sara into the station and went to the front counter.

The receptionist said without looking up at her, "Can I help you?"

Anna said, "I need to speak to someone about some domestic fear?"

The lady looked up, confused. "Are you being hurt by your spouse?"

Anna said, "I have nowhere to go."

The lady said, "Wait over there and I'll get someone to talk to you."

A female officer came over, and she saw her nametag said "Officer Trout." Anna took a deep breath and followed her with Sara into a small office in the back. Anna faced away from the door.

With a caring look, the officer said, "My name is Laura. Could you tell me your name and why you're here?"

Anna said, "This may sound strange, but I feel I am in danger from my husband and his father. I have been investigating the death of my mother-in-law, and I feel she was murdered, and now that I am investigating it, I fear they will hurt me, too."

Anna suddenly felt a presence behind her and looked back to see Jeff, as if the day was not strange enough.

"What are *you* doing here?" she said.

Jeff put his arm around Anna's shoulders, and she remembered his warmth and loving nature and felt comforted. Jeff said, "Anna, are you okay?"

"I don't know," she said, "but what are you doing here?"

He looked at Laura and said, "It's okay. I can take it from here."

Laura got up and walked out of the office, saying, "You're in good hands now."

He sat down next to her as she looked up and suddenly saw Sue come down the hall with handcuffs on. Anna said, "What is happening?"

Jeff said, "Remember when you saw me a few months ago?" Anna nodded. "I'm a prosecutor for this county, and I just happened to be at a meeting at the station. Well, after I saw you, I asked Officer Lott why you were here. He told me that you'd been investigating the Lawrence case. So I looked into the case myself and brought Lynn back in. She brought me the letter Katrina wrote to her and confessed she never did give it to Officer Lott, like she told you. Well, due to the new evidence, we reopened the case."

Anna thought, *Am I dreaming this? It is all so strange!*

He said, "Did you know Mr. Lawrence gave the insurance money to Katrina's favorite charity? He may be a philanderer, but he is not a murderer. Katrina was scared of Sue, Jake's mistress. She had threatened her and wanted her to leave Jake, and when she didn't, she took things into her own hands. We found she drugged Katrina, and *she* was the one who pushed her down the stairs."

Anna felt so confused. Her head was pounding. Jeff put his hand on hers. "I brought Lynn in to talk to her, and she broke down. She said that she knew her daughter was Jake's mistress and was trying to help Katrina get better so she would leave Jake. I don't think Lynn knew how sick her daughter was. I brought Dave back in as well. He told us his father, Jake, wasn't at home at the time, but he was. He said he found his mother after the fall. He didn't see Sue push her. But he did see Sue's car pull out of the driveway after he found his mother. He confessed he didn't tell us that the first time to protect his father from that pain and he was confused at the time. He called 911, and his voice on the call was devastated. Without you, Anna, Sue would still be free. Mr. Lawrence and Dave aren't the bad guys you thought, Anna."

Anna looked at Jeff. "I don't understand why Lynn would give the letter to you now if she was protecting Sue?"

He said, "I asked her that, and she said that she has been living with this secret and couldn't do it anymore. She said Sue was a manipulative narcissist and she had to do something before she hurt someone else."

Anna felt her thoughts racing around. She got up and sat back down and looked at Jeff. "Why did you do all this, Jeff?"

"I will always love you, Anna. I had a chance to look after you, and I did. I have always wanted you to be happy. Plus, there was a chance I could have sent your husband to jail and then maybe I would have another chance with you." He smiled. "But the right thing is the right thing."

Kathy and Dan suddenly arrived and came into the room. "Thanks for calling us, Jeff." Kathy put her arm around Anna as she saw Dave come around the corner.

"Hi, everyone," Dave said. "Could I have a minute with Anna?" They all left the room.

He sat down, tears running down his face. "Anna, do you know how hurt I am that you thought my father and I could have hurt my mother? You actually thought we were at the house to hurt you? You never even gave me a chance to talk to you. I wasn't ready to reopen that painful chapter in my life."

Anna looked around and thought, *I feel safe here, so I'd better just do it.* She took her wedding ring off her finger and gave it to him. "Dave, you're right. I did think the worst of you and your father. You don't deserve to have a wife that thinks you're capable of abuse or even of murder. You never did open up to me like you did with Jen. You never let me have a voice, and I cannot cloud my vision that I wasn't happy with you and we were never right for each other. I cannot be the wife you need or want, and no one will be happy, least of all our little Sara. If anything, I did learn that from my own parents."

Jeff was lurking in the hallway, and Dave looked around the room. Anna felt comforted that he couldn't have a bad reaction in a police station. He got up, and she watched him take a deep breath and seem to be running through his thoughts. "You make me so angry, Anna. I love you. I will let you go, though, if that is what you want. I am grateful that my mother's murder is solved and without you, well, that wouldn't be the case. I knew Sue was guilty, but I never did tell my father that she was there. I knew she did it when I saw her car drive away and my poor mother was left there. I was so confused at the time and didn't know what to do."

Anna watched Dave as he fell to the chair and put his head to his hands and started to bawl. She texted Jen to come to the police station right away, and she stayed with Dave until Jen arrived. Jeff filled her in briefly, and Anna said, "He could use you now."

Anna left them alone and brought Sara out to the waiting area as Jeff came out and said, "I have some paperwork for you to fill out if that is okay?" Anna nodded as he placed his hand on her back, and she thought, *I'm safe and loved. I'm a good person and deserve a good relationship.*

That night, she slept at her mother's house and thought, *For the first time, I don't have to be on pins and needles in my own house. I am home.*

CHAPTER 22

Conclusion

Anna started her new job as she shared custody of Sara with Dave. She filed for a divorce, and Dave had no choice but to give her what was legally available to her. She stayed living with her mother and Sara. Anna came home one day and found Eve in the kitchen with Kathy. Anna felt shocked and sat down as Eve brought her some water.

Kathy said, "Anna, I'm not sure why you're so shocked. You wanted me to do this all along. Your father and I are actually getting a divorce now. I think I understand why I have stayed with Dan and allowed them to have an affair. I was never really in love with your father. I know that Dan and Eve were in love, but Eve wouldn't allow Dan to leave me all those years. It was Eve who felt obligated that he stayed married to me to take care of me. She thought she was protecting me, but now she understands she wasn't. Anna, your father and I haven't been intimate since Luke was conceived. That was the last time. I never did hold it against him to have affairs, but I know that Eve was the only affair he ever did have. I want them to be together now. I am fully at peace with things. I have always been okay on my own."

Eve kept silent but was sitting down listening as well, tears running down her face. "I have my sister back. There is nothing more that I want now, except maybe my niece and her new baby."

Anna got a text as they were talking. "Hi, Anna. I have been giving you some time, but now I'd like for you to go to dinner with me, please."

Anna laughed and showed the text to her mother and newfound aunt. She looked at Sara, who was in her seat, playing with her squeaky toy. "Well, what do you all think? Am I ready to open this adventure up?"

Eve and Kathy said at the same time, "Only if you feel ready, and only you can answer that."

She texted Jeff, "Hi Jeff, I am not ready at this time. I am going to be alone for a while and learn to rely on myself. I need to get out on my own and take care of myself and Sara. I never want to hurt you again. You have helped me in countless ways and I will never forget what you have done for me. Maybe, down the road our paths will cross again. I hope. Love Anna."

The next week, Alia and Luke came home, and Alia gave her another bear hug. Anna reciprocated, and Alia whispered, "I'm finally going to be your sister, legally."

Anna grabbed Luke and said, "Well, it's about time, Luke. I've been waiting for this day since you brought her home."

"In that case, I take it back," Luke joked.

Alia said, "Not on your life."

Anna wrote in her journal, *I have learned so much about the power I have when something happens, I can pause and relax and decide what to do in any situation. I have the power not to react from emotions but to use my rational thoughts to make a good decision for myself. I will continue my journey to keep learning from my past and to be intentional in my decisions. I am ready to go to therapy and not try to do it on my own. I have so much more to learn, and I am excited to learn and to change and find my own happiness. Anyone can do this and not be hostage to past experiences and painful emotions. What a world we would live in if no one reacted to each other. Amazing.*